John S. Blackie

Horae Hellenicæ

essays and discussion on some important points of Greek philology and antiquity

John S. Blackie

Horae Hellenicæ
essays and discussion on some important points of Greek philology and antiquity

ISBN/EAN: 9783337390358

Printed in Europe, USA, Canada, Australia, Japan

Cover: Foto ©Andreas Hilbeck / pixelio.de

More available books at **www.hansebooks.com**

HORÆ HELLENICÆ:

Essays and Discussions

ON SOME IMPORTANT POINTS

OF

REEK PHILOLOGY AND ANTIQUITY

BY

JOHN STUART BLACKIE, F.R.S.E.,

FELLOW OF THE SOCIETY FOR ARCHÆOLOGICAL CORRESPONDENCE, ROME ;
HONORARY MEMBER OF THE SOCIETY FOR THE SPREAD OF GREEK LETTERS, ATHENS ;
AND OF THE GREEK PHILOLOGICAL SOCIETY, CONSTANTINOPLE ;
PROFESSOR OF GREEK IN THE UNIVERSITY OF EDINBURGH.

London:

MACMILLAN & (

1874.

Δύο καιροὺς ποιοῦ τοῦ λέγειν, ἢ περὶ ὧν οἶσθα σαφῶς, ἤ περὶ ὧν ἀναγκαῖον εἰπεῖν. ἐν τούτοις γὰρ μόνοις ὁ λόγος τῆς σιωπῆς κρείττων, ἐν δὲ τοῖς ἄλλοις ἄμεινον σιγᾶν ἢ λέγειν.—Isocrates.

TO

WILLIAM EWART GLADSTONE, M.P.,

STATESMAN, ORATOR, AND SCHOLAR,

𝔗𝔥𝔢𝔰𝔢 𝔓𝔞𝔤𝔢𝔰 𝔞𝔯𝔢 𝔇𝔢𝔡𝔦𝔠𝔞𝔱𝔢𝔡

BY

THE AUTHOR.

University, Edinburgh.
May 1, 1874.

CONTENTS.

PREFACE.

THE present volume consists of Essays and Discussions on some points of Greek philology and antiquity which appeared to me to have been unduly subordinated, or altogether neglected, by British scholars, or unwisely handled by men of acknowledged talent and reputation. Originally published in the Transactions of learned Societies and Philological Reviews, they laboured under the double disadvantage of being with difficulty consulted and with facility ignored. As they are the product of hard reading and hard thinking, and raise some questions worthy of being seriously grappled with by English scholars, the author, whose professional position forces him to desire that truth should be stated and error combated on as open a field as possible, hopes that their present collected publication in a form adapted for a wider circle of readers will not be attributed to any undue amount of self-esteem.

There are some other papers on similar or cognate subjects, which, for various reasons, I have excluded from the present collection; but, as they contain matter that might reward a glance from persons interested in the subjects which they discuss, it may be useful to give an index to them here. They are as follows :—

1. On English and German Scholarship.—Foreign Quarterly Review, January 1839.

2. On Greek Metres.—*Ibid.*, April 1839.

3. On Euripides and his Dramatic Art.—*Ibid.*, January 1840.

4. On the Rhythmical Declamation of the Ancients.—Classical Museum, vol. i. 1844.

5. On the Teaching of Languages.—Foreign Quarterly Review, April 1845.

6. On the Character, Condition, and Prospects of the Greek People.—Westminster Review, October 1854.

7. The Philosophy of Plato.—Edinburgh Essays. Edinburgh : Black, 1856.

8. Plato and Christianity.—North British Review, November 1861.

A lecture on the classical affinities of the Gaelic language, published some years ago and now out of print, which met with a very favourable reception from competent judges, I have not reprinted here, partly because I hope soon to be able to carry on my studies of Gaelic philology to more worthy conclusions; partly because I have some reason to believe that Professor Geddes of Aberdeen, the Rev. Alexander Cameron of Renton, and other labourers in this much neglected field, will set their hands so seriously and stoutly to the work that any further excursions on my part into a domain not specially mine may be rendered unnecessary.

Two other remarks it seems proper to make. If any person shall be surprised that, in the paper on Homeric theology, I have made no allusion to the genial labours of Mr. Gladstone in this same field, the answer is ready, that my Essay on this subject was completed and published several years before the Homeric Studies appeared; and besides, my Essay is so much an affair of pure induction from a collection of Homeric passages, placed in detail before the reader, that a comparison of concordant or conflicting opinions did not fall naturally within its scope. At the same time I may say that, so far as my memory serves me, there is no important point in the Homeric theology, as deduced by me, from which Mr. Gladstone will feel himself called on to dissent. How far it has been my misfortune to differ from him in regard to certain of his mythological speculations, the discourse on that subject will sufficiently indicate. The other remark I have to make is, that, so far as my antagonism to certain philological and mythological speculations of my distinguished friend, Professor Max Müller, is concerned, I have seen nothing either

from his pen or from that of any other person, that in
the slightest degree moves me to any qualification of
what I have distinctly stated on these points; and as for
Mr. Grote, highly as I value the apology for the Athenian democracy, which is the characteristic feature of his
great work, it has always appeared to me that there are
some matters in the intellectual history of the Hellenic
people with which the unpoetical character of his mind,
and the negative philosophy which he professed, rendered
him incompetent to deal.

ON THE THEOLOGY OF HOMER.

Πάντες τε θεῶν χατέουσιν ἄνθρωποι.

BY the theology of Homer, as distinguished from his
mythology, I understand those grand general principles
with regard to the nature of the gods, and their relation
to men, which are common to all the individual gods that
compose the many-faced system of Greek polytheism. The
special character of the separate gods, their functions and
actions, have nothing to do with the present inquiry ; as
little the ceremonial details of worship with which the gods
are honoured : for these belong manifestly to the practical
religion, not to the doctrinal theology, of the ancient
Greeks.

The theology of the Homeric poems is not the theology
of an individual, but of an age ; and this altogether irrespective of the Wolfian theory, which, in a style so characteristically German, with one sublimely sweeping negation removed at once the personal existence of the supposed
poet, and the actual coherence of the existing poem. The
principal value of Wolf's theory in the eye of many genuine lovers of poetry, is that, while it robbed us of the poet
Homer and his swarms of fair fancies, it restored to us the
Greek people, and their rich garden of heroic tradition,
watered by fountains of purely national feeling, and fresh-
ened by the breath of a healthy popular opinion, which,

A

precisely because it can be ascribed to no particular person, must be taken as the exponent of the common national existence. To have achieved this revolution of critical sentiment with regard to the Homeric poems; to have set before the eyes of Europe, the world-wide distance between the poetry of a Shelley or a Coleridge writing to express their own opinions, and the songs of a race of wandering minstrels singing to give a new echo to the venerable voices of a common tradition; this were enough for the great Berlin philologer to have done, without attempting to establish those strange paradoxes, repugnant alike to the instincts of a sound æsthetical and of a healthy historical criticism, which have made his name so famous. The fact is, that the peculiar dogmas of Wolf, denying the personality of the poet, and the unity of the poems, have nothing whatever to do with that other grand result of his criticism to which we have alluded,— the clear statement of the distinction between the sung poetry of popular tradition, and the written poetry of individual authorship. Not because there was no Homer, are the Homeric poems so generically distinct from the modern productions of a Dante, a Milton, and a Goethe; but because Homer lived in an age when the poet, or rather the singer, had, and from his position could have, no other object in singing than to reflect the popular tradition of which his mind was the mirror. As certainly as a party newspaper or review of the present day represents the sentiments of the party of which it is the organ, so certainly did a Demodocus, or a Phemius, a Homer, or a Cinæthus, the public singers at the public banquets, of a singing, not a printing age,—represent the sentiments of the parties, that is, the people in general, for whose entertainment they exercised their art. 'Tis the very condition, indeed, of all popular writing in the large sense, that it must serve the people before it masters them ; that while entertainment is its direct, and instruction only its indirect object, it must above all things avoid coming rudely into conflict with public feeling and public prejudice on any subject, especially on so tender a subject as religion ; nay, that it must rather, by the very necessity of its position, give up the polemic attitude altogether in reference to public error and vice, and be content, along with many glorious truths, to give immortal currency to any sort of puerile and perverse fancy that may be interwoven with the motley texture of popular thought. A poet even in modern times, when the great public contains every possible variety of small publics, can ill afford to be a preacher ; and if he carries his preaching against the vices of the age beyond a certain length, he changes his genus, and becomes, like Coleridge, a metaphysician, or, like Thomas Carlyle, a prophet. But in the Homeric days, corresponding as they do so exactly to our mediæval times, when the imaginations of all parties reposed quietly on the bosom of a common faith, to suppose, as Herodotus in a well-known passage (II. 53), does, that the popular minstrel had it in his power to describe for the first time the functions of the gods, and to assign them appropriate names, were to betray a complete misconception both of the nature of popular poetry in general, and of the special character of the popular poetry of the Greeks, as we find it in the pages of the *Iliad* and *Odyssey*. So far as the mere secular materials of his songs are concerned, Homer, we have the best reason to believe, received much more than he gave ;[1] but in the current theology and religious senti-

[1] Compare the history of the growth of the famous mediæval Epos " of Reynard the Fox," as it has been gradually revealed by the labours of Jacob Grimm. *Foreign Quarterly Review*, No. XXXIV. Art. 3.

ment, we have not the slightest authority for supposing that he invented anything at all. Amid the various wealth of curious and not always coherent religious tradition, he might indeed select this and reject that, as more or less suited for his immediate purpose; he might give prominence to one aspect of his country's. theology while he threw another into the shade; he might even adorn and beautify to some extent what was rude, and here and there lend a fixity to what was vague;[1] but whatsoever in the popular creed was already stable, his airy music had no power to shake; whatsoever in the vulgar tradition had received fixed and rigid features, his plastic touch had no power to soften. Nay, we are rather certain, that as in the geological formations of later birth, boulders of strange granite will sometimes appear, so there are incorporated into the body of the Homeric theology, fragments of an older and more crude Pelasgic creed, that assort ill with the higher organism of the poet's own faith, and the faith of the age to which he belonged; while it seems equally certain, that with the large receptive capacity so characteristic of great imaginative minds, he had hung up in his mythological gallery not a few pictures, to whose original significance —whether physical or moral—he in common with the heroes of his melody had lost the key.[2] We may therefore attempt an articulate statement of the principal heads of Homeric theology, with the most complete conviction

[1] I believe, for instance, that the Ἄτη of *Il.* XIX. 91, and IX. 501, so distinctly an allegorical personage (*Nägelsbach,* p. 67), may have been a creation of the poet's fancy (acting, however, in unison with the whole tendency of the Greek religion), which afterwards becoming stereotyped, received a prominent individuality among the persons of the celestial aristocracy from the tragedians.

[2] To the former class may belong the strange-sounding myth of Briareus Ægeon delivering Jove from the chains imposed on him by the other gods (*Il.* I. 399, on which see Welcker's *Anhang Trilogie,* p. 147); to the latter, the description of the connubial embrace of Zeus and Hera (*Il.* XIV. 346), on which see Müller.

that we are giving the religious faith of an age and of a people, not the private speculations of a person.

One good use to be made of this consideration is, that we shall start on our inquiry in no wise expecting a metaphysical precision, or a philosophical consistency in all points. Even formal confessions of faith, drawn up by subtle systematic theologians, are often far from preserving a rigid consistency through all their articles, much more the floating variety of an imaginative creed without a Bible, like that of the ancient Greeks. Popular poets like Homer assert the fundamental moral and religious instincts of human nature, without attempting to prove them where the foundation may appear weak, or to reconcile them where they may sound contradictory; and the profoundest philosophers have generally contented themselves with doing the same thing, only in a more elaborate and ambitious style.

In setting forth the theological views of the Homeric writings, attempts have been made by some writers to draw a broad line of distinction between the *Iliad* and the *Odyssey*. It is alleged that the religious conceptions of the former are as inferior to those of the latter, as its poetic glow is more intense, its flight of winged words more rapid, and its pictures more vivid; and it is conceived that this difference, or rather contrast, is so great as, along with other considerations, to justify the conclusion, that these two immortal works were the productions neither of one author, nor of the same age.[1] But the

---

[1] This is the conclusion of Benjamin Constant, and of Dr. Ihne, in an otherwise admirable paper in Dr. Smith's Biographical Dictionary (London 1844), *Art.* HOMER. "A great and essential difference, which pervades the whole of the two poems, is observable in the notions that are entertained respecting the gods. In the *Iliad* the men are better than the gods: in the *Odyssey*, it is the reverse. In the latter poem, no mortal dares to resist, much less to attack and wound a god; Olympus does not resound with everlasting quarrels. Athene consults

minute comparison which I have made of all the passages in both poems that have any bearing on religion leads me most certainly to the conclusion that such a notion is untenable. I shall, on the other hand, I flatter myself, be able to prove distinctly, that there is no prominent and characteristic feature of Hellenic theology in the one poem which does not appear in the other ; and that, though some traits of a crude creed are put forward with more glaring offensiveness in the *Iliad* than in the *Odyssey*, these naturally arose from the nature of the subjects treated, and from the dominancy of its own particular idea over the

humbly the will of Zeus, and forbears offending Poseidon, her uncle, for the sake of a mortal man. Whenever a god inflicts punishment or bestows protection in the *Odyssey*, it is for some moral desert, not as in the *Iliad*, through mere caprice, without any consideration of the good or bad qualities of the individual. In the *Iliad* Zeus sends a dream to deceive Agamemnon ; Athene, after a general consultation of the gods, prompts Pandarus to his treachery ; Paris, the violator of the sacred laws of hospitality, is never upbraided with his crime by the gods ; whereas, in the *Odyssey*, they appear as the awful avengers of those who do not respect the laws of the hospitable Zeus. The gods of the *Iliad* live on Mount Olympus ; those of the *Odyssey* are further removed from the earth ; they inhabit the wide heaven. There is nothing which obliges us to think of the *Mount* Olympus. In the *Iliad*, the gods are visible to every one, except when they surround themselves with a cloud. In the *Odyssey*, they are usually invisible, unless they take the shape of men. In short, as Benjamin Constant has well observed (*de la Relig.* III.), there is more mythology in the *Iliad*, and more religion in the *Odyssey*."

After writing the remarks in the text,

I lighted on the following admirable observations in Nägelsbach, p. 103:— "In the *Odyssey* there is no strife among the Olympic gods ; for the principal divine personages that take interest in the action, Zeus and Athena, are united, (*Od.* XXIV. 472) ; and Hera has nothing to do with the plot, so that Poseidon alone stands on the opposite side. In the *Iliad*, again, the struggle on earth is only the counterpart of the struggle in heaven. The celestial personages, who are independent and free to choose their own part, come thus into a state of mutual hate and hostility ; and this gives the gods of the *Iliad*, *in appearance*, a different character from those of the *Odyssey*. For all the evil passions, which war raises in human breasts, must in consequence of this hostile attitude be stirred in the bosom of the gods, to whose essential nature, holiness in no sense belongs." The author therefore agrees with me, in representing the theological system of the *Odyssey* and the *Iliad*, as different only *in appearance* (*scheinbar*). The italics belong to the author, showing distinctly that he placed great weight on the word, and is not to be understood for a moment as favouring the views of Benjamin Constant and Dr. Ihne.

general tone and character of each poem. As a song of
war and battle among mortal men, the *Iliad* could not
but exhibit the sympathizing gods as animated by all those
violent and more or less undignified passions, without
which war in any shape, and especially in an age of warriors, cannot be conceived to exist; while, in the *Odyssey*,
a narrative of domestic fortunes, and an example of severe
retribution exercised on the guilty violators of social laws
in times of peace, it could not but be that the poet should
cause the motley confusion of inferior Olympic personages
to recede before the awful presence of Jove the avenger,
and his wise daughter Athena.[1]

These preliminary observations may be necessary to
anticipate misconception in the minds of some, whose particular line of study may not have familiarized them with
investigations of this kind. Without further preface, I
now proceed to state the theological system of Homer as
compactly as I may be able in a series of propositions.

PROPOSITION I.—The gods are a race of beings externally of human form and appearance, but in quality and
energy superior to mortal men, enjoying an existence
supremely blissful in its nature ($\dot{\rho}\epsilon\hat{\iota}a$ $\zeta\omega\acute{o}\nu\tau\epsilon\varsigma$, *Il.* VI. 138),

---

[1] "In the *Odyssey*," says Archdeacon
Williams (Homeros, App.,) "there seems
to have been embodied the Homeric
creed concerning the social and political
duties of man, and the certain punishment which is sooner or later to over-
take the impenitent violators of the
moral law." Of the justice of this remark there can be no doubt; only it
must always be borne in mind that,
though this creed is most certainly embodied in the poem, the exposition of it
was not the only, perhaps not the main,
object of the bard in composing his
poem. His simple object was to sing
the adventures of the far-wandering
Ulysses, as he himself intimates in the
invocation. That he was able to inter-
weave this story of marvellous adventures with a grand exhibition of retributive justice on the part of Jove
shows at once to what order of poets
he belonged; proves that he was one
of those who so incorporate light entertainment with serious instruction, that
it is hard to say, whether it be their
main object to help the trifling to season a listless hour, or the serious to
solve a moral problem.

and controlled by no superior power; the wide welkin is their habitation, and Mount Olympus in Thessaly, their home. That which most peculiarly distinguishes them from human beings is their immortality (μάκαρες θεοὶ αἰὲν ἐόντες, *Od.* v. 7); by which, however, is meant, not that they have always existed, but that when once they begin to exist, they may not in anywise cease to exist. Though begotten like men, and holding their power by right of succession from more ancient celestial dynasties no longer acknowledged, they are not subject to death or mutation; and their dominion, once established, can never pass away.

In stating this proposition, I have followed Nägelsbach [1] in specifying immortality as that attribute by which the divine nature, according to the Homeric conception, is most distinguished from the human. For though, as we shall see afterwards, the attribute of power comparatively infinite belonging to the highest gods stands in a no less striking contrast to the weakness of mortals, than their eternal blessedness to our ephemeral and sorrow-chequered existence, yet this extraordinary degree of power is by no means possessed by all the gods, and some of the inferior tribes of them are not a tall remarkably endowed in this way: immortality, however, of soul and body, without the necessity of that sorrowful change which we call death, characterizes all the superhuman race, from Zeus to Calypso, and forms the most prominent quality that distinguishes them from mortal men. In most other respects they are human enough in their passions, their purposes, and their actions; and indeed it is this humanity which makes them not only take such an ardent interest in all human affairs, but even leads them to seek that con-

---

[1] *Homerische Theologie,* Nürenberg, 1840, p. 38.

nexion with mortal women, from which one of the greatest
blessings of earth, a race of heroes and demi-gods, is produced. With regard to their origin, Homer is not at all
curious, practical piety, not metaphysical theology, being
his province ; he only indicates in the line (*Il.* xiv. 201),

'Ωκεανόν τε θεῶν γένεσιν καὶ μητέρα Τηθύν,

that they are all descended from the two sea-powers,
Ocean and Tethys, as from a common father and mother.
He also intimates with sufficient clearness, that they did
not arrive at the height of power where they now stand
without passing through previous struggles and convulsions of a very serious kind (the struggle with Kronos and
the Titans, *Il.* xiv. 204, viii. 479) ; but, once established,
he has no idea (such as that with which Prometheus feeds
his pride in Æschylus) that they can ever be overthrown,
any more than a Christian has that the world can ever
revert from Christianity to Judaism. In reference to
their habitation, though they are generally styled in the
Odyssey οὐρανὸν εὐρὺν ἔχοντες (a style, however, occurring
also in the *Iliad,* xxi. 267), there is not the least
foundation for Dr. Ihne's remark, that this designation
furnishes one ground of distinction between the theology of the *Odyssey* and that of the *Iliad,* as if that of
the former were of a more spiritual and refined nature ;
for a *Mount* Olympus is distinctly described in *Od.* i. 102,

βῆ δὲ κατ' οὐλύμποιο καρήνων ἀΐξασα,

in the very language of the *Iliad* (iv. 74, xxii. 187), besides *Od.* v. 50, vi. 42, and other places where Olympus
is mentioned (and ὀλύμπια δώματα, xxiii. 167), without the
slightest reason to suppose that anything else can be
meant than the *Mount* Olympus of the *Iliad.*

PROPOSITION II.—The gods are the supreme rulers of

the world, the dispensers of good and evil to men, and the directors of their fates.

A habitual piety, characterized by the special reference of all events in life, whether prosperous or adverse, to the divine providence, is not less characteristic of the writings of Homer than of the Old Testament Scriptures; and, indeed, this is one of the many remarkable and extremely interesting points of resemblance, that strike the most superficial reader in works otherwise so dissimilar in their tone, and opposite in their tendency. "Nothing," says Nägelsbach (p. 53), "is further from the Homeric man than to look upon himself as isolated and separated from the gods, or to look on the divine government as a dead system of laws and rules once for all implanted into the nature of things. The relation of men to the gods is rather to be looked on as an uninterrupted living intercourse." And accordingly, we find that whatsoever a man is and enjoys is constantly and instinctively attributed by Homer to the gods, as if it could not be otherwise; birth, marriage, and death (*Od.* IV. 7, 12, XVI. 211); health (v. 397), and strength (*Il.* I. 178); good and bad weather (*Od.* IV. 351); luxuries (VII. 132); good sport in hunting (IX. 158); and even a good jest and a hearty laugh (XVIII. 37). In the same way every sort of bad luck is immediately referred to the wrath of a god; as when a marksman misses his aim (*Il.* v. 191, VIII. 311), or when a fleet runner slips his foot, even where the direct cause of the fall may be quite evident (XXIII. 782). The Homeric man is always more deeply impressed with the first and originating than with the second and mediating cause of things. The old Hellenic voyager knows that he has been driven out of his course by the east or other unfavourable wind; but the

Zeus or Poseidon who caused the wind to blow is the grand object of his attention,—and so of everything else. In consistency with this view, all persons who enjoy great prosperity, that is, on whom the gods shower many gifts, are said to be dear, and very dear (μάλα φίλοι, *Od.* VI. 203) to the gods : while misfortunes are a manifest evidence of the celestial disfavour (IV. 755, *Il.* VI. 200); and in the same way, if a person is distinguished by any natural gift, as Helen by beauty, he is said to be dear to the god or goddess from whom, as from a divine perennial fountain, this gift flows. As to phraseology, θεοί, θεός, θεός τις, and δαίμων, seem to be used indiscriminately by the poet, when talking of the divine source of all the good that men enjoy, or the evil that they suffer ; often, also, the particular deity is named through whose instrumentality, as standing in a peculiar relation to this or that human being, the blessing is dispensed. In this way Athena appears everywhere as the presiding deity of the *Odyssey.* She sends sleep to Penelope (I. 364), speeds the departure of Telemachus (II. 382, 420), and is with the hero in all the critical turns of the perilous and bloody catastrophe.

PROPOSITION III.—This providence, or supreme control of all human things by the gods, is not confined merely to the circumstances of the external world by which human happiness or misery is affected, but reaches also all the thoughts, purposes, and passions of men ; which thoughts, purposes, and passions, accordingly, the evil and the good indifferently, are looked upon as the direct effect of an immediate divine agency ; specially, however, all great and glorious thoughts, and impulses leading to actions of extraordinary energy and excellence, come from a god ; and these actions themselves, though achieved visibly by mere human agency, are οὐκ ἄνευ θεῶν, not without the instigation, assistance, and directing control of the gods.

It is remarked by some theologian,—I forget by whom, —that among all the objections made by the heathen philosophers to the doctrines of the Gospel, no exception was ever taken to the doctrine of divine influence, or the operation of the Holy Ghost on the human mind. This doctrine, which has been looked upon in modern times by Arminians, Pelagians, and others, with a sort of jealousy, could not excite any suspicion, or appear even in the light of a novelty, in an age when all the higher minds in the moral world were initiated into the philosophy of Plato or Zeno,[1] and when the great Catholic Bible of popular religious tradition, viz., Homer, recognised the doctrine of direct spiritual action of the divine mind on the human as one of its most familiar truths. That a man's genius and inclinations are all divinely implanted is a truth sufficiently obvious, and which, stated as an abstract proposition, few men now-a-days will deny ; but the difference between our time and the Homeric in this matter lies not so much in any abstract doctrine as in the comparative frequency of a correspondent phraseology in his language, and its unfrequency in ours. Thus, for instance, when Ulysses (*Od.* XIV. 227) says :—

αὐτὰρ ἐμοὶ τὰ φίλ᾽ ἔσκε τά που θεὸς ἐν φρεσὶ θῆκεν
ἄλλος γάρ τ᾽ ἄλλοισιν ἀνὴρ ἐπιτέρπεται ἔργοις,

he uses in the first line a distinctly marked Homeric

---

[1] No doubt there was a something of *self-containedness* in the *Stoic*, which did not so readily suit devout connection with the divine mind, as the high aspirations of the Platonist ; but how far the Stoics were from wishing to isolate man from the divine mind, on which he depends, may be seen from the arguments put into the mouth of Balbus by Cicero, in the second book *de Natura Deorum.*

phraseology, while the second line contains only what any of us in our common talk might say any day, and what in fact we do say every day. "*Those things are dear to me which a god put into my heart*"—this style refers the likings and dislikings of the human heart directly to a divine influence ; while the other proposition, "*one man delights in one thing, another in another*," merely asserts a human fact without giving any hint of its divine causation. Now, the habitual assertion of this divine causation in all the more notable movements of the human mind is one of the grand prominent features of that atmosphere of religion (or religiosity, as some may prefer to say) which gives such a peculiar colour to the Homeric epos. In the language of an obsolete criticism (perhaps not yet altogether obsolete in certain quarters), the Olympian personages are termed the "machinery" of the poem ; if this word, however, is to be used, it is much more near the truth to say that, in Homer's view, the mortal men are everywhere the mere machinery of the great drama of existence of which the gods are the real actors. The constant occurrence in the Homeric page, with reference to human purposes, of such phrases as ἐνὶ θυμῷ βάλλειν (*Od.* I. 200), ἐπὶ φρεσὶ θῆκε (V. 427), νόημα ποίησε (XIV. 273), θεοῦ ὑποθημοσύνησιν (XVI. 233), and ἐνέπνευσε φρεσὶ δαίμων (XIX. 138), shows how familiar to the old Hellenic mind was that famous sentiment afterwards expressed by Cicero :—"*Nemo vir magnus sine aliquo afflatu divino unquam fuit ;*" and not only so, but a sentiment far more extensive than this, viz., that a man can in fact think nothing worth thinking, except by virtue of a direct divine impulse or inspiration. This is a method of viewing things to which the somewhat mechanical English mind (since the days of Cromwell at

least) has shown a great aversion;[1] but how far it is
from being contrary to a high Christian philosophy, the
single text, Luke XII. 12, may suffice to show. But
Homer, in his views of divine influence, is far from stop-
ping where the language of a pious Puritan of the six-
teenth century, or a fervid evangelical of the present day,
mutatis mutandis, would readily go along with him.   He,
in fact, goes so far as to attribute foolish, and even vicious
actions, to an impulse proceeding from above, to such an
extent as seemingly to destroy altogether the idea of
human responsibility.   When, for instance, a man thought-
lessly (ἀφραδέως, *Od.* XIV. 481) goes out without his cloak
on a frosty night, so that he is in danger of dying, or at
least catching severe rheumatism from cold, he exclaims
quite naturally, παρὰ μ' ἤπαφε δαίμων, *a god deceived me
that I did this thing.*   This is a very peculiar phraseology,
and sounds to a modern ear very strange, from an author
whose general tone, as we have said, is sufficiently devout.
And in like manner, instead of exclaiming, as a modern
Englishman would, *what a fool am I!* Telemachus, when
reviewing his conduct, says, *truly Zeus hath made me a
fool!* (*Od.* XXI. 102.)   Nor is this all : Antinous, when
blaming Penelope for wilful obstinacy and evil cunning,
instead of confining the blame to her, which would have
pointed more keenly his reproach, does not hesitate to

---

[1] Some, however, of our most practical writers, have not hesitated to
assert a belief in presentiments and
warnings divinely impressed on the
soul.   Thus DE FOE, in *Robinson
Crusoe*, writes,—"Let no man despise
the secret hints and notices of danger
which sometimes are given him, when
he may think there is no possibility
of its being real.   That such hints and
notices are given us, I believe few that
have made any observations of things
will deny ; that they are certain discoveries of an invisible converse and a
world of spirits, we cannot doubt ; and
if the tendency of them seems to be
to warn us of danger, why should we
not suppose they are from some friendly
agent (whether supreme, or inferior and
subordinate, is not the question), and
they are given for our good ?"

name the gods as the true authors of her so reprehensible conduct (ὅντινά οἱ νοῦν ἐν στήθεσσι τιθεῖσι θεοί) ; and stronger still, the fair Helen, whose infidelity to her Spartan lord brought so many woes on her countrymen, and sent so many noble souls to Hades, speaks of her own conduct with the utmost coolness, as having been the result of a pernicious infatuation (ἄτην) placed in her heart by Aphrodite ;[1] and in this judgment old Priam (*Il.* III. 164), who might be expected to be a more severe moralist, fully agrees :—

οὔτε μοι αἰτίη ἐσσὶ· θεοί νύ μοι αἴτιοί εἰσιν.

This sentiment, indeed, that not the doers of an evil deed, but the gods who inspire the purpose of doing it, are the real criminals, seems a standard commonplace in the Homeric morality ; for Agamemnon (*Il.* XIX. 86, a famous passage to which we shall have again occasion to refer) uses it with regard to the unhappy cause of his breach with Achilles. After such passages, one might be apt to think that the doctrine of divine influence in Homer was such as to confound light with darkness, and obliterate the universal instincts of the human breast with regard to right and wrong ; and that it did so to a certain extent, as well in the Homeric days as in the days of Puritan enthusiasm, to which reference has been made, is not to be doubted ; but as the world is full of mysteries, and the human heart full of contradictions, we must not rush to a hasty conclusion in this matter, till we come to treat specially of human responsibility, of the dependence of morals on religion, and of the punishment due to evil works. In the Old Testament, also, we read that " God hardened Pharaoh's heart " (Exod. vii. 3), and that " the

---

[1] Contrast this language with that of the apostle James (i. 13), with regard to temptation.

Lord sent a lying prophet" to a certain Hebrew king (I Kings xxii. 22, *apud* Wolf. *Proleg.* 37). Mere surface consideration will not settle matters of this kind, lying as they do so deep in the darkest roots of our moral nature, which our finite wit certainly will never be able, in all points, with complete satisfaction to fathom.

PROPOSITION IV.—The gods are in an especial manner the authors of all extraordinary phenomena in nature, as also of all events of which there is no visible human agency, or to which human agency is considered inadequate.

Strictly speaking, according to the religious philosophy so characteristic of the Homeric age, there is no part of nature, or of the vast system of things, which is not sacred or divine,—the sea, the shore, the land, the night, the day, are all governed by a god, and inspired with whatsoever is great or beautiful in them by a special divine energy; polytheism being, in fact, only a ramified and variously divided pantheism; but in the common, and anything but strictly philosophical style of talking which Homer uses, only the grandest objects and more striking phenomena of nature are specially referred to a direct divine energy. It is not poetry, as the Bishop of Thessalonica has it (παρεκβολαὶ, vol. i. p. 9, edit. Roman.), but the general style of thinking and feeling in the Homeric age, of which it may be justly said, that πᾶν τὸ παρηλλαγμένον καὶ ξενίζον καὶ ἐξαίρετον, καὶ τεράστιον ἢ καὶ τερατῶδες εἰς τὸ θεῖον γένος καὶ εἰς θεὸν ἀποκαθιστᾶ. There is a natural and deeply-seated tendency in all men at all times to recognise God in strange, startling, and unaccountable phenomena; while in the more plain and intelligible manifestations of his every-day power, he is apt to be overlooked. Even the severe Stoics admitted the justness of the argument for the existence of the gods drawn from this tendency (see the words of Cleanthes in Cic. *de Nat. Deorum,* II. 5) ; but in Homer it encounters us at every turn. The whole science of augury, and the interpretation of omens, so necessary at every critical moment in Homer, depends on this principle. Hence also it is that dreams, especially remarkable dreams, which are altogether independent of our common reason and volition, come from Jove (*Il.* I. 63), or from some other god (*Od.* IV. 796). Hence also madness is ascribed directly to the gods (μάργην σε θεοὶ θέσαν, *Od.* XXIII. 11), and all violent exertions of energy akin to madness (οὐχ ὁ γ' ἄνευθε θεῶν τάδε μαίνεται, *Il.* V. 187). Poetry especially, as one of the most striking effects of what we call genius as opposed to talent, is the direct product of divine teaching (*Od.* XXII. 347). Even we in modern times, talk in a loose sort of way of the inspiration of the divine Shakespeare ; but such was the reverence of the old Ionic minstrel and his age for every manifestation of the divine power in the masque of humanity, that he could talk with a more serious and pregnant religious meaning of the inspiration of a ship-carpenter or a shoemaker than we do of a great poet. A swineherd to him was more divine than a high priest or a hero is to us. But especially all extraordinary events, inexplicable effects without any apparent cause, are the plain operation of a god, as if a fair marksman should shoot twenty arrows at a mark, and all should fail ! In such an extraordinary result, even a child, καὶ ὃς μάλα νήπιός ἐστιν (*Il.* XVII. 629), may discern the finger of a god. And in extraordinary escapes from imminent danger, in sudden and unaccountable disappearances of persons well known, not man, or ordinary causes, but the gods themselves (θεοὶ αὐτοὶ with emphasis, *Od.* XXIV. 400), are plainly at work.   On the same principle sudden and painless deaths are ascribed with an especial emphasis to the shafts of Apollo and Artemis (*Od.* XV. 410).   In one word, all uncommon things are more divine than what is common, and very uncommon things are explicable only on the supposition of an extraordinary divine inter-position for the nonce.

PROPOSITION V.—From all that has been said on the extent and variety of the influence of the gods on human fates and affairs, it plainly follows that the Greeks, in their theology, have no place for a being corresponding to our Christian idea of the Devil, as a powerful super-mundane spirit, energetic for evil, and for evil only ; so that the significant English phrases of, " *the devil's in the fellow,—to play the devil with a thing,*" are expressed in Homeric (and also in general) Greek, by the phrases, " *a god's in the fellow,—a god's in the business.*"

This proposition is a necessary corollary from what has been already stated in Propositions II. and III. ; but there is no harm in its standing here separately, as it serves to bring out with greater distinctness the contrast between ancient Homeric and modern English ways of thinking.   Let it be understood, then, as a most charac-teristic trait in the system of Homeric theology, that there is, and can be no devil, properly so called ; for the very plain reason, that the same gods are the general authors of evil and good to men, and serve them now with the right hand now with the left, as the Muse served the Phæacian bard Demodocus, giving him sweet song, but taking away the light of his eyes :—

Τὸν πέρι Μοῦσ᾽ ἐφίλησε δίδου δ᾽ ἀγαθόν τε κακόν τε
ὀφθαλμῶν μὲν ἄμερσε, δίδου δ᾽ ἡδεῖαν ἀοιδήν.

Hence the striking difference in the Jewish and Greek methods of expression with reference to the common phenomena of disease. The Jew said of a woman bent with weakness, and unable to look up with the common privilege of humanity to the skies, that she was *bound by Satan* (Luke xiii. 11, 16) ; the Greek, of one pining under a protracted and painful illness, that he was *plied by a hateful god* (στυγερὸς δέ οἱ ἔχραε δαίμων, *Od.* v. 396), or simply that one cannot escape a disease sent from mighty Jove (IX. 411). Nor is the στυγερός in the passage just quoted, or the κακός in another (x. 64), applied to δαίμων, indicative in any sense of a special *cacodæmon*, or spirit essentially evil, like the unclean spirits of the New Testament, such as the later theology of Greece might acknowledge ; these designations in Homer are only descriptive expletives, which, for all theological purposes, had as well been omitted. The only semblance, indeed, of a real devil in Homer is that Ἄτη already mentioned (*Il.* XIX. 91), on whom Agamemnon so unceremoniously throws the blame of his untoward quarrel with the swift-footed son of Thetis ; but even of her, and in the time of the tragedians, the Greeks never speak as of *the* source of evil, but only as *a* source. In Homer, however, she is an allegory, scarcely less transparent than the Harpies or the Κῆρες, where we find the polytheistic fancy of the early Greeks in the very act of impersonating and incarnating the gods of a future generation ;[1] and in the very passage where so much is made of her in the shape

---

[1] "In κήρ, and some other such words, we catch fancy engaged in the work of shaping forth ill-understood, incalculable effects, into separate persons; for never in these cases is the image completely finished, and clad with the full personality of a perfect god."—NITZSCH, on *Odyss.* III. 236.

of a distinct person, the infatuation, which is said to have
been the result of her evil inspiration, is ascribed in the
common phraseology of the Homeric men to Jove,—καί
μευ φρένας ἐξέλετο Ζεύς (XIX. 137). The old minstrel who
first worked out this divine personage from the common
state of mind, or result of a state of mind denominated
ἄτη, which any of the gods might produce (*Od.* IV. 261 ;
Il. IX. 18), was in the fair way, had the popular creed
allowed him, to have worked out a Hellenic Trinity akin
to that of the Hindus, with Ate for its Siva ; but he
made not the most distant approach to the Christian idea
of the devil. The bard of the *Iliad,* had he written the
gospel history, might have said that Ate put it into the
heart of Judas Iscariot to betray Christ (John xiii. 2) ;
but he might have said with equal, or rather greater
readiness, that Jove or any of the gods had deprived him
of his senses, and driven him to do this act. In the
Christian theology, God is essentially opposed to the
Devil ; in Homeric language, Jove and Ate are convertible
terms.

PROPOSITION VI.—Zeus is the supreme ruler both of
gods and men, and stands to the former exactly in the
same relation that an absolute monarch does to the aristocracy of which he is the head. His will is the grand
originating centre of all great movements in the physical
and moral world; and besides the peculiar functions which
he exercises as god of the upper air, he has a general
superintendence over the conduct of all the other gods,
and over all the thoughts, purposes, and actions of men.
He is in an especial manner the friend and protector of
those who have none to help them, and the enforcer of all
the great rights and duties by which the framework of

society is knit together. He is the rewarder of those who do well, and the punisher of those who do evil.

The supremacy of Jove, as stated in this proposition, is the strong key-stone of the polytheistic arch in Homer, without which, indeed, polytheism in heaven, like a pure democracy on earth, would be sure to start asunder, and rush blindly into absolute chaos and dissolution. It introduces in fact, to an extent greater than is generally imagined, for many practical uses, the monotheistic principle into polytheism. The right of the son of Kronos to this high position is founded, by Homer, on the single fact of his superior strength, just as the right of Agamemnon to be king of men stands upon no other foundation, so far as one can see, than that he is the strongest among the strong (*Il.* I. 281). The most notable passage in which this doctrine is stated is that famous appeal made to the assembled deities by the celestial autocrat himself in the beginning of *Iliad* VIII., where he tells them plainly, that if they were to suspend a golden chain from heaven, and endeavour to pull the Father down, they would not succeed with all their united endeavours; while, on the other hand, if he were to fix the one end of the chain round a crag of Olympus, he would hold all the gods dangling in vacancy at the other end, with earth and sea to boot !—

τόσσον ἐγὼ περί τ᾽ εἰμὶ θεῶν, περί τ᾽ εἴμ᾽ ἀνθρώπων.

This is a homely, and to us an infantile simile; but it expresses significantly enough the central celestial fact, to which, as a pole-star, all the conflicting and divergent materials of both the epics are made finally to point. In the *Odyssey* the jealous wrath of Poseidon against the tempest-tost hero is at length forced to yield to the con-

summated counsels of the supreme Father, and his like-
minded daughter (*Odys.* XXIV. 477). In the *Iliad* the
Διὸς δ' ἐτελείετο βουλή, with which the song is commenced,
rides over the whole action with a dominancy, only the
more triumphant that it meets with constant and combined opposition from the strongest of the other Olympian
powers, specially Poseidon the brother, Hera the spouse,
and Athena the unmothered daughter of the great Olympian ; but the more that these inferior deities fret and chafe
against the divine decrees of the Thunderer, with the more
unshaken serenity does the high administrator of war to
men (ταμίης πολέμοιο, *Il.* IV. 84) sit on his throne apart
(*Il.* I. 499), and over the murmurs of hostile gods, and the
heaps of dead and dying men, measure with his thought
the march of his high purpose till it be fulfilled (*Il.* XI.
80).   All the passages in the *Iliad* that seem to indicate
anything contrary to this practical supremacy of Jove's
high will in heaven and in earth, when accurately examined, throw their weight into the opposite scale. Of
all the gods, Poseidon is that one who, with the fairest
show of reason, might have asserted his right to control
the obnoxious decrees of the Olympian ; but the "liberty,
equality, and fraternity" of which he boasts in one famous
passage (*Il.* XV. 185), like its human counterpart in
modern French democracy, is found to exist only in
theory ; when the hour comes for action, he is as ready as
Diomede, or any mortal man, to say,

> οὐκ ἂν ἔγωγ' ἐθέλοιμι Διὶ Κρονίωνι μάχεσθαι
> ἡμέας τοὺς ἄλλους, ἐπειὴ πολὺ φέρτερός ἐστιν.
>
> Il. VIII. 210.

With which compare XV. 211. In VIII. 440, where he acts
as equerry to Jove, his inferiority is yet more markedly
shown. As little can be made out of the famous myth of

Briareus Ægeon (*Il.* I. 396) against the absolute supremacy
of the Father. Here, also, the three most important members of the celestial assembly, Hera, Poseidon, and Pallas,
are leagued against Jove, and wish to bind him. But
he is delivered from this formidable conspiracy, says the
myth, by the sea-goddess Thetis, and the hundred-armed
strong man of the floods (see Welcker, p. 4, above), and *de
facto*, he still remains supreme. In a similar strain, we
are told that the stout Thracian Lycurgus so frightened
Dionysos, that he was obliged to take refuge in the sea,
and in the bosom of the same Thetis (*Il.* VI. 135); but
with all this display of momentary weakness, the divine
power of the wine-god over men waxed strong, and an
unblissful end was his who dared to strive with immortals.
These monstrous myths, bearing as they do some analogy
to the portentous figments of the Hindus (see the *Curse
of Kehama*), were in all probability invented by the licentious imagination of rude religionists for the express purpose of magnifying the power of the gods, by showing
that though they could be humbled and even persecuted ·
for a season, they must certainly triumph in the end.
Besides that, such rich collections of popular tradition as
are incorporated into the Homeric poems cannot possibly be expected to be homogeneous in all details. The
comprehensive genius of the arch-minstrel whom we
call Homer, has doubtless taken into his caldron some
strange materials which he could not, or cared not to
fuse. Homer was not professionally a theologian, but a
poet; and if in some parts of his works he has admitted
tales of the gods not altogether consistent with the more
exalted character of his general theology, he has only
erred, as the most pious poets will err, when more intent
on sport for the moment than on edification.

One circumstance which more than any other tends to show how much of the monotheistic element was practically inwoven with heathenism, is the habitual reference to Zeus when there is no special call for mentioning his name more than that of any other deity. The passages are innumerable, where Jove, as the ordinary administrator of the world, is said to send sorrow or sadness, blessing or bane, when the polytheistic phraseology θεοί would have been equally appropriate (*Od.* III. 132 ; IV. 34, 208). He indeed it was whom the pious heathen was taught by the Homeric poetry habitually to look up to, as the dispenser of all the bounties of Providence on which the existence and the happiness of man depends.

Ζεὺς δ' αὐτὸς νέμει ὄλβον 'Ολύμπιος ἀνθρώποισιν
'Εσθλοῖς ἠδὲ κακοῖσιν, ὅπως ἐθέλησιν ἑκάστῳ.
Od. VI. 188.

But it is as the supreme moral governor of the universe that the monotheistic influence of Zeus is chiefly manifest. All the other Olympian gods were elemental or material powers, personations of vast wavy tides of physical or sensuous surges, but without law or restraint, subordination or rule. Poseidon is then most himself, when his white-crested billow spits wrath most bitterly ; Aphrodite has her special glory when the strongest man, a Cæsar or a Napoleon, is for a season unmanned by the witchery of a pretty face ; the triumph of such gods is the triumph of mere unreined impulse, physical or moral as the case may be ; but Jove, besides his physical virtue as ruler of the sky and lord of the thunder, knows and acknowledges law, and by his patronage of social rights and duties, reclaims man from savagery, and renders society possible. This is everywhere most distinctly indicated both in the *Iliad* and the *Odyssey*, but especially in the *Odyssey*,

whose moral and retributive character, as already remarked, has been justly pointed out by Archdeacon Williams.   The connexion between Zeus and Themis is prominently set forth in *Iliad* xx. 4 ; and when, in the
second book of the *Odyssey*, Telemachus, having called a
public assembly of the islanders, is about to state the
wrongs which he suffered at the hand of the suitors, he
commences most solemnly by an invocation of Jove and
Themis, without whose presidency an ἀγορά could not
exist,—

$$\Lambda ίσσομαι\ ἠμὲν\ Ζηνὸς\ 'Ολυμπίου\ ἠδὲ\ Θέμιστος$$
$$ἥτ'\ ἀνδρῶν\ ἀγορὰς\ ἠμὲν\ λύει\ ἠδὲ\ καθίζει.$$

The statutes (θέμιστες) of Zeus (*Il.* i. 239) exercise a strong
influence in the *Odyssey*, even over godless men, preventing them from proceeding to those extremes of bloody
daring which lead directly to the subversion of all society,
and the confusion of all right (*Odys.* xvi. 403) ; and it is
only such ferocious cannibals as the Cyclopes ὑβρισταί τε
καὶ ἄγριοι οὐδὲ δίκαιοι, who altogether disregard them, and
in a state of unsocial independence do every one what is
right in his own eyes (*Od.* ix. 112).   The supreme god
further strengthens the links of society, by conferring on
earthly kings a divine title to rule on earth, judging between the right and the wrong (*Il.* ix. 99), similar to
what himself enjoys in Olympus :

$$τιμὴ\ τ'\ ἐκ\ Διός\ ἐστι,\ φιλεῖ\ δέ\ ἑ\ μητιέτα\ Ζεύς.—Il.\ \text{II. 197.}$$

And king-killing to the Homeric chiefs was no light business (*Od.* xvi. 401), any more than to the Puritans who
sat in earnest and prayerful judgment over the ill-starred
Charles.   We may observe further, in respect to the
moral functions of Zeus, that it is his high prerogative to
visit with retribution unrighteous deeds of whatsoever

description; he is the avenging Jove, and the giver of just recompence to all who have been unrighteously treated either in their persons or property (*Odys.* I. 379; *Il.* III. 321). He is, moreover, specially invoked to sanction the obligation of an oath (*Od.* XIX. 303; *Il.* III. 276); he protects with special care the houseless wanderer, and penceless mendicant (*Od.* VI. 207), and with the significant surname of ἱκετήσιος keeps an open ear for the cries of the friendless suppliant. He protects the rights of hospitality under the hallowed title of Ξένιος (*Od.* XIV. 283), and his altar lends a sacredness to the domestic hearth (XXII. 335). Whatsoever, in short, either in the shape of stern law or of mild equity, renders man an object of interest and of love to man, comes from Jove. He is God in a sense that belongs to no other deity. Without him men would be wild beasts, life an uninterrupted war, and Olympus a sublime bedlam.

PROPOSITION VII.—Though the absolute power of Jove is not to be questioned by any of the gods, and all opposition to his supreme will vain, yet in the general course of his divine government, a large liberty of action is allowed to all the members of the celestial aristocracy, who have each his separate rights, with which, except on great occasions, and for high providential purposes, Jove will not willingly interfere; and thus an individual god may often be found involved in a course of action opposed to the will of Jove, and persevering for a long time in this course of opposition, till in the fulness of the destined years (περιπλομένων ἐνιαυτῶν, *Od.* I. 16), he submits himself to the will of Jove, and the general council of the gods.

A notable example of this we have in the conduct of

Poseidon throughout the *Odyssey* (I. 19, and many other places), which of itself is sufficient to show the fallacy of Dr. Ihne's remark, that in the *Odyssey* "Olympus does not resound with everlasting quarrels." This circumstance, that there is less of brawl and bickering in the Olympic assembly of the *Odyssey*, is, as we have observed, purely accidental, and resulting from the nature of the subject ; for Poseidon, the most important member of the celestial senate next to Zeus, is as active and unabated in his hostility in the one poem as in the other. A division of the celestial counsels is, in fact, the natural, and unavoidable result of a polytheistic system of divine government, and the supreme ruler will be more or less thwarted in carrying out his views, just as on earth most monarchies which are nominally absolute, are in practice limited by the aristocracy of whatever nature, hereditary or bureaucratic, that encircles the throne ; and in this matter of government, as in all other points except immortality, the Homeric heaven is only the highest power of the Homeric earth. If our nice modern sense of propriety is startled by the rude language which Achilles casts in the teeth of the king of men (*Il.* I. 225), we cannot expect to find speech much more courteous in the mouth even of the wise Athena, when she stands in a hostile relation to her father Jove (*Il.* VIII. 360) ; and if Jupiter's one daughter Ate (like the homunculus in the second part of Faust') turns her pernicious activity against the mighty father that bore her (*Il.* XIX. 95), it is only because, in heroic and feudal times, such ungracious things are sometimes done on earth, and because man has, in all ages, been fond of being governed by gods, created as much as may

---

[1] " Am Ende hangen wir doch ab
Von Creaturen die wir machten."

be in his own likeness.   Liberty of thought and feeling,
speech and action, belongs as essentially to the gods in
heaven, as to men on earth; and it is only when this
liberty is carried so far as to threaten the dissolution of
the firm framework of things, that the omnipotent will
of Zeus interferes to prevent fatal collisions, and to restore
a necessary peace.   We are not, therefore, to be surprised
at the great length of tether allowed to Poseidon (*Il.*
XIII. 10, XIV. 510), when Jove is absent among the milk-
fed just men of Thrace; nay, it is plain that the theoretical omnipotence of Zeus is sometimes practically limited
by the decidedly expressed dissent of the other gods, as,
for instance, in the matter of Sarpedon (*Il.* XVI. 440),
and in the often repeated threat, ἔρδ᾿· ἀτὰρ οὔ τοι πάντες
ἐπαινέομεν θεοὶ ἄλλοι.   In another very singular passage, to
which we shall have to recur (*Il.* IV. 1-72), something of
the nature of compromise, from motives of mere expediency
and for the sake of peace, regulates the conduct of the
omnipotent Olympian at a most important crisis of the
strife; in fact, Zeus here comports himself less like an
absolute monarch than like a prime minister of such an
aristocratic constitution as that of Great Britain, who,
when he appears to lead the nation, is in fact led by a
party.   These are inconsistencies, which it was not
Homer's business, and therefore it cannot be ours, to
reconcile; we only remark that "*die Welt ist voller
Widersprüche*"—the world is full of contradictions, as a
wise German poet sings; and that that philosopher is by
no means nearest the truth, whose cosmologic doctrine is
the most simple and the most consistent.

Our next propositions shall proceed to set forth more
distinctly some of the most striking of the divine attributes, as exhibited in the pages of Homer.

PROPOSITION VIII.—Next to immortality, that which most strikingly distinguishes the gods from mortal men is POWER. Though not formally omnipotent, no pious mind will allow itself to suppose a limitation to their power. In this quality alone no mortal man can dare to enter into competition with them. In moral qualities they seem to stand pretty much on a level with their worshippers.

'Tis an old saying of the philosophers with regard to popular religions—

"Primus in orbe deos fecit Timor :"

and with regard to the baser sort of minds, that is, the majority (οἱ πολλοὶ κακοί), it is no doubt true. Cleanthes, in *Cicero* (*de Nat. Deor.* II. 5), states as the third of the four causes why the belief of the gods is universal amongst men, this, that "the minds of men were terrified by lightnings, tempests, snow, hail, devastations, pestilence, earthquakes, sudden sinkings of the earth, portentous births, meteors, comets," and other dreadful phenomena of that sort; and, under the influence of this fear, he continues, they were led to suspect the existence of some divine and celestial power. The prevalence of this feeling of fear before superior power, is sufficiently manifest in the character of the Homeric gods, and the temper of Homeric piety. But the full development of this ugly side of old Hellenic religion we must defer till we come to make some remarks on that feeling of jealousy towards mortal men which so strongly characterizes the Homeric gods. Meanwhile, it may be sufficient to remark that, for all practical purposes, without affecting metaphysical curiosity, the θεοὶ δέ τε πάντα δύνανται of *Od.* X. 306, may be taken as a general expression of Homer's opinion with regard to the gods. How much also mere power is re-

garded as the distinguishing characteristic of the divine
nature, appears most strikingly from this, that the sons
of the gods often differ from mortal men only in superior
strength ; in virtue they may be much inferior, as in the
familiar case of Polypheme—

ἀντίθεον Πολύφημον ὅου κράτος ἐστὶ μέγιστον
πᾶσιν Κυκλώπεσσιν.—*Od.* I. 70.

Such passages as *Od.* XII. 107, where it is said that
not even a god could do so and so, are, with reference to the
supposed power of the gods, not to be pressed curiously,
they being merely loose colloquialisms perfectly identical
with our English style, when we say, *it would defy the
devil to do so.*   The only thing that the gods cannot do, is
to save from death (*Od.* III. 236) ; but this also, I suspect,
is not to be pressed further than the fact that, in the
general case, the gods never do save from death.   Had
Homer been catechised curiously with regard to his belief,
whether it was within the power of the gods to save from
death, there is little doubt that he would have given as
orthodox an answer as any Christian that repeats the
Nicean creed.   It appears, indeed, from the *Iliad*, that
Jove was both able and willing to rescue Sarpedon from the
fate that cut him off, and was restrained from doing so
only by a regard to the representations of his yokefellow,
Hera, whose constant habit it was to thwart her husband's
plans.   Omnipotent in all points he evidently was not,
as he never could have been so without nullifying the
rights of the other gods.   In her own domain, of course,
Aphrodite would brook no rival, and even Hypnos has
power over the Eternal (XIV. 352).   But all this does not
touch his practical all-sufficiency as the Supreme Governor,
moral and physical, of the universe.   Whatever grades,

distinctions, and rights might have been among the gods themselves, these differences affect not the general relation in which the mortal stands to the immortal, viz., a relation of complete and absolute dependence. How far the gods themselves, and even Zeus, may have been secretly subject to some dim unknown power called Fate or Fortune, we now proceed to inquire.

PROPOSITION IX.—Of an omnipotent Fortune, or all-controlling Fate, as a separate independent power, to which gods and men must equally yield, the practical theology of Homer knows nothing ; nevertheless there are certain dim indications of an irreversible order of things—it is not said how arising—to which even the gods submit. This the later theology of the Greeks seems to have worked up into the idea of a separate independent divine power called FATE.

The common idea, that the Greek theology represents the gods as subject to a superior power called Fate or the Fates, is derived from the tragedians, and from later writers generally, certainly not from Homer. In the Homeric poems, Jove and the gods are the only prominent and all-controlling actors in the great drama of existence. None of Homer's pious heroes, when narrating their fortunes, set forth,—

" Fortuna Omnipotens et ineluctabile Fatum,"

VIRGIL, *Æn.* VIII. 334,

as the great authors of their bliss or bane. On the contrary, it is certain that μοῖρα or αἶσα is merely the lot or portion dealt out by the supreme providence of the gods, and that whatsoever is μόρσιμον or fated to a man, is so because it is θέσφατον, or spoken by the divine decree. These words are, in fact, identical (*Od.* IV. 562, x. 473).

Zeus is especially named as the sender of a man's μοῖρα, (*Od.* XI. 559), and in the same style occurs Διὸς αἶσα (*Il.* XVII. 321, IX. 604 ; *Od.* IX. 52), and θεοῦ μοῖρα (*Od.* XI. 292). And these passages come to us, not only with their own distinct evidence, but with the whole weight of the general doctrine of the overruling providence of θεοὶ and Ζεύς, which we find under every possible variety of shape in almost every page of the Homeric writings. There is no such sentiment in Homer as that in Herodotus, quoted by Nägelsbach,—Τὴν πεπρωμένην μοῖραν ἀδύνατά ἐστι ἀποφυγέειν καὶ θεῷ (Clio, 91), nor that which Æschylus puts into the mouth of Prometheus (v. 516),—

Οὔκουν ἂν ἐκφύγοι γε (*i.e.* Ζεὺς) τὴν πεπρωμένην,

and though it be quite true that the idea of μοῖρα, like that of "Ατη and Κήρ, is in some places impersonated (*Il.* XIX. 87 ; xx. 128 ; *Od.* VII. 197), I can see no proof that the poet looked upon this Αἶσα, the spinner of fatal threads, as any more substantial person than "Ατη ; much less can I see the slightest reason to exalt her above those very supreme rulers, of whose functions she is only a cloudy and half-developed incarnation. I say *half-developed*, because, as above remarked, there is a great difference in Homer between the full-grown gods, clad with all the dignity of a person, and such personages as "Ατη, Μοῖρα, and the Harpies, who, like the Egyptian frogs mentioned by Diodorus, if gods at all, have not yet acquired strength enough to shake themselves free from the slime out of which their physiognomy has to be shaped.

Altogether, Homer is a poet of too sunny a complexion to deal much in the dark idea of a remorseless Fate ; and if, on a sad occasion (*Il.* VI. 487), Hector comforts

Andromache by saying, that no one can take away his life ὑπὲρ αἶσαν, and that no one can escape his μοῖρα, this manner of speaking is not Turkish any more than it is Calvinistic ; it is only human. Such a thought occurs to all men under certain circumstances. That no man can escape death when his day is come (*Il.* XII. 326) is what any man may say as well as Sarpedon.

But though I cannot allow that anything like a regular doctrine of Fate superior to Jove is taught by Homer, it is not to be denied that there are expressions and situations in his poems from which the Hellenic mind, if so inclined, might easily develop such a doctrine as we stated above (p. 19) that the tragedians had shaped out from the idea of Ate. And there is nothing more obvious than the necessity of thought which led the Greeks to work out this idea of Fate to the stature which we find it has attained in that passage of Herodotus, and in the tragedians. For, to the thoughtful mind, in reference to many things that daily happen in this world, the divine power being first postulated as unbounded, the question will always arise,—*if the divine power* COULD *have made the world otherwise, why* DID *it not do so?* This question the Homeric men, if they had no tradition of the doctrine of Moses, that the world lies under a curse for the sin of the first man, and if they did not believe, as they certainly did not, in a devil, could only answer by saying, *that things are what they are, and as they are, by some inherent necessity of nature,* and not even a god could make them otherwise than they are made. That some dim idea of this kind may have hovered before Homer's mind is extremely probable, though he certainly has not worked it up into any definite system which his reader can lay hold of. Homer, as the event proved, had

C

said enough to feed the metaphysico-imaginative wit of his countrymen, and had dropt the seed out of which a regular personal Μοῖρα or 'Ανάγκη might grow; and, if there were theological sects in ancient Greece inclined to wrangle about the comparative powers of Μοῖρα and Ζεὺς, as even our theologians draw swords about liberty and necessity, both parties, with that ingenuity of which religious sects are seldom void, would readily find in the Homeric bible texts sufficiently pliable to their several opinions.[1]

PROPOSITION X.—The gods know all things. This proposition, however, like that respecting the divine omnipotence, must not be pressed curiously, but understood with reference to the uses of the divine knowledge in the moral government of the world.

The practical omniscience of the Homeric gods is implied in their general control and superintendence of human affairs, which, without such an attribute, could not possibly be exercised in the grand style which is characteristic of Homer; the special doctrine, however, θεοὶ δέ τε πάντα ἴσασιν (*Od.* IV. 379), was as familiar to the Greek ear as the θεοὶ δέ τε πάντα δύνανται already quoted, and this quality of superhuman knowledge not limited by the vulgar barriers of space and time, though

---

[1] Nägelsbach, after reviewing the passages which seem to speak for the independent functions of the Μοῖρα, with a more serious and favourable eye than I have been able to do in the text, concludes thus :—"The will which rules the Olympian commonwealth is not so absolute as that every existing might necessarily retreats before it. For the human mind is formed with an irrepressible desire to give a head to the multiform congregation of the gods, to provide a principle of unity, which shall hold together the articulated organism of the celestial society ; and the product of this desire is the Μοῖρα, a power made superior to the gods; *another essay of the human mind to satisfy its innate longing for a monotheistic view of the universe,*" p. 127. I cannot see that Homer had anything so very definite in view when he talks of the Μοῖρα. It appears to me that he never conceived of it distinctly as anything independent of the will of the gods.

it belongs to all the partakers of an immortal nature, is, with peculiar emphasis, applied to the elemental god, Helios, ὅς πάντ' ἐφορᾷ καὶ πάντ' ἐπακούει (*Od.* XII. 323), and to Zeus, the moral governor of the world (XV. 523). It is not to be expected, however, that the sense-bound poet of an early stage of civilisation should be able, on all occasions, to preserve in fact the consistency of this high ideal of the celestial intellect, which he lays down theoretically. On the contrary, as Nägelsbach well observes, the spectacle of a self-constituted but continually self-baffled ideal of supersensuous perfection, is that which the Homeric gods (and I may add, the theological doctrines of nations much more highly cultivated) present. Examples are frequent; but *Il.* XVIII. 168, and XIX. 112, show more vividly than any other passages how even the father of gods and men may, at times, be blinded and circumvented by the agency of his own ministers.

PROPOSITION XI.—The gods are easily offended, wrathful and jealous. Their hatred is the more to be dreaded in proportion as they are more powerful than mortals; and their high resolves, when once made, are carried out with a relentless firmness, that can be appeased only by the greatest possible sacrifices on the part of the guilty or unfortunate offender.

Nothing strikes the Christian reader of Homer with more astonishment, and it may be loathing, than the extremely low moral character of the celestial personages who are held up to view as the objects of popular reverence; and of the base feelings by which the bosoms of these high persons are continually actuated, that of a purely selfish jealousy on private grounds of quarrel, and an unrelenting spirit of personal hostility, is to a well-

constituted moral nature the most odious. One is at
times tempted, considering these things, to say of the
Homeric gods generally, as Dr. Ihne says of the gods of
the *Iliad*, that they are "worse than the men." Certainly, whatever be the temper of the gods of the *Iliad* in
this respect, that of the *Odyssey* is nothing better; for
what wrath can be more relentless and persecuting than
that of Poseidon against Ulysses? (*Od.* I. 20 ; XIII. 125 ;
&c.), and what motive for this anger can be less noble and
more akin to the meanest humanity, than that assigned
by the poet, *Od.* I. 69 ? Polypheme is a godless monster
and a cannibal; and because Ulysses, to save himself and
his comrades from being eaten alive, deprives this em-
bruted hulk of his eye-sight, he incurs the indignation of
the deity, who happens to be the monster's father, to such
a degree, that nothing but the lives of all his trusty comrades can satiate the divine appetite for revenge. Nor is
this a solitary case; but it goes through the whole poetry
of Homer with such a pervading inspiration, that, though
living in an age when more just ideas of the divine character were entertained by not a few, Virgil did not think
that he could scheme out the characters of his immortal
Epos, without having a Juno to perform the like part.
Nor is the wrath or fierce hostility of the gods the worst
feature in the divine character. The mean selfish jealousy
with which Poseidon regards the commercial prosperity of
the Phæacians, is comparable to nothing so fitly as the
spirit with which the members of close corporations in
this country, without the slightest regard to the public
good, defended their exclusive privileges before a committee
of an aristocratic House of Commons. What shall we say
to all this ? Only one thing can be said, that the men
who could so conceive, and so picture their gods, were

themselves in a very low state of moral development. Whether Homer himself was not a little advanced in ethical insight beyond the men whose traditionary theology he received into his verse, is not easy to say; certainly some of the most glaring instances of moral deformity in the character and actions of his divine personages may be conveniently explained on the supposition already mentioned, that he is there giving us the crude and unassimilated elements of an old Pelasgic creed; but this consideration will not help us very far, as the conduct of Achilles himself—a fair specimen of the popular hero of those days—is, in point of inexorability and passion, no unworthy type of the "*tantæne animis cælestibus iræ*" which marks the characters in the Olympian drama. If Achilles may immolate his thousands being a mortal, Poseidon, being a god, may swallow up his tens of thousands. We are forced, therefore—if we will have a palliation for this monstrous theology—to fall back upon this proposition, that, in the Homeric conception of the gods, holiness, or moral excellence of any kind, forms no essential element. Superior strength is their characteristic attribute, and fear rather than love the inspiration of their worshippers. The gods, in fact—except in the single case of Zeus, as moral governor—are only incarnations of the powers and forces that we see everywhere at work around us in nature; and as such it is not to be expected that they should manifest any moral feelings whatever. The wrath of Poseidon, therefore, though represented to us by the poet as the evil passion of a being like to our evil selves, is fundamentally nothing but the violence of the ocean waves, which, at the present day, rages and roars with as little regard to any moral principle as it did in the age of Homer. The god Poseidon, as he stands in

Homer, is a clumsy union of two incompatible characters ;
an unruly elemental power, and a being formed after the
image of man, and therefore properly with a moral nature ;
but the poet, partly because he was himself unacquainted
with a high moral type of humanity, partly because he
could not shake the gods free from that merely physical
character which originally was their only one, was able to
produce nothing but a gigantic incongruity, to which all
the harmony of his numbers, and all the magic of Phidias'
chisel, could not afterwards reconcile the growing practical reason of his countrymen.

PROPOSITION XII.—The gods are capable of acting
falsely, and of deceiving the expectations which they had
raised in the breasts of mortals. A wise man should not
trust absolutely to a god, but, on slippery occasions,
exact an oath for the greater security.

This proposition contains the culminating point of
odious immorality in the character of the Homeric gods as
depicted by Homer ; and though it is no doubt true that
the most glaring instances of divine want of faith occur
in the *Iliad*, and that for sufficient reasons already mentioned, there are examples enough of the same principle
in the other poem, to show that the author of both was
either the same, or had fundamentally the same conceptions of the divine character. In the *Odyssey*, Ulysses
exacts an oath both of Calypso and Circe, because he
could not trust them without it ; and so much accustomed is he to the idea of deceit on the part of the gods,
that even when the benign daughter of Cadmus appears
over the rush of waves to save him from a watery death,
the first thing he does is to suspect that one of the gods
is *weaving a wile for his ruin* (*Od.* v. 356). Telemachus,

in the same way, will not believe that Ulysses is his
father, but fears that some god is bewitching him—θέλγει
(*Od.* XVI. 195)—to his woe. In the *Iliad*, again, Jove
sends οὖλος ὄνειρος to deceive Agamemnon, and Agamemnon is a fool (νήπιος) for believing him (II. 38). The king
of men, in another place, charges the king of gods and
men with an evil deceit, κακὴ ἀπάτη (*Il.* IX. 21), and the
fair Helen, in speaking to the fairest Aphrodite, uses
a word—ἠπεροπεύειν (*Il.* III. 399)—which, according to
Homeric usage, is applicable only to swindlers and seducers
of the lowest kind (*Od.* XV. 419). But worse remains.
Athena, the incarnated wisdom of "the father"—one of
the most perfect characters in Hellenic theology—on two
distinct occasions, perpetrates a very gross act of deceit
and falsehood, from which every honourable and manly
feeling revolts; in the *first* place, she solicits and
obtains from Zeus (the ὅρκιος, the avenger of violated
truth !) the permission to tempt Pandarus to violate the
treaty solemnly sworn to by the leaders of the Trojans
and the Greeks, which treaty is accordingly broken, and
the daughter of Zeus is guilty of tempting a mortal man
to commit an act of pure perjury, her father consenting
(*Il.* IV.). In the *second* place (what Hermann, in his Latin
argument, calls an "*atrox dolus*"), by personating
Deiphobus (*Il.* XXII. 227), she draws away the unsuspect-
ing Hector into that unequal conflict with the son of
Peleus, in which he was to meet his sad fate. Now, with
regard to these truly monster traits of divine character as
occurring in the two last passages of the *Iliad*, we must
make the special remark, that these extraordinary acts of
divine perfidy are all made in favour of the Greeks, whose
poet Homer was by strong preference, as every book of
the poem shows. The cases, therefore, fall within the

extensive category of abnormal moral states caused by
self-love, national vanity, and party-preference, so that,
in fact, the poet merely says, in a rude unqualified way
(being accustomed to plain speaking), what all parties,
and especially all religious parties, in all ages, have supposed and acted on—that when Heaven is interested in
a cause (or the church, as we say now) justice may become injustice, and truth and falsehood be confounded.
Still it must be admitted that there is a wide moral gulf
between Homer, who makes his gods do these things,
and our modern religious parties, who only do them in
the name of God.   These, by their evil deeds, make void
their own scriptures ; the countrymen of the old poet, for
every diabolic deed, might plead a divine precedent in the
only scripture of which they were in possession.   With
regard to the other less glaring instances of divine deceit,
the observations made under the former head apply.   In
a warlike and semi-savage people, cunning and stratagem,
lies and deceit of every kind, must ever—of course, within
certain recognised bounds—be in high esteem; and Ulysses,
no less than Achilles, will find his pattern and his patron
in Heaven.   It is also to be borne in mind, when considering these matters, that the devout Greek habit of
referring every internal change of feeling, or external
change of circumstance, to direct divine agency, almost
necessitated the extraordinary language which they sometimes use, of their gods.   As, for instance, when in an
adverse position, one of the Homeric warriors exclaims—

$$Ζεῦ \ πάτερ, \ ἦ \ ῥά \ νυ \ καὶ \ σὺ \ φιλοψευδὴς \ ἐτέτυξο$$
$$πάγχυ \ μάλ'.$$

Il. XII. 164.

" O father Zeus, you are fond of lies above all measure,"

these impious-sounding words, when translated into modern language, merely mean, "*gracious God, how have I been deceived in all this; how have my expectations been disappointed!*" Zeus, in the view of the Homeric men, was at once the inspirer of the hopes which this man had entertained (*Prop.* III.) and the arranger of the external circumstances (*Prop.* II.) by which they had been frustrated; therefore he says bluntly, "*O Jove, thou hast deceived me signally!*" instead of "*O God, how signally have I been deceived!*"

PROPOSITION XIII.—The gods, as the givers of all good things, are to be regarded as habitually inspired with a benevolent affection towards the human race; and though, on certain occasions, and against particular persons, their indignation is terrible, and their vengeance not easily satisfied, still their general character, in reference to offending mortals, is placability.

The passages which I have to adduce in support of this proposition from the Homeric writings are comparatively few; but we are not on that account to suppose that it contains a sentiment less familiar to the minds of the Greeks, than those of a less amiable character contained in the immediately preceding propositions. As those years are often the happiest in a nation's history which furnish fewest materials for the pen of the dramatic historian, so those attributes of the Hellenic gods are not to be regarded as the least influential, which give occasion to the fewest startling events in the narration of a popular Epos.[1] It is in the nature of things that the wrath of gods, like

---

[1] I scarcely think Nägelsbach has sufficiently regarded this when he states in such strong language, that "love to God could not arise in the Hellenic mind, as it appears in Homer, because there is no love of the gods to men presupposed from which it could arise," p. 201.

the wrath of men, just because it is an exception from
the common order of proceedings, should give rise to
critical situations, strange concatenations, and striking
catastrophes, such as form the natural raw materials for
an Epic poet to work up. So the divine wrath consequent
on the sin of Adam supplied a theme of appropriate
grandeur for Milton's lofty Muse ; so the miseries of a
thirty years' war became pictorial in the hands of Schiller ;
and in the same way, Poseidon ἀσπερχὲς μενεαίνων furnished
Homer with a series of the most varied adventures, which
he might have sought for in vain among the stores of rich
bounty spread on groaning boards by the θεοὶ δωτῆρες ἐάων
(*Od.* VIII. 325). The general benevolence of the Homeric
gods, notwithstanding the special instances of wrath just
mentioned, is to be inferred not so much from a special
designation to that effect, as from the general tone of
cheerful gratitude with which their goodness is continually
acknowledged by their worshippers on all the occasions of
common life. Notwithstanding the strong expressions
quoted under the previous heads, no person can rise from
the perusal of the Homeric poems, with an impression
that there is anything stern and forbidding in the habitual
aspect of the gods, or that fear was the only strong feeling
in the minds of their worshippers. Though power is their
principal characteristic, it is never supposed that they use
that attribute maliciously, or wantonly, merely to vex
mankind. On the contrary, Zeus, even when in the mid-
career of his predestined course, looks down with pity on
the mortals whose fate it is to suffer sharp sorrows, that
the purposes of the Almighty one may be fulfilled ; and
the prayer of the labouring good man prevails, if not to
avert the blow altogether, at least to blunt the point of
the weapon which inflicts it (*Il.* VIII. 245). That the gods,

though not easily turned from their purposes (*Od.* III. 147),
are yet to a certain extent, with the single exception of
Hades (*Il.* IX. 158), στρεπτοί (*Id.* 497), is so much an
essential doctrine of Homeric theology, that it is expressly
stated as the only ground on which prayers, sacrifices, and
other acts of divine worship proceed—

> Καὶ μὲν τοὺς θυέεσσι καὶ εὐχωλῇς ἀγανῇσιν
> λοιβῇ τε κνίσσῃ τε παρατρωπῶσ᾽ ἄνθρωποι.

Il. IX. 500.

And in general, we may say that, though the gods of the
Greeks, as portrayed by Homer, present many individual
traits in common with the lowest theology, or rather
demonology of the most savage peoples, their general
character is as mild and beneficent as the necessities of
their physical original, and the habitude of a warlike
atmosphere allowed.

The few propositions that remain relate to the method
of communication between gods and men, and the obligations arising out of the relation in which men, as dependent and responsible creatures, stand to the gods, as the
supreme disposers of all things, and the moral governors
of the world.

PROPOSITION XIV.—The gods maintain an intercourse
with men as part of the ordinary course of their providence, and this intercourse consists principally in revelations of the divine will, and specially of future events,
made to men by oracular voices, dreams, and sacred signs,
the transmission and interpretation of which belongs generally, though by no means exclusively, to certain persons
peculiarly set apart to sacred functions, called soothsayers
and priests.

There is no necessity for marshalling an array of pas-

sages to prove matters so familiarly known to every reader
of Homer as those mentioned in the first part of this proposition.   But the second part of it is very important, not
only in reference to Homer, but in reference to the whole
genius and character of social religion, as exhibited in the
history of the ancient Greeks.   There is no appearance of
a caste of priests in Homer, such as is in India and Egypt;
no far-reaching closely-banded corporation of priests, fenc-
ing society round with a bristling rampart of artificial ortho-
doxies, such as exists now in many parts of Christendom.
Völcker, it seems from a quotation in Nägelsbach (p. 176),
has lately hazarded the assertion, that there is a " certain
hierarchy of Homeric priests;" but this emphatic word
hierarchy is precisely what no unprejudiced reader will
ever witch out of Homer, any more than he can extract
the same doctrine out of the New Testament.   Priests
there are, no doubt, in Homer, as we see in the very
opening scene of the first book of the *Iliad*, but they seem
always attached as stationary ministers to some particular
temple or shrine; and nowhere do they come forward in
that position, and with that importance, which belongs to
a body of sacerdotal men, banded together for such social
purposes, as we find the Romish priests in Roman Catholic countries now banded.   Against all such pretensions
on the part of the Homeric priests, it is sufficient—we
entirely agree with Nägelsbach—to mention the single
fact, that these functionaries are nowhere, in Homer, represented as *the only and indispensable mediators between
earth and heaven*, and that, wanting this, they want the
grand condition precedent to the possibility of a hierarchy
properly so called.   No modern Plymouth brother or
Quaker could have less exclusive ideas on the subject of
priesthood than the old Hellenic Homer; he mentions

priests, indeed, and with respect, as persons existing and performing honoured functions with benefit to the community, but he has not the most remote conception that the divine Spirit, like the electric fluid, has any exclusive preference to being conducted through a sacerdotal channel. Such an idea is, in fact, altogether precluded by the habitual direct operation of the divine Spirit on the mind of all men described in Proposition III.; besides, we find constantly the functions of priests and soothsayers performed in a voluntary way, without apology, by all sorts of persons. The right of laic divination is asserted by Athena as a thing well known (*Od.* I. 200), and exercised by Helen (xv. 172), while acts of public (*Il.* III. 271) and of family devotion (*Od.* III. 418) (see Nägelsbach, p. 180) are everywhere performed by the chiefs without the intervention of a priest, in a manner which, in a sacerdotal country like modern Spain, could in nowise be tolerated. We may take it with us, therefore, as an undoubted fact from the earliest records of the most cultivated nation of antiquity, that freedom from sacerdotal bonds existed among them in the earliest times, as the indispensable condition of that luxuriant growth and bloom of intelligence to which they afterwards attained.

PROPOSITION XV.—The gods visit the earth, and often appear in a visible shape to mortals, generally, however, under some human mask, in such a manner that, while their godhead is veiled to the general eye, they are capable of being seen and recognised in their divine character by the unfilmed eye of their pious worshippers.

Dr. Ihne, in the passage above quoted, lays down a distinction in this matter of theophany, which he has observed between the *Iliad* and the *Odyssey.* I can find none. " In the *Iliad*," says he, "the gods are visible to every one, except when they surround themselves with a cloud ; in the *Odyssey* they are usually invisible except when they take the shape of men. How the first of these assertions should have been made in the face of the well-known lines, *Il.* I. 197—

στῆ δ' ὄπιθεν, ξανθῆς τε κόμης ἕλε Πηλείωνα,
οἴῳ φαινομένη—

I do not know. This passage, indeed, represents a grand condition of every theophany, both in the *Iliad* and the *Odyssey*, that the god does not appear to the profane-staring many (in this view contrast Leviticus ix. 23), but only to the particular favoured mortal with whom he stands in a spiritual relation—

οὐ γάρ πω πάντεσσι θεοὶ φαίνονται ἐναργεῖς.

Od. XVI. 161.

As little have I been able to observe any difference between the two poems, in respect of the human mask which the gods generally assume. This, so far as I can see, is the rule in the *Iliad* as much as in the *Odyssey* (see *Il.* v. 462, 604, XIII. 45, XIV. 136, &c. &c.) ; and, indeed, there are few extensively believed creeds, of which the appearance of the divine Being in a human shape does not form a characteristic element. The Epicureans were not so far wrong here as in some other points of their theology, which they made to float so uselessly in the air. Had they brought down their anthropomorphic divinities to walk the earth with a human sympathy as well as with a divine power, they might certainly have calculated on a thousand worshippers, for one that would have been attracted by the "round gods"[1] of the Stoics. The impor-

---

[1] *Mundum ipsum sensibus præditum the sneer of the Epicurean interlocu-
rotundum volubilem ardentem Deum,* tor in Cicero (*De Nat. Deor.* I. 8).

tant fact with regard to theophany in Homer is, that it is regulated in all respects like the apparition of ghosts in modern demonology. Modern ghosts, like the ancient classical idols, appear always in a human shape ; and, like the ancient gods, they appear not at random to any person or all persons, but to certain persons, on special occasions, for special reasons, and for special purposes. Only to certain highly-favoured tribes, in this respect elevated above the general level of humanity, do they appear publicly and ἐναργεῖς ; as to the Phæacians (*Od.* VII. 202), a people who are ἀγχίθεοι, or " near to the gods," pretty much in the same way that Adam and Eve in paradise stand before the mind of the devout Christian in modern times, as living and walking with God after a fashion to which not the most highly-favoured saint in this age of moral decadence can attain. One other remark with regard to divine theophany, Nägelsbach makes, which did not occur to me. The mighty Zeus never appears in his own person on the stage of human affairs. Between him and his wise daughter, the nearest to him of the celestial conclave, there is a mighty gulf in this respect. Jove sits apart. In Homer, as in Horace, he has nothing like to him in all the universe, and nothing second—

" Nec viget quicquam simile aut secundum."

To a being so highly exalted, converse with such ephemeral creatures as mortal men is possible only through mediators.

PROPOSITION XVI.—Worship is due by mortal men to all the gods, with Jove supreme at their head ; but more especially to the patron god or goddess of particular places and functions, with whom the worshipper is under any

particular circumstances brought into more particular connexion. The gods have a special delight in receiving such
reverential acknowledgments from men (*Od.* III. 438),
come bodily to receive the sacrifices that are offered to
them (*Id.* III. 435), and remember the pious offerer,
rewarding him in due season.

In the Homeric idea of worship by sacrifice, there is
something particularly simple and unsophisticated. The
share which is given to the gods of the wine that flows,
and the flesh that smokes on the festal board, proceeds
from a combination of the two ideas, that man owes an
acknowledgment of some kind to the powers by whom his
existence is sustained; and that these powers, being essentially human in their habits and sympathies, can enjoy
such offerings of gratitude as one mortal would offer to be
enjoyed by another.[1] This case is precisely analogous to
that of the departed spirits, who are represented in Hades
as sipping nourishment from the pools of streaming blood
which Ulysses had shed on entering their domain (*Od.* XI.).
The feeling of grateful dependence on which this worship
depends is a characteristic of every healthy mind in the
Homeric page :

οὐδὲ συβώτης
λήθετ᾽ ἄρ ἀθανάτων φρεσὶ γὰρ κέχρητ᾽ ἀγαθῇσιν.

And on the due performance of such acts of pious acknowledgment rests a sort of claim on the part of pious men
to receive assistance from the gods in the hour of need
(*Od.* I. 65, XIX. 365, *Il.* I. 39).

PROPOSITION XVII.—Even of more ˌimportance in a
religious man than external acts of ceremonial worship is

---

[1] The idea of vicarious atonement
by sacrifice, so clearly indicated in the
sacrifice of the scape-goat (Lev. xvi. 21),
is not to be found in Homer.

his duty to cherish that feeling of dependence on the celestial powers, from which all acts of acceptable worship proceed. Nothing is more characteristic of a pious man, according to the Homeric idea, than the habitual deep impression which he carries along with him, of the infinite distance between the divine and the human condition. Of this feeling the natural expression is prayer (to which the gods generally, though not always, lend a ready ear), as of its absence the natural indication is pride and arrogance, and a boastful spirit : qualities of mind altogether inconsistent with the condition of humanity, and therefore rendering man peculiarly obnoxious to the divine displeasure.

That humility of mind is not a characteristic of heathen, but only of Christian piety, is a proposition which we sometimes hear stated in a declamatory way from the pulpit, or even in serious works of moral philosophy ; but every page of Homer, as of the tragedians, cries out against such a representation, the fact being, that few virtues are more prominently brought forward by Homer than humility ; and in the words of his wisdom, as in those of Solomon, pride, insolence, and haughtiness are the universal forerunners of a fall. In the first place, the continual recurrence of prayer under all the varied circumstances of life, is of itself an indication of a state of mind from which lofty looks and vain self-sufficiency are far. " *Who knows, but that with the help of God* (σύν δαίμονι) *I may prevail?* " is the modest language of a Homeric hero when undertaking a difficult mission (*Il.* xv. 403) ; and in the ethico-religious language of the poet, ὑβρισταί, insolent, haughty, and overbearing men are coupled with ἄγριοι and οὐδὲ δίκαιοι, and contrasted with those whose mind is θεουδής, or godly (*Od.* vi. 121). Nothing is more conspicuous in the character of the wise Ulysses, than the humility with which he throws off all those compliments paid him by his admiring entertainers, in which they liken him to the immortal gods :

οὐ γὰρ ἔγωγε
ἀθανάτοισιν ἔοικα, τοὶ οὐρανὸν εὐρὺν ἔχουσιν.—*Od.* VII. 209.

a beautiful contrast to the sounding impiety with which Greek kings of the East in later days allowed altars to be erected to their honour, and caused the epithet ΘΕΟΣ to be stamped upon their coins ! It is the most certain of all doctrines with Homer, that no man whose breast is possessed with this superhuman conceit will long escape the anger of the gods, with whose perfections he provokes an impious comparison. So Eurytus the bowman, puffed up with self-sufficiency on account of his prowess, dies prematurely by the shafts of Apollo (*Od.* VIII. 225) ; so Thamyris was blinded by the Muses (*Il.* II. 595) ; so Ajax was whelmed in the waters of Poseidon, for the insolent boast (like that of Capaneus in Æschylus),--

φῆ ῥ᾽ ἀέκητι θεῶν φυγέειν μέγα λαῖτμα θαλάσσης.—*Od.* IV. 504.

No doctrine, therefore, is more essentially Homeric than that of Sophocles in the first chorus of the *Antigone :*

Ζεὺς γὰρ μεγάλης γλώσσης κόμπους
ὑπερεχθαίρει·

and if there be any apparent exceptions to this rule, they are easily explained. It is quite true that man does not stand at such an infinite distance from the divine nature in a polytheistic, as under a monotheistic system ; and therefore it is nothing surprising to find gods of an inferior order sometimes even made subject to mortal men for the nonce, as Proteus, *Od.* IV. ; but with all this the grand doctrine remains, that with the gods in council, or with Jove as their natural head and representative, no mortal may dare to contend (*Il.* VI. 129, XVII. 98) ; and of this the example of Diomede in the fifth book of the *Iliad*, which seems to indicate the contrary, is the strongest proof. The actions done by the Etolian hero in that remarkable book are all done by the special advice, and under the direct guidance of the daughter of Jove, and the responsibility of the deeds committed belongs, in the eye of the poet, altogether to her, and not at all to the son of Tydeus. The wounding of Aphrodite proves nothing ; the goddess of beauty, like all the other heathen gods, is powerful only in her own province. The attack made on Apollo is a more serious matter, and the poet treats it accordingly ; the impetuous mortal listens to the wise warning of the god, and retreats from the unequal combat (*Il.* V. 440-44). With the same pious instinct he retreats from Ares once (v. 606), and again (819) ; and when the god of war is at last worsted at his own game, it is not the hand of a mortal, but of a superior goddess, that, with the point of her divinely-tempered spear, causes him to shake heaven and earth with his million-voiced roar (v. 856) ; and so Ares himself complains in the presence of Jove, that it is not Diomede, but the father's own mad daughter, that is the cause of such sorrow (v. 882). The very next book also shows how far Homer was from imagining that in the previous descriptions he had compromised the character of his hero, as a humble and a pious-minded man. It is not a Capaneus, or an Ajax that says,

Οὐ γὰρ ἔγωγε θεοῖσιν ἐπουρανίοισι μαχοίμην.—VI. 129.

Is there, then, no difference between Christianity and

the Homeric heathenism, in respect of the temper of mind
with which the mortal looks on the immortal, the human
on the divine ?   Assuredly there is ; but the peculiarity
of the heathen lies not in his underrating the virtue of
humility, but in the narrower basis on which he plants it.
Hellenic humility rests solely on a feeling of dependence ;
Christian humility rests on this indeed also, but primarily
and characteristically,—unless I am much mistaken,—on
a feeling of guilt, or at least self-prostration, in the consciousness of sin before a perfect moral ideal.   There is
also to be noted a certain air of familiarity in talking to
the gods, which to an ear tuned by the perusal of the
Hebrew and Christian Scriptures is apt to appear irreverent.   Witness the light tone in which Helen is made
to address Aphrodite (*Il.* III. 399), and of Diomede to the
same goddess (v. 348).   But that which has excited the
greatest scandal among the reverent admirers of the poet
is the language of Hera to Jove (*Il.* XIV. 332), and the
famous adventure of Aphrodite and Ares, told with such
humorous gusto in *Odyssey* VIII.   Of this we shall say
nothing, except that it is perfectly consonant with the
familiar tone with which polytheism allows the gods to be
handled on occasions ; and that it is most admirably suited
to the purpose for which it is introduced, viz., the sooth-
ing down of the angry feelings which threatened to disturb the harmony of the Phæacian board by the narration
of a jocular myth.[1]   That jocular religious myths, however, of any kind, should have been tolerated by a piously-
disposed people like the Phæacians, brings before us in
the strongest possible light the truth, that the deepest

[1] Lloyd in *Class. Mus.*, No. XXII. p. 395, has with great ingenuity traced the adaptation further ; but it is safer to remain content with the statement that I have given in the text.

habitual awe and reverence for the divine power can be felt only under a system of strict monotheism. Even in Christian Spain and Italy traits of a somewhat light and familiar piety. are occasionally observed, from which the sternly consistent monotheism of Protestant Britain revolts.

PROPOSITION XVIII.—There is an essential distinction between good and evil in human character and conduct. Man is responsible for his sins, and the gods inflict punishment on the guilty, sometimes directly, sometimes by the hands of their fellow-men.[1]

That the Homeric poems, making allowances for a few peculiarities belonging to the age in which they were composed, exhale a general atmosphere of sound and healthy morality, will be doubted by no one. Their morality as a whole is much better than their theology; for which indeed, in the nature of things, there is this plain and obvious reason, that man requires a certain soundness of the moral feeling in order to exist at all as a social being, while the orthodoxy of his theological views is, among all nations, more or less without influence on his practical conduct. At all events, God has so ordained matters in this world, that the most extraordinary aberrations of human intellect in the domain of theological speculation do not necessarily carry along with them that amount of practical evil consequence which a man reasoning in his chamber might be apt to imagine. The doctrine, for instance, which has been already stated in Proposition III., that the gods are the authors of all the evil thoughts and purposes that stir the

[1] It is not demanded by the title of the present paper to follow the Homeric system of ethics into detail. Many matters of this kind that I have not alluded to will be found in Nägelsbach under the title of *Die practische Gotteserkenntniss.*

bosom of man, would, if consistently followed out, necessarily
lead to the confounding of all moral distinctions, and the
denial of all human responsibility.   But it is not the curse
of poets, as it is of very logical philosophers, to be forced
to follow a wrong principle into all the wrong consequences that naturally flow from it.   No doubt the ever
ready, "*Not I am to blame, but a god who instigated my
actions*," was a convenient opiate for the conscience of the
Homeric man, when forced, by public evil result, to admit the folly of his private deed; and tricks of this kind
the self-love even of good men in the present day plays
off on their consciences, though, of course, in a less direct
form, and under a more refined verbal disguise; but the
sound moral faculty of Homer's age did not allow this
palliative view of the origin of moral evil to rob the
human mind of its instinctive judgments concerning the
character of human actions ; nay, the highest authority in
moral matters, Jove himself, in a remarkable passage, distinctly repudiates the doctrine that evil comes from the
gods, and throws it back directly on the self-originated
perverseness of the human will :

> ᾿Ω πόποι οἷον δή νυ θεοὺς βροτοὶ αἰτιόωνται.
> ἐξ ἡμέων γάρ φασι κακ᾽ ἔμμεναι· οἱ δὲ καὶ αὐτοὶ
> σφῇσιν ἀτασθαλίῃσιν ὑπέρμορον ἄλγε᾽ ἔχουσιν.
>
> Od. I. 32.

These words, like the inscription on Dante's Hellgate,
stand a striking text before the opening scenes of the
Odyssey, that the reader may be impressed with the
serious lesson of moral retribution which is to be taught by
the bloody catastrophe.   And not only the insolent and
riotous suitors, but the companions of the sea-tost hero,
are represented as having suffered what they suffered in

consequence of their own folly.[1] This also is prominently set forth in the very opening lines of the poem—

αὐτῶν γὰρ σφετέρῃσιν ἀτασθαλίῃσιν ὄλοντο.—I. 7.

No less clearly is the truth enunciated, that the gods see with observant eyes the evil deeds of men, and recompense them accordingly. The most distinct utterance on this subject is put by the poet into the mouth of Eumæus, "the divine swineherd,"—

οὐ μὲν σχέτλια ἔργα θεοὶ μάκαρες φιλέουσιν
ἀλλὰ δίκην τίουσι καὶ αἴσιμα ἔργ' ἀνθρώπων
Od. XIV. 83.

and in another remarkable passage it is said—

καὶ τε θεοὶ ξείνοισιν ἐοικότες ἀλλοδαποῖσιν
παντοῖοι τελέθοντες ἐπιστρωφῶσι πόληας
ἀνθρώπων ὕβριν τε καὶ εὐνομίην ἐφορῶντες.
XVII. 487.

and, as if to avoid all possible misconception of his meaning on the part of the most obtuse, the grand moral of the whole poem is again distinctly repeated before the final work of retributive slaughter (XXII. 39) ; and this work accomplished is declared by the old Laertes to be an undeniable proof that there are gods in the vast Olympus—

Ζεῦ πάτερ ἦ ῥα ἔτ' ἔστε θεοὶ κατὰ μακρὸν "Ολυμπον
εἰ ἐτεὸν μνηστῆρες ἀτάσθαλον ὕβριν ἔτισαν.
XXIV. 351.

With regard to the gods, to whose office the function of retribution falls, though in cases of special sins against particular gods the punishment naturally comes from the

---

[1] It is well remarked by Nägelsbach, that sin in Homer is often characterized as folly (ἀφραδία), and want of sense. See the passages collated in p. 270.

quarter where the offence lies, yet in the common transactions of life, as already mentioned, it is Jove who
grants παλίντιτα ἔργα; so much so, indeed, that even the
mighty god Helios (*Od.* XII. 376), when sinned against by
the companions of Ulysses, instead of inflicting vengeance
with his own hands, betakes himself to Zeus, and states
his case, adding, that if justice be not done to him in
this matter, he will leave the heaven, and, descending
into Hades, spend his light henceforth on the dead. We
have only to add further, with respect to the inflictors of
divine vengeance, that in certain very gross cases, as
offences against a father or a mother, the Erinnyes, or
singly, "the Fury that walketh in darkness," is called
into play. These Furies, from the manner in which they
are mentioned, seem to have been at first merely the impersonations of the ἀραί, or curses which parents, when
sorely irritated, vented on their unnatural children (*Il.*
IX. 454, 567); but the idea seems afterwards to have
been extended, so that even poor persons who are under
the special protection of Zeus are said to have their
Ἐρινύες or avengers (*Od.* XVII. 475).

PROPOSITION XIX.—The souls of men exist after death
in the subterranean abodes of Hades, or the invisible
world, but in a dim, shadowy, unsubstantial state, by no
means to be looked on with envy by those who behold the
sun in the upper regions, and tread with firm foot on the
stable earth. A few special favourites of the gods rise
above this common fate of the vulgar dead, and partake
in Heaven, or in the isles of the west, of a state of substantial beatitude; while, on the other hand, a few
atrocious monsters, or men of reckless and impious character, sinning daringly in the face of the gods, are condemned

to excruciating woes in Tartarus or Hell. This terrible retribution, however, has no reference to common men, or common crimes, which are punished by the gods in the present life, the proper theatre of human fates.

Among the many remarkable coincidences that a thoughtful observer might point out between the religious condition of the early Greek and that of the Hebrew mind, none is more notable than that which relates to the views entertained by both nations with regard to a future state. In a legislative capacity, of course, Moses had nothing to do with futurity ; but it is remarkable, that in many of the psalms, too many to require special quotation, the state of the dead is spoken of precisely in the same dim, comfortless way that characterizes the language of Homer. The well-known exclamation of Achilles,

$$\mu\grave{\eta} \ \delta\acute{\eta} \ \mu o\iota \ \theta\acute{a}\nu a\tau\acute{o}\nu \ \gamma\epsilon \ \pi a\rho a\acute{\upsilon}\delta a, \ \phi\acute{a}\iota\delta\iota\mu' \ '\text{O}\delta\upsilon\sigma\sigma\epsilon\hat{\upsilon}, \ \&c.$$

Od. XI. 488.

where Ulysses, the live visitant of the dead, is endeavouring to console him in regard to what he had lost by death, contains a complete revelation of the early Greek ideas with regard to a future existence. Homer was no Plato. A distinct and practical realist, he had no conception of any existence worth having, without a substantial body of flesh and blood. To him the Christian doctrine of the resurrection, so derided by the Stoics and Epicureans of the apostolic days (*Acta Apost.* xvii. 18), would have appeared the necessary condition of the immortality which the gospel preached. I am scarcely inclined to go so far as Nägelsbach (§ VII.) who says that the dead in Homer, except when roused to a momentary revival, are to be considered as utterly exenterated of that consciousness which is our real self in this terrene state; but it is plain, from the whole of Book XI. and the other places where the dead are incidentally mentioned, that their state is so dim and cloudy, feeble and pithless, that for all the purposes which, to the energetic Homeric man, made life valuable, it was little better than absolute annihilation. When "darkness covers the eyes" of an old Hellenic hero, wounded in the red strife of war, the curtain has fallen on all his glory for ever; and nothing now remains of that substantial energetic organism called man, but, as it were, a floating cloud or a dream.

If this be Homer's general view of the state of the dead, we are not to wonder that he does not delay the punishment of the wicked in a future state, but rather completes their suffering in that state, where they are alone capable of any substantial enjoyment. Whether the twenty-fourth Book of the *Odyssey* be genuine or not, the procession of the εἴδωλα of the suitors to Hades, and their reception there, is quite in keeping with the whole Homeric representation of the state of the dead. We do not find that these wicked men, punished with such sanguinary vengeance in the present state, are subjected to any further tortures in the region to which they are conducted by Hermes. Homer has no hell for the mass of men, plainly enough, because he has no heaven. The instances of Sisyphus, Tantalus, and a few others, mentioned in Book XI., prove no more a Homeric hell with regard to the mass of men, than the deathless transference of Menelaus to Elysium (*Od.* IV. 561) proves a general Homeric heaven. Only for perjurers some peculiar punishment of an awful nature seems reserved in a future life (*Il.* III. 278); but the passing allusion to the judicial functions of Minos (*Od.* XI. 568), and that in a place peculiarly liable to interpolation, will never, by any man who understands the

poet, be esteemed strong enough to warrant the assertion
that he had any firm belief in a general state of retribution after death.   The gods of Homer are too substantial
to waste their wrath on such pithless phantoms as float in
his Hades.

These, as rapidly as the union of completeness, with a
certain degree of interest, would allow, are the most important theological views which a careful study of the
Homeric writings suggests.   In arranging them I proceeded on the principle of the greatest possible independence, by making a careful collation of all the passages in
both poems that have any bearing on religion, and marshalling them under different heads, before I looked into
any writer on the subject.   After completing this labour, I
took a careful view of Nägelsbach's most accurate and judicious work, so often quoted, and was happy to find that,
while in one or two places I was enabled, through his
observations, to give a greater completeness to my own,
on very few points had I arrived at conclusions different
from his.   This agreement will, I hope, serve as a sort of
presumptive guarantee to scholars, that both our sum-
maries may be regarded as substantially correct.   I have
not had an opportunity of consulting any other of the
learned tracts and monograms with which the Germans
have enriched this, as other curious departments of philological research ; but this is the less to be regretted in a
matter where the materials are not to be collected from
remote regions, and where all that is attempted may be
satisfactorily achieved, by diligent collation, a certain
moral sympathy, and a fair amount of common sense.

ON THE PROMETHEUS BOUND OF ÆSCHYLUS.*

"*Omnis scriptura sacra,*" says Thomas à Kempis, or whoever he be that bears that name—*Omnis scriptura sacra, eo spiritu debet legi quo scripta est*—a most admirable rule of interpretation, not for the Bible only, but for all books, and a rule to the neglect of which may well be ascribed the creation of full nine-tenths of the follies of inane criticism and impertinent commentary, under which the biblical and philological shelves of the libraries groan; but, like all very wise general maxims, this hermeneutical principle of the good Thomas, even when once thoroughly acknowledged and adopted, leaves a more wide region of doubt and difficulty behind, viz., in its own application.

* 1. Die Æschyleische Trilogie Prometheus: von F. G. Welcker. Darmstadt, 1824.

2. Nachtrag zur Trilogie: von F. G. Welcker. Frankfurt-am-Main, 1826.

3. De Æschyli Prometheo Soluto Dissertatio: scripsit God. Hermann; edita 1828 (Opusc. IV. 253).

4. Commentatio de Æschyli Prometheo: auctore Dr. B. Toepelmann. Lips. 1829.

5. Theologoumena Æschyli Tragici: exhibuit R. H. Klausen. Berol. 1829.

6. De Æschyli Ternione Prometheo: auctore C. F. Bellmann. Uratislav. 1839.

7. Prometheus und sein Mythenkreis: dargestellt von B. G. Weiske. Leipzig, 1842.

8. Prometheus: die Sage und ihr Sinn; ein Beitrag zur Religionsphilosophie: von G. von Lasaulx. Würzburg, 1842.

9. Des Æschylus Gefesselter Prometheus: von G. F. Schoemann. Greifswald, 1844.

10. Correspondence between Dr. Julius Cæsar and Professor Schoemann on the Prometheus, in the *Zeitschrift für die Alterthums-Wissenschaft*, 4ter Jahrgang. October 1846. Cassel.

11. The Prometheus of Æschylus, translated into English Verse by (1.) Captain Medwyn. London, 1832.—

It is a great point gained, no doubt, in the interpretation of ancient writings, when we can get men to commence formally with an act of self-exenteration, to put themselves in the attitude of receiving instead of giving, not of mastering but of being mastered. In theology, warped as our judgment so often is by preconceived notions, how few attain to even this preliminary step! but, after all, the real difficulty, in many cases, is in what spirit was this or that book originally written, this or that march of imagery originally projected? Sometimes the drift of an author may be plain enough, and then self-exenteration, coupled with the necessary capacity of sympathy, will do the perfect work of hermeneutics; but in those cases, not unfrequent in the higher literature of all nations, where such a wild thing as a poet's fancy has wedded itself to such a loose thing as a popular mythology, then, to discern clearly by what spirit the phantasmal progeny of such conjunction is inhabited, requires sometimes no vulgar divination. In investigations of this description a curious accuracy and a philosophical profundity will often lead us as far out of the true path as a loose and ramb-

(2.) Mrs. Browning. London, 1833.—
(3.) Chapman in *Blackwood's Magazine*, 1836.—(4.) Swayne. Oxford, 1846.—
(5.) Prowett. Cambridge, 1846.

N.B.—It is not intended in the following remarks to make a formal review of the above works; but they are placed here merely to indicate that the writer of the present article has read them all, has reaped the benefit of their researches, and has had them in view in the expression and arrangement of his own opinions. It has at the same time been his desire to make the present paper, without being cumbrous, one of as extensive reference as possible to the results of learned speculation on the subject. The works named contain as various a range of conflicting views as is necessary for exhausting everything of importance that can be said on the cardinal point; nevertheless the writer regrets extremely that it has not been in his power to add to the above list a review of Schoemann's work in the *Wiener Jahrbücher* for 1845, vol. 109, called "able" by Grote, *Hist. of Greece*, vol. i. p. 104. The most recent opinions of Hermann also he has not seen; but Schoemann, in the *Correspondence*, No. 10, above, says that he has adopted the views of Cæsar, the merits of which will be discussed below.

ling superficiality ; and, if it should happen also that the artistical creation which we would comprehend exists no longer in its perfect shape, but only as a trunk with head and legs cut off, a yet more perplexing element of confusion and dubiety is introduced ; for it is seldom or never the case with imaginative works, as with the fossil organizations which belong to the science of geology, that the glance of a Cuvier can reconstruct the harmony of a whole from the wrecks of a part.   A combination of all these elements tending to trouble the æsthetical vision, and to perplex the judgment, is presented in the PROMETHEUS BOUND of Æschylus ; and the consequence has been, that in few fields of philological criticism—always excepting the great Homeric and Roman questions started by Wolf and Niebuhr—has the recent literature of luxuriant Germany been more prolific.   England also, as became a country in which classical literature is a sort of national watchword, has not been altogether silent ; but our direct and practical character has on this, as on so many other occasions, shown itself averse to enter that region of moral and religious speculation to which the profounder intelligence of the Prometheus belongs.   We accordingly have more to show in the way of translation than of speculation ; and if we will boast of our imaginative sympathy with the Æschylean Prometheus—for we speak not here of mere verbal criticism—are wise to turn from the ranks of the philologers to the poets, proud to compensate ourselves for the lack of the cumbrous erudition of a Bellmann, the acuteness of a Weiske, and the ingenuity of a Welcker, with the possession of a genius at once so subtly Hellenic, and so grandly Æschylean, as Percy Bysshe Shelley.

It is indeed not the least remarkable feature of the

Promethean legend, that, while it received a more than common prominence in antiquity, from being adopted at different and most diverse periods by the genius of a Hesiod, an Æschylus, and a Plato—not to mention the popular persiflage of a Lucian in later times—it has, in the age which has just gone by, been transferred into the popular currency of modern literature by four men so high above the vulgar mark, as Goethe and Herder in Germany, and among our own countrymen, Byron and Shelley. This contemporary appropriation of an exotic theme by men in many respects far from similar, deserves the attention of the philosophical critic, as a most important testimony to the deep human interest and moral significancy of the myth ; and, while it brings the subject out of the narrow circle of antiquarian disquisition into the wide range of living European sentiment, excites further the curious and interesting inquiry, how far the general impression of the Æschylean drama made on the mind of the greatest European poets has been identical with, or different from that which, there may be good reason to believe, it must have made on an Athenian audience. Such a question is one of the most interesting that possibly can be raised in the criticism of the classics ; and we shall not, therefore, crave the pardon of the more learned reader, if we introduce the more strictly philological part of the present inquiry, by a distinct statement of the place which the Prometheus holds in the general sympathy of European readers, by virtue of the genius of the great poets just mentioned. We shall thus propose for ourselves a distinct critical problem to be solved,— how far the popular impression of the Promethean legend is, or is not, consistent with the spirit in which it was originally conceived.

No reader interested in such questions, we may well presume, will require from us in this place a detailed narrative of the plot of the Prometheus, as it is presented in the play of Æschylus. The action is at once so simple in itself, and so familiar to every cultivated imagination, that to set it forth in curious detail would seem but a pedantic attempt to fritter away the impression of a gigantic whole, that stands like a permanent background in the picture gallery of the mind. The "high-counselled son of Iapetus and Themis" chained to a rock in wintry Scythia, for a crime that appears no crime,—the stealing of fire from heaven, and teaching the use of it to mortal men, contrary to the will of Jove; the calm defiance which he breathes against his Olympian adversary, and the spirit of firm self-sustainment by which, through ages of unmitigated torture, he is supported; the wide untrodden waste of solitude around him, interrupted only by the sympathetic utterances of the Ocean maids, and the friendly but fruitless expostulations of old father Ocean himself; then, like a darker shade upon the grand picture (remaining stationary and unchanged through the piece), the shrieking lamentations of the "many-wandering" Io, the "horned maid," the persecuted daughter of Inachus, the innocent victim of the love of Jove, and the jealousy of Hera; and lastly, the messenger sent direct from the Olympian himself to besiege the constancy of the rebellious Titan with threats of thunder and precipitation into Tartarus; and the catastrophe of the piece in the actual execution of these threats :—all this stands in grand and vivid outline so familiarly before the imagination of the scholar, that a more detailed statement of the general argument may well be spared, while particular passages will more conveniently be brought forward under the different heads of the discussion to which they belong. We proceed, therefore, without preface, to inquire what is the general impression which the Æschylean play has made upon those who, *primâ facie*, are the fittest representatives of the moral effect produced by it on cultivated minds in modern times ; we mean Herder and Goethe, Byron and Shelley, in the first place ; and second to them, the English translators, who, not being scholars by profession, have accompanied their versions by remarks on the æsthetical and moral character of the piece ; to whom we shall add Schlegel, as representing the modern dramatic critics. We shall then bring the opinions of these parties—not the less valuable in some views because they represent in this question the laity, and not the clergy of scholarship—into contact and collision with the results of the most recent learned investigation on the subject ; and out of these conflicting elements endeavour to inquire what harmonious reconciliation of apparently incompatible views may be producible.

First, therefore, let us hear Byron, the poet who of all others in modern times has produced and re-produced a type of character in his works, that in its tones of lonely grandeur, high defiance, and self-sustained isolation, bears a strong resemblance to the Prometheus of Æschylus.[1] Byron's conception of the character of the Titan is the more interesting that we have his own assurance for the fact, of the deep impression which the Æschylean drama, at an early period, made on his mind.

[1] MANFRED, as Lord Jeffrey well remarked, is, in "tone and pitch," a true modern Prometheus. This essential kinship Byron himself at once avowed, while the connexion of the same poem with Goethe's *Faust* belongs to the form of the first scenes merely, scarcely more.—See Byron's own notes to *Manfred*.

E

" Thy godlike crime was to be kind,
    To render with thy precepts less
    The sum of human wretchedness,
    And strengthen man with his own mind ;
    But baffled as thou wert from high,
    Still in thy patient energy,
    In the endurance and repulse
    Of thine impenetrable spirit,
    Which earth and heaven could not convulse,
    A mighty lesson we inherit :
    Thou art a symbol and a sign
    To mortals of their fate and force ;
    Like thee, man is in part divine,
    A troubled stream from a pure source ;
    And man in portions can foresee
    His own funereal destiny ;
    His wretchedness and his resistance,
    And his sad unallied existence :
    To which his spirit may oppose
    Itself—an equal to all woes,
    And a firm will and a deep sense,
    Which even in torture can descry
    Its own concenter'd recompense,
    Triumphant where it dares defy,
    And making death a victory."

The author of *Manfred* therefore saw in Prometheus a type of human nature, and that in its noblest aspect ; activity hallowed by love, and suffering consecrated by endurance.   Prometheus is the martyr of humanity, the champion of intellectual freedom against all brutish, unreasoning powers ; " faith which worketh by love," to adopt an apostolic phrase, oppressed beneath the temporary ascendency of evil, but not prostrate.   In this view Prometheus is an ideal of moral perfection, as his adversary is an incarnation of malignity.

" —— The inexorable Heaven
    And the deaf tyranny of Fate,
    The ruling principle of HATE,

> Which for its pleasure doth create
> The things it may annihilate."

To the same purpose Shelley—

> " To suffer woes which hope thinks infinite,
> To forgive wrongs darker than death or night,
> To defy power which seems omnipotent,
> To love and bear, to hope till Hope creates
> From its own wreck the thing it contemplates ;
> Neither to change, nor flatter, nor repent :
> This, like thy glory, Titan, is to be
> Good, great and joyous, beautiful, and free.
> This is alone life, joy, empire and victory."

Substantially identical with these views, though different in a not unimportant point, which we shall notice anon, is the idea of Herder, who, in the Preface to his *Prometheus Unbound*,[1] finds the most noble, and perhaps the most natural, sense of the myth to be " the progress of the human race in every sort of culture ; the continued striving of the Divine Spirit in man for the awakening of all his powers." Akin in the main tendency, though singularly modified by the peculiar mental constitution of the writer, is the representation of Goethe, who, out of the rich fulness of moral excellence embodied by Byron and Shelley, in the character of Prometheus, has selected the one element of artistic activity, and made it the subject of a lyrical composition, as classically chaste in the execution as it is sublime and original in the conception. The whole poem, though very far removed from the Æschylean idea of Prometheus, agrees with it strikingly in one point, an attitude of defiance towards the Olympian powers and a tone of irreverence, real or apparent, which escapes many a modern reader in the Greek drama, only because

---

[1] *Dramatische Stücke und Dichtungen ; Aesthetische Werke*, vol. vi. Edit. 1806.

he lives habitually in the conviction that Jove is " nothing in the world," a mere idol, perhaps a devil,

> " And devils to adore for deities,"

towards whom reverence were a greater moral perversion of sentiment than contempt.

> " Deem'st thou that I should hate my life,
> And into deserts flee,
> Because I could not see
> All blossoms of my dreamings rife ?
> Here sit I, and with life inspire
> A race that shall be like their sire ;
> Who shall know beneath the skies
> To suffer and to weep,
> To enjoy and to rejoice,
> And thee and thine even so despise
> As I do !"[1]

The reader will observe, what is a point of main importance to start with, that all these representations agree in exhibiting Prometheus as a heroic character of the highest order, a martyr, and a champion worthy of our most unqualified love and admiration. Nor are we allowed to forget, in these modern reproductions of the pregnant old myth, the quality so essential to the conception of Prometheus, that, while he is the spokesman and representative of man, he is in his own nature no man, but a god, at least a demigod ; a being with all the gigantic, intellectual, and moral proportions, but without the moral perversity of Milton's Satan. This similitude and contrast has been vividly perceived, and felicitously expressed by Mrs. Browning in the following passage :—

> " —— But Prometheus stands eminent and alone; one of the

---

[1] Goethe, in this passage, has adopted that comparatively modern exaggeration of the myth, which represents its hero as the creator of man. Hesiod knows nothing of this, and Æschylus as little. —See the masterly historical development in *Weiske.*

most original and grand and attaching characters ever conceived by
the mind of man. That conception sank deep into the soul of Milton,
and, as has been observed, rose from thence in the likeness of his Satan.
But the Satan of Milton and the Prometheus of Æschylus stand upon
ground as unequal as do the sublime of sin and the sublime of virtue.
Satan suffered from his ambition ; Prometheus from his humanity :
Satan for himself ; Prometheus for mankind : Satan dared peril which
he had not weighed ; Prometheus devoted himself to sorrows which
he had foreknown. " Better to rule in hell," said Satan ;" " better to
serve this rock," said Prometheus. But in his hell Satan yearned to
associate man, while Prometheus preferred a solitary agony ; nay, he
even permitted his zeal and tenderness for the peace of others to
abstract him from that agony's intenseness."

After this strongly put antithesis, we shall not be surprised if other students of the Prometheus have ventured
upon a comparison that to some may appear bold, and
even profane ; they have instituted a comparison between
the tortures of Caucasus and the agonies of Calvary, and
have not hesitated to employ language in reference to the
mythical demigod of Greek fiction, similar to that which
Christians are every day in the habit of using with regard
to the historical founder of their faith. This comparison,
we have said, may appear unwarrantable and even profane
to some ; but it is only an appearance. Nothing indeed
could be more obvious than the parallel : and the simplest
way to dispel all suspicion of irreverence in the writers is
to read what they have written. Toepelmann, for one, in
his excellent little tract, has the following observations
(p. 69, 70-1) :—

" Nemo tam obtuso est ingenio quin animadvertat ad quantam
Promethei Aeschylei argumentum aliorum populorum revelationis
divinae accedat similitudinem. Dico autem doctrinam quae Dei filium
in terram descendisse, homines a malis liberaturum, et meliora de
rebus divinis docturum exponit. Ac certe si Christiani σωτῆρος
vitam et facta cum Prometheo comparemus, primum in eo conveniunt
quod deorum quisque erudiendo generi humano operam navabat, Chris-

tus autem spiritualem, Prometheus temporalem hominum mortem prohibebat :—

$$—— \; \dot{\epsilon}\xi\epsilon\rho\upsilon\sigma\dot{\alpha}\mu\eta\nu \; \beta\rho\sigma\tauο\dot{\upsilon}s$$
τοῦ μὴ διαββαισθέντας εἰς "Αιδου μολεῖν.—v. 244-5.

tum vero cuique eorum propter beneficia quibus genus humanum cumu-laverat cruciatus erant subeundi. Praeterea autem, quod per interest multum Christi perfectionem inter, et Promethei non perfectam natu-ram, hoc etiam magnum inter eos discrimen esse apparet, quod ille a Deo patre ad opus in terrâ patrandum legatus sit consentiente eodem perfecit, Prometheus, invito deorum patre et irato, generi humano multis modis benefecit, ejusque jussu poenâ est affectus. In quo dis-crimine si internam rei Christianae praestantiam in comparationem non vocamus, sed solum spectamus utriusque et voluntatem et auda-ciam, non possumus Graeci quam de generis humani sospitatore sibi conformaverant sententiam Christianâ quanquam minus sanctam piamque, tamen audaciorem esse non judicare. Nam quod Prometheo propter τὸν φιλάνθρωπον τρόπον, et διὰ τὴν λίαν φιλότητα βροτῶν a Jove timenda erant, ea non erant Christo, cui cruciatus illi in coelis reduci a patre amantissimo resarciebantur. ILLE DEOS LAESIT, UT HOMINES BEARET ; HIC HOMINES BEAVIT, UT SUAE DEIQUE PATRIS OBSECUNDARET VOLUNTATI."

To the same purpose, though in a different connexion, a recent English translator :—" Prometheus himself is the personification of Divine love, willing, for the sake of man, to suffer to the utmost what divine justice could inflict or require."[1] In the same direction, though not so far and so decidedly, do the well-known observations of A. W. Schlegel point ; from which, as translated by Black, and adopted by Captain Medwyn, we extract the following :—

" The chained Prometheus is the representation of constancy under suffering, and that the never-ending suffering of a god. Though the scene exhibits the principal person exiled to a naked rock on the shore of the encircling ocean, this drama still embraces the world, the Olym-pus of the gods, and the earth of mortals, all scarcely yet reposing in a secure state above the dread abyss of the dark Titanian powers. This idea of a self-devoting divinity has been mysteriously inculcated

[1] Swayne's Introduction, p. 12.

in many religions, as a confused foreboding of the true. Here, however, it appears in a most alarming contrast with the consolations of revelation. For Prometheus does not suffer in an understanding with the powers by whom the world is governed, but he atones for his disobedience, and that disobedience consists in nothing but the attempt to give perfection to the human race. He is thus an image of human nature itself, endowed with a miserable foresight, and bound down to a narrow existence without an ally, and with nothing to oppose to the combined and inexorable powers of nature but an unshaken will, and the consciousness of elevated claims."

But the most remarkable, and in every way the most interesting, parallel drawn between the mythical tortures of Caucasus and the real agonies of Calvary, is that drawn by our countryman Shelley, who, in his supra-mundane poem of the "Prometheus Unbound," introduces a chorus of Furies, endeavouring to terrify the dauntless Titan into submission, by conjuring up the phantasmal representation of the good and the great in all ages who had suffered for the advancement of humanity, but, according to the interpretation of the chorus, had suffered, and could not but have suffered, in vain. How striking are the following lines, in which Christ appears as a preacher of righteousness, but a righteousness so super-excellent, that in the hands of abusive mortality, the antidote is changed into a poison!—"Like a jewel of gold in a swine's snout," so is a good thing in the hands of a bad user.

> " One came forth of gentle worth,
>   Smiling on the sanguine Earth :
>   His words outlived him, like swift poison
>   Withering up truth, peace, and pity.
>   Look where round the wide horizon
>   Many a million-peopled city
>   Vomits smoke in the bright air.
>   Mark that outcry of despair !
>   'Tis his mild and gentle ghost
>   Wailing for the faith he kindled."

And again—

FURY.

" Behold an emblem : those who do endure
    Deep wrongs for man, and scorn and chains, but heap
    Thousandfold torment on themselves and him.

PROMETHEUS.

    Remit the anguish of that lighted stare ;
  Close those wan lips; let that·thorn-wounded brow
  Stream not with blood ; it mingles with thy tears !
  Fix, fix those tortured orbs in peace and death,
  So thy sick throes shade not that crucifix,
  So those pale fingers play not with thy gore.
  O horrible ! thy name I will not speak ;
  It hath become a curse.   I see, I see
  The wise, the mild, the lofty, and the just,
  Whom thy slaves hate for being like to thee,
  Hunted by foulest lies from their heart's home," etc. etc.

But of this enough : we have now seen as the first grand element in the interpretation of the Æschylean drama, what general impression it has made on the intellects of the present age, who, being touched with a living poetical sympathy, were the most likely to be free from those perverse subtilties and unsound refinements which are so often wont to perplex the judgment of the learned.   But the poets also, and the poetical translators, have their peculiar professional fallacies, " their idols of the tribe," as Bacon phrases it.   What love and sympathy with a grand idea can understand and appreciate they will appreciate ; but they are a wayward and a wanton and a licentious race, and oftentimes are themselves the father of the child, which they seem but to adopt; the brand which they flourish is taken piously from the altar of the god, but the fire with which it is kindled is not seldom their own.   One must therefore look, not suspiciously indeed, but narrowly, into their handling of ancient myths; ready to find in the general case a true reflection of foreign imagery, but not surprised if here and there we are deceived by a home-grown delusion. To guard ourselves, therefore, against their one-sidedness, in the present inquiry we shall now make a similar review of the opinions of the learned; and in doing so we shall do ourselves the pleasure to recall and to present prominently, as one of the last legacies of the scholarship of the past century to the present, the opinion of Schütz : not because we think that opinion of much value as a result, but because it connects itself most naturally with the views already given, and will serve as a most useful stimulant to thought in the contrast which it presents to some more recent views which we shall have immediate occasion to bring under review.

"Cum primum poëta animum ad scribendam hanc tragoediam appulit, id potissimum egisse nobis videtur, ut Atheniensibus acerrimum tyrannidis odium inspiraret, verumque libertatis, qua tum maxime fruebantur, amorem tanti mali metu in eorum animis excitaret confirmaretque. Quo consilio Jovem deorum novum regem seu tyrannum impotentem finxit, omnia pro arbitrio agentem, jura sibi data negantem, omnia suae majestati arrogantem, inexorabilem, asperum, et in amicos quoque bene de se meritos, propterea quod suspectos omnes habeat, ingratum atque crudelem.   .

"In Prometheo vero spectatoribus utilissimum hominis vere popularis exemplar proposuit, quem, ut ait Horatius, nec vultus instantis tyranni, nec civium ardor prava jubentium mente solida quatiat; qui propter generis humani caritatem praepotentis tyranni odium suscipere nullus dubitaverit, susceptum autem excelsa animi magnitudine ac robore sustineat. Itaque illius humanitas cum Jovis crudelitate, illius cupiditas cum hujus bene de omnibus merendi studio, illius effrenata ferocia cum hujus moderatione et fortitudine praeclare comparatur.

"Jupiter universum hominum genus extinguere voluit : Prometheus omnium mortalium vitae ac felicitatis auctor, parens, deus exstitit. Prometheus Jovis ad regnum obtinendum adjutor fuerat ; Jupiter Prometheum, immemor beneficii, nec ullam ob causam, nisi quod eum ob nimiam humani generis caritatem suspectum haberet, indignis modis vexat, acerbissimisque poenis affligit. Jupiter in summo dignitatis et imperii fastigio constitutus omnia libertatis jura diis eripuerat, aequitatem ac justitiam negligebat, sanctissimas antiquissimasque leges pedibus conculcabat; Prometheus ne summa quidem miseria sic induratur, ut ingenitum humanitatis sensum ex animo amittat; non irascitur hominibus, quorum propter amorem tanta se calamitate oppressum videt, non exuit pristinam miseris succurrendi voluntatem; et quamquam se immensis malorum fluctibus mersum videt, idem tamen se quam plurimos malorum socios optare candide negat. Jovem ne summa quidem potentia a timore liberat, id quod haud obscuro indicio prodit, cum vaticinio Promethei perterritus Mercurium ad eum ablegat, omnibusque minis ac terroribus, pertinacissimum quo ille nuptias Jovi periculosas premebat, silentium vincere atque expugnare cupit; Prometheum vero, quamvis omnibus artubus deligatum et constrictum, non Chori sollicitudo benevolentiae plena, non Oceani mitiora remedia suadentis amica consilia, non Iûs miseris furoribus vagisque cursibus unius Jovis ob noxam agitatae horrores, non saevae Mercurii comminationes, non denique aëris marisque tumultus, non coeli terraeque ruinae molliunt ac frangunt. Ecce justum illum ac tenacem propositi virum! Ecce virum fortem cum mala fortuna compositum!"

This view of Schütz, which substantially agrees with that of Byron and Shelley, may stand also for the opinion of a great German Hellenist, whose leading sympathies seem rather to go with the philologists of the last century than with those of the present;—we mean Godfrey Hermann. This writer, in his dissertation on the Prometheus Unbound,[1] while he has expended his strength on many debated polemical points of lesser moment, has, with regard to the main idea of the drama, contented himself with repeating Schütz's view in the single sentence, that the ancient tragic poet wished to please and to instruct, " *non per enigmata abstrusae cujusdam sapientiae, sed per viva constantiae, fortitudinis, animi magnitudinis exempla.*" Thus

---

[1] *Opusc.* iv. 253.

far, therefore, the academical men, and the imaginative
men, seem to be at one; only, as is fitting, the former
give themselves a less various scope, and confine themselves within a more narrow range. They take the individual instance as it is presented in the individual play,
and content themselves with admiring the heroic representation of virtuous fortitude; the comprehensive glance
of the poet sees in the fate of the individual the type of
the whole, in the torture of the son of Iapetus the destiny
of the sons of Adam. Unquestionably the prominence
given by Æschylus to the merits of his hero, as the inventor
of the useful arts (v. 436-506), must force us to admit the
general idea of human progress, as no less essential than
that of fortitude to the Æschylean conception of the
myth; and it is with pleasure, therefore, that we find in
Bellmann, a man of learning and speculation,[1] who launches
largely out with all the cumbrous equipments of German
erudition, into the wide region over which the winged
Muse of Shelley delighted to wander; and in the striv-
ings and sufferings of the mythic Titan sees clearly adum-
brated the "*historia generis humani qualis omni tempore
obtineret*" (p. 59). The men of learning, therefore, with
Bellmann to supply the deficiencies of Schütz and Hermann,
so far as we hitherto see, give their cordial support to the
view of the Promethean legend generated in the greatest
poetical minds of modern times. All agree in conceiving
the Æschylean Prometheus as an ideal, either of moral
perfection and human progress generally, "*summa quam
mente animoque complectaris perfectio*" (Bellmann, p. 44),
or of the special virtues of disinterested generosity and

---

[1] We concur, however, heartily with
Schoemann's pithy characteristic of the
313 pages "*de ternione—ein schwer les-*
bares Buch."—The author is one of
those writers who would have been much
more intelligible in his mother tongue.

manly fortitude.   And there can be little doubt, further, that this view of the matter is not the opinion of Hermann's party in Germany only, or of the Byronic school of poetry in England; it is in a most wide and comprehensive sense the general opinion.   Ninety-nine hundreds of all the thousands of European youths who have read the Prometheus, in school or college, since the days of Erasmus and Melanchthon until now, never formed any other opinion.   There is therefore a presumption established in its favour, to which, if we are not strangely pledged to our own conceits, we are bound to pay no idle respect.   If we dissent from such a weight of old established authority and precedent, we are bound, in lawyer's phrase, to show strong cause; we must come, like Niebuhr, with a club in our hand that will become stronger the more blows it deals.   Let us proceed, therefore, to inquire what the grounds are of the new views, which have within the present century, and mostly within the last few years (specially by Welcker, Klausen, Lasaulx, and Schoemann),[1] been propounded on this subject.

In commencing this inquiry, the first question is, What gave occasion to these views?   Was it the mere restless spirit of German speculation, ever eager for a new cobweb? or did they spring from the natural and legitimate source of new speculation—from any felt insufficiency in the received theory—from any secret, but not the less formidable, difficulty which the current hypothesis left unexplained?   If this question be fairly asked, fairness will also answer, that the new theories, whether true or false, were anything but uncalled for.   There is, in fact,

---

[1] *Weiske's* closely reasoned and thorough work was unfortunately interrupted by the death of the writer, just when it had arrived at the point from which Æschylus started. We have read it, however, with much profit.

a great stumbling-block and offence in the received explanation, which has been felt not oftener, only because those
who are inclined or forced to feel it are, from the nature
of the case, necessarily few. So long as a man looks
at a noble range of mountains merely as a prospect, the
most barren rocks may be the most beautiful ; but when
he walks up to them, and sits down to dwell among them,
other considerations force themselves very seriously on his
attention. An Englishman reads the *Prometheus Bound*
as a play, and is delighted, carried away, and possessed by
the idea of self-sustaining virtue that seems incarnated in
the principal character ; it never enters his mind to inquire
how an Athenian, beholding this sacred opera (for such the
Greek tragedy was), represented at the feast of Dionysus
as an act of religious worship, was religiously moved by the
exhibition. If, according to the view of all the authors
hitherto quoted, Prometheus appears as the most oppressed of martyrs, and Zeus as the most unjust of tyrants,
the question arises, how an Athenian audience, an audience proverbially remarkable for δεισιδαιμονία (*Act. Apost.*
xvii. 22), at a solemn religious festival on the public stage,
could tolerate such a representation ? This is a grave
difficulty certainly; and it is a difficulty which the received
theory of the Prometheus either altogether overlooks, or
in a way not very satisfactory endeavours to obviate. The
majority of general readers, little concerned to maintain
the honour of Jove, have, in all probability, never proposed
to themselves the question. A certain school of theologians also may have been well satisfied to have it believed,
that the refined audience of the most highly cultivated
city of the ancient world could be content to sit quietly
on the seats of the public theatre, and hear their supreme
deity, "the king of gods and men," openly blasphemed.

This view of the matter, if it be the real one, were certainly a rare illustration for those partial declaimers who know no more cunning way of exhibiting the brightness of Christianity, than by smearing the face of heathenism indiscriminately over with pitch ; but the philologists by profession were bound, as a matter of duty, not only not to overlook this formidable difficulty, but to do something, if it might be done fairly, to redeem Greece from the monstrous reproach of a theology altogether without moral distinctions, and a religion altogether without reverence. It is this very natural, and we may say necessary feeling on the part of the philologists, that has given rise to much of the recent discussion on the subject ; a discussion, the reader will observe, of the most vital importance, not only to the classical scholar, but to the theologian and the philosopher ; and which at once transfers the Promethean myth from the vague floating limbo of poetical fancy into the earnest central point, a point to be found only in a man's own heart, of religious philosophy.   Not without a very significant propriety, therefore, has Professor Lasaulx entitled his recent tract on this subject " a contribution to the philosophy of religion ;" and, though we may not pledge ourselves to all his views, we cannot but think there is a great general truth—and a truth specially applicable to the Prometheus—contained in the following observations with which he ushers in his treatise :—

" The mythology of the heathen nations of antiquity stands before us as a mysterious dream-like depicturement of ante-historical humanity, a dreamy prophecy, of which the true significance was given only, when the destined ages were completed, in the person of Him who was more than all prophets, in Christ,—of Him whose victorious voice broke the charm of the old serpent, and, redeeming the hitherto unblest race of mortal men from the slavery of sin and of the law, brought them into the perfect freedom of the children of God. The beginning, and the first-born of every creature, the image of the invisible God, the pattern at once of us and of the world, did, in His character of the first-born Son of the God of all gods, embrace in Himself all gods that afterwards appeared.

" Considered in this light, profane history, no less than the history of the Hebrews, appears as invested with a typical character fore-shadowing Christianity; and from the history of the religions of anti-quity there may be restored and reconstructed a second apocryphal Old Testament, which, along with that canonical one which we already have, finds its progression and its fulfilment in the New Testament. To show how in the collective world, before Christ actually appeared, the germ of His coming was contained—how it was clearly prophesied in Judaism, and in Heathenism everywhere divined and anticipated ; how the desired of all nations was revealed, under different forms, both among the heathens and among the Jews : to set forth this in detail, is the problem of a Christian philosophy of religion, to which the present remarks on the Prometheus are to be regarded as a con-tribution."

No doubt this view, which sees in heathenism a sort of imperfectly foreshadowed and dimly anticipated Chris-tianity, is capable of very great abuse in its application, and must be received as true only to some extent, and in some cases ; but in so far as it asserts the essential religious unity of human nature in all ages, though it be a unity that manifests itself by gradations, the philo-sophic mind will readily acknowledge it as a most pregnant and most significant truth. Such a mind certainly will not rashly exclude the common religious sentiment from the heart of a whole people, any more than it will expect to find an identity of religious insight in nations the most diverse in capacity and in situation. It will be disposed to handle a religious question among heathen Greeks and Romans no less than among Christians, seriously as a reli-gious question ; and it will not be inclined gratuitously to suppose that a nation, in every other respect the most

highly developed, should in religion only present a confusion of the most abnormal aberrations, and a farrago of
the most portentous monstrosities.   So far, and so far only,
do we request the English reader to receive with favour
the views of those German writers, such as Lasaulx and
Schoemann, who have prominently brought forward the
religious and the peculiarly Christian element in the
Prometheus, in a way, as we shall see, quite opposed to
that glorification of man, as it should almost seem, at the
expense of Jove, which we have found in Shelley[1] and
Bellmann.   For, to enter upon the wild domain of mythology, even in cultivated Greece, so full of moral crudities
of all sorts, with a systematic predetermination to make
the " wisdom of the ancients " appear to have been in
all cases as great as possible, were an extreme equally
remote from the chance of truth, with the negative and
unfruitful principle to which it is opposed ; and in this
regard the caution of Hermann, against seeking in every
old legend *" enigmata abstrusae cujusdam sapientiae,"*
is most necessary ; though certainly, with regard to this
particular matter of the Promethean myth, the darkest
enigmas of the most abstruse wisdom are not more worthless in the way of elucidation than the flat prosaic explanation—after the manner of Euhemerus—which Hermann
himself, in his dissertation " on the most ancient mytho-

---

[1] This observation applies strictly to
Jove as the god of Æschylus and of
Greece.   As for Shelley personally, he
has, in his Prometheus (Act II. Sc. 4),
nobly shaken himself free from that
strange atheism, which is enunciated in
Queen Mab.   This great poet, indeed,
is in no wise chargeable with the consequences that flow from the assumption, that Æschylus meant to represent
Prometheus as a moral ideal.   In his
Preface he distinctly states, that in his
poem he delineates Prometheus as he
would wish to see him delineated, not
exactly as Æschylus, following the prescribed course of the mythologic legend,
would have worked out the catastrophe.
The whole passage will be given in a
more appropriate place below.

logy of the Greeks" (*Opusc.* II. 186), has enunciated.   But
to proceed :—

Schütz, who, in common with Byron and Shelley,
represents the supreme god of the Greeks as a cruel and
unprincipled tyrant, was not, as a philologist, altogether
blind to the grand religious difficulty which we have stated;
but in attempting to cut gallantly, it appears to us that
he only grazes lightly by the Gordian knot, and allows
himself to be deceived by an unsubstantial glamour.   His
words are these :—

" Quod vero Æschylus sub Jovis nomine, quem deorum hominumque
regem venerabatur populus, tyrannorum injustitiam et crudelitatem
castigavit, id sane, si res ad veram aetatis nostrae de Dei numine philo-
sophandi rationem exigenda esset, impium et sceleratum, populique
moribus perniciosum fuisset ; cum autem istis de Jove opinionibus tota
Graecorum natio dudum imbuta esset, non magis in poëta nostro quam
in Homero reprehendi debet, eum humana potius ad Deos, quam quae
vere divina essent, ad homines transtulisse."

And to the same effect Hermann (*Opusc.* IV. 256),
" neque utile quærere (et quæsivere quidam) quomodo in
Jovis persona crudelissimi tyranni exemplum proponere
potuerit poëta.   Neque habuerunt ista apud Græcos offen-
sionem, nec potuerunt habere, ut in religionibus quæ totæ
ex hujuscemodi fabulis essent compositæ."   We are not
to express surprise, says Hermann, at the glaring impiety
and irreverential audacity of the Prometheus, *" because
the whole Greek religion is full of such things."*   Now there
is a great general truth in these words, but which, when
narrowly examined, will be found insufficient to explain
the phenomena of the present case.   It is quite true that
in many of the theological legends of the Greeks no ideas
of a character entitled to the name of moral are discover-
able.   Every school-boy feels this.   As little is it to be

denied that, in many familiar instances with which the pages of Homer teem, the relation between man and God seems to have appeared to the most ancient Greek mind rather as a relation of contrariety and opposition than as one of submission and subjection, much less of love. The gods, according to the rude popular conception, seem more ready to fear the greatness of man than to approve his virtue. Their justice shows rather like jealousy; and their wrath has the inspiration of revenge. Crude ideas of this kind are common to the theological conceptions of all barbarous or semi-civilized peoples. In the *Iliad* a Diomede encounters Mars in the fight; the mortal routs the immortal; and it is nothing strange. Why then should we allow our fastidious moral sense, trained as it has been and cultivated by the Christianity of 2000 years, to take hasty offence at the quarrel between the son of Iapetus and the son of Kronos, and the freedom of speech which the bold-mouthed poet allows the former? Such is the argument of Hermann and Schütz, stated as strongly as we can put it. Still we say it throws only a pleasant mist about the subject, and does not approach the difficulty. For, in the first place, it does not follow, according to the Homeric theology, that because a mortal like Diomede, *with the assistance* of one god—Pallas Athene —may get the better of another, therefore a mortal, or an inferior god, like Prometheus, may ride triumphantly over the supremacy of Ζεὺς ὕψιστος, μέγιστος; much less does it follow that a *modern* poet like Æschylus—for such he was to the Greeks who witnessed his plays—may seize upon any old religious legend which seems to place the supreme god of the country in an odious light, dress up and systematically exaggerate its odiousness, and, upon the open stage of a religious metropolis, hold up the

object of general worship to public hatred and contempt.
There is manifestly a great and most unallowable jump
in this logic.　It is one thing to say that a popular
mythology contains many unworthy and immoral stories
of the gods; another and altogether a different thing to
maintain, that a dramatist in a religious country shall,
without offence, exhibit a native religious tradition in
such a shape and manner, that its whole theme shall be
rebellion, its drift impiety, its spirit the spirit of scoffing,
and its eloquence the breath of blasphemy.　A public
exhibition of this kind is, in our opinion, as man is
constituted, morally impossible; not even the Bushmen,
almost or altogether atheists, of South Africa, of whom
Moffat tells,[1] could achieve such a portent.　With regard
to Greece, making full allowance for the crudities of its
early theology, the considerate student will have no difficulty in adopting the language of Toepelmann (p. 57),
" *Non licebat poëtis tragicis deos religionis vulgaris,
nedum majorum gentium, malos pravosque exhibere et de-
pingere, ut licitum erat comoediae eos ludibrio laedere.*"
The distinction here made between tragedy and comedy
has been overlooked by some; but those who know
human nature in all its moods, and who have watched it
specially in some of its religious phases in Italy and Spain,
will not be slow to acknowledge its important bearing
on the present question.　The manner in which Plautus
handles Jupiter in the Amphitryo can supply no rule
whereby to gauge the relation of Æschylus to Zeus in the
Prometheus.　On the freedom with which *poets* before the
Reformation handled churchmen see Dr. M'Crie's *Life of
Knox*, c. i.　But they never attacked the fundamentals of
the popular faith.　The case, therefore, as Schütz and

[1] *Missionary Labours and Scenes in Southern Africa*, c. xvi. xvii.

Hermann and Bellmann and also Welcker[1] put it, is hope-less. Æschylus did not, and could not, in a free country, represent the supreme god as an odious tyrant, nor in a religious country hold up a daring blasphemer as an object of unqualified admiration. Writing under the influence of a theology which acknowledged POWER as the distinctive attribute of the supreme god, and relative weakness as the characteristic quality of all other beings, whether divine or human (see *Iliad*, VIII. *init.*), under the influence of such a universally received conception, the poet of the Prometheus did not, and could not intend to represent the disobedience of the crafty demi-god as a thing absolutely right, much less as a well-grounded rebellion of which the success might be conceived probable or even possible. Were this the case we might with justice revert

---

[1] "The Zeus of this tragedy, and with him the main part of the mythical substratum, is taken from the theogony; but he has changed his character. For whatever ideas the theogony may include under the type of different celestial dynasties, one thing is certain, that it excludes all idea of moral estimate and sequence. Æschylus is not slow to perceive his advantage, and uses the materials provided for him by the old poet, for the filling up of a far more comprehensive plan. He brings studiously into the foreground every circumstance purely human, that was interwoven with the theologic legend, for the purpose of connecting one symbol with another; everything that can be found in it tending to place Jove in a disadvantageous light. The supreme god, accordingly, appears in this drama, not as more godlike, only as more powerful than Prometheus, only as the recently elevated despot before the unbending freeman; the hero that, like an Achilles among the gods, breathes a spirit of haughty defiance in a pure though not quite understood consciousness of good deeds. Both are absolutely equal under the eternal and just sway of destiny.— The Zeus of this tragedy is represented strictly according to the pattern of a tyrant, and that in the most glaring outline: whether in thus painting him the Persian invader was in the imagination of the soldier who fought at Marathon, or, as I rather think, only Grecian history and politics in general, that by this representation of the free-minded Titan, he might fan the flames of freedom in the hearts of his countrymen; or finally, his object might be only to give free scope to his own feelings as they had been fostered during his residence in Sicily, a country in which he had the image of a just and equitable sovereign before him, which might readily suggest its counterpart in the character of the despotical son of Kronos."—*Tril.* p. 21-2.

to the ready criticism of the old French school, and give our verdict coolly in the words of La Harpe, "*Le sujet de Prométhée est monstrueux.*"

We have called Prometheus a demi-god. He calls himself a god in the play (v. 92), and Hephæstus bears testimony to the propriety of the addition (v. 14). Some persons have been eager to make much of this point, and to bring it forward as a key to the otherwise inexplicable impiety of the piece. Had Prometheus been a mere man, they argue, Æschylus, in writing as he has written, would have been justly chargeable with blasphemy; but a god may surely be allowed to battle with a god, not with words only but with blows, and, according to the Greek ideas, no offence result. But, in the first place, the supremacy of Jove, according to the idea of the *Iliad*, whatever changes of celestial dynasty may have preceded, is an established fact that admits no question.[1]   Gods, in the Homeric theology, may justly battle with gods ; but Zeus is god in a higher sense, sitting apart from the vulgar throng—

> Ἀκροτάτῃ κορυφῇ πολυδειράδος Οὐλύμποιο,

serene where all are troubled, supreme where all are subordinate. And if the dynasty of Jove—though a thing that had an acknowledged beginning—was, in the days of Homer, a power beyond the power of popular conception or poetic fancy to shake, how much more in the days of Æschylus ?   In the second place, the rank which Pro-

---

[1] Such representations as that in *Iliad*, I. 400, where Here, Poseidon, and Pallas are said to have conspired to bind Jove, are, in our opinion, to be looked on as fragments of the old amorphous theology of the rudest Pelasgi, long before the age of Homer, and as forming no living element of religious faith in the time of Homer, much less in the age of Æschylus. Besides, in all such legends—even in the portentous heaven-stormings of Hindu Yogees— the supreme god always retains his seat. The fiction of possible dethronement seems to have been devised partly to show the stability of the throne.

metheus held as a god in the popular faith of Greece was
practically very low; theoretically indeed, that is to say,
according to the genealogy of Hesiod, he appears as the
contemporary and the equal of Jove, the son of Iapetus,
and the son of Kronos, being, in fact, brothers' sons; but,
as in the aristocratic arrangements of modern society, the
elder and younger branches of the family often share very
different fates, so in the world-upheaving turmoil of Titanic
contention, the lines of lineal and collateral relationship in
the celestial family were strangely disturbed; and, as ages
rolled on, the degree of divinity in competing candidates
for popular homage was estimated, not by the descent, but
by the event.   Thus, in the days of Æschylus, the cousin
of Jove had become a local demi-god, the patron-saint of
the potters in the Ceramicus—scarcely a degree more.[1]
In the third place, let Prometheus be perched as high as
we will in the scale of divinity, we never can overlook the
fact, that not only in the representation of Æschylus, but
in the old popular representation, so far as we know it,
everywhere and characteristically Prometheus appears as
the representative of man.   Whatever his original descent,
he has in the course of the fated æons identified himself
with man, and stands forward as the living impersonation
of human interests as opposed to divine.[2]   This character
of the legend is admitted by all who have been at pains
to receive it into their imaginations purely as it is given
by the Greek authorities; and if so, the struggle of the
Titan against the Olympian is in fact not merely a new

[1] See the whole subject of the worship of Prometheus in Athens, admirably handled by *Weiske*, pp. 497-521.

[2] This essential contrast between Prometheus, as the representative of man, and Zeus, as the highest celestial power, is altogether lost sight of by allegorizers like *Swayne*, who arbitrarily makes Prometheus the representative of *divine* love, satisfying the demands of divine justice. See above.—This licentious Christianizing of Hellenic myths can lead to nothing but confusion.

scene in the great primeval battle of the gods, but an ominous collision between earth and heaven, an unequal contest between the weakness of man and the omnipotence˜ of Jove. If free in his own right to rebel—although even this can scarcely be supposed—yet as the representative of man, Prometheus, according to Greek ideas, was not blameless, and could not be prosperous in his contumacy.

The office and virtue of *Μοῖρα*, or Fate in the Greek theology, is another point which has been brought forward prominently by those who, assuming the perfect rectitude of the moral position of Prometheus, are necessitated to find in the popular conceptions of religion a superior power which may adjudicate between the oppressed Titan and the tyrannical son of Kronos. Thus Welcker (p. 88) ; thus Bellmann (p. 53) ; nor had they far to go for their arbiter ; Prometheus himself had put into their mouths the remarkable passage—

CHORUS.

Τίς οὖν ἀνάγκης ἐστὶν οἰακοστρόφος.

PROM.

Μοῖραι τρίμορφαι, μνήμονές τ' Ἐρινύες.

CHORUS.

Τούτων ἄρα Ζεὺς ἐστιν ἀσθενέστερος.

PROM.

Οὔκουν ἂν ἐκφύγοι γε τὴν πεπρωμένην.

In the hands of a modern Christian, or christianizing speculator, it requires very little stretch of idea to metamorphose this dim dark power called πεπρωμένη, of which we hear so much in the Greek drama, into a regular πρόνοια, or clear and distinct superintending providence, which shall hold the balance of fates human and divine much more equitably than Zeus does in the *Iliad.* But to prove that the Greeks in the days of Æschylus, or the ancients indeed anywhere (except here and there, perhaps, in the pious paragraphs of a Marcus Antoninus), had any idea of a superintending and retributive πρόνοια, above and beyond, and even contrary to the will of Jove, who is emphatically called μητίετα Ζεὺς—the counsellor; this is a very different affair, and will, we fear, go far beyond the strength of those who shall attempt to make it out. Hesiod very significantly makes the Μοῖραι daughters of Night (*Theog.* 217); and in darkness, doubtless, they were involved, to the ancient Greek mind, too deep to admit of their being employed as definite and legitimate arbiters in a strife between the supreme god and a contumacious demi-god. Altogether the Μοῖραι seem to present themselves in classical writers more as an unfathomable background in which the origin of all things may be supposed to lie concealed, than as a prominent personal agency fit for the purposes of the dramatic poet; and with regard to Zeus, it is like to prove a very delicate investigation how far the doings of the Μοῖραι in the general case are not identical with his own will. On this point Schoemann in a note has put forward a statement (p. 110) with which we are inclined to concur.

" Why," says Bauer (*Symbolik,* II. 340), " may the Μοῖρα not have been an intelligent principle? A moral harmony, the idea of an eternal justice dispensing to each his proper lot, and with severity anticipating every transgression of the appointed limits of different agencies. Such an idea, what is it but the great law of the universe which preserves in constant equilibrium the world of gods and

men, the world both of intelligent beings and of unconscious nature?"   " I am of opinion, however, that, according to the Greek conception, this great law of the world
had never attained to a clear embodiment in the person of
any individual god, not even in the Μοῖραι.   Such a law,
indeed, rules from the beginning, and determines in the
last instance all that is and happens ; it is the regulating
norm of the whole course of the universe : but among all
the powers endowed with a distinct personality which in
the course of ages have been evolved, there is no one being
whose intelligence completely embraces this all-compre-
hensive law, and possesses it with distinct consciousness
as a matter of knowledge.   Zeus alone stands so high,
that in the province which belongs to him his intelligence
invariably harmonizes with that law of the world ; where-
fore, also, the theogony makes Themis, the conservatrix of
that law, his spouse, and the Μοῖραι, the dispensers of the
lots of individual beings, his daughters ; that is to say, by
means of Jove only are these beings elevated into the sphere
of intelligence, and from mere physical mights become intelligent and moral beings.   The same relation is expressed
by others when they represent the Μοῖραι as associated
round the throne of Zeus (Διὸς παρὰ θρόνον ἀγχόταται θεῶν
ἑζόμεναι.—Eurip. *Fr. Pel. ap. Stob. Ecl. ph.* I. 6, 10).   But
that, in any being standing above and beyond Jove, the
great law of the world became a fact of consciousness in a
higher degree than in him ; such an imagination is altogether foreign to the faith of the Greeks."

Thus far this sensible and very valuable writer.   But
it is not necessary for our present purpose to enter with
metaphysical curiousness into the exact idea of the ancient
Greek Μοῖραι.   Sufficient for our argument, if in the habitual conception of the pious Greeks they possessed no such

powerful and prominent personality as to entitle them to be brought in at a *dignus vindice nodus* when a strife was to be laid and a controversy adjudicated between the omnipotent autocrat of the skies, and an inferior deity recusant.   At all events we shall not adopt this theory so derogatory to the just supremacy of the king of gods and men, till other and more obvious ones, presently to be stated, shall have been proved untenable.

The personal character and religious convictions of Æschylus form another element in the consideration of this question too important to be omitted.   In what relation did Æschylus stand to the popular creed of his country ?   Have we any reason to believe that he wrote his *Prometheus Bound* in the same spirit that Shelley wrote his *Prometheus Unbound*, as a protest against established authorities and consuetudinary ideas of all kinds ?—or was he a pious believer in that Zeus whom his Prometheus blasphemes ?   On this subject some notions have been propounded by Welcker (*Trilog.* p. 111), which, if they could be established, would not be without influence in reconciling us to the startling idea that Æschylus, in the Prometheus, really intended to enter a protest against the Jove of the multitude, and publicly to ridicule the theology of Hesiod :—

" Summing up all that we have said, and keeping in view specially the fact that Æschylus, both as a philosopher and a person initiated into the Eleusinian mysteries, occupied a position, at least in not a few views, hostile to the popular creed ; on these premises we are authorized to conclude, that in the *Prometheus Bound,* while handling the chief points of Hesiod's theogony, it was his object to declare himself decidedly (*sich nachdrücklich zu erklären*) both against that system and against the Zeus, which is a part of it; that by the free representation of the connexion of the different parts of the theogony, it was his purpose to show that the legends of the gods contained in it are to be taken only as poetical fictions, and to be carefully separated from that which really belongs to the divine nature. Spectators who knew all these relations, and who were at the same time previously familiar with the personal character and the views of the poet, would, without difficulty, recognise in the Zeus of the Prometheus, not the supreme god (*den höchsten Gott*), but a poetical personage of the theogony; and they would at the same time feel that Æschylus had gone beyond the plan of the ancient fable, and adapted it to his own purpose of an allegoric poem, perhaps not without a passing stroke of satire directed against the popular superstitions (*oder auch in satyrischer Nebenabsicht*").

These words state the views of a most acute and ingenious man—a man whom all scholars respect; but we shall not refute in detail the baseless theory which they contain, not knowing but that the learned author himself may have long ago seen the insufficiency of the facts known of the life of Æschylus to sustain so strange a conclusion. We know, indeed, that the poet was a Pythagorean; Cicero tells us so (*Tusc.* II. 10); it is highly probable also, both from external testimony and internal verisimilitude, that he was initiated in the mysteries of Eleusis:[1] but there is not the vestige of a proof, either that the philosophy of the son of Mnesarchus, when imbibed most deeply, had a tendency to excite in its votaries a feeling of hostility towards the polytheistic form of religion; or on the other—especially after the investigations of Lobeck—that the hierophants of Eleusis were a secret conclave of Attic Deists, and the mysteries of the goddess of corn fields a discourse on free thinking. As little can be concluded from the words of Ælian (*Var. Hist.* v. 19), Αἴσχυλος ἐκρίνετο ἀσεβείας ἐπὶ τινὶ δράματι, and the other versions of the same story. That a bold and daring genius like Æschylus,

---

[1] The internal evidence arises from the connexion of Æschylus with Eleusis, his birthplace, along with his strong religious sympathies. The external is based on Aristoph. *Ran.* 886, taken along with Aristot. *Nicom. Eth.* III. 2, as expounded by Welcker (*Trilog.* 106). Against these, on the other hand, we have the positive declaration of Clemens (*Strom.* II. 166, Sylburg), and the opinion of Lobeck, *Aglaoph.* I. 82.

amid his many flights into untried regions, should have stumbled upon some small matter that might give offence to the nice sensibility of Athenian δεισιδαιμονία, or, perhaps, offer a wished-for handle to the eager malignity of Athenian δημοκοπία, is the most natural thing in the world. Dante, with a temperament much akin to the Greek tragedian, said many things in his divine poem sufficiently offensive to the ultra-Romanists, and yet remained a very pious bard. It is indeed altogether to run counter to the obvious probabilities of the case, in an early poet like Æschylus—a poet certainly belonging to the more ancient rather than the more modern aspect of Greek culture—with a theology so imaginative, so various, and so pliant as the Greek, with the natural tendency of all highly poetical minds, to adapt and assimilate, rather than to reject and disown the received religion, under such circumstances to admit, without the most distinct proof, the theory of a direct hostility between the faith of a popular writer, and the faith of a people to whose moral or religious feelings he appealed. When distinct proof, however, is asked, it appears plainly enough, that we know nothing in fact, and can know nothing, of the religious opinions of Æschylus, except in so far as he has indicated them in his works ; and to judge by this standard, Luther himself, in his Lutheran hymn-book, is not more a Lutheran than Æschylus in all his plays—except this enigmatical one—is a pious and godly worshipper of Zeus.[1]

---

[1] Since writing the above, we have read with much pleasure an article in the *Quarterly Review*, vol. lxiv. p. 387, which advocates a mild modification of Welcker's view :—" We speak from the writings of the poet, in saying that the very depth of his religious feelings made him dissatisfied with deities, whose nature he could fathom, whose character he could despise. *Not that he was truly an unbeliever ; the elastic nature of ancient systems saved him from that ; and he could acquiesce in the* de facto *dynasty, so to speak, of Olympus, while his heart and his allegiance were elsewhere.* There was an earlier, a more dread and mys-

The proof of this assertion of course is the general impression left on the mind of those who read his works frequently and sympathetically: those who wish for a detailed and tangible deduction on the subject will find ample satisfaction in the well-known work of Klausen. For one, the present writer, after not a few years' familiar occupation with the plays of Æschylus, can only express his conviction of the utter improbability, to use the words of the most recent English translator, "that Æschylus, the most religious poet of antiquity, should have attempted to enlist the sympathies of his audience against the gods of his country;"[1] and nothing but the happy felicity of ingenious theory in finding arguments to prove itself, can explain how a scholar of Welcker's stature should have found only "a sublime Lucian" in the poet of the

---

terious theology—πρὶν ὤν,—*Agam.* v. 170, which had passed away, and been superseded indeed, but which still lingered in the background of the Hellenic system; and to this he devoted himself with the more energy, in proportion to his disquiet, perhaps with the more zeal, for that the old faith seemed neglected. The real gods of his devotion were EARTH, with her Titan brood, of whose time-honoured inheritance the Olympic dynasty had possession but questionably and precariously — the FATES—the FURIES—and above all, the dread power of DESTINY." This passage avoids the offensive harshness of Welcker's language; and the sentences we have given in italics seem to bring the writer's view, to a certain extent, into harmony with that unquestioned supremacy of Jove, which we allege to be a characteristic of Æschylus and the Prometheus, as much as of the ancient poetry of Homer and Hesiod. We much fear, however, that the representation thus given of the relation of Æschylus to Zeus is only a hasty generalization from the Prometheus, as it affects us in its present truncated shape. The very passage of the *Agamemnon* quoted by the writer proves the devout allegiance of the poet to Zeus as distinctly, at least, as any expressions in the Prometheus prove his disaffection. As little can we see, in the juridical pleadings of the Eumenides, any concerted irony against the received gods: we perceive only the necessary awkwardness into which a dramatist falls, whose plot leads him to put into a legal and argumentative shape the thousand and one absurdities of a purely legendary faith.

[1] Prowett, *Introduction*, p. 8. So also Mr. Whiston, in Smith's *Biographical Dictionary*, art. ÆSCHYLUS, "The religious views and tenets of Æschylus, so far as they appear in his writings, were Homeric."

very solemn and devout opening chorus of the Agamemnon.[1]

In vain, therefore, as it should seem, is every argument tried, and every hypothesis ventured, to reconcile the commonly received notion of the Æschylean Prometheus, either with the religious opinions of Greece generally, or with the theological views of the poet. Turn where we will in search of a satisfactory explanation, we are baffled. It therefore remains only that we carefully review our facts, that we recur to our original impression, and see whether there may not be good reason to question its accuracy. Our sympathies, as we read the piece, are confessedly altogether with Prometheus, while our unmitigated hatred is centred on Jove. But is it absolutely necessary, is it in any view imperative, that we should suppose the same representation to have made the same impression on the minds of the Athenians? For were it possible to imagine, that from difference of position and susceptibility, the sympathies of the Athenians were different from ours, perhaps ran altogether in the opposite direction, then there is an end of the question; literature and religion being no longer at war, neither learning nor ingenuity are necessary to reconcile them.

Now, on this head, it is most obvious to remark, that of all the component parts of a foreign and distant literature, that which concerns religion is the most difficult for the stranger student to realize. The squabbles of the marketplace, and the wranglings of the forum, being pretty much the same in an ancient or a " modern Athens," will be easily understood by a reader of any time and place; but

---

[1] On the opening words of the invocation to Jove in that chorus—Ζεὺς ὅστις ποτ' ἐστὶν—Welcker remarks,— " *Sicher schrieb er dies nicht ohne Iro-* *nie!*" (p. 104). A case must be very hopeless that requires such perverse ingenuity as this.

between Christianity and heathenism the gulf is so wide, that a perfect recognition of the ancient by the modern can be achieved only in the case of the studious few, and that not without much labour, and a peculiar emotional sensibility. We are bound, therefore, to approach problems of this kind with a certain cautiousness and self-suspicion, quite the reverse of the indifferent carelessness by which, in respect of them, our judgment is generally possessed. In particular, we are bound not merely to dispossess ourselves of all modern notions which have grown with our growth, but to possess ourselves of all corresponding ancient notions which grew with the growth of the Athenians; we must put a force upon our own convictions, and conjure up in our souls a factitious reverence for names that were once powers and virtues and mighty agencies in the moral world. We must approach the reading of the *Prometheus Bound,* as the pious Athenian came to witness its representation, with a mind prepossessed, and that strongly, not in favour of Prometheus, but in favour of Zeus. This prepossession alone will go far to change the whole aspect of the case ; but we can happily go much further : we are in a condition to come to the reading of the *Prometheus* with the same detailed knowledge of the legend, and the same received interpretation of it, that possessed the mind of the ancient Athenian. The potters and the torch-runners of the Ceramicus, in all likelihood, knew no more of it than we do. We possess, in fact, the Greek *Bible* on the subject ;—so far, at least, as the floating fanciful religion of the Greeks could be said to have a Bible,—we possess HESIOD.

What then does the pious old Ascræan say on the subject ? This is the preparatory question from which every thorough investigation into the theology of the

Æschylean drama must start. The Athenian came thus
prepared; and to place ourselves in the same position, so
must we: not with a portentous logical deduction, like
Bellmann, who (p. 37) boasts that he will bring out the
idea of the play, "*solo scriptore duce*," as if the writer
himself ever dreamt of addressing blank minds, and did
not rather calculate upon the preconceived ideas and tendencies of his audience, as on a main matter on which the
effect of his artistical exhibition depended! Well; Hesiod
tells the story, as we all know it in the facts, not once,
but twice, with considerable breadth of detail, in the
Theogony (507), and in the *Works and Days* (48); but the
tone in which he tells it, and the moral with which he
couples it, are less known, and for the most part not at
all present to the mind of the general, or even the learned
reader; so completely with his bold and daring grandeur
has the more modern dramatist thrown the simple-hearted
theologer into the shade. But this tone and this moral
are the very soul of the legend: they represent the religious mind of Greece on the subject; or, if they do not,
nothing else does; and it is from this source only that we
can learn, at the present day, the feelings with which an
Athenian audience, in the days of the Persian war, came
to witness a theatrical exhibition, of which the fire-filching
demigod was the hero. Let any man, therefore, read the
Theogony from the beginning to the conclusion of the
Promethean Episode, and say how he is affected by the
representation there given. It is plain the pious old
genealogist—and this is the main point—approves no
more of the conduct of the son of Iapetus than of the host
of other Titans: these strove by violence against Zeus, he
by cunning; but they were both rebels against him whom
the Greeks worshipped as both omnipotent and omniscient,

as not merely the highest physical force, but the supreme moral power in the system of the world;[1] and in the character of rebels they were both punished.   Which was the greater guilt, whether to oppose Zeus by force or by fraud, the bard does not inquire; but if there be degrees in wickedness of this kind, the sinner who endeavours to deceive the all-knowing one will scarcely seem less guilty than he who vaunts himself to subdue the all-powerful. Such certainly was the notion of Hesiod, who concludes both his narratives with the distinct moral,—

$$\text{`}Ω\text{ς οὐκ ἔστι } Δ\text{ιὸς κλέψαι νόον οὐδὲ παρελθεῖν—}$$
(*Theog.* 613; *Op.* 92)

a moral, be it observed, no less characteristically Christian than Heathen, and in which the true Christian significance of the Prometheus indicated by Lasaulx lies; though indeed the distinct enunciation of this moral was not at all necessary, as the whole tone and connexion of the narrative in both works prove the same thing.   Wherein, then, according to the old poet, does the guilt of Prometheus consist?   Plainly, in the impious attempt to deceive and to defraud the supreme god, with an obstinate perversity of cunning, on two several occasions; first, in regard to sacrificial rites—which circumstance, by the way, Æschylus has thought fit to drop—and then in the great matter of using celestial fire for terrestrial purposes. No doubt the result of both these attempts is in favour of man; the benevolent end seems to sanctify the unworthy means; but the piety of the poet is nowise affected by this circumstance.   He only knows that Jove is supreme; and

---

[1] We do not, of course, mean to say that the Homeric idea of Jove was precisely that of a Christian's idea of God; but the familiar epithets of ὅρκιος, ξένιος, etc., altogether preclude the idea of looking on him as merely an impersonation of supreme *power* in the physical world.

that every boon, however gracious, conferred without his consent and against his will, cannot be without guilt on the part of the giver, and danger on the part of the receiver. That Prometheus is guilty forms in fact the foundation of the whole legend, according to Hesiod.[1] This is so manifest, that even among those modern commentators who consider Jove as tyrannical in his conduct, there are many who equally admit the guilt of Prometheus. That the Athenians, at least, must have started with this as an undeniable axiom seems as certain as that a modern Christian reads the third chapter of Genesis with the undoubting faith that Adam and Eve, and the serpent, sinned grievously in what they did. " *Persuasum erat auditoribus reum luere justam pœnam,*" says Toepelmann (p. 37). So even Herder admits the guilt of Prometheus partially, though he represents Jove as having been much more blameful, putting forth Themis, strangely enough (one of Jove's wives !), or eternal justice, to adjudicate betwixt them. So Welcker also ;[2] only not Byron and Bellmann, Shelley, and Schütz, and Goethe. What, then, let us inquire further, the Athenian mind being thus fore-armed with Hesiodic views, was the moral effect of the Æschylean Prometheus on the spectators ? The answer to this question depends on the answer to another one, Is the Æschylean Prometheus the same as the Prometheus of Hesiod—morally, we mean, of course—or is he different ? He is the same in every respect substantially ; only Æschylus brings his better qualities, his fortitude and

---

[1] So, in a much later age, true to the moral of the old legend, Horace—

" Audax omnia perpeti
   Gens humana ruit per vetitum nefas ;
  Audax Iapeti genus
    Ignem fraude malâ gentibus intulit."
                 Od. i. 3. 25.

[2] " The proper crime of Prometheus, the one great deceit by which the mind endeavours to lay violent hold of what is divine (*das Göttliche an sich zu reissen*"), p. 73, and a great deal more to the same effect in the chapter—*über die Bedeutung des Ganzen*—well worthy of study.

self-sustainment, into the foreground, while a shade is
cast over his cunning and his crime. These bad qualities,
however, are in nowise withheld. . He is called the THIEF
of fire, and charged again and again, by mouths commanding respect, with rashness and pride; with audacity
and obstinacy, and ὕβρις in every shape. The modern
reader, indeed, may not choose to give any weight to this
judgment; but with the ancient spectator it was at once
the ground and the body of all orthodoxy. Æschylus
therefore does not deny the moral of Hesiod; and if he
does not do it, either expressly or by implication, most
assuredly his audience would not do it for him. Every
believer in a popular theology—no matter whether wise
or absurd—is slow to have his faith shaken. A direct
attack must be made before he will be roused; then indeed
his vengeance is terrible.

But the chorus, the impartial spectator, the spokesman of all morality, and the preacher of all propriety in
the Greek drama, does he—or in this case rather, does
she—not sympathize with the suffering Titan, and express
her detestation of the tyranny of Jove? One passage
there certainly is in this view very strong; it is as follows. We quote the whole, for it is short:—

CHORUS.

λεύσσω Προμηθεῦ· φοβερὰ δ' ἐμοῖσιν ὄσσοις,
ὀμίχλα προσῇξε πλήρης
δακρύων, σὸν δέμας εἰσιδούσᾳ
πέτραις προσαυαινόμενον
ταῖσδ' ἀδαμαντοδέτοισι λύμαις·
νέοι γὰρ οἰακονόμοι κρατοῦσ' Ὀλύμπου·
νεοχμοῖς δὲ δὴ νόμοις Ζεὺς ἀθέτως κρατύνει
τὰ πρὶν δὲ πελώρια νῦν ἀϊστοῖ.—vv. 144-51.

These are certainly distinct words—*ΑΘΕΤΩΣ*; and if

there were no other statement from the same quarter to a different effect in the same play, the question might be considered as triumphantly settled in favour of the popular view. A consistent verdict of this kind from an ancient chorus could not have brooked contradiction from any modern critic. But the persons of the chorus in the Prometheus are scarcely to be looked upon as judges. No busy actors are they indeed, and parties directly interested, like the fell-snorting, black-banded sisterhood in the Eumenides; but they are simple ocean-maids, amiable, kindly, and tender-hearted, and, like all proper women, eager for nothing so much as to sympathize always with all affliction, ever pleading for mercy, without inquiring curiously into the claims of justice. They therefore confine their office, in the present drama, almost altogether to the expression of sympathy with the sufferer, and that, as was necessary in noble characters, not by word only, but by deed. They pretend, however, to no judgment in so gigantic a strife; or, if they judge at all, express an opinion on the side of Zeus; for the strong words above quoted are more than negatived by the decided language of an opposite tendency that occurs as the action of the play advances.

But it may still be argued, if the chorus gives no opinion in the matter, does not Æschylus himself do so? Has he not drawn the whole portraiture, determined every attitude, thrown every light with the view, and to the effect, of engaging the whole stream of our sympathies in favour of the sufferer? Assuredly he has drawn a strong picture of manly fortitude, and in doing so, unquestionably he wished to excite sympathy in behalf of the sufferer; but the conclusion, therefore, is not legitimate, which Schütz and Bellmann have drawn, that he wished to exhibit Prometheus as in all respects a moral model, in the fashion somewhat of the stoical wise man. There are great and manly virtues in Macbeth and Richard, which our greater Æschylus meant that we should admire, without prejudice to our condemnation of the main character of these persons. So, also, Milton has tricked out the devil with more of the trappings of heroism than is agreeable to many. Goethe's *Mephistopheles*, it has been thought, is a much more proper devil; a fiend whom you can hate thoroughly, without being tempted to admire. In the same way, we may feel that the crafty fraudulent Prometheus of the theogony is a much more fit subject for the pillory of the Caucasus than the

" High-minded son of right-decreeing Themis,"

whom the father of Greek tragedy has elevated to the culminating point of the sublime in endurance. But Æschylus and Milton alike, in this modification of the character of their heroes, followed their lofty genius, not the popular conception. Wise in doing so; and safe from misinterpretation of their main scope, by the strength of general prepossession, and the stability of the popular faith.

One most important point in the Athenian conception of the Promethean myth still remains to be noticed. The Greeks learned more from Hesiod than the unquestionable guilt of Prometheus, and the justice of his punishment. They learned, at the same time, the palliation of that guilt, and the limit of that castigation. He had opposed the will of the supreme; therein his guilt was great; but his main object was not essentially base or selfish; his theft was from the gods, but for the benefit of man : fire, the " mother of arts," was a gift that the giver of all good things—the δωτῆρες ἐάων, could not mean finally to withhold from creatures who so much required it; Prometheus, therefore, sinned in the form rather than in the drift and result of his offending; and for him, according to all reasonable ideas of a divine procedure, mercy was reserved. The old myth accordingly taught that Prometheus, after suffering unexampled woes, was finally to be liberated, and that even by the agency of the great Hellenic liberator, Hercules. This the Athenian audience distinctly knew from Hesiod (*Theog.* 526); but it is announced also with no less distinctness in our drama (v. 772); and the effect of this annunciation must necessarily have been to remove from their minds any appearance of harshness and severity on the part of Zeus, which the terrible nature of the punishment seemed to wear. The degree of punishment, no doubt, in theological legends of this kind, is popularly estimated, not by any curious admeasurement of the magnitude of the crime or the capacity of the sinner, but by the transcendental nature of the being against whom the offence is committed. Still the offence of Prometheus was one which, in the most severe view, could scarcely seem worthy of never-ending torture. The

" Sedet æternumque sedebit infelix Theseus"

of Virgil applies to a crime of much more flagrant atrocity. Final pardon, therefore, the Athenian spectator looked for confidently; as ages rolled on, the period would certainly come when it would be consistent with the sovereignty of the supreme god to temper his stern justice with mercy; when a reconciliation between the offending demigod, having expiated sin by suffering, and the justly offended deity, would take place. The previous know-

ledge of this final satisfactory settlement of the great controversy was sufficient to quiet the conscience of a pious
Athenian, if at any time the whetted words of the tortured Titan seemed to cast reproaches in the ear of Zeus,
more bitter than might be grateful to pious ears to hear.
The poet when he represented, and the people when they
beheld, painted with glaring colours individual aspects of
the portentous myth, only the more decidedly that their
heart rested with perfect faith in the acknowledged righteousness of the anticipated catastrophe.

But there is more than this,—the spectators of the
Prometheus Bound not only knew what the catastrophe
should be, but there is every reason to believe that they
actually saw it. That Æschylus wrote three, and perhaps four plays on this significant myth has long been a
patent and well-known fact to scholars. That he wrote
a *Prometheus Unbound* is the most certain tradition of
all; for we actually have a translation from it in a
work so commonly read as the Tusculan Questions of
Cicero (II. 9). Of this fact, not a single scholar, probably, who has criticised the *Prometheus* for the last three
hundred years, has been ignorant ; but, in recognising the
bearing of so important a fact on the interpretation of the
now existing play, many writers, even in the most recent
times, have been strangely deficient. If the Bound Prometheus is only introductory to an Unbound Prometheus,
which, in the actual representation, immediately followed,
as itself was introduced by a fire-bringing Prometheus, it
is manifest that we are not. at present in a condition to
judge of the total effect of the trilogy, any more than
from one act of a modern play the spectator can always
divine—for *sometimes* certainly he may divine—the whole.
Our modern critics, however, even those who may the

least suspect it, have proceeded too generally on the assumption that the present play contains within itself the elements of a just judgment as to its tendency. So prepossessed with this very natural notion does Hermann, for instance, seem to be, that he expends not a little forced ingenuity of labour in endeavouring to disprove against Welcker the natural continuity of the play which follows with that which precedes. There is no direct testimony, indeed, from the ancients, either that the Prometheus Unbound was in actual representation given directly after the play which we now possess, or that the Προμηθεὺς πυρφόρος immediately preceded it. Hermann also insists that this first part of the assumed trilogy was identical with the Προμηθεὺς πυρκαεύς, mentioned by Pollux,[1] and which we know from the argument of " the Persians " to have been a satiric drama, the last in the tetralogy there given. But leaving this point undecided—as most likely it never can be decided—the hypothesis, that the Προμηθεὺς λυόμενος, which forms so natural a sequel to the δεσμώτης, was disjoined from it in the actual exhibition, is so forced and gratuitous, that not even the name of Hermann will induce the sound-minded student to give it a serious consideration. In criticism as in morals, probability, not possibility, must be our guide. The conclusion that the λυόμενος was exhibited immediately after the δεσμώτης, is not only the most obvious and natural in the case, but it is a supposition which the admitted theological difficulties of the introductory play imperatively demand. The catastrophe thus evolved, irrespective altogether of what we know from Hesiod, were sufficient of itself to remove every objection arising from the apparent impiety of the piece ; the supposition of a continuous trilogy, or,

---

[1] ix. 156 ; x. 64.

at least, of a second play following the present, is, in fact, a theory which satisfactorily explains all the phenomena; while the opposite theory explains nothing, being useful only, so far as a plain man may see, to prop the crumbling consistency of ancient error, and to enable the old school of philologists to be gathered to their fathers with the comfortable assurance that they have not been vanquished by the new.[1]

As to the precise manner in which the reconciliation between Jove and his stout-hearted adversary was brought about by the poet in the last piece of the trilogy, there exist materials large enough to justify a few probable conjectures, but too scanty to admit of any approach to certainty.[2] The most satisfactory attempt to reconstruct the lost framework of Æschylus, the German scholar will find in Schoemann's very valuable work; an author with whose views on almost every point of the Promethean question we are disposed to coincide; and to whom the present writer owes it more directly, that his own long-revolved imaginations on this subject have at length organized themselves into the present tangible shape.

[1] "If there ever was a case in which it was justifiable to assume positively the existence of a connected trilogy it is this case of the Prometheus."—*Quart. Review*, vol. lxx. p. 353. *N.B.*—I had not read this when I wrote the text. The coincidence of independent opinion has of course a certain value.

[2] Those who have read Shelley's Prometheus need not be told that no attempt is there made to reconstruct the lost play of Æschylus. From any attempt of this kind the poet's instinctive good taste, as well as his bold and original genius, were sufficient to deter him. It is of importance to us, however, to remark specially, with what a just poetic discernment he perceived the necessity of the lost play to evolve the catastrophe of the present piece, and how clearly he perceived that the poet must have brought about the catastrophe by a reconciliation of the contending parties. Adhering, however, strictly to the idea that Zeus is to be looked on only "as the oppressor of mankind," it is no wonder he could find in the Æschylean sequel no theme worthy of his genius. The following is from the Preface :— " The Prometheus Unbound of Æschylus supposed the reconciliation of Jupiter with his victim, as the price of the disclosure of the danger threatened to his empire by the

Before concluding these remarks, it will be necessary
to advert for a moment to a view of the moral connexion
of the Bound and the Unbound Prometheus, first proposed by Dissen in a letter to Welcker (*Trilog.* p. 92),
and brought forward again by Dr. Julius Cæsar in opposition to the views of Schoemann.   Professor Schoemann
does not assume any more than ourselves that it is necessary, in the final reconciliation of the contending parties,
to suppose any confession of error or change of character
on the part of Jove.   We both suppose with Hesiod that
the punishment suffered by Prometheus was merited;
and with the Greeks generally that the moral sovereignty
of Zeus is not to be questioned; nor the degree of punishment which he chooses to inflict on the offender a
matter about which the curious casuistry of human wit can
legitimately be exercised.   But there are scholars who,
agreeing with us in the point of the guilt of Prometheus,
are not able to shake themselves free from the impression
of gross tyranny which is left upon the modern reader by
the perusal of the present truncated work.   These per-

consummation of his marriage with
Thetis. Thetis, according to this view
of the subject, was given in marriage
to Peleus; and Prometheus, by the permission of Jupiter, delivered from his
captivity by Hercules. Had I framed
my story on this model, I should have
done no more than have attempted to
restore the lost drama of Æschylus;—
an ambition which, if my preference to
the mode of treating the subject had
incited me to cherish, the recollection
of the high comparison such an attempt
would challenge might well abate. But,
in truth, I was averse from a catastrophe so feeble as that of reconciling
the champion with the oppressor of
mankind. The moral interest of the
fable, which is so powerfully sustained
by the sufferings and endurance of Prometheus, would be annihilated, if we
could conceive of him as unsaying his
high language, and quailing before his
successful and perfidious adversary.
The only imaginary being resembling
in any degree Prometheus is Satan;
and Prometheus is, in my judgment, a
more poetical character than Satan, because, in addition to courage, and majesty, and firm and patient opposition
to omnipotent force, he is susceptible of
being described as exempt from the
taints of ambition, envy, revenge, and
a desire for personal aggrandizement,
which, in the hero of *Paradise Lost*,
interfere with the interest."

sons, therefore, have been driven to the invention of a sort of middle hypothesis between the two views contrasted in this paper; a hypothesis conceived purposely so as to admit on the one hand the penitent submission of Prometheus, and on the other the progressive amelioration and final perfectionation of Jove. The following are the words of Dissen :—

" What has always offended me most in the Prometheus is the total giving up of the character of Jove, which seems to be the effect of the poet's representation; and I have never been able to convince myself that it was the intention of Æschylus to exalt the world of Titans without qualification, and to depreciate the presently existing gods. The first idea that occurred to me, to remove this difficulty, was, that the principal actors in the Promethean myth are not heroes, with gods introduced only as a sort of machinery; but here we have a contest of gods against gods; and a god is freely allowed to bring accusations against Jove, such as would have constituted blasphemy in a mortal. But this explanation is not satisfactory. We have two questions to answer. Can the controversy between Jove, a tyrant of the world, and his accusers, be looked on as a matter of personal feeling between the parties concerned; or is it meant that we, the spectators, and in our person the Greek religion, henceforth are to look upon Jove under the same aspect of tyranny in which he appears to the principal actor in the play? The one supposition is insufficient; for Jove is made to do that which actually *is* tyrannical, so manifestly that the spectator cannot look upon it as a collision arising out of personal animosity. The other supposition I cannot prevail upon myself, without more ado, to adopt. I have accordingly been forced to another view of the subject, which is this,—I look upon the whole as a *Titanomachy*, as the last great struggle of that mighty time; as, indeed, we find that the myth of Prometheus, according to the theogonic chronology, follows immediately after the battle of the Titans, and forms in fact their conclusion. In such an age—in the early epoch of mundane development—when the elements of the future system of the world were not yet in equilibrium, violence and exaggeration on both sides are quite natural; and as Prometheus, on his part, was not free from blame, so Jove also erred in the exercise of a tyrannical authority. I therefore look upon the tyrannical character of Zeus, exhibited in the Bound Prometheus, as only a transition state of things which is to vanish with the final establishment of the new order of things, to be represented in the third piece. In this epoch, if the system of the world is still felt as tyrannical, it can only be so in the feeling of an individual ; in a higher view of the whole, the tyranny disappears ; and in this regard I imagine Æschylus could never have meant to represent the government of Jove as a permanent tyranny—a representation which would have been at war both with the Greek tragedy and with the Grecian world.   Prometheus, in the exercise of an excessive benevolence, has given to men that which belongs to the gods ; and in as much as he has thereby planted man on a more commanding platform, as against the gods, Jove, jealous of his power, persecutes him, and will not tolerate the higher elevation of man till such time as he—so I view the relation—being reconciled to Prometheus, is at the same time reconciled to the new order of the world, and is brought to the insight that it is better for him to reign over ennobled men, than over creatures little better than the brutes.   For Jove also must have come forth from that terrible Titanic struggle, not in his original character, but with a higher consciousness.   Force and forcible rule were essential elements of the Titanic period, in which one celestial power after another dethroned its predecessor ; in perfect keeping with which general character it is, that the Jove of that epoch is suspicious, haughty, despotical, etc., even because he forms the transition between the old and the new, till, with the conclusion of the Titanic struggles, a higher phasis appears.   When I contemplate the whole trilogy in this light, it appears to me a profoundly-conceived glorification of the new order of the world, as having put an end to the licentious exaggerations of the preceding period.   Sluggish insensibility (*Stumpfheit*), oppression and tyranny, have come to an end : the free development of the mind in the unfolding of the arts commences ; everything marches to meet a higher destiny.   And this feeling, I may add, is precisely that which would naturally be predominant in the poet's mind at the time when he wrote.   The period immediately following the Persian wars was accompanied with an expansive movement in the Greek mind, which corresponds happily with the sublime idea of mundane development, as I imagine it represented in the trilogy."

The objection to this theory, according to our view, is, that if we have proved anything by the preceding remarks, it is altogether unnecessary, being invented, according to the declaration of the author, to obviate a difficulty which never existed in the Athenian mind.   The

Athenians, we have distinctly stated—for this is the point
on which the whole discussion hinges—did not, and could
not, look upon the conduct of Jove as tyrannical in the
matter. The general impression of the tyrannical character of Jove is the mere offspring of modern partial
conceptions, formed in the total disregard both of Hesiod
and of the *Trilogy*. Independent of this objection, however, the hypothesis is faulty, because it is too fine-spun
and metaphysical; abstract and speculative, rather than
practical and popular. In modern times a theologian of no
common notoriety has written a work on " the development of Christian doctrine ;" and no doubt all religious
doctrines and ideas, Christian as well as heathen, are subject to what may be called a development ; that is, they
are understood differently, more narrowly or more largely,
more grossly or more spiritually, according to the capacity
of the minds into which they are received ; but a formal
exposition of such a development of intellectual and moral
phases in a faith generally received would seem to fall
within the province of the theologian and the philosopher
rather than that of the poet. The dramatist, certainly, of
all men who come in contact with a popular religion, is the
least hopeful person to make a physiological unfolding of
its growth and a public demonstration of its anatomy.
He receives it as a thing given, and makes the best of it.
It is a general moral element which all his fantastic personages must breathe ; not a separate theme for himself
to handle. The Greek religion, no doubt, so purely imaginative and emotional, afforded a philosophical dramatist
a wide field for inoculating mythical personages with
abstract notions, such as a definite and closely-reasoned
creed would have barred ; but it is going too far to maintain that the writer of a publicly exhibited sacred opera

—standing somewhat in the position of Metastasio at
Vienna—should have presumed to set before a pious
audience the process of growth of their supreme god, and
to show them, step by step, how Zeus the cruel, in the
course of years and by power of destiny, became Zeus the
just, somehow as a modern physiologist will expound
leisurely how a tadpole, which is substantially a finny fish,
can in the course of days, by the benign influence of light,
become a footed frog.   All this forced and unnatural
theorizing is avoided by the simple supposition that the
Athenian audience believed in Homer and Hesiod ; and
that the fortitude and constancy of the sufferer, which in
the more popular modern view colours the whole of the
Æschylean drama, was in fact but a strong dramatic point
in the mind both of the ancient dramatist and his audience ; while the religious soul that inspired the complete
legend was the solemn conviction of the Greek, as it is
also of the Christian mind,[1] that whether in man or in
demi-god—the representative of man, every function is
to be exercised, every energy put forth blissfully, only
under subjection to the will of the Supreme ;

$$\text{ὅττι μάλ' οὐ δηναιὸς ὃς ἀθανάτοισι μάχηται.}$$

---

[1] Besides Lasaulx and Schoemann,
Völcker also, in his *Mythologie des Iape-
tischen Geschlechts* (Genev. 1824), recog-
nises in the Promethean myth, as given
by Hesiod in the *Works and Days*, a
heathen account of the Fall of Man. We
shall best forestall contradiction by saying, that the sin of Adam in Genesis iii.,
and the sin of Prometheus in Hesiod
and Æschylus, however they may differ
in form and in effect, are in conception
and principle substantially the same.

ON THE PHILOLOGICAL GENIUS AND CHARACTER OF THE NEO-HELLENIC DIALECT OF THE GREEK LANGUAGE.

PROPOSITION I.—All spoken language is a growth, subject, like the creature who uses it, to a constant course of mutation; it is a living organism, developed according to certain laws, partly inherent, partly superinduced; and, though it is liable to decay, disintegration, and death, this disintegration, except in special cases of extermination, becomes the soil of a new growth, and this death the cradle of a new life. The historical action of this process of mutation is to produce either new varieties or dialects of one language, or new species of one family of languages.

PROPOSITION II.—Though no living language is capable of an absolute stoppage, and, according to the Heraclitan doctrine of πάντα ῥεῖ, must either go on growing or be exterminated, yet there are certain influences at work in the constitution of human society that may retard the process of change to an indefinite period, creating a more or less fixed type, from which deviations are few and far between. These influences are of two kinds, internal and external, or as we may say, intellectual and political: intellectual, proceeding from the predominant and authoritative force of great creative intellects, such as Homer and Dante; political, proceeding from the unifying effect of a stable form of government, and a permanent type of social order. In other words, the changes that naturally go on in language, as in everything vital, will be impeded and retarded by the traditions of the past so long as these retain a firm hold on the national habit of thought and expression. And the duration of the type of any language will be in the direct ratio of the force of the controlling influences, internal and external.

PROPOSITION III.—In the case of the Greek language, while the internal conservative influences were peculiarly strong, the external were loose and variable. An absolute political cohesion in the Roman style the Greeks never had. Variety by expansion, and dispersion, and consolidation round a number of special social nuclei, was during their most brilliant period the law of their external growth; but during this period, the influence, first of an Ionic minstrelsy in Asia Minor, and then of an Attic culture in south-eastern Europe, was so strong that it controlled in a very imperial fashion the separative and particularizing forces of independent political centres; and afterwards, when a strong central government was established, and continued for many centuries at Constantinople, this unifying influence, acting with the double power of Church and State, though disturbed at first by the intrusion of a strong Roman vein, combined, with an unexampled weight of intellectual and moral tradition, to retard and impede, or practically to ignore, the changes which, by a process of nature, were naturally going on in the Greek language, in an increasing ratio, from the overthrow of the political and intellectual supremacy of Athens by the Macedonians, to the taking of Constantinople by the Turks, and from that time by natural propagation, though with diminished force, up to the present hour.

PROPOSITION IV.—These retarding forces, however, being in a manner artificial, and acting contrary to the natural law of variation by growth, are necessarily limited in their operation, and can, of course, act only where they are felt; that is to say, in those classes of society which are kept constantly under the moulding and controlling influence of the inherited traditions of the past, or, in common language, in the well-educated classes of the community. The uneducated classes, on the contrary, by whom the controlling power of this traditional culture is not felt, or felt only indirectly and with greatly diminished force, go on, partly breaking down old forms of speech, partly sending forth new shoots, so as to form what becomes a distinctly marked dialect of their own; and in this way the language of a whole people in a state of imperfect and inadequate culture may be propagated in two distinct parallel lines, like an upper and a lower stratum in geology, without coalescing into any common type.

PROPOSITION V.—This bistratified condition of a spoken language is exactly what we find realized in the capital of the Byzantine Empire at the time of the Crusades. For here, while a remarkably strong and unbroken chain of literary and ecclesiastical tradition had preserved, with very trivial alterations, the Catholic dialect of the Greek tongue, of which Attic is the most finished type, the gradual disintegration of an ill-governed

H

empire had combined with various influences, topographical and commercial, social and political, to shake
the language of the great mass of the illiterate masses
loose from all precedent, and to favour the growth of a
corrupt and hybrid dialect, which, with the aid of favourable circumstances, might in due season shape itself, like
the barbarous Latin of the middle ages, into a new language. Of this we have happily the most distinct and
clear evidence in the two short poems of the monk
Theodore Ptochoprodromus, written in the popular dialect, and addressed to the Emperor Manuel, who came
to the throne in the year 1143.   These poems are
composed, not only, like the Annals of Constantine
Manasses, who wrote about the same period, with a
total disregard of the old classical rhythmical laws, but
with a phraseology, and in a style so corrupt and so
hybrid, that, even after the lights thrown on the work
by Du Cange, Koraes, and other scholars, not a few passages still remain obscure, and would be much more so,
were it not that the Latin, which forms one of the chief
corrupting elements, is a language with which the readers
of Byzantine Greek are generally familiar.

PROPOSITION VI.—We must not suppose, however,
from the fact of Theodore, or any other stray writer of
the Byzantine period, having taken it into his head to
write a book or two of verses in the corrupt popular
dialect, that this dialect had at that time asserted for
itself a place, and received a certain recognition in the
world of books. Quite the contrary. In those dreary
days, there arose no popular genius to stamp the popular
dialect with a certain character of limited classicality;
but even had the Byzantines of those times had strength

to produce a Burns, the traditional Greek of the court, the Church, and all educated intellects, was too strong to allow a mere lyrical variety, fostered in the hotbed of barbarism and corruption, to claim for itself more than a very little corner in a very large vineyard. The consequence was, that while the lower stratum of the spoken language was ripening from day to day into the well-marked form of a new dialect, or even a new language, it does not appear to have advanced a single step out of its ignored position as a literary organ, from the time of Theodore down to the taking of Constantinople by the Turks in 1453. Byzantine Greek was classical Greek from beginning to end, with only such insignificant changes as altered circumstances, combined with the law of its original genius, naturally produced.

PROPOSITION VII.—By the fall of the last Palæologus, the bond of unity which held the motley provinces of the Byzantine Empire together was broken; one of the two strong external links that connected the degraded present with the glorious past was snapped; and with the ruin of the Greek Empire, if the example of the Western Empire was to be a precedent, the death of the Greek language might naturally be expected to follow. But this result did not follow, and that principally from the action of three very powerful forces. The system of government introduced by the conquering Turks was not such as to render a fusion of the dominant and subject races possible; here was the first element of repulsion; in the domain of religion the repellent force on the side of the vanquished was even stronger; and, if we add to these two influences the fact, that the accumulated intellectual forces of ages were all on the same side, we shall have no difficulty in perceiving how the taking of Byzantium by the Turks could have no such effect on the language of the Greeks, as the Lombard reign in Italy had on that of Rome, or the Norman invasion of England, in a much more decided way, on the speech of the Anglo-Saxons. Nor were matters much different in the south-western division of the Greek Empire, where the Venetians and other Franks had parcelled among themselves, in governments of greater or less permanency, the dismembered inheritance of the Byzantine Cæsars; for the Greeks hated the Pope, who had on various occasions endeavoured to deprive them of their ecclesiastical liberties, scarcely with less intensity than they did the Turks, who had deprived them of all liberty; and thus, in Frankish Greece also, the new forces introduced by external conquest were not strong enough to effect the disintegration of the old linguistic inheritance, and the construction of a new language, or even the general recognition of a new dialect.

PROPOSITION VIII.—But in spite of the strong and long-continued action of these retarding forces, nature would have her way; a process of growth was slowly going on, which could not but issue in the formation either of an entirely new language, or of a well-marked species of an old language; and under the continued action of the strong conservative forces indicated, the latter was the only result possible. The matter was brought to a practical decision, like so many other significant events in modern times, by the invention of printing and the diffusion of books. By means of these powerful engines, the great storehouses of knowledge were no longer confined to the few, but gradually, as by a well-organized system of irrigation, the refreshing waters were brought down from the far hills, and dispersed through the plains; and an essential part of such a machinery, of course, was the adoption of a language understood by the great mass of the people. If the Greek people were to be raised from the state in which they were kept by their political oppressors, the great preparatory instrument, till an opportunity for physical resistance should present itself, was popular education; and popular education remained impossible so long as the learned wrote in a dialect artificially fed from reservoirs of dead tradition, not beating with the living pulses of the present. Under the influence of this patriotic necessity, books of various kinds, especially theological and ecclesiastic, had been issued from the Greek· press in a popular dialect, somewhat similar to, but not nearly so corrupt as that used by Ptochoprodromus; and works originally written in classical Greek, like the well-known Church History of Meletius, Bishop of Athens (*ob.* 1714), were translated into Romaic or modern Greek, just as we modernize Chaucer for the benefit of the million. These patriotic exertions for elevating the popular intellect were brought to a distinctly marked and generally recognised climax by the learned Adamantine Koraes (*nat.* 1748), a Smyrniote Greek of great learning, philological talent, and ardent patriotism. This distinguished man, living under the inspiring influence of the great French Revolution, showed his countrymen, by precept and example, how it was possible to use the popular dialect according to its own now fully formed type, while preserving a well-balanced medium between the classical norm familiar to scholars and the gross barbarisms practised in the most remote districts, and by the rudest portion of the community.

This wise and patriotic example, followed generally by a succession of accomplished men, has issued in planting modern Greek, or Neo-Hellenic, as it is now called in its perfect form as one of the recognised types of the great Greek language, on the same platform with the Ionic of Homer and the Doric of Theocritus.

PROPOSITION IX.—In attempting now to state scientifically the specific characteristic differences between the Neo-Hellenic dialect and what we are accustomed to call ancient Greek in all its extent, two important questions occur on the threshold. *First,* what do we mean by a *dialect of a language,* as distinguished from a new language formed from old materials ; and from what sources, as a standard, are we to make our inductions with regard to the real philological character of modern Greek ? The first question is one which, in theory, it may be very difficult to answer ; but practically we may say, that whenever the old materials of a language are so modified as that only a very few words remain in their original form, and that more accidentally than systematically, and when the obscurity arising from this source is increased by the admixture, in larger or smaller quantity, of foreign materials, in this case, as in the case of *Spanish* and *Italian,* a new language has been created.[1] But whenever the changes induced on the old materials are comparatively slight and more sporadic than penetrating and pervading

---

[1] The lines in Italian—
  " In mare irato, in subita procella,
    Iuvoco te, nostra benigna stella,"
often quoted (C. Lewis's "Romanic Languages," 2d edit. p. 246) to prove the nearness of Italian to Latin, are no proof of the rule in that language, but are altogether exceptive, as any one may perceive by taking a stanza of *Ottava rima* either in Tasso or Ariosto, and counting how very few words in the eight lines have retained the unaltered form of the Latin from which they are derived.

in their character, with only a very spare admixture of foreign materials, in this case we shall have only a *new dialect*—not a new *language*. The second question, as to what we may take as a fair standard of modern Greek, can be answered as a matter of fact only by hitting a judicious medium between the two extremes of gross corruption, and that greater or less approximation to the standard of classical Greek, which the practice of some writers presents. Topographical and political causes conspired to create different shades, grades, or types of modification in the popular Greek dialect, which had more or less of a local character. The Byzantine Greek of Theodorus, the Albanian Greek of the Epirotic Klephts, and the Cretan Greek of Cornaro, who wrote the romance of Erotocritus, in the first half of the eighteenth century (first edition, Venice, 1737), are in some characteristic points, essentially different. These constitute what, according to a botanical analogy, we might call local varieties of a common species ; and such varieties, as a rule, present a greater amount of deviation from the normal classical type than the floating mass of modern Greek common to all the existing race. On the other hand, since the time of Koraes, there has commenced a process of purification and restoration which tends to remove from the modern language some of those peculiarities which are its most distinctive characteristics. In judging of the language as a whole, therefore, it is wise to take some work or book of an essentially popular character written for general circulation in the last century, before the appearance of Koraes ; and I have used for this purpose a translation of the *Arabian Nights* into modern Greek, published at Venice by the well-known house of Glycys, in the year 1792. This choice, however, was dictated purely with a view to the conclusions of philological science; for practical purposes, it is manifest that the best type of the Greek actually now spoken in Greece is contained in the Greek newspapers destined for general circulation. But neither can the philologer, though he refuses to accept local varieties, as part of the general norm of the dialect, overlook them as a fact. They are part either of the disintegration of the old type, or of the growth of the new, of which, in all its stages, he is bound to take cognizance; the more that the phenomena of linguistic change, which are the most interesting to him, present themselves more strikingly in the more corrupt than in the less corrupt forms of the language.

PROPOSITION X.—In examining the processes of modification through which the Neo-Hellenic language has attained its present type, the most obvious helps are, of course, the dictionaries of mediæval Greek by Du Cange and Meursius, the learned commentaries of Koraes on Theodorus, the dictionary of Byzantine Greek by Sophocles, the dictionaries of modern Greek by Gerasimus, Bentotes, Kind, De Heque, Byzantius, and others, with the grammars from Thomas downwards to that of Sophocles and Mullach, which is the most complete. Besides the grammar, Mullach has edited the *Batrachomyomachia* of Demetrios Zenos, from which the student will reap benefit; and with him should be taken the collection of mediæval Greek chronicles and poems by Ellisen. Great zeal has been shown in the same department of Hellenic study by the French, of which the *Collection de Monuments pour servir à l'Étude de la langue Neo-Hellénique*, by Monsieur le Grand, and the Paris association for the same object, of which Monsieur d'Echthal is the moving genius, furnish ample evidence.* English scholars as a rule have paid little attention to the subject. Pashley, Tozer, and the late Viscount Strangford, with the late Professor Felton in America, were the only English names known to me in connexion with this branch of scholarship, till the publication last year of the highly original and ingenious work of M. Geldart; in Scotland special praise is due to Dr. Clyde, and after him to Donaldson.† The late Cornewall Lewis, unfortunately, was altogether ignorant of this branch of philology: otherwise, as is evident from a note in his Essay on the Romanic Languages (p. 237, second edit.), he was prepared to have made an admirable use of it.

PROPOSITION XI.—When scholars talk of a type of language, such as the strange events of long centuries

---

* 1. Koraes ἄτακτα.—2. Sophocles' Glossary of Byzantine Greek ; London, 1860.—3. Gerasimi Thesaurus quatuor Linguarum ; Venet. 1723.—4. Kind, Handbuch der Neu-griechischen Sprache; Leipzig, 1841.—5. De Heque ; Paris, 1825.—6. Λεξικόν Ἑλληνικὸν καὶ Γαλλικόν ; by Byzantius ; Athens, 1846. —7. Λεξικόν τρίγλωσσον ; by Bentotes and Blante ; Venice, 1820.—8. Nova Methodus Linguæ Græcæ vulgaris ; auctore Thoma ; Paris, 1709.—9. Méthode pour étudier la langue Grecque moderne, par David ; Paris, 1821.—10. Grammatica linguæ Græcæ recentioris ; Franz, Romæ, 1837.—11. Sophocles' Modern Greek Grammar ; Hartford, 1842. —12. Grammatik der Griechischen Vulgar Sprache ; Mullach ; Berlin, 1856.— 13. Analekten der Mittel und Neu Griechischen Litteratur, Ellisen ; Leipzig, 1855.—14. Demetrii Zeni ; Paraphrasis Batrachomyomachia, Mullachius ; Berolini, 1837.—15. Collection de monuments pour servir à l'étude de la langue

Neo-Hellénique, par Émile le Grand ; Paris, 1869. — 16. Mediæval Greek texts ; the Philological Society's extra volume ; by W. Wagner ; London, 1870.—17. Association pour l'encouragement des Études Grecques en France ; Annuaires ; Paris, 1868-71.

† 1. Pashley ; Travels in Crete ; London, 1837.—2. Tozer ; Researches in the Highlands of Turkey ; London, 1869.—3. Viscount Strangford on the Cretan Dialect, in Spratt's Travels in Crete ; London, 1865. See also collected works of Viscount Strangford ; London, 1871.—4. Clyde ; Romaic and Modern Greek compared ; Edinburgh, 1855.—5. Donaldson ; Modern Greek Grammar ; Edinburgh, 1853.—6. Geldart ; the Modern Greek Language in its relation to Ancient Greek ; Oxford, 1870.—7. Professor Felton published a collection of pieces in modern Greek, which was once in my possession, but of which I cannot now recover the title.

have produced in modern Greece, they are apt to talk of
it altogether as a *corruption*, and as the pure result of
phonetic decay.   But this is only a part, and a small part
of the truth.   A language is corrupt when it abandons
its own natural analogies, or adopts foreign ones, which do
not harmonize with its original type, or when it is defaced
and disfigured in various ways by sheer ignorance and
carelessness.   In this sense it is quite correct in Italian,
for instance, to say, that *donna* is a corruption of *domina*,
avuto of *habitum*; and in the same way, in Neo-Hellenic,
to say that ἐγβάλλω is a corruption of ἐκβάλλω, and μαθαίνω
of μανθάνω; and of such corruptions, no doubt, a large
part of Italian, and a certain much less considerable part
of modern Greek, is composed.   But, on the other hand,
it is no corruption when, in the progress of time, an old
word comes to be used in a modified, or perhaps altogether different sense; as when κάμνω, in modern Greek,
takes the place of ποιῶ, when σηκόω, which in Plutarch
signifies to *weigh*, in modern Greek signifies to *raise*,
when φθάνω is used generally for ἀφικνέομαι, to arrive, or
παιδεύω for μαστιγόω, as they are not only in modern
Greek, but in the New Testament.   Such progressions
and transmutations of meaning are always going on in all
living languages, of which ample illustrations could be
produced from English and every spoken language, if it
were necessary.   As little can it be called a corruption,
when new forms blossom out from old roots, so long as
these new forms follow the fair analogies of the language.
No one, for instance, supposes that the English language
is corrupted when we bring into currency such words as
solidarity, complicity, utilize, and similar French formations from Latin roots long ago acknowledged in both
languages.   In the same way, χρησιμεύω, νοστιμεύομαι, and

other such words, are perfectly legitimate formations, even though it be true that the Attics were not in the habit of affixing the termination εύω to verbals in μος ; for the Athenians at all times had their peculiar local idioms, just as London has its Cockneyisms ; and the mere Attic usage could prescribe the law to the common Greek tongue, only so long as Athens remained the political and literary capital of Greece, which it ceased to be exclusively when the centre of intellectual activity was transferred first to Alexandria and then to Byzantium. To write pure Attic Greek, after the Athenian literary dictatorship had ceased, was an affectation of which only pedantry or a false fastidiousness could be guilty. The barbarism to which, in a general way, a certain class of scholars would consign such words, is more justly regarded as an overgrowth of lusty vitality. Such new-coined words may not indeed be necessary ; the old words might have served all purposes equally well ; but they are the natural and legitimate product of the right of a living organism to put forth new shoots according to its type. If it be said that a word is always barbarous till it be stamped by the authority of a great classic of the language, I answer this may be a very healthy limitation which a writer at a certain period of the adult growth of a language may choose to put on his choice of vocables ; but it is to the eye of the philologer an arbitrary procedure of which science can take no account. To him *claritudo*, and *gratitudo*, and *beatitudo* are perfectly good Latin words, whether Cicero happens to use them or not ; and in such words—what a nice Ciceronian of the Bembo school would brand as a departure from the norm of Latin purity—a philologer may often have cause to recognise a natural extension and fair enrichment of a meagre and inadequate medium of expression. If, therefore, Homer uses not only γλυκύς, but γλυκερός, there is no reason why a scholar should condemn as barbarous varieties of a similar description in the existing Greek tongue ; and if the ancients, in their exuberant play of terminational affixes, chose to say ἀληθινός as well as ἀληθής, shall it be forbidden to the modern Greek to say ταχινός as well as ταχύς, and βρωμερός as well as βρωμώδης ? So in English one writer may say *kingliness* and another *kinglihood* (Tennyson), with equal right. But further, even in the case of corruptions properly so called, that is not a new growth of the language, but a breaking down of the old structure from sheer carelessness, or the intrusion of some extraneous element, there is a great and vital distinction to be made between those corruptions, which, to the eye of a philologer, look like a scar or a patch, and such as easily take their place and fit into the old structure of the language. Thus the word γεμάτο, from γέμο, to be full, is a gross barbarism, for it attaches to a Greek root a Latin participial termination, which is at once recognised as something foreign and incongruous. It is as if, instead of the word *obesity*, we should talk of the *fattosity* of a corpulent person, a combination at once felt to be barbarous, though certainly our English tongue, through its loss of native terminations, has an excuse for incongruities of this kind, which could not be pleaded by the Greek. On the other hand, the modern Greek habit of substituting the diminutive for the simple word, and then cutting off the final or unaccented syllable, as when παιδίον is used for παῖς, and then παιδί for παιδίον, is an offence against the ancient tradition readily condoned ; for by the emphasis of the accent on the accented syllable, the ear is already accustomed to the sound, which becomes final when the short ultimate syllable is dropped. In the same manner, the favourite diminutive termination ἀκι, appearing in γεροντάκι, κοντάκιον, δενδράκι, and scores of other words, where analogically it is not the diminutive termination pertaining to such roots, passes lightly into the habit of the ear from the analogy of μειράκιον, and other such words, where the ακ is part of the root. Of superficial and false analogies of this kind, both in flexion and in syntax, the structure of all languages presents sufficient instances.

PROPOSITION XII.—Following out the principles just stated, the first noticeable characteristic that strikes us in the Neo-Hellenic dialect is the remarkable change and extension that has taken place in the usage of certain words, giving rise to significations either altogether different from classical usage, or deriving from that usage only their late and scarcely apparent germ. Of these I shall here set down some of the more remarkable :—

	MODERN.	ANCIENT.
σηκόω,	to raise,	weigh, balance.
βαστάζω,	to refrain, restrain,	carry.
καμαρώνω (όω),	to give one's-self airs, to admire,	vault or arch.
τάσσω,	to promise,	arrange.
συντρέχω,	to assist,	run together.
ἰδίωμα,	manners,	a peculiarity.
λαλῶ,	sing,	prate.
χώνω,	conceal,	heap up.
σώνω (σώζω),	suffice,	save.
κύριος,	a father,	a master.
κομβόω,	deceive,	to bind up, gird.
χωνεύω,	digest,	cast metal.
ψοφάω,	to die (of an animal),	to make a slight noise.
βραδί,	the evening,	slow.
πρόξενος,	a match-maker,	patronus (in politics).

	MODERN.	ANCIENT.
πλακόω,	oppress, overwhelm,	lay with flat plates.
ἐξωτική,	a fairy,	extraneous, foreign.
ἀψυχῶ,	to spare life,	to die.
μετεώρισμα,	an amusing tale,	floating in the air.
βασιλεύω,	to set (of the sun),	reign.
ποδαπύς,	a person of no account,	from whence.
χάνω,	lose,	gape.
αὐγή,	morning,	brightness.
βάνω (βαίνω),	place, set,	go.
φθάνω,	to arrive,	to get before.
ἄνοιξις,	the spring,	opening.
πλάτη,	shoulder,	flat part of an oar.
ὑποκείμενον,	a person,	a subject.
ἀράσσω,	to land,	to crash.
σκιάζομαι,	to be afraid,	to shade one's-self.
ἀδειάζω,	to fire a gun,	to give an amnesty.
πνευματικό,	a clergyman,	windy.
ταχύ,	the morning,	swift.
γεῦμα,	dinner,	taste, smack.
τὰ σωστά,	sense, wits,	things saved.
συμπάθεια,	pardon,	sympathy.
σκοτίζω,	stun, astonish,	darken.

PROPOSITION XIII.—But these changes of meaning
and application in old words, however strange, and however important to be noticed as presenting a practical
difficulty to a student passing from the classical to the
modern dialect, are only what must take place in any
language, which for the space of more than a thousand
years has been allowed to float freely on the surface of the
popular mind without any central authoritative control.
More characteristic of the peculiar genius of the Greek
tongue is the luxuriant growth of new terminations to
old roots, especially verbal, which the living dialect presents. This habit of luxuriating in a variety of verbal
forms differing nothing in signification, but displaying
only, to adopt a botanical phrase, a greater breadth of

terminal blossom, was characteristic of Hellenic speech from the earliest times. Thus, from the adjective ὅμαλος we have the three equivalent forms ὁμαλίζω, ὁμαλύνω, and ὁμαλόω, for which our meagre English is only too happy to find that it possesses the single *equalize;* and in the same way, from the root σεβ, we have the verbal forms σέβομαι, σεβάζομαι, σεβίζω, and later σεβασμιάζω (in Zonaras), all perfectly identical in signification. And though, no doubt, it may seem that ἀζω, as in ἑλκυστάζω, and ύζω as in ἑρπύζω, had originally a frequentative meaning, yet this distinctive feature was lost in the growth of the language ; and between στένω and στενάζω there is only a difference of sound, as, in Latin, between *claritas* and *claritudo.* Following out this instinct of rich terminational ramification and efflorescence, the current Greek vocabulary presents such varieties as the following :—

MODERN.	ANCIENT.
ἀρχίζω and ἀρχινίζω,	ἄρχομαι.
δακρύζω,	δακρύω.
πασχίζω,	πάσχω.
φοβερίζω,	φοβέω.
τρομίζω,	τρομέω.
ξυραφίζω,	ξυρῶ.
ἀραχνιάζω,	ἀραχνιόω.
λαβόω, to catch, hit, wound,	λαμβάνω.
λογιάζω,	λογίζομαι.
μελανιάζω,	μελανίζομαι.
σκοτεινιάζω,	σκοτίζομαι.
χορταίνω,	χορτάζω.

All these are legitimate formations, being either parallel forms from the original root, or secondary verbs from the substantive of a primary verb, or the adjective connected with the substantive. Not unfrequently this luxuriance of terminational blossom shoots out into pregnant new formations, which have no parallel in the classical tongue, as in

πλαγιάζω,	to fling one's-self down across the mattress and sleep.
ξεκαρδίζομαι,	my heart leaps out of my body, as with violent joy.
ἀρκουδίζω,	to go on all-fours like a bear, as children do.

A similar lustihood of terminational vitality—a point in which our English tongue is so remarkably feeble—displays itself in the terminations of adjectives and substantives, some of which are authorized by ancient analogy, as in βρωμερός, for δυσώδης, and others are a separate creation of the modern linguistic instinct, as in φρονιμάδα, νοστιμάδα, and the whole family of abstract nouns in άδα.

PROPOSITION XIV.—But it is not only in terminational variety that the ample vitality of the living Greek tongue asserts itself. As in the ancient, so in the modern dialect, the tendency to a florid growth of ever new compound words is irresistible. It is in the domain of the verbs again where this tendency exhibits itself most strongly. Here, of course, the compounding elements are often prepositions; but other elements are not excluded; and not a few very expressive compounds are formed from elements of which, for this purpose, the ancients made little or no use. Let the following serve as examples:—

ἀνακατόνω (όω),	to turn upside down.
στρεφογυρίζω,	to turn round and round.
ἀποκαμαρόνω,	to contemplate with admiration.
ξανθογυρομάλλος,	having red and curly hair.
πολυσκουριάζω,	to cover with rust.
χειλημουκτρίζω,	to neigh.
ἐκκοκκινίζω,	to turn pale, *lit.*, to go out of the red.
καλοκυττάζω,	to look favourably on.
γλυκυφιλῶ,	to give sweet kisses.
γλυκυχαράζω,	to break sweetly, as of the dawn.
γλυκυκυττάζω,	to look sweetly on.

κακοκαρδίζω,	to displease.
κακοκυττάζω,	to look with an envious eye on.
κακοφαίνεται,	it displeases me.
ἀστροπελεκίζω,	to lighten, *lit.*, to send down meteor-axes.
χαμογέλασμα,	a slight smile.
χαροκόπος,	a bon-vivant, a man of pleasure, a voluptuary.
μοσχομυρίζομαι, μοσχοβολῶ, }	to be fragrant, odorous.
κλωθογυρίζω,	to spin round and round and lose one's way.
ὀφθαλμοφανῶς,	for ἐναργῶς, *i.e.* clearly, distinctly, bodily.
ἀναποδιάζω,	to do a thing perversely, awkwardly.
ψυχοπαιδίον,	an adopted son, son of my soul.
ψυχοπονέω,	to sympathize.
μονοπάτιον,	a footpath.
παλαιογουρνομύτης,	a swine-snouted old sot.
κοσμογυριστής,	a world-perambulator, said of the sun.
ἀναποδογυρίζω,	to turn upside down.
συμποσόω,	to amount to.
βρεφουργῶ,	to make incarnate.
σπαταλοκρομάδης,	an onion-gourmand.
βομβοκτυπίζω,	to din the ears, *obtundo*.
μοσχοκάρυον,	nutmeg.
ἐποφθαλμιῶ,	to cast an envious eye on.
ἐκμυστηριάζομαι,	to reveal.
κρασοπατέρας,	a wine-bibber.

These examples, and a host of others that might be adduced, show how absurd it is to class under the head of corruption those changes in a long-lived language, which indicate a buoyant juvenescence rather than a withered decrepitude of expression. Let us now turn our attention to those changes in the form of the language, which fall distinctly under the category of LOSS or ABATEMENT, though by no means necessarily under that of DEFACEMENT and DISFIGUREMENT.

PROPOSITION XV.—As language, in long ages of neglect and semi-barbarism, is used by the masses principally for purposes of convenience, it is plain that considera-

I

tions of an æsthetical nature, such as influence men of genius and high culture in their use of language, will be subordinated ; and the purely scientific considerations, on which the philologer puts a high value, will not influence the popular mind at all. Carelessness, convenience, custom, and sometimes mere freak, fashion, and the itch of novelty, will produce important changes in the structure of a language which a delicate sense of harmony, and a scientific perception of organic completeness, would alike repudiate. Among the phenomena of this kind which continually tend to ·break down the classical form of words, those known to grammarians under the heads of *aphæresis*, *apocope*, and *syncope*, are the most frequent. But, not to encumber a plain subject with learned phraseology, we shall say simply, that all cultivated languages, when used merely for convenience, without the continued check of a higher aim, are liable to have their vocabulary changed by a process of CURTAILMENT which makes a part of the word serve for the whole. Thus in America, from the rattling haste in which the people delight, " an acute man" is called " a 'cute man ;" from the same careless instinct, the ignorant English peasant, or the sharp London street boy, talks of the " varsity" instead of the " university ;" and the familiar words, *bus* and *cab*, are only the tail and head respectively of two polysyllabic words, borrowed the one from the Latin, the other from the French. That this is a corruption, not of a very elegant kind, no person will deny ; for even when the original form of the word may have died out from the popular memory, it requires only a little bookish culture to make one feel that a segment has been cut from the full sound of the thing, the absence of which makes itself felt. Curtailments of this kind are obvious everywhere in French

and Italian, and in not a few German words also derived
from Latin and Greek, as in *probst* for *propositus*, *pfingst*
for πεντηκοστή, and such like. Now, it is manifest that
these corruptions may be made in various ways. Sometimes only a weak initial or final letter or short syllable
may be dropt, which leaves the word not much the
worse; sometimes a half, and that not the most important half, may be left, after the amputation, and in such a
fashion it may be, that only a scientific eye can recognise
its original identity. One of the commonest forms of
curtailment in Greek is that of an initial short vowel,
of which the following list contains some of the most
common :—

λίγος,	for ὀλίγος.	πωρικά,	for ὀπωρικά.
μαλιά,	„ ἅμιλλα.	βρίσκω,	„ εὑρίσκω.
μιλῶ,	„ ὁμιλῶ.	βλόγια,	„ εὐλόγια.
πές,	„ εἰπές (ἐιπέ).	λη’μέρι,	„ ὁλημέρι.
νός,	„ ἑνός.	βαγγέλιον,	„ εὐαγγέλιον.
ψηλός,	„ ὑψηλός.[1]	πεθυμιά,	„ ἐπιθυμία.
μέρα,	„ ἡμέρα.	γούμενος,	„ ἡγούμενος.
μερόνω,	„ ἡμερόω.	σφαλίζω,	„ ἀσφαλίζω.
διόμα,	„ ἰδίωμα.	παντυχαίνω,	„ ἀπαντυχαίνω.
πανδρεύομαι,	„ ὑπανδρεύομαι.	φετεινός,	„ ἐφέτινος.
σκύπτω	„ εἰσκύπτω.	ματώνω,	„ αἱματόω.
γιαλός,	„ αἰγιαλός.	ῥημοκλῆσι,	„ ἔρημα ἐκκλησία.
ῥέγομαι,	„ ὀρέγομαι.	πετραχήλι,	„ ἐπιτραχήλιον.
σάζω,	„ ἰσάζω.	γειά,	„ ὑγίεια.
σώθικα,	„ ἐσώθικα, *i.e.* ἐντόσθια.	πίσω,	„ ὀπίσω.
μβαίνω,	„ ἐμβαίνω.	μᾶς,	„ ἡμᾶς.
μπορῶ,	„ ἐμπορῶ.	λάμνω,	„ ἐλαύνω.
τέρι,	„ ἑταῖρος.	γλυτόνω,	„ ἐκλυτόω = ἐκλύω from λυτός.

In these cases of initial curtailment it will be seen
that the vowel which falls off, as in the case of the
American "'cute," is generally a very feeble one, such
as in rapid pronunciation is little missed. Sometimes,

---

[1] The highest peak of Mount Ida in Crete is now called *Psiloriti*, or High-mount.

however, it is a diphthong, though never an accented one, as in ματόω for αἱματόω, δὲν for οὐδὲν, γιαλός for αἰγιαλός, and some others. It may even be a whole syllable, like the Italian *scuro* for *obscuro*, as in δάσκαλος for διδάσκαλος.[1]

PROPOSITION XVI.—But the end of the word presents to a hasty speaker even greater facilities than the beginning for a popular amputation, of which tendency the final *m* and *s* of the ancient Roman poets afford familiar examples. And here we find a remarkable analogy pervading old Roman, Italian, and modern Greek. As the Roman dropt his final *m*, producing the Italian *domino* from the perfect form *dominum*, so the modern Greek regularly drops the final *v*, which with him corresponds to the Latin *m*, and says καλό for καλόν; and not only so, but in diminutives he drops regularly the complete last syllable *ov*, so that all diminutives which are paroxytones in classical Greek come out with a sharp acute accent on the final syllable. Thus παιδίον becomes παιδί, κρασίον, κρασί,[2] just as in Italian *amavit* becomes *amò*, *potestatem*, *podestà*, and so forth. When the original word has the

---

[1] The following examples from Italian illustrate the same tendency to initial curtailment in languages set free from the control of strict literary aristocracy:—

bieco	for	obliquum.	stimare	for æstimare.
scuro	„	obscurum.	state	„ æstate.
sciocco	„	exscuccus.	sperto	„ experto.
badia	„	abbadia.	spietato	„ dispietato.
cagione	„	occasione.	sbarcare	„ disbarcare, and other compounds with *dis*.
stivali	„	æstivale.		
ricciò	„	cirricius.	romita	„ eremita.
Lamagna	„	Alemannia.	stra (French *très*)	„ extra, as in straordinario, and other compounds.
rame	„	æramen.		
nemico	„	inimico.	mentre	„ dum-interim (Diez).

[2] The historic steps in the process were παιδίον, παιδίν, παιδί, the intermediate form appearing generally in Theodorus.

oxytone accent, as in ποταμός, κεφαλή, the accent of the curtailed diminutive lies on the penult ποτάμι, κεφάλι, and many others. Similarly, a final oxytone in prepositions may fall off, as in ἀπ for ἀπό.

PROPOSITION XVII.—It is manifest that both these kinds of amputation, by head and by tail, may be exercised upon the same word; and then there arises sometimes a new word consisting only of the middle syllable, or two middle syllables of the amputated diminutive, which it requires an exercised eye to detect. Of this double curtailment the following are a few familiar examples :—

shore,	γίαλι,	from αἰγίαλιον,	αἰγιαλός.
eye,	μάτι,	„ ὀμμάτιον,	ὄμμα.
fish,	ψάρι,	„ ὀψάριον,	ὄψον.
companies,	τέρι,	„ ἑταῖρος,	
oil,	λάδι,	„ ἐλάδιον,	ἔλαιον.
vinegar,	ξίδι,	„ ὀξύδιον,	ὀξύ.
house,	σπίτι,	„ ὀσπίτιον, (Lat.) hospitium.	

A perfect analogy to this system of double amputation occurs in many English words, when their present form is compared with the original German word. Thus, our "*fought*" is "*foughten*" in old English, and *gefochten* in German.

PROPOSITION XVIII.—As the Greek verb is the part of speech in which the formative instinct of that rich language blossoms out most luxuriantly, we should expect that in this domain the pernicious, or it may be in this case perhaps, the beneficial effects of amputation will best appear. And so in fact it is. For not only have individual verbal affixes and prefixes been lopped off, but whole tenses and moods totally disappear, to supply whose place auxiliary verbs after the fashion of the modern languages are freely used. But as this is a matter that affects largely the syntax of the language, I shall reserve what is to be said on these organic losses for another section. In this place it will be sufficient to say, that of verbal curtailments falling under the heads of aphæresis and apocope, and not affecting the syntax of the language, the three following seem to be the principal :—(1.) The very irregular use and frequent omission of the augment. In this, however, it is superfluous to mention that the moderns follow the example of Homer, and that the loss is mostly as unimportant as that of the reduplicated second aorist of the poet was to the Athenians. (2.) The reduplication before the perfect participle passive is omitted—γραμμένος for γεγραμμένος. This is a change precisely analogous to that which the German has suffered in passing into English, as in *given* for *gegeben*, and so forth. (3.) The infinitive of the present infinitive active, after cutting off the terminative ν, becomes ει, as γράφει for γράφειν, and that of the first aorist passive, in the same way after cutting off the terminal ναι, becomes ῆ, as ἐλευθερωθῆ, for ἐλευθερωθῆναι. This again forms a perfect analogy to the process by which the ν, which originally belonged to the full form of the infinitive, as ἔμμεναι, ἔμμεν, εἶναι, and which appears in the German, *lieben*, *geben*, is dropt in English, so that only the monosyllables *love* and *give* remain.

PROPOSITION XIX.—A very peculiar and characteristic species of initial curtailment is that which takes place when a preposition precedes the definite article, and being absorbed by it, is pronounced as one word. Thus, εἰς τὴν πόλιν, *to the city*, by curtailment of the initial diphthong and absorption of the remaining consonant by the following article, become στην πόλιν, or, where the Dorism of *a* prevails, σταυπόλιν, whence the vulgar *Stamboul* arising from a misunderstanding of the Franks. In the same way the ancient Cos was supposed to have been metamorphosed into *Stanco* (ἐς τὰν Κω) ; and in Crete, according to Spratt,[1] they have actually Νήδα from εἰς τὰν Ιδα. A similar error, arising from the ignorance of the Lowlanders, occurs in the Highlands, where *Loch Nell,* for instance, near Oban, receives its barbarous and unintelligible Saxon designation from the absorption of the definite article *na* by the substantive *eala,* signifying a *swan,* as is the case also with *Loch Ness, Moness,* and other such names, occurring not unfrequently in the topography of the Highlands, where the Gaelic *ais,* signifying a waterfall, attaching to itself the *n* of the definite article, presents to the uninstructed the false appearance of an independent word *ness.* In the same way the substantive verb vanishes into the following noun : as *smellum so = is maith leum so, this is good with me, I like ;* and *spik orm,* for *is beag orm, this is little on me, I dislike.* It is remarkable that in German it is not the preposition in such cases, but the article that is absorbed. Thus *zu der* becomes *zur, zu dem, zum, in das, in's,* and so forth. In Italian sometimes both the article and the preposition are curtailed, as in *pel* for *per lo, nel* for *in illo.*

PROPOSITION XX.—Of *syncope,* or the dropping of consonants in the middle of a word, and of *synizesis,* or the slurring of two consecutive vowels into one syllable, there are not wanting examples in Romaic ; but, as they are neither so frequent as the initial and final curtailment,

---

[1] *Travels in Crete,* by Captain Spratt. London, 1865.

nor occasion the same difficulty to the student, they may
be slightly mentioned here. As in Homer we have κάβ-
βαλε for κατέλαβε, and such like, so in Romaic we have
συβάζω for συμβιβάζω, σπίθη for σπινθήρ, κάνω for κάμνω, νύφη
for νύμφη, φάιτο for φάγετο, λάινι for λαγένιον, πεντήντα for
πεντήκοντα, and with a large initial curtailment σαράντα for
τεσσαράκοντα. Two of the most familiar examples of this
medial curtailment are those which take place on the verbs
λέγω and ὑπάγω. When I was living a lodger in Athens,
about twenty years ago, a little girl, the landlord's daughter, as I was going out, used to say to me ποῦ πᾶτε. When
I heard this first I was considerably puzzled, and began at
once to think of πατέω and *pattens;* but this scent led me
far astray, and on inquiry I found that the mystical dissyllable was only a curtailed form of ὑπάγετε, as that word
is used in the New Testament (Matthew xvi. 23). The
same habit of dropping the medial gamma, I afterwards
found, led to the forms λές, λέτε, λέν, familiarly used for
λέγεις, λέγετε, and λέγουν; and in like manner φᾶν stands
for φάγουν. (So in Chaucer *han* for *haben* = *have.*) As to
synizesis, or the slurring of two vowels into one syllable,
which the readers of the Attic plays are quite familiar
with, the modern Greek makes a systematic use of this
figure in words of the first declension, such as σοφία,
φωτία, καρδία, accompanying the slur of the slender vowel
with the transference of the accent to the strong final
vowel καρδιά. Sometimes in such cases the slight
vowel is omitted altogether, as κυρά for κυρία, *lady,*
mother.

Closely connected with *synizesis* is the practice of
crasis, so perplexing to the tyro in Sanscrit, and familiar
to the ancient Greek in such cases as ἁνήρ for ὁ ἀνήρ, ὦνερ
for ὦ ἄνερ, and others. The most common phenomena of

this kind in modern Greek, and on which a classical
scholar will be apt to stumble, are such forms as—

νᾷσαι,	for	ἵνα εἶσαι,
νάλθῃ,	,,	ἵνα ἔλθῃ,
νάχει,	,,	ἵνα ἔχει,
τώχει,	,,	τὸ ἔχει,
πώρχεται,	,,	ὅπου ἔρχεται,
τῶπα,	,,	τὸ εἶπα,

and others of a similar description, which occur frequently
in the Erotocritus.

PROPOSITION XXI.—These remarks, taken singly, might
naturally lead to the idea that modern Greek is a sort of
amputated ancient Greek, as the Saxon half of English is
a sort of amputated German—a meagre dialect in which
every dissyllable has been cropped down into a monosyl-
lable, and every trisyllable into a dissyllable. But this is
by no means the case. Miserable and meagre, in point of
vocal swell and syllabic roll, as our truncated Saxon tongue
would have been, had it not been reinforced by the strong
intrusion of the sonorous element from the classical languages, the tongue of the ancient Hellenes has suffered no
such loss as to produce any bald disfigurement of this
kind. The explanation of this is obvious. The words of
the Greek language are so exuberantly polysyllabic, that
the abstraction of a single syllable from each word would
leave the great body of the language still distinctly polysyllabic; thus, 'πιθυμῶ falls upon the ear with pretty much
the same amplitude as the full form ἐπιθυμῶ. But further,
the fact is that the curtailments of which we have spoken
affect only a limited class of words ; and, singularly enough,
the largest class to which apocope is applied contains a
compensation which leaves the apocopated word as many
syllables, or perhaps more than the original word of the

classical tongue. This apparent paradox arises out of that substitution of diminutives for the original word, which we have already noted as characteristic of the modern dialect. For the diminutive in Greek, and all the Aryan languages, while it lessens the idea, increases the magnitude of the word, as in βρέφος, βρεφύλλιον, μεῖραξ, μειράκιον, σάρξ, σαρκάριον, and so forth, from which the consequence follows, that where a diminutive is systematically substituted for the simple word, and afterwards apocopated, the syllabic magnitude of the word is not diminished. Sometimes it may even be increased, as παιδί, παιδίον, παῖς ; ποτάμι, ποτάμιον, ποταμός ; γεροντάκι, γεροντάκιον, γερόντιον, γέρων. If to these considerations we add the exuberant, amplificative and expansive tendency of the Greek language, and its delight in the formation of new compounds (p. 128 above), we shall be prepared to believe that the existing Greek language is no wise inferior to its classical prototype in point of syllabic amplitude, and the student of Aristophanes, whose ear swells with pleasure at the σφραγιδονυχαργοκομήτης, and other sesquipedalian luxuries of the jovial Attic comedian, will not be surprised at encountering χαβιαροκατελυτος, σκουμπροπαλαμιδοπαστός, ἐγγραυλοπαστοφάγος, and such like, in his meagre Byzantine follower.

PROPOSITION XXII.—The practice of substituting the *diminutive* regularly for the simple word, which we have just mentioned, deserves further the special remark, that, besides being a characteristic of Italian, as in *sorella*, *fratello*, *uccello*, etc., it had its origin in the earliest classical times, as we see in the Latin *oculus*, from the old root ὄκκος (Hesych.), Sanscrit *akshi*, in *auricula*, Italian *orecchia*, for *auris*, and in the classical Greek θηρίον, πεδίον, and a few others. In Aristophanes the frequent use of the diminutives must strike every reader; and we see here, as in most other instances, that what we call modern Greek is merely the natural development and full growth of tendencies deeply rooted in the heart, if not always visible on the surface of the classical tongue.

PROPOSITION XXIII.—The chapter of curtailment on which we have been dilating, so common in the progress of all languages, suggests, as its natural complement and counterpart, that of *addition* or *increment*, whether this addition be real, that is, an appendage posteriorly added to the root, or only a part of the root, by change of circumstance brought to the surface after a long period of concealment, as happens to seeds sometimes by the process of deep trenching. It is a well-known fact in the classical Greek language, that familiar words sometimes appear in two forms, the one differing from the other only by the addition of an appended letter or syllable,—an appendage which, when it appears in the front of the word, is technically called *prosthetic*, and when at the end *paragogic*. Thus we have χθές and ἐχθές, κεῖνος and ἐκεῖνος, μαυρόω and ἀμαυρόω and not a few others. The same phenomenon appears largely in the comparison of different languages of the same family, as in *dent*, ὀδόντ, ὀφρύς and our *brow*, ἀστήρ (Gaelic, *bruach*), *star*, Sanscrit *tara*, τείρεα (Hom.) Now, though in many of these cases it is quite plain that curtailment has taken place, as when *pater* becomes *athar* in Gaelic, and *plenus lan*, it seems pretty certain that in others the taste or fashion of some particular time and place has added a letter to the original root. For this addition there may be various causes, demonstrative emphasis perhaps, as in the *celui-ci* and *celui-là* of the French, or mere euphony, as in the favourite habit of the Italian ear, which

leads them to avoid a consonantal ending ; thus *sunt* becomes not *son*, but *sono*.   To determine the history and
significance of these prosthetic and paragogic letters is in
many cases one of the most difficult tasks of scholarship ;
and on some of these problems the masculine erudition of
one of the greatest of German scholars has been not un-
worthily spent ;[1] but to enter into such discussions here
would lead too far from the main purpose of this discourse ;
so I shall merely set down a few of the more notable of
these enlargements of the old Greek form which the existing popular dialect presents, without speculating curiously
on their origin.   In the first place, we have sometimes,
though far from regularly, a vowel appended to the third
person plural of the indicative mood, λέγουνε for λέγουν,
ἐλέγανε for ἔλεγαν, quite in the Italian fashion.   Similarly,
among the pronouns we meet frequently with τόνε for τὸν,
just as the Athenians said οὑτοσί for οὗτος, and ἐκεινοσί for
ἐκεῖνος ; then for αὐτοῦ we have αὐτουνοῦ, for αὐτῆς, αὐτηνῆς,
and αὐτηνῆς τῆς.   Among the particles we have ἀντίς for
ἀντί, and τότες for τότε.   This final ς appears in the imperative of certain verbs, as in εἰπές, by apocope 'πές, following the ancient analogy of δός and θές.   The accusative
of the pronouns of the first and second persons presents
the lengthened forms of ἐμένα and ἐσένα.   The demonstrative, on the other hand, is lengthened only in the
front, and τοῦτο becomes ἐτοῦτο.   Τοῖος is subject to a reduplication, and becomes τέτοιος.   A prosthetic ι before two
initial consonants, of which the first is σ, is familiar to the
student of the Romanic languages, and appears in the
modern Greek ἴσκιον for σκία.[2]   This initial σ itself is added

---

[1] *Pathologia Græci Sermonis.*— Lobeck, Königsberg, 1853.

[2] This prosthetic *i* appears regularly

in Italian when the previous word
ends in a consonant, as *con isdegno* for
con sdegno. But this is only the occa-

in some words, as in σκόνη for κόνις, just as in the classical dialect μικρὸς and σμικρὸς appear in friendly company. The letter γ, which appears sometimes as a prosthetic letter, seems to be a modification of the rough breathing, as in γυιός for υἱός, γιεράκι for ἱεράκιον, from ἵεραξ. But this γ has a tendency to show itself not only in the front of words, but specially in the middle between two vowels, by the figure known to the old grammarians as epenthesis. Thus we have—

σαλέυγω,	for	σαλεύω.
γυρεύγω,	,,	γυρεύω.
ἀγοῖρος,	,,	ἄωρος.
καβαλλικεύγω,	,,	καβαλλικεύω.
αὗγον,	,,	ὦον.
θηργιό,	,,	θηριό = θηρίον.
λάγουτα,	,,	λαοῦτα (lute).
πλέγω,	,,	πλέω.
ῥαγίζω,	,,	ῥαίζω.
στέργιος,	,,	στέρεος.
βογγάω,	,,	βοάω.
ἀγναντεύω,	from	ἐναντίος.

That this epenthetic γ is a relic of the famous digamma, which plays such a redoubtable part in the criticism of the Homeric text, is a favourite notion with scholars. That it actually is so in some cases seems probable ; scarcely in all, I should think, or in the majority of cases.

One of the most notable epenthetic lengthenings of classical words occurs in the present indicative of certain classes of verbs, by the insertion of ν. Thus, in all liquid verbs ; for στέλλω, στέλνω, for φέρω, φέρνω, κολνάω for κολλάω, a fashion clearly traceable in the New Testament. There we have δέρνω for δείρω, ὀπτάνομαι for ὄπτομαι, χύνω for χεω,

sional form of the word for the sake of euphony ; the rule is, that, while in Italian the initial *e* or *i* in such cases is never added, but regularly rejected, in Provençal, Spanish, and early popular French, it is always prefixed, even where no traces of it are found in Latin. Cornewall Lewis on the *Romanic Languages*, 2d edit. p. 107.

and others. In fact, this peculiarity is as old as Homer, who has θύνω and δύνω for θύω and δύω, and the lengthened form of ἀγινέω for ἄγω. We need not therefore be surprised at its great prevalence in modern Greek. From the Alexandrians downwards, the people have always been in the habit of inserting a ν before the final vowel of the large class of verbs in όω; as in the common σκοτόνω, to *darken one's day-lights*—to *kill*, φανερόνω, καμαρόνω, and many others. But this ν is found also in other and less marked cases, as in ἀφίνω from ἀφίημι, σώνω for σώζω, βάνω for βάζω, χαρίνω for χαρίζω, ψένω for ἔψω, ψάχνω for ψαύω. This is a peculiarity, indeed, to which every one must tune his ear who wishes to read modern Greek with any comfort.[1]

The remarkable paragoge of κα, which appears in the vulgar form of the first aorist passive, ἐγράφθηκα for ἐγράφθην, appears to have arisen from an illiterate confusion of the terminations of the past forms of the active and passive voice.

PROPOSITION XXIV.—The process of partial disintegration and reconstruction to which modern Greek, like Italian and French, owes its birth, is governed by a law which seems to belong naturally to all human speech under similar circumstances, what I may call the LAW of SIMPLIFICATION and REGULARISATION. All language, by the natural action of the human mind, is constructed originally on the principle of likeness and analogy; but when, by the mixing of diverse tribes, or from other

---

[1] Mr. Geldart (c. iv.) remarks that, "in ancient Greek we may regard αίνω as a strengthened form of έω, and άνω as a strengthened form of άω." This may be quite true; only in such verbs as λευκαίνω the ν is retained throughout all parts of the verb, whereas in the modern σκοτόνω, and such like, it belongs only to the present indicative.

causes, irregularities and anomalies have once got a place in it, which disregard or contradict its characteristic analogies, the establishment of a classical norm of speech, by a succession of authoritative writers, may stereotype such irregularities as a recognised part of the language for an indefinite period. Thus in English the irregular plurals —fragments, by the way, of an old regularity—*men, women, oxen,* and a few others, remain fixed ; and so in Greek, the aoristic forms in κα, ἔθηκα, ἔδωκα, ἦκα, contrary to the general rule of verbal formation. But so soon as the firm control of intellectual authority is weakened, as by the removal of some artificial constraint, the popular ear falls back on the familiar analogy, and abolishes the anomaly ; and thus in modern Greek, ἔθηκα becomes ἔθεσα, ἔδωκα ἔδωσα, ἀνέγνων ἀνέγνωσα (also in ancient Ionic), and so forth. A familiar example of this tendency is the *seèd* for *seen, coomed* for *come,* etc., of the common people in England. Similarly we find in Greek ἐφέρθην from φέρω, βαλμένος for βεβλημένος, καλεσμένος for κεκλημένος. To the same category belongs the total abolition of all verbs in μι, the relic, as is well known, of the oldest form of the verb in the Aryan languages. Thus, as early as the New Testament epoch, from the general use of ἔστηκα as a present, the new regular form στέκω had been produced, which is the only form of the old ἵστημι now used in the Greek tongue. So for δίδωμι we have now δίδω, for τίθημι, a secondary verb, θέτω, formed from the verbal adjective θετός, like ἀστατέω (1 Cor. iv. 11) from ἄστατος, and στατός, for ἀφίημι, ἀφίνω, and for παρίστημι, παρισταίνω (Rom. xii. 1). So much for the verbs. Among the nouns this tendency displays itself most strikingly, as in Italian, in the habit of taking the objective case of nouns of the third declension, and turning it into a new nominative, to be declined after the fashion of the first or second declension.[1] Thus,—

ἡ μητέρα,	from	μήτηρ.
ἡ πεδιάδα,	,,	πεδιάς.
ἡ ἀγελάδα,	,,	ἀγελάς.
ἡ φλέβα,	,,	φλέψ.
ἡ φτέρα,	,,	πτερίς.
ἡ φοράδα,	,,	φοράς.

And this termination άδα, when it had once caught the popular ear, became a favourite norm for the formation of abstract substantives even when there was no objective case of the third declension from which to make the transfer.   Thus,—

For	λαμπρότης,	λαμπυράδα.
For	φρόνησις,	φρονημάδα.
From	νόστιμος	νοστιμάδα.

In the same way with masculines,—

For	ἔρως,	ἔρωτας.
,,	πατήρ,	πατέρας.
,,	ἀήρ,	ἀέρας.
,,	βασιλεύς,	βασιλιάς.
,,	rex (Lat.)	ῥήγας.

For, in fact, ς in non-Attic Greek was the favourite termination of masculine agents, as we see in *Cosmas*, *Ducas*, and other proper names of the Middle Ages.   So for the Attic ἀρτοποιός, they preferred the shorter form ἀρτάς, for ὡρολογοποιός, ὡρολογάς, and many others.   The

---

[1] Cornewall Lewis, in his essay on the Romanic Languages (2d edit. 1862, p. 91), while tracing this tendency to prefer the accusative case through all the Romanic languages, says that " he is unable to suggest any very satisfactory explanation" of the phenomenon. The explanation seems simply to be that, in the case of most nouns, which are not agents, we think of them regularly as *objects* of our thoughts and feelings, that is, grammatically, we generally use the objective case; and even in the case of agents, we feel more strongly, and have to express more frequently, our action on them than their action on us ; as, *I like* HIM, *I hate* HIM, *I* TELL HIM, *I order* HIM, *I forbid* HIM, etc.

prevalence of this termination is specially marked by the systematic use of the form βλέπωντας for βλέπων as the nominative of the participle, and that in both genders. The termination ος of the second declension is sometimes used in the same way, as γέρος for γέρων, δράκος for δράκων ; of which confusion we have examples also in the classic authors, as ἀλάστορος (Homer, Æschyl., and Soph.) for ἀλάστωρ, μάρτυρος for μάρτυρ. To the same category of regularisation belong, of course, the forms καλήτερος, πολλότατος, μεγαλήτερος, μεγαλότατος, for the well-known irregular forms of the classical grammar.

PROPOSITION XXV.—The previous observations relate exclusively to the changes that time has wrought on individual words, apart from their relation to one another. The elements of language which indicate the method of the connexion of one word with another, or of one sentence with another, are chiefly the cases of nouns, the tenses and moods of verbs and prepositions and conjunctions. Every change, indeed, made on a verb by diminution or increase, does not mark a change in the law of the dependence of words on each other, or of sentences on sentences ; but for the sake of a complete view (in addition to what was said above), it will be convenient to note the principal changes made on the verb in this place. Now, every one who bears in mind the prodigal luxuriance of form in the Greek verb will be prepared to find that the change here falls almost exclusively under the category of loss. Thus the common third person plural of the present indicative in ουν, sometimes ουνε, is a manifest curtailment of the old Doric οντι, Latin *unt.* This οῦν of the indicative is then transferred to the subjunctive, and we have πράξουν for πράξωσι, and

similar forms. The next thing that strikes us is the
total disappearance of that double form of the aorist,
which gives so much annoyance to young students of the
classical tongue. The first aorist with the *a* as its final
syllable has gained a decided victory over the *o* form in
the active voice; and in the passive the aspirated form
which appears in ἐστάλθην is preferred to the Attic
ἐστάλην. Thus, even when the second aorist is retained,
because no first aorist existed, it assumes the *a*, which is
the characteristic of the first aorist. So ἔλαβαν for ἔλαβον,
a peculiarity already prominent in the Septuagint. But
the two most striking amputations which the verb has
suffered, and which most prominently affect the syntax,
are those of the optative and the infinitive mood, both
changes for which the way was fully prepared in ancient
times, as the student of the New Testament must be
aware. The loss of the *optative* as the natural and sym-
metric form, of the conjunctive after a past tense in the
leading clause, is no doubt in an æsthetical point of view
to be lamented. Its effect in modern Greek is the same
as if in English we should say, "*I* GAVE *you this property
that you* MAY *enjoy yourself on it.*" Practically, however,
it occasions no ambiguity, and accordingly we find that,
in the language of the New Testament, the place of the
optative in such dependent clauses is almost always taken
by the subjunctive; and not in the New Testament
only, but frequently in Plutarch, and not seldom even in
Thucydides. It may be said, therefore, with perfect
truth, that the dropping of the optative is in the end an
improvement, rather than a corruption of the language;
as it is better that a person should be dead altogether
than that, being alive, his occasional presence should
serve only to remind us with the more acute pain of his

habitual absence. But the loss of the *infinitive mood* is something to which the thoroughbred classical scholar will feel it much more difficult to reconcile his ear. If there is one thing more than another that distinguishes the flexible grace of Greek syntax from the somewhat formal dignity of the Roman, it is the frequent use of the infinitive mood. And one cannot but express a wonder at first blush, that a form of expression so convenient and so flexible as the infinitive certainly is, should have given place to the lumbering form of a conjunction with the subjunctive or indicative mood. But so it is; for even the Greeks in their best days said οἶδα ὡς or ὅτι, instead of the less circuitous infinitive or participle; and the Romans, who, for a special class of cases well known to school-boys, had prescribed the accusative before the infinitive as the only form, before the time of St. Augustine began pretty generally to say, *Scio quod Petrus est vir doctus,* or even *quia,* which is the mother of the French *que* and the Italian *che.* Whence the habit now so characteristic of modern Greek took its rise of using *va* (for ἵνα), with the subjunctive instead of the old infinitive, it seems useless to inquire. I have sometimes thought it might be by a contagion caught from the Roman syntax; but the relation of the two languages was of such a kind as to create a current of contagion from Greek upon Latin syntax (as indeed we see in Tacitus) rather than the reverse. I shall say, therefore, it was only a change of fashion. Certain it is that the partiality for ἵνα with the subjunctive mood appears already largely developed in the New Testament in cases where a classical ear feels the want of the familiar infinitive. But custom, which exercises a despotic authority in such matters, soon reconciles us to the change; which, indeed, when considered apart from the habit of the ear, is anything but an important one, and quite in harmony with the commonest grammatical phenomena, both in ancient and modern languages. When I say in English, for instance, *it is too bad that you should do so and so*, I am merely using the modern Greek syntax of δεινὸν νὰ τὰ τοιαῦτα κάμῃς for the classical δεινὸν τὸ τὰ τοιαῦτα σέγε πράττειν; and the apparently more awkward syntax, διὰ τὸ να πραχθῶσι ταῦτα, for πραχθῆναι ταῦτα, is again only the English *on account of the fact that*, and the Latin *propterea quod*. There is only one other amputation in the Greek classical verb which must be mentioned, for it is certainly the most grievous of all. I mean the loss of the future and the pluperfect, with the substitution therefor of the auxiliary verbs, θέλω or θά, and ἔχω. Now, it is no doubt true that the particle ἄν, so familiar in the classical dialect, and κε in Homer, could have been nothing in their origin but auxiliary verbs; and so θα may plead a classical precedent. True also it is that the verb ἔχω is not unfrequently in the tragic writers joined with the past participle in a way that has some analogy to the function of an auxiliary verb; but it is in reality very different; and as there is nothing in modern Greek that so offends the polite ear of the elegant scholar as the presence of these auxiliary verbs, it is matter of congratulation that the best modern writers know so rarely and so dexterously to use them, that the offence is practically reduced to a minimum, and with some writers appears to cease altogether. There is another characteristic of Neo-Hellenic prose closely allied to such essentially modern syntactic combinations. I mean the use of such modern turns of speech as βάλλω εἰς πρᾶξιν, *to put into execution*; χάνω τὴν στράταν, *to lose the way*; κάμνω πανία, *to make sail,* etc. ; and in respect of these also it is comfortable to remark, that even in the lowest phase of the language they are much fewer than might have been expected, and in the more cultivated forms are becoming fewer and less prominent every day.

Another severe syntactic loss which the modern dialect has suffered is the disappearance of the *dative case,* and the confounding of that case, not only with the accusative, as in our English pronoun *him,* but with the genitive. The loss of the cases, as is well known, takes place naturally from the relations originally expressed by the terminational affixes having become obscured to the popular ear ; a process which was sometimes precipitated by a confusion in the pronunciation of cognate diphthongs, as when τοῦ was pronounced τῷ, or the contrary. This loss is repaired, in the first place, by the use of *prepositions* along with case-affixes, in which conjunction they are in fact tautological, as in the Homeric phrase ἐξ ἐμέθεν. Afterwards, when the removal of all authoritative control and the weakening of precedent have allowed the affixes to be dropt or confounded, the prepositions take their place as the alone significant element, and attach themselves prominently or exclusively to the accusative as the dominant case. Thus, in modern Greek, ἀπό takes the accusative, and εἰς, usurping the function of ἐν, is joined with the same case, whether its signification be *in* or *into.* This is the case in Scotch also, as we say, "*a head wi' a muckle lot in till't,*" i.e. *in it;* and both in Latin and in German there is only one form for εἰς and ἐν.

In reference to the connexion of clauses there are only two observations more to be made ; one, that the relative ὅς is in the modern dialect frequently replaced

by ὁ ὁποῖος (the Italian *il quale*), or simply by the inde-
clinable ὁποῦ, somewhat as in English we say, *whereof*
and *wherefrom*, instead of *of which* and *from which*. In
German the adverb *so* is used in the same way ; and
among ourselves, with the uneducated, *as* often serves
the same purpose. The other point is the confounding
of ὡς ἄν or σάν with ὡς ; and combined with this the formation of some new conjunctions, of which the most
common are,—

ἀγκαλά,	though.
ἀμή,	but.
ὡς τόσον,	meanwhile.
εἰς τόσον ὁποῦ,	the while—while that.
μὲ ὅλον τοῦτο,	nevertheless.

Some new prepositions and adverbs, or old forms curtailed, may also here be noticed, as,—

συμμά,	near.
μέ,	with.
μαζί,	with.
μέσα,	in, into, within.
ὁλόγυρα,	for περί.
δίχως,	for χωρίς, ἄνευ.
τὰ ἰσία (*soeben*, German),	for αὐτίκα.

This phenomenon appears also in the Romanic dialects,[1] and seems to belong naturally to a language in a
state of nascent or complete disintegration.

PROPOSITION XXVI.—Not the least important element
in the new phasis of an old language is that which
either does not appear at all, or is only partially represented in the Dictionary—viz. the *pronunciation*. This
is a matter with regard to which, from the Reformation

---

[1] See Cornewall Lewis, chap. v., for   Provençal prepositions, adverbs, and
an analysis of the French, Italian, and   conjunctions.

downwards, very fierce battles have been fought between
the living Greeks and the great majority of classical
scholars; but after three centuries of ink-shed, and now
that in the great German school an accurate philology has
been added to a large philosophy, we feel warranted in
asserting that the great salient points of the question
have been planted before the thinking scholar in their
right aspect. No person who has examined the subject
will now deny that, while correct Greek speakers pronounced their prose orations both according to accent and
quantity, in prose the accent was the dominant element,
while quantity prescribed the law to poetry.[1] Then as to
the sounds of the individual vowels and diphthongs, while
on the one hand no sensible person will suppose or attempt
to prove that the present vocalisation of the Greek tongue
has remained in all respects unchanged from Homer downwards, on the other hand, such a person will regard it as
no less certain that the comparative tenuity, the so-called
itacism of the modern dialect, is a peculiarity of very
ancient date in the language, being in fact clearly noted
by Quinctilian in the marked contrast which he draws
between the *strong* Roman language and the *slender*
Hellenic.[2] As little will any well-informed scholar in
these days be bold enough to assume the advocacy of that
altogether arbitrary pronunciation of Greek which has
obtained currency in this country—a pronunciation which
both corrupts vocalisation by the insular anomalies of
John Bull, and travesties intonation at almost every step
by the arbitrary substitution of the Latin for the Greek
accent. On this basis, and emancipated formally from

---

[1] For the detailed proof and illustration of this, I must refer to my paper
on the *Power and Place of Accent in
Language*, Transactions of Royal
Society, Edinburgh, March 1871, and
in this volume below.

[2] *Non possumus esse tam* GRACILES;
simus FORTIORES.—*Instit. Orat.* xii. 10.

the evil habit of our English school utterance, we may state
the position of the modern Greek with regard to *accent,
quantity, and vocalisation,* very simply thus.   The accent,
with a very few exceptions, has asserted its supremacy on
those very syllables of the word where its emphasis was
marked by the grammarian, Aristophanes of Byzantium,
in the early days of the Ptolemies ; and the circumstance
that, wherever a word is curtailed by dropping an initial,
or final syllable, or both, the accented syllable always
remains, as containing, to use Diomede's phrase, "the
soul of the word ;"[1] this circumstance of itself were sufficient proof, though all others were wanting, that emphasis
or stress, in the modern sense, and not mere elevation, as
some English scholars hastily assume, was the essential
element in that affection of articulate speech which the
Greeks called τόνος (*stress* or *strain,* from τείνω).   When
we reflect what extensive changes in English accentuation
have taken place with us since the time of Chaucer, we
shall consider this persistency of the same element in the
Greek, during a period of more than two thousand years,
a phenomenon not a little remarkable, and we shall rejoice
to think that the great Byzantine grammarian, if not in
the general practice of English scholars, certainly in the
living tradition of his people, and in the practice of the
national Church, has received the reward which he
deserved.   But the accent, like other strong forces, having
lost the salutary control of a hereditary school of music,
has not only maintained its position, but invaded the
domain of quantity ; so that with the modern Greek the
word ἄνθρωπος, for instance, is pronounced not like the
English word *lándhölder,* as it was by Demosthenes, but
like the English word *abbacy,* or *atrophy,* that is, with

---

[1] *Accentus est anima vocis.*—Diomede ; Putschius, *Gram. Lat. Auct.,* p. 425.

the middle syllable curtailed of its natural volume of sound. The fact of the matter is, that there is in all language a popular tendency to cheat the unaccented syllable of its full quantity, especially when it comes immediately after an accented syllable ; and to this tendency Latin yielded at an early period (as we see from the short final ŏ in Martial) and Greek probably about the same time. Along with this abuse, there crept in also in Greek that other one, of dwelling, in many cases, upon the accented syllable in such a manner as to change its natural quantity from short to long ; just as the Scotch, who as a rule speak slower than the English, draw out the accented syllable in many words, such as *májesty, nátional,* which the English pronounce short. The consequence of this excessive emphasis of the accent is, that in their rhymed poetry the Greeks find no offence in echoing αἶνα by ἕνα, μένος by μῆνος, and so forth ; which is just the same as if we were to abolish the difference between *hare* and *her, mane* and *men, pope* and *pop.* Then again as to the vowel sounds. In the face of the distinct gamut of the vowels given by Dionysius of Halicarnassus (*De Structurâ Orationis,* xiv.), it is impossible to maintain that the itacism now universally prevalent was considered correct speaking (though it might perhaps have been the vulgar fashion) in the days of Augustus Cæsar. We must say, therefore, that the present fashion of pronouncing η like *ee* is a corruption and an enfeeblement of the classic speech, in so far as it substitutes a weak and feminine for a strong and masculine sound. The like verdict must be pronounced on the itacising of the delicate sound of υ, which was equivalent to the German *ü* in *Brüder,* and the Scotch *ui* in *bluid, guid*—a vulgarizing of a fine sound to which the descent, when corruption once sets in, is very prone ;

as we find even now in Saxony, where *Brüder* is commonly pronounced *breeder*, and in Aberdeen, where the south country *guid* is squeezed out into *gweed*.

PROPOSITION XXVII.—It is another question altogether, how far the euphony of the Greek language, considered as an æsthetical product, has been affected by these corruptions. Latin was corrupted in a similar fashion, and came out of the process, not only not less, but, as some think, considerably more euphonious, in the shape of Italian and Spanish. The mere change from quantitative to accented poetry implies no absolute cacophony; it is merely the introduction of a new rhythmical law, and the transference of the musical weight of a word in verse from one syllable to another. This the beautiful hymnology of the Latin Church sufficiently attests; and no man of taste, who knows how to read these compositions, will speak less favourably of the unrhymed accented chants of the Byzantine Church, except, of course, in so far as he may feel the want of the pleasant recurrent sweetness of rhyme.

> χαῖρε ἀστὴρ, ἐμφαίνων τὸν ἥλιον.
> χαῖρε γαστὴρ ἐνθέου σαρκώσεως·
> χαῖρε, δι' ἧς νεουργεῖται ἡ κτίσις,
> χαῖρε δι' ἧς βρεφουργεῖται ὁ κτίστης,
> χαῖρε, νύμφη ἀνύμφευτε.[1]

Then, as to the effect of the excessive frequency of the feeble sound of ι, expressed by the term itacism, we must bear in mind that, though the modern pronunciation applied absolutely to certain picked lines of the ancient classics might produce a very petty vocal effect, it does

---

[1] SERGII, ὕμνος ἀκάθιστος τῆς Θεοτόκου. Anthol. Græca Carminum Christianorum. *Christ et Paranikas.* Leips. 1871, p. 140.

not at all follow that the same result will be produced
when the modern language is used by those who know
how to handle it. Such a sequence of weak identical
sounds, for instance, as occurs when the law of itacism is
applied to a word like πληθυνθείη, does not exist in the
Neo-Hellenic verb; for the optative is obsolete. But
further, it seems to be quite certain, that, if certain lines
in classical Greek have their music marred by the application of the modern itacism, the harmony of the whole
language is destroyed by the barbarous English pronunciation of the diphthong *ov*, in which the rude canine *ow*
is substituted for the soft and velvety *oo*. And with
regard to this beautiful *ov*, which the English so pervert,
it is a noticeable fact, that not only is it one of the most
prominent sounds in classical Greek, but it has extended
its sphere in the modern dialect so as to produce some
new and sonorous terminations. How beautiful, for
instance, are the diminutives in *ούλα*, as—

ῥαχούλα,	for	ῥάχη.
μανούλα,	,,	μάνη.
αὐγούλα,	,,	αὐγή.
φωνούλα,	,,	φωνή.
περδικούλα,	,,	περδίκιον.
παλαιὰ κλησούλα,	,,	παλαιὰ ἐκκλησία.
καρδούλα,	,,	καρδία.
λαλούλα,	,,	λάλημα.
βρυσούλα,	,,	βρύσις.

No man with an ear will deny that in these cases,—and
they are abundant enough to give a marked character to
the modern dialect,—the classical type of the word has
been corrupted into a decided improvement. A similar
euphony strikes the ear in the words with the less common termination *ούδα*, as in ἀρκούδα and καλιακούδα. The
same favourite diphthong appears in βροντούνε for βροντῶσι,

in ζοῦνε for ζῶσι, and others of the same kind, which may be picked out of the Klephtic ballads. The ranks of the same diphthong are further swelled by desertions from the ancient υ and ω, as in

φουσκόνω,	from	φύσκοω.
κουδούνιον,	,,	κώδων.
βρουχίζω,	,,	βρύχω.
σκούζω,	,,	σκύζω.
σκούβαλον,	,,	σκύβαλον,

and others.

Nor is the sonorous sound of *a*, according to Dionysius the most musical of the vowels, but which the English in many cases degrade into the feeble rank of η (Scotch), less prominent in the modern than in the ancient dialect. On the contrary, many beautiful new substantive forms are used with a marked preference to which this rich vowel gives the key-note, as in

σημάδι,	for	σημεῖον.
σκοτάδι,	,,	σκότος.
ποτάμι,	,,	ποταμός.
εὐμορφάδα,	,,	εὐμορφιά.
νοστιμάδα,	,,	νοστιμότης.
φρονημάδα,	,,	φρόνημα.

With the troop of favourite diminutives in άρι and άκι.

And I must say, generally, that in reading through the Erotocritus, I was more struck by the predominance of these two rich musical sounds of *a* and *ov*, than by any offensive accumulation of itacised syllables; and both in that poem and in the Klephtic ballads, my ear not seldom rested on lines of a full and masculine melody, not inferior to the best in Homer. Thus we read—

Ὀλημερούλα πολεμᾷ τὸ βράδυ καραούλι.

" *All day we fight, and all the night we waste in sleepless watches.*"

And

Σκοτόνει τοὺς Ἀγαρηνούς πεζούρα καὶ καβάλο.

" *He mows them down, the Agarenes, both foot and horse he mows them.*"

And again,

Πολλὴ μαυρίλλα ἔρχεται, μαυρὴ σὰν καλιακοῦδι.

"*A blackness sweeps across the plain, black as a troop of ravens.*"[1]

And what can be more vigorous and powerful, so far as sound is concerned, than the following lines from the Erotocritus, describing the impatient steeds at a battle, eager to start at the first blast of the trumpet?

Κτυποῦν τὰ πόδια τοὺς στὴν γῆν, τὴν σκόνη ἀνασηκόνουν,
Τὸ τρέξιμον ἀναζητοῦν, ἀφρίζουν, καὶ δριμώνουν.
'Η γλῶσσα μὲ τὸ στόμα τους παίζει τὸ χαλινάρι,
Τόνα καὶ τ' ἄλλο ἀγριεύετο, σὰν κάνει τὸ λιοντάρι.
Τἀρθούνια τους καπνίζουσι, συχνὰ τ' ἀφτιὰ σαλεύουν,
Καὶ νὰ κινήσουν βιάζονται, νὰ τρέξουσι γυρεύουν.

Or, again, take the beautiful little χελιδόνισμα, or swallow song to welcome the spring, from Kind's collection—

'Ο 'Απρίλης ὁ γλυκὺς ἔφθασε, ἐὲν 'ναι μακρυά·
Τὰ πουλάκια κελαδοῦν, τὰ δενδράκια φυλλανθοῦν,
Τὰ ὀρνίθια νὰ γεννοῦν ἄρχησαν καὶ νὰ κλωσσοῦν,
Τὰ κοπάδια ἀρχινοῦν ν' ἀναβαίνουν 'ς τὰ βουνὰ,
Τὰ καιζίκια νὰ πηδοῦν καὶ νά τρώγουν τὰ κλαδιά.[2]

So that, upon a broad practical estimate of the whole, I scarcely think any impartial person, who has taken the trouble to train his ear to the euphony of language (which I am sorry to see even great scholars don't always do), will pass any other verdict than this, that the old language of Homer, and Plato, and Demosthenes, whatever amputations and transmutations it may have suffered in the course of centuries, remains still among the organs of human expression one of the most vigorous and the most harmonious; as a magnificent tree with full luxuriant leafage may bear much lopping, and still remain very beautiful.

---

[1] Passow: *Popularia Carmina Græcorum*, ix. 2, lxxxii. 12, xcvi. 6.
[2] Kind: *Neugriechische Anthologie*, p. 72. Leipzig, 1847.

PROPOSITION XXVIII.—In connexion with the ortho-epy of the existing Greek language, one or two other points deserve mention. The first is that the present race, while allowing the *spiritus asper* to drop, have shown no tendency to narrow the sphere of that consonantal *aspiration* so favoured by their ancestors, but have rather increased it. For not only do φ, χ, ψ, and θ remain with their full aspirated force in the words which originally had them, but many words which had a slender consonant in classical usage, now regularly receive an aspirate. This specially happens where two slender consonants come together, in which case, in the modern practice, the former is always aspirated ; thus,

For κλέπτης,	they say	κλέφτης.
βλάπτω,	,,	βλάφτω.
πίπτω,	,,	πέφτω.
δείκνυμι,	,,	δείχνω.
πτωχός,	,,	φτωχός.
πτέρυγες,	,,	φτέρουγες.
ῥίπτω,	,,	ῥίχνω.
ῥάπτω,	,,	ῥάφτω.
ἅπτομαι,	,,	ἅφτω.
πταίω,	,,	φταίω.

And many more. The same tendency to aspiration—closely connected with the sibilation so common in classical Greek—has led to the lisping of every δ, and the softening of β into our English *v*, which often produces a very pleasant effect, as when *voblomæ*, the Romaic pronunciation of βούλομαι is compared with the rude and canine English *boulomai*. And if the modern Greek has shown no objection to the classical aspirates, as little has he felt inclined to soften down the masculine ξ—κς—after the fashion of the Italians, into a double sibilant. Besides retaining the ancient ξ in all cases where it existed,

he has new created a large class of compound verbs with
ἐκ or ἐξ, of which the characteristic is, that the initial
vowel is omitted or transposed, so that εκ becomes ξε, and
the word appears commencing with the double consonant.
Of this class the following are characteristic examples :—

ξαγαπῶ,	to cease loving—grow cool.
ξακουστοσύνη,	celebrity.
ξαστερία,	clear starry brightness.
ξαφεγγαρία,	moonlessness.
ξεβάπτω,	to take out the colour.
ξεβουλλόνω,	to unseal.
ξεδοντίζω,	to draw teeth.
ξεκαρδίζω,	to dishearten.
ξεκαρφόνω,	to take out nails.
ξεμανθάνω,	to unlearn.
ξεμναλίζω,	to put one's brain out of shape—madden.
ξεσπαθόνω,	to draw the sword.
ξετραχηλίζω,	to break one's neck.
ξεψυχέω,	to give up the ghost.
ξημερόνει,	the day breaks.

PROPOSITION XXIX.—In the above analysis I have
made no allusion to one element of corruption, which
from the analogy of Italian one might expect to find in
the modern Greek dialect. I mean the element of *adulteration* from foreign sources. In the purest modern
languages, as in German, for instance, this adulteration
is considerable, and, except on a principle of pedantic
purism, to which utility and good taste are equally
opposed, could not be dispensed with. But it is different
with Greek. For not only do all nations borrow their
scientific terminology from the language of Aristotle and
Hippocrates, while the language of these great master-
builders of early science borrows from no one, but the
foreign elements which at different periods crept into use
as part of the current Hellenic, did so only by way of

external attachment, so to speak, not by way of inocula-
tion; they did not infuse themselves into the blood, or,
to use a legal simile, they were not fixtures.   And thus it
came to pass, that with the change of masters one adopted
element was readily thrown off, and another as readily
assumed, and as loosely retained.   The colloquial style of
the Byzantine Greeks thus became superficially Latinized,
or spotted rather with Latinisms; that of the Frankish
chroniclers included a sprinkling of French words; that
of the Cretans flirted with Italian; while that of the
Acarnanian, Thessalian, and Epirotic Klephts was forced,
for the sake of convenience, to tolerate a certain admixture of the Turkish element, which their most deeply
rooted principles and their most powerful associations
would have led them to reject.   But the number of
these foreign words was at no time considerable; and as
one immediate result of the grand national resurrection
in 1821, the unseemly crusts and blotches of this foreign
accretion instantly fell off like the scurf of a cutaneous
disease, and the pure Hellenic came out of the caldron of
a barbarous broth as clean and bright, and pure from all
stain, as the god-like Ulysses out of his bath.   In the
current Greek newspapers which present the language
in its ultimate type, not one of those Latin, Italian, Albanian, and Turkish words is to be found, which raise a not
unfrequent stumblingblock in the way of the student of
mediæval and Venetian Greek; much less do those
hybrid compounds occur which bristle in Theodorus, made
by the addition of the Latin terminations ἀτωρ, and ἀτος,
and ἀριος, to a Greek root.[1]   At the present time, a little
girl in the street, if you ask for a flower by the Albanian

---

[1] Of this barbarism, the name of an
illustrious Fanariot family, Maurocor-
dato—*black-hearted*, is a familiar example.

word λουλούδι, may surprise you by saying that you must say ἄνθος; and if you wish a boat to shoot across from the Piræus to Ægina, you may find that you have to ask in Thucydidean phrase for a λέμβος, and not for a *barchetta*.

PROPOSITION XXX.—With regard to the materials of which the modern dialect consists, as well as the physiognomy which it presents, a question has been raised, in how far it represents any of the ancient dialects, Doric, Ionic, or Æolic; for Attic it certainly is not. Now, it seems quite plain that, looking at the conditions of the case, nothing would have been more strange than that some considerable traces of these non-Attic varieties of Greek speech should not have presented themselves in the modern new formation. For Attic, we ought to remember, was a dialect originally confined to a comparatively small portion of the Greek-speaking population; and the breadth of space which it afterwards occupied was a purely literary phenomenon, leaving untouched the great popular substratum of a distinctly diverse-featured speech, spread out in large reaches of country from Tænarus to Trebizond. Byzantium specially, the centre of non-Attic Hellenism in later days, was a Doric colony; in Africa, neither Alexandria nor Cyrene could lay any claim to a native Atticism; and on the sunny shores of Asia Minor, as well as the bright isles of the Ægean, Doric, Æolic, or Ionic varieties of Greek speech were everywhere at home.[1]

[1] How much of the peculiarities of the Alexandrian Greek has passed, either directly, or through the influence of the Church and the Alexandrian translation of the Old Testament, into modern Greek, the student of the Septuagint will readily convince himself. It is notable also, that not a few of the rare words used in the Septuagint, though unknown to Attic Greek, are found in Polybius, Herodotus, and Diodorus, as Schleusner, and other Biblical lexicographers, have been careful to note. The Biblical Greek which issued from Alexandria is, in fact, a sort of half-way house between Attic Greek and Romaic;

Now, in what proportions these local peculiarities might mix themselves up in a new dialect to be formed after the long and disturbed action of centuries, so as to serve for a common medium of understanding, no man could dare to prophesy ; but that the traces of their existence should appear in some shape and to some extent, seemed certain. And so, in fact, it has proved. Putting out of view the local dialect of the Tzacones[1] in Eastern Laconia, as something isolated and deserving special consideration, the general dialect of the modern Greek, from the Byzantine lingo of Ptochoprodromus to the Cretan of Cornaro, and the Epirotic of the Klephtic ballads, certainly does present certain features of an Æolo-Doric physiognomy. . Of this the dominance of the broad vowel a, not only in the nominative of all masculine agents, as above mentioned (p. 144), but in a large class of verbs, as in ζητᾷ for ζητεῖ, μετρᾷ for μετρεῖ, φοβᾶται for φοβεῖται, is in itself sufficient evidence. But besides this, we have the well-known Doric peculiarity of forming all verbs whose future is in ξ from a present in ζ instead of a double σ, according to the Attic usage ; thus, instead of τάσσω we have τάζω ;[2] and in this way has been formed a large class of modern verbs, as, φωνάζω φωνάξω, φοβερίζω φοβερίξω, τρομάζω τρομάξω. Of Æolism, the accusative plural of the first declension in αι instead of ᾶ, as Μούσαις for Μούσας, is a familiar example. On the other hand, it is not to be denied that there are some traces of Ionic also in modern Greek, as in the conversion

and in this view it is certain that a familiarity with the living dialect of Greece would be of more value to our young theologians than many of the branches of philology which at present occupy their attention.

[1] On the peculiarities of the dialect of the *Tzacones*, which Mullach identi-

fics with the *Caucones* of the ancient topographers, see Mullach, *Grammar*, p. 94, and *Das Tzakonische von Professor Moriz Schmidt in Studien zur Griechischen und Lateinischen Grammatik, herausgegeben von Georg Curtius*, vol. iii. p. 347.

[2] Ahrens, *De Dialecto Dorica*.

of *o* or *ω* into *ου*, and the use of the slender *η* for the broad *a* in certain adjectives in *ρος*; but I have not been able from my observation to confirm the strong remark of the late Viscount Strangford on this point—one of the best authorities no doubt—to the effect that "it would be easy to show two Ionisms for one Æolism or Dorism in modern Greek."[1]

A kindred point to this dialectic physiognomy of the modern tongue is brought out by the occurrence in it of certain words, or forms of words, which anciently were confined to poetic usage, but have now passed into general circulation. The following is a short list of this type which 1 have collected :—

σιγαλός,	(Pindar).
βροχή,	for ὑετός.
ὀμμάτια,	ὄμματα, Homer, for ὀφθαλμός.
τρικυμία,	storm at sea, for λαῖλαψ.
νόστιμος,	for τερπνός.
κτυπάω,	έω, Hom., for τύπτω.
κτίριον,	κτέαρ, Hom., for κτῆμα.
ἄρμενα,	tackling, rigging, for ὅπλα.
λιβάδιον,	from λιβάς, for λειμών.
δροσερός,	for ἡδύς.
τάχ.νός,	(Callim.), for ταχύς.
αἴθουσα,	a hall.

The transference of such words from poetical into common usage is not a phenomenon that need excite any surprise. The popularity of a great national poet, or the affectation of some fashionable writer, may readily achieve this; but we must bear in mind also, that what we would justly mark as poetic in an Attic writer may, in some of the widely scattered provinces occupied by the Greek race, have been a word which was generally current in the mouth of the people. That Homer himself, as being a popular

[1] *On Cretan and Modern Greek*, in the Appendix to Captain Spratt's *Travels in Crete*, vol. i.

minstrel, addressed the inhabitants of the eastern shores
of the Ægean, to which country he belonged, not in a
peculiarly and distinctly marked so-called poetical style,
but, like our own Burns, in a language familiar to the
common people, we cannot for a moment doubt; and in
this view any Homeric element in the existing Romaic
may have come down by direct descent from the pre-
Homeric popular dialect, not by degradation from the
peculiar poetic and epic style used by literary Greece.

PROPOSITION XXXI.—In conclusion, it seems not im-
proper, in the case of a famous language of such remarkable
longevity, to cast an eye into the future, and calculate
the chances of its permanence.   And in this divination
past experience certainly entitles us to say with confidence, that a language which has survived so many
changes, and resisted such a succession of destructive
forces, will maintain its vitality unimpaired, so long as the
moral motive power of the world is mainly Christian, and
the science of the world is proud to root itself in Greek
traditions.   For whether the present little Greek kingdom shall have strength enough to grow into an independent political integer, or whether, which seems its more
probable destiny, it shall at no distant day be attached
to the great Russian Empire in the manner of an outlying
principality, as Cymric Wales was attached to Saxon
England, it does not appear that it will have to contend
with any disintegrating or exterminating force in any way
so strong as those which it successfully resisted when
under Turkish and Venetian supremacy.   The conservative force of the Welsh language in the south-western
corner of our insular triangle is a fact of such potency, as
to have been deemed worthy of special notice and wise

concession by our administrative council in London ;[1] but if Cymric, which is no doubt as old a language as Greek, with its scanty stores of literary tradition, still flourishes in a green old age, the extinction of Greek, with its immense momentum of intellectual and moral force, not less intense in kind than extensive in operation, is not a thing to be looked for within any assignable period. If the Greek kingdom should unfortunately not be able to maintain its position against the combination of internal faction and external aggression, which may at any moment break it up, there is nothing in the antecedents of any of the great powers into whose hands a dismembered Greece might fall, to warrant the apprehension that they would employ any severe measures for the purpose of stamping out the national language. Russia certainly, which in religion is full sister to Greece, would have neither desire nor interest to look upon the language of Athens with the same jealousy that she looks on that of Warsaw. Under Russia the Greeks might readily become the founders of an enlightened Broad Church party in that country, just as under the Turks they became first the necessary interpreters, and then the wise governors of great and important provinces. As for the form in which it seems most desirable that this noble language should be transmitted to distant ages, it seems necessary, on the one hand, to warn against any forced and affected recurrence to the classical type, and on the other to invite literary men to the culture of the popular dialect as the fittest for a cer-

---

[1] In the winter of 1872 a representation was made to the British Government on the evils arising from the appointment to judicial situations in Wales of barristers unacquainted with the language of the natives ; and the Government pledged themselves to have respect to the representation in future, in so far as it might be possible to do so with a due regard to the legal knowledge of the persons appointed, *i.e.* that a Welsh-speaking barrister should in future be preferred, if his abilities and learning were equal.

tain style of lyrical and essentially popular poetry. As in Scotland the language of popular song runs in its own channel, apart from the English used as a general literary medium, so the Greek of Coraes and the newspapers might still continue to occupy a middle place between the Greek of classic tradition and the Greek of the popular ballads. Variety was one of the distinguishing features of the Greek family of languages from the beginning, and it may well remain so to the end. Whether or not the course of affairs shall ever be so ordered by Divine Providence, as that, according to the pious aspirations of Monsieur d'Eichthal, and other eminent French Hellenists, it may at no distant period be prepared to take the place of Latin as a catholic medium of correspondence between cultivated men of all countries, it seems in vain to speculate; but, in the form that it has now assumed, and in all likelihood will maintain for centuries, there is no reason why it should not be much more extensively studied by all classes than at any previous period. When our classical scholars shall have become ashamed of their false methods and narrow prejudices, and when a succession of intelligent travellers shall have been practically convinced that it is as easy to learn Greek in Athens, as to learn German in Berlin, or French in Paris, the sons or grandsons of Monsieur d'Eichthal and his French associates may behold with joy the probable advent of that kingdom of Pan-Hellenic brotherhood of which it is now only permitted to dream.

ON SCIENTIFIC METHOD IN THE INTERPRETA-
TION OF POPULAR MYTHS, WITH SPECIAL
REFERENCE TO GREEK MYTHOLOGY.

OF all the branches of interesting and curious learning,
there is none which has been so systematically neglected
in this country as mythology—a subject closely connected
both with theology and philosophy, and on which those
grand intellectual pioneers and architects, the Germans,
have expended such a vast amount of profitable and un-
profitable labour. The consequence of this neglect has
been, that of the few British books we have on the subject, the most noticeable are not free from the dear seduc-
tion of favourite ideas, which possess the minds of the
writers as by a juggling witchcraft, and prevent them
from looking on a rich and various subject with that
many-sided sympathy and catholic receptiveness which it
requires. In fact, some of our most recent writers on
this subject have not advanced a single step, in respect
of scientific method, beyond Jacob Bryant, unquestionably
the most learned and original speculator on mythology of
the last century; but whose great work, nevertheless, can
only be compared to a grand chase in the dark, with a
few bright flashes of discovery, and happy gleams of sug-
gestion by the way. For these reasons, and to make a
necessary protest against some ingenious aberrations of

Max Müller, Gladstone, Inman, and Cox in the method of mythological interpretation, I have undertaken the present paper; which, if it possess only the negative virtue of warning people to be sober-minded and cautious when entering on a path of so slippery inquiry, cannot be deemed impertinent at the present moment.

For the sake of distinctness and compactness, I shall state what I have to say in a series of articulate propositions.

PROPOSITION I.—By the mythology of a people I understand the general body of their traditions, handing down from the earliest times the favourite national ideas and memories, in a narrative form, calculated to delight the imagination and stimulate the affections of love and reverence.

PROP. II.—The dress of all mythology, as appealing to the imagination, is necessarily poetical; the contents of it are generally fourfold—(1.) Theological; (2.) Physical; (3.) Historical; and (4.) Philosophical and Moral.

PROP. III.—In the theological and moral myth, the idea is the principal thing, the narrative only the medium; in the historical and physical myth the fact is the principal thing; what goes beyond the fact is mere scenic decoration or imaginative exaggeration.[1]

PROP. IV.—A myth intended to convey an idea is distinguished from an allegory or parable by the consciousness

---

[1] Sometimes, however, a historical person, like Faust, may be seized on by the people, merely as a convenient vehicle for embodying a floating mass of mythological notions. In this case the person is really a secondary consideration : a real person he remains, no doubt; but, for a legendary nucleus, any other person would have done as well.

of purpose with which allegories and parables strictly so called are put forth and received.

PROP. v.—As it has been well said of popular proverbs, that they are the wisdom of many and the wit of one, so theological and moral myths grew up in the popular imagination, and were nursed there till in happy season they received a definite shape from some one representative man, whose inspiration led him to express in a striking form what all felt to be true and all were willing to believe.

PROP. vi.—The first framers of myths were, no doubt, perfectly aware of the real significance of these imaginative pictures ; but they were aware as poets, not as analysts. It is not, therefore, necessary to suppose that in framing their legends they proceeded with the full consciousness which belongs to the framers of fables, allegories, and parables. A myth is always a gradual, half-conscious, half-unconscious growth ; a parable is the conscious creation of the moment.

PROP. vii.—During a certain early stage of national life, which cannot be accurately defined, but which always precedes the creation of a regular written literature, the popular myth, like a tree or a plant, becomes subject to a process of growth and expansion, in the course of which it not only receives a rich embellishment, but may be so transformed by the vivid action of a fertile imagination, and by the ingrafting of new elements, that its original intention may be altogether obscured and forgotten. How far this first significance may in after times be rightly apprehended depends partly on the degree of its original obviousness, partly on the amount of kindred culture possessed by the persons to whom it is addressed.

PROP. VIII.—As of essentially popular origin and growth the myth cannot, in the proper sense, be said to have been the creation of any poet, however distinguished. Much less could a popular minstrel, like Homer, using a highly polished language, and who manifestly had many predecessors, be said to have either created the characters or invented the legends about the Greek gods, which form what the critics of the last century used to call the machinery of his poems. In regard to theological myths, which are most deeply rooted in the popular faith, such a poet as Homer could only turn to the best account the materials already existing, with here and there a little embellishment or expansion, where there was no danger ot contradicting any article of the received imaginative creed.

PROP. IX.—The two most powerful forces which act on the popular mind, when engaged in the process of forming myths, are the physical forces of external nature, and the more hidden, though fundamentally more awful powers of the human will, intellect, and passions. It is to be presumed, therefore, that all popular myths will contain imaginative representations of both these powers; and, in their original shape, they are in fact nothing more than the assertion of the existence of these two great classes of forces in a form which speaks to the imagination—that is, in the form of personality ; and there will be a natural presumption against the adopting of any system of mythological interpretation which ignores entirely either the one or the other of these elements. If this

proposition be correct, the objections of Max Müller
(*Chips*, ii. 156) to the Greek derivation of 'Ερινύς, from
the old Arcadian ἐρινύειν (Pausan. viii. 25, 26), are un-
founded.

PROP. X.—The most fertile soil for purely theological
myths is polytheism ; and the most obvious as well as the
largest field for a religion of multiform personalities is
external nature. In the interpretation of such myths,
therefore, we shall be justified in searching primarily for
the great forces and phenomena of the physical world, as
underlying the imaginative narrative and imparting to it
its true significance ; and in proportion to the prominence
of these phenomena, and the potency of these forces, will
the probability be that we shall find them fully represented in any body of polytheistic theology.

PROP. XI.—As the essence of polytheism thus consists
in the habitual elevation of what we call physical facts
and forces into divine personalities, the line betwixt a
purely physical myth and a theological myth will naturally
be extremely difficult to draw. Zeus, for instance, as the
Thunderer, represents a physical fact as well as a theological doctrine ; nevertheless, it would be wrong to assume
that there is no such element in tradition as a strictly
physical myth. Certain striking facts of volcanic action
or geological change, strange and grotesque shapes of rocks
and other natural objects, unusual conformations of land-
scape, not to mention the occasional discovery of gigantic
fossil bones, and even entire skeletons of animals no longer
existing, might well form the basis of what is properly
termed a physical or a geological, rather than a theological
myth ; and, as Hartung well remarks (*Gr. Myth.* i. 168),

notable recurrent events in nature, such as the heavy
rains at the end of summer, are peculiarly calculated to
impress the popular imagination, and to produce myths.

PROP. XII.—But as to man there is, after all, nothing
more interesting and more important than man, it is in
the highest degree unreasonable, in the interpretation of
myths, to proceed on the assumption that all myth is idea,
and that no myth contains any historical element. It may
be true, no doubt, that in the case of some particular
nation all action of the popular imagination on human
personalities has been excluded; but such a one-sided
action is not to be presumed; it must be proved; and
that in such a rich and various mythology as the Greek
all reference to human characters and human exploits
should be systematically excluded is in the highest degree
improbable. In a country where the gods descended so
easily into humanity, it were strange if men had not occasionally ascended into godhood.

PROP. XIII.—In a theology so thoroughly anthropomorphic as the Greek, the distinction between the divine and
human element will sometimes be difficult to trace; for
the same feelings, situations, and actions will necessarily
belong to human gods and to godlike men. But this
state of the case, in the interpretation of any particular
myth, is a ground for doubt, not for dogmatism. It includes the possibility or the probability of one of two
explanations, but the certainty of neither.

PROP. XIV.—The incredible exaggerations or embel-
lishments with which the name of any national hero may
have been handed down in a popular myth afford no pre-

sumption against the genuine historical character of its nucleus. On the contrary, it is just because extraordinary characters have existed that extraordinary and incredible, miraculous and even impossible stories are invented about them. A plain, sober, critical, matter-of-fact account of its early popular heroes is not to be expected from any people.

PROP. XV.—The error of certain ancient rationalizing interpreters of the Greek myths did not consist in presuming historical fact as the nucleus of some myths, but in the indiscriminate application of the historical interpretation to all myths, and that often in a very prosaic and altogether tasteless way.

PROP. XVI.—The error of certain modern idealizing interpreters of the Greek mythology does not consist in endeavouring to recover the ideas which originally lay at the root of some myths, the full significance of which had been lost so early as Homer, but in the partial and one-sided application of a few favourite ideas to all physical facts, and in the broad denial of any historical elements underlying any personality of early tradition.

PROP. XVII.—Among the ancients the extreme of the rationalizing interpretation of the Greek theological myths is what may be called the irreligious, godless, and altogether prosaic system of Euhemerus (B.C. 300), who wrote a book to prove that all the Greek gods, not even excepting Jove, had been originally dead men deified. The error of this system consisted, not in the assertion that the elevation of extraordinary human characters to a divine rank with religious honour after death is an element traceable in the Hellenic, as in some other popular theologies, but in the wholesale declaration that religious worship had no other origin, and that this element, which is always secondary and derivative in the popular creed, is primitive and exclusive.

PROP. XVIII.—In order to ascertain how far the principle of Euhemerus may apply to any particular case, the general religious tendencies and habits of the nation or people must be considered in the first place, and then the whole circumstances and features of the mythical narrative must be accurately surveyed and carefully weighed, and a separation of the canonized man from the deified nature element with which he may have been mixed up, made accordingly.

PROP. XIX.—Euhemerus, however, was altogether wrong in supposing that this system of interpretation could be applied on any extensive scale to the mythical theology of the Greeks ; and the few French and English writers who, in the flatness of the last century, gave a limited currency to this idea, have found no followers in the present.

PROP. XX.—An opposite theory to that of Euhemerus, much in fashion with the Germans, is, that whereas he said the gods were elevated men, we ought rather to say that many men, perhaps all the heroes of legendary story, are degraded gods. That in the course of religious development, especially when mixed up with great changes in the political relations of different races, such a degradation may have taken place, is certain ; that it has taken place in certain special cases will be a just conclusion from an analysis of the character and worship of certain heroes, when a cumulative view of the myths connected with them suggests the theory of a divine rather than a human significance ; but there is no scientific warrant for the assertion which it is now the fashion to make (Baring Gould on *Religious Belief*, vol. i. p. 167), that the old heroic names of a country, as King Arthur, for instance, are in the mass to be treated as degraded gods.

PROP. XXI.—The best authorities for the facts of a myth are not always the poets, nor even the most ancient poets, as Homer, who in the exercise of their art often take large liberties with sacred tradition; but the reliable witnesses are rather such as Pausanias, who record the old temple lore in its fixed local forms. This distinction, often forgotten, has given rise to not a little confusion, and created some needless difficulty in mythological inter-pretation; and Hartung (i. 184) has done important service to comparative mythology by drawing attention emphatically to the difference between sacred LEGENDS as believed by the people, and religious MYTHS freely handled by the poets.

PROP. XXII.—In the interpretation of any popular myth, the first thing to be done is to ascertain carefully what the thing to be interpreted actually is ; and this can only be done by collecting all the facts relating to it, working them up into a complete, and if possible consis-tent picture, and not till then attempting an explanation. Now, as the facts relating to any single god, let us say in the Greek Pantheon, are scattered over a wide space, and come from various sources, to attempt the explanation of these facts without the previous labour of critical and well-digested scholarship, may be an ingenious amusement, but never can be a scientific procedure. All the facts must be collected, and all the criticisms weighed, before a verdict can be pronounced.

PROP. XXIII.—But the mere collection of facts will never help a prosaic or an irreverent man to the interpretation of what is essentially poetic and devout. A book supplies what must be read; but the eye that reads it can see only what by natural faculty and training it is fitted to see. As the loving and reverential contemplation of nature was the original source of the polytheistic myths, so the key to them will often be recovered by a kindred mind acting under influences similar to those which impressed the original framers of the myth; and if this may be done with a considerable amount of success by a poetical mind, acted on by nature in any country, much more will such success be achieved by such a mind in the country where the myths were originally formed. But as the aspects of nature are various, and the fancies of poetic minds no less so, it will always be necessary to verify any modern notion of an ancient deity thus acquired, by confronting it accurately and continuously with the traditional materials contained in books and works of art. Highly poetical minds, such as Shelley, Keats, and Ruskin, when dealing with Greek mythology, without the constant correction of accurate scholarship, are not seldom found using Greek myths to represent modern ideas, rather than human ideas to interpret Greek myths. And the example of the Germans proves, that in minds naturally fertile and ingenious, no amount of erudition affords a safeguard against the besetting sin of mythological interpreters, to find in all myths a select field and enclosed hunting-ground for the pleasant disport of an unfettered imagination. Discoveries are easy to make in a region where plausibility so readily gains currency as proof.

PROP. XXIV.—An important aid in the interpretation of myths will often be supplied by the etymology of the names of the mythological personages ; and in this way new deities will sometimes be found to have arisen from the mere epithets of old ones, as Jacob Bryant saw clearly nearly 100 years ago ; nay, even magnificent myths may at times be traced to no more sublime origin than a false etymology which had taken possession of the popular ear. The significance of divine names must, of course, be sought in the first place in the language to which the mythology belongs ; but in applying this test, with the view of obtaining any scientific result, great care must be taken to avoid treating doubtful etymologies in the same way that certain ones may be treated. For where the etymology is uncertain, that is, does not shine out plainly from the face of the word (as in the case of the Harpies in Hesiod), then the elements of doubt are often so many, that it is wiser to abstain altogether from this aid, than to attempt founding any serious conclusions upon it. For, in the first place, we may not have the word in its original form ; and, in the second place, two or three etymologies may be equally probable. The best etymologies, whatever theorists pleasantly possessed with one idea may say to the contrary, are only accessories of mythological interpretation, not the chief corner-stone.

PROP. XXV.—If the mythological names have no significance in the language to which they belong, then recourse may be had to cognate languages ; and in the

M

case of European tongues, with propriety to the Eastern sources from which they are demonstrably derived. But here a double caution is necessary ; for accidental resemblances may be found in all languages, and extensive learning, coupled with a vivid imagination, may readily supply the most plausible foreign derivations, which are merely fanciful.

PROP. XXVI.—By referring to another, and it may be a more primitive and ancient language, for the etymological key to a religious myth of any people, we are treading on historical ground extrinsic to the people with whose myths we may be dealing. For comparative philology, like archæology, recovers the earliest history of a people before writing was known ; and this raises the inquiry, whether a mythology which bears a foreign nomenclature on its face may not convey foreign ideas in its soul—that is, to take an example, whether the Greek mythology, if the names of its personages are more readily explained in Hebrew or Sanscrit than in Greek, may not, in respect of its ideas and legends, be more properly interpreted from original Hebrew or Sanscrit than from native Greek sources ? And may we not hope, in this way, in the Hebrew Scriptures, or the Sanscrit Vedas perhaps, to put our fingers on the ancient germs of those anthropomorphic myths which Homer and Hesiod present to us in adult completeness and full panoply ? and thus the highest end of scientific research will be obtained, not only to dissect the flower, but to trace it to the seed, and follow it through every stage of its rich and beautiful metamorphosis.

PROP. XXVII.—The prospect thus held out of tracing

famous European religious myths to their far home in the
East is extremely inviting.[1]   It satisfies at once scientific
minds by the promise of going to the root of a matter which
has hitherto been treated superficially, and that not incon-
siderable class of literary men and scholars who have a
keener eye for an ingenious novelty than for a stable
truth.   When we bear in mind also the significance of the
homely proverb, that " far birds have fair feathers," and
the well-known fact, that every mother is apt to prefer
her own bairn to others which may be more healthy and
beautiful, we shall see reason to proceed, not without hope
indeed, but with more than Scottish caution, in this
Oriental adventure.   There is a class of persons in the
world who have a strange pleasure in travelling a thousand
leagues to quarry out a truth which they might have
picked up from beneath their nose.   Against these
seductions, therefore, in the first place, while prosecuting
this foreign chase, we must be on our guard.   We ought
to know that we are hunting on very deceitful ground ;
that we are dealing with a class of phenomena, that,
like clouds and kaleidoscopic figures, are very apt to
change their shape, not only by their own nature, but
specially also according to the position of the observer ;
and that the same nebulous conglomerate may at one
moment look very like a whale, at another moment
very like Lord Brougham, and at a third moment very
like Olympian Jupiter.   And in the prospect of such a
possible ridiculous conclusion to the sublime adventure on
which he is starting, every inquirer into the remote origin
of European myths ought to take with him these
cautions---

[1] " The whole theology of Greece was derived from the East."—Bryant,
vol. i. p. 184.

(1.) That there is no necessity and no scientific warrant for seeking a foreign explanation of deities, which already sufficiently explain themselves by the character which they bear, or the symbols which they exhibit in their own country.

(2.) That the formative power by which myths were created, viz., the imagination, possesses a wonderful magic, in virtue of which the materials on which it acts, especially with a quick and vivid people unfettered by formal creeds, are subjected to a perpetual process of transmutation, which renders the recognition of the original identity of two diverging myths an extremely difficult and not seldom an altogether hopeless task. In this respect the recognition of the original identity of different words in cognate languages by comparative philology is a much more safe and scientific process than a similar recognition of the identity of different persons of two Pantheons through the shifting masks of comparative mythology.

(3.) That the principal relations under which the great objects of nature, such as the sky, the sun, the sea, etc., may appear, when subjected to the process of imaginative impersonation, are in many cases so obvious that two different polytheistic peoples may easily hit upon them without any historical connexion. Even in the free exercise of poetical talent in the case of individual poets of highly potentiated imagination, we constantly stumble on comparisons which have been made independently by other poets at other times or in distant countries, and which superficial critics are sometimes eager to fasten on as plagiarisms; much more, in the vulgar exercise of the imagination, by the mass of the people on certain given natural objects may we expect frequent instances of coincidence without connexion. This consideration will restrain a prudent investigator in this department from building any theory of foreign origin of myths on a few points of natural similarity.

Taking these cautions along with us, we now observe, in reference to the probable Eastern origin of certain Greek myths—

PROP. XXVIII.—That the borrowing of one nation from another in the province of mythological ideas, as in the case of philological materials, may take place in a twofold fashion, either in the way of original descent from a common stock, far back in the cradle of the race, or by importation through the medium of commerce or great religious revolutions and invasions. Of these two methods of borrowing, it is impossible to say, à priori, which promises the greater amount of gain to the adventurous inquirer; for, while the advantage of greater closeness belonging to the original identity of stock may be in a great measure neutralized by the distance of time and place, and the changes which they induce, the disadvantage of a more loose connexion which belongs to the foreign importer may be amply compensated by the firm hold which the commerce, and polity, and intelligence of a superior may take of an inferior people.

PROP. XXIX.—It must be borne in mind, also, that the recognition of a supposed identity between the gods of any two polytheistic peoples may easily take place without any real borrowing. For the desire of harmonizing and classifying discordant phenomena, which belongs to the very nature of intellectual action, is particularly displayed in the field of popular religion—to such an extent, indeed, that it became a fixed habit of the Greek and

Roman mind to identify the deities of foreign countries
with their own native deities by certain signs more or
less superficial. The testimony of the Greeks, therefore,
with regard to the supposed identity of certain personages
in their Pantheon with certain gods or goddesses in the
Egyptian or Phœnician, and their consequent foreign ex-
traction, will require to be examined with the severest
scrutiny.

Prop. xxx.—In deriving any god from a foreign
source, even though his foreign origin should appear in some
respects perfectly certain, we must not conclude that all
the phenomena which his person and character present
are to be explained from abroad. Nothing is more
natural than that he should be a compound god, one-half
native and one-half foreign, or even a monstrous conglomerate of many gods.

Prop. xxxi.—Of all the foreign sources to which the
Hellenic mythology has at different times been referred
by the learned, Egypt is at once the most reputable and
the least likely. For here we have neither original connexion by identity of stock, nor any such commercial or
political action of the more ancient over the more modern
people, as would lead to the importation of religious ideas.
The ancient Greeks had a great respect, and a sort of
awful reverence for the wisdom and the antiquity of the
Egyptians ; but this respect and reverence was more
likely to lead them, as in fact it often did, to the recognition of superficial resemblances (as in the case of Io and
Isis) than to the trace of original identity. Modern researches have added nothing to the probability of the
favourite notion of Bryant and Blackwell, that the prin-

cipal persons and legends of Hellenic mythology came
directly from the land of Ham.

PROP. XXXII.—For the Hebrew origin of some of the
Greek theological ideas—the darling notion of Church
Fathers and Protestant theologians, and which has been
recently revived by a statesman of distinguished character,
talent, and erudition—there is even less to be said. For,
in the first place, here we are comparing a polytheistic
system with a monotheistic, where antagonism rather
than similarity is to be looked for; the elements of
original or superinduced connexion between the two
peoples are altogether wanting; and the original unity of
the human family, which is the only link that binds the
Greek to the Jew, is so remote that it requires no incon-
siderable amount of hardihood to drag them into the
arena of the present comparison. This hardihood, however, has never been wanting; and, besides its own
virtue, has always found great favour with the religious
public, which is pleased with nothing so much as the idea
that everything good, beautiful, or excellent in any way
that heathen religions may be allowed to possess must
have come either from the Hebrew Scriptures directly, or
from some more ancient source of primeval revelation.
And no doubt there may be a certain truth in this view;
but it is a truth which affects the monotheistic element,
that in the person of Zeus lies as the background of the
Hellenic polytheism, rather than the polytheistic personages to whom it has been applied. A consciousness
of this truth led the early mythological interpreters of
this school to apply the principle of Euhemerus largely
to the Old Testament, in such a way only as to recognise
the venerable Hebrew patriarchs under various masks of
old Pelasgic gods or demigods.

PROP. XXXIII.—For the Phœnician influence on the formation of the early Greek theology there is much more to be said. We can, indeed, scarcely imagine a race of such distinguished merchants and navigators, commanding the Greek seas in the early ages of European civilisation, without supposing some such contagion and ingrafting of religious ideas, as the genius of polytheism was on all occasions prone to invite. We shall, therefore, be disposed to receive favourably any distinct proof, or even probable indication, of the derivation of Greek gods from a Phœnician source; but we must bear in mind at the same time, that the Phœnicians were known to the Greeks as mere traders, with temporary settlements on the coast of the Mediterranean, and that their character, as exhibited in the *Odyssey*, was by no means possessed of such attractions as might aid to allure the Greeks to the adoption of any of their peculiar objects of worship.

PROP. XXXIV.—The last source of Greek myths, for which a strong claim has recently been put forth by a German of distinguished talent, taste, and learning in this country, is Sanscrit. And here at last some people seem to think, that with all certainty we have got at the true source of the many-winding mythological Nile. But after looking into this matter with all possible care, and with no prejudice whatever (for nothing would please me so much as to catch the infant Mercury in the bosom of a cloud, floating over the shining peak of the Hindu Kush, or to hook Proteus in one of his many forms at the mouth of the Ganges), I must honestly confess, that hitherto the interpreters of Hellenic myths from Sanscrit roots and Vedic similes have inspired me rather with distrust than with confidence. The principal characters of the Hellenic Pantheon tell their own story, to a poetical eye, more obviously and effectively than with the help of a Sanscrit root; and those few of them which are more doubtful, such as Hermes and Athena, seem to be precisely those in which the Sanscritizing mythologers have most egregiously failed. I consider, therefore, that, while the Vedic mythology, preferably to any other polytheistic system, presents an ample field from which some of the Hellenic legends may be aptly illustrated, and a few, perhaps, correctly interpreted, the attempt to explain the great and prominent phenomena of the Greek Pantheon, by an ingenious application of a few favourite physical ideas variously impersonated by the fancy of the Vedic poets, must be regarded in the meantime, at least, as a failure.[1]

PROP. XXXV.—Without, therefore, in the slightest degree wishing to throw discouragement on the delightful and interesting study of comparative mythology,—a study which promises the most fruitful results in the domain of theology and moral philosophy,—the procedure of exact science seems to demand that, before venturing on extensive excursions into foreign regions, we should, in the first place, carefully survey and exhaust our home domain—that is to say, that the Greek traditions with respect to their gods, interpreted by themselves, and the general principles of mythical interpretation laid down in the above propositions, afford a surer basis for this branch of mythological science than hints suggested by Oriental etymologies, or analogies from the Vedic hymns. And in order to make this more clear, I will select a few examples

[1] The interpretation of certain personages in the Greek Pantheon from sources of Sanscrit etymology, to which Max Müller has given currency, is not at all confirmed by the judicious sobriety of our countryman Dr. Muir. See his paper in Edinburgh Royal Society Transactions, vol. xxiii. p. 578.

of personages from the motley theatre of Hellenic legend, which may be best adapted for testing the value of the different methods of interpretation.

PROP. XXXVI.—As examples of how the elemental significance of the Hellenic gods reveals itself to a sympathetic eye, from the mere presentation, epithets, attitudes, and badges of the mythologic personages, we need do no more than mention *Zeus, Poseidon,* and *Apollo,* in whom all the ancients, who exercised reflection at all on the matter, recognised, with one voice and by an unerring instinct, the great elemental powers of the sky, the sea, and the sun.   And these are precisely the powers which, from their prominence, might *à priori* have been predicated as certain to obtain a conspicuous place in an anthropomorphic Pantheon of elemental origin.   Of these three great gods also be it noted, that the first is the only one of which we can trace the etymology with any certainty; but neither does this one etymology, when recognised in the Sanscrit word *Diva,* to *shine,* add anything to the already recognised idea of the Hellenic Zeus, nor does the lack of an etymon in the other two cases render our perception of the character of the two gods less clear, or our knowledge of their significance more certain.   With regard to Poseidon, Mr. Gladstone's recent attempt to fix on him a Phœnician pedigree must be regarded as unsuccessful.   The people who at an early period sailed to Colchis and to Troy did not require to borrow a lord of the flood from the merchants of Tyre and Sidon.

PROP. XXXVII.—In *Hera,* who, to the people and the people's poet, was simply the spouse of Zeus, a large class of ancient speculators, as is well known, were inclined to recognise the lower region of the atmosphere, of which Zeus represented the αἰθήρ, or upper region. But a little consideration has convinced most modern interpreters that this idea was a mistake. When by the completion of the anthropomorphic process the original οὐρανός had become "Father Jove," it was most natural that his elemental counterpart Γῆ, Mother Earth, should become the matron Hera ; and with this supposition, the well-known description of the sacred marriage of Zeus and Hera (*Il.* XIV. 345), together with the cow-symbolism belonging to the Βοῶπις, and her Argive priestess Io, notably harmonize. It is no objection to this view, that Ceres or Demeter is also the anthropomorphosed earth ; for "the many names of one shape," πολλῶν ὀνομάτων μορφὴ μία, characteristic of the oldest elemental theology could easily and did often crystallize into two or more shapes of one power. We shall, therefore, say with no rash confidence, that the Hellenic Hera means the earth ; and we readily allow the etymological conjectures connected with her name to remain conjectures.

PROP. XXXVIII.—On *Athena*, Max Müller says, " The Sanscrit root AH, which in Greek would regularly appear as ACH, might likewise then have assumed the form of ATH; and the termination ENE, is Sanscrit ANA" (*Science of Language*, vol. ii. p. 503); and again, "How Athena being the *Dawn*, should have become the goddess of wisdom, we can best learn from the Vedas. In Sanscrit, *Budh* means to *wake* and to *know*" (*Ibid.* p. 504).

But this is manifestly following out a favourite idea upon theories of the most flimsy texture. If any etymology is to be sought for the syllable ΑΘ, the native root αἰθ which signifies to glow, corresponding as it does with the familiar epithet of γλαυκῶπις, or "flashing-eyed" (which I think Welcker suggests), is preferable to that suggested by the distinguished Sanscrit scholar. But here, as in other slippery cases, the principles laid down in the preceding propositions lead me to set etymology aside, and to look at the finished figure of the goddess, with her badges, relations, and actions, as the natural and sure index to her significance. Now if Zeus, according to the Greek conception, was the strong, stormy, and thunderous element of the sky—as his epithets κελαινεφής, and ἐριβρεμέτης, and τερπικέραυνος, sufficiently declare—his flashing-eyed daughter, who alone is privileged to wield his thunderbolt (Æschyl. Eumen. 814), must be some action or function of the sky. Let her, therefore, be the flashing lightning, or the bright rifted azure sky between the dark rolling thunder clouds, or both if you please, and you have at once an elemental theory which explains adequately her anthropomorphic parentage and presentation. As to her moral and mental significance, that follows necessarily from her Jovian fatherhood. When the all-powerful was recognised as at the same time the all-wise and the great counsellor (μητίετα Ζεύς), his daughter, as a matter of course, became the goddess of practical wisdom, that is, of the great arts of peace and war (as the vases largely show), the patron and protector of all men of valour like Achilles, and of sagacity like Ulysses.

PROP. XXXIX.—The Hellenic *Hermes* is one of those mythological personages who from an originally simple root has grown up into such a rich display of graceful ramification, that, when we approach him from his most familiar side we are the least likely to interpret his true significance. But if we attend to the earliest indication of his functions as found in Homer, and as displayed in the familiar phallic symbol (Herod. II. 51), we can have no difficulty in evolving, by a series of graduated expansions, his final avatar as a god of eloquence, from his original germ as a pastoral god of generation and increase (Hom. *Il.* XIV. 491). As the god of shepherds and mountaineers, he was necessarily the guide of all wanderers through the many winding glens, and across the many-folded hills of the Arcadian Highlands. This early function accordingly appears in Homer : he is the friendly guide of all persons who have lost their way or who wander in the dark (*Od.* X. 277 ; *Il.* XXIV. 334). His connexion with music and with wrestling, the natural recreations of a pastoral people, of course belong to this his earliest Hellenic character. Afterwards, when in the necessary progress of society the patriarchal shepherd of the hills resigned his social position into the hands of the rich merchant of the great towns, Hermes became the god of gain generally ; and, with gain, of all those arts of adroitness and sharpness which belong to the career of a successful trader. The kindly guide of night-wandering shepherds has now become the expert negotiator, and the trusty messenger ; he is the winged servant of the gods above ; and among men his oaten pipe is exchanged for the charm of winged words, which sways the counsels of the wise, and soothes the clamours of the turbulent. With this natural and obvious interpretation of a purely Hellenic deity, as given within the bounds of Greece itself, we shall raise only a brilliant confusion, if we follow Max Müller across the Hindu Kush, and curiously attempt to find the germ of the Pelasgic shepherd-god in the breeze of the early dawn, which ushers in the march of the busy day. Such remote conjectures may be both beautiful and ingenious, but they are a mere play of fancy, and travel obviously far out of the way of a sober, a scientific, and a stable interpretation.

PROP. XL.—*Dionysus* was a god of comparatively recent introduction into Greece (Herod. II. 49), confessedly of Asiatic origin, and in whom the union of fervid wine with the phallic symbol and violent orgies can leave no doubt as to his true character. He is the male god of generation, according to the Asiatic conception, as the Syrian goddess of Lucian (*De Dea Syria*, 16) was the female one; and the old Heraclitan principle that fire is the origin of all things, rudely conceived by the popular imagination, is manifestly that which in this god identifies the glow of the vine juice, the brewst of the sun, with the fervour of the generative process. The fact that the worship of Dionysus was not native in Greece, but imported from the East, naturally led to the representation of this god as a wonderful conqueror, in the fashion of Sesostris and Alexander the Great; from which analogy, coupled with his preaching the gospel of wine, Bryant and other speculators have been eager to find in him a perverted Noah; but the application of the principle of Euhemerus in this case evidently rests on too slender a foundation to afford any grounds for a scientific interpretation.

PROP. XLI.—*Aphrodite* is that goddess in whose case Mr. Gladstone's favourite idea of Phœnician influence on the Greek Pantheon has long been recognised as the most certain (Herod. I. 105 ; Pausan. I. 14-6). The recognition of this Phœnician element, however, does by no means imply that the existence of an original Hellenic impersonation of the passion of love, and the seductions of personal beauty, should be denied. On the contrary, the female deity whom the Phœnicians were seen worshipping in their factories on the coasts of the Mediterranean would most probably be accepted by the ancient Pelasgic tribes chiefly because they found in her attributes a striking identity with their own native Aphrodite.

Prop. xlii.—Phœnician influence is also undoubtedly to be acknowledged in the very complex and composite mythology connected with the name of *Heracles.* But the person of Heracles, as we find him in Homer, exhibits nothing beyond the exaggerated traits of a stout and muscular humanity in combat with fate and circumstance, and the wild beasts of the forest—a plain Hellenic counterpart, in fact, to the Hebrew Samson, of whose historical reality, to a mind not violently possessed by German theories, there cannot be the slightest reason to doubt. The exaggerations connected with his story are the natural and necessary effects of the excited popular imagination brought to bear on such a character ; but these exaggerations, taken at their highest, are exhibited on a very small platform in Homer, and present a very modest array of achievements compared with the multiform mass of myth that afterwards accumulated round this representative Greek hero. The principle of growth, of such luxuriant vitality in popular myths, has been obviously at work here ; and the sort of omnipresence latterly attributed to this wandering queller of monsters is most readily explained from the influence of the Phœnician factories in the Mediterranean, in whose Melcarth the Greeks delighted to recognise their own stout son of Jove and Semele. And if this Tyrian Hercules, as Phœnician scholars incline to believe (Moevers, vol. i. p. 385), really was a sun-god, the twelve labours of Hercules will, of course, only be the symbolical expression for the progress of the Titan sun through the twelve months of the solar year. This the ancients themselves, in the Orphic theology at least, distinctly recognised.

PROP. XLIII.—In *Bellerophon* the Germans find a favourite example of their theory, that all the heroes of the so-called heroic age are the degraded gods of an early elemental worship. How this theory is worked out in the present case it may be instructive to consider. The winged steed, of course, brings you at once into the region of the sun. Then you turn up Eustathius' commentary on the well-known episode of the Corinthian hero in the sixth book of the *Iliad* (v. 181), and you find there that there was an old Greek word ἔλλερος, used by Callimachus, which is equivalent to κακός or *bad*; but bad things are black things; therefore, with the help of the digamma, transmuting ἔλλερος into βέλλερος, we arrive at the conclusion that βελλεροφόντης means the slayer of darkness, and, of course, can be nothing but the light, or the sun. Bellerophon is thus, by a dexterous etymological feat, already a solar god in full panoply; and when, in addition to this, we find that the worship of the sun was much practised at Corinth, the native place of the hero, and that he died in Lycia, a country famous for its devotion to the same deity, the case for a degraded Ἥλιος seems to be satisfactorily made out. But, on the other hand, the oldest version of the story in Homer has no hint of the winged horse, and for the rest, looks in every trait as much like a purely human history of those early Greek times as the story of St. Columba shows like a real legend of a real Catholic apostle in early Christian times. We shall, therefore, in my opinion, more wisely say that the airy flight of the grandson of Corinthian Sisyphus on his winged Pegasus is only the imaginative painting out of a real human journey made from such real and natural causes as those which Homer details; and, if the winged horse has anything to do with the worship of the sun at Corinth, it is more reasonable to suppose that such a blazon should have been added for the glorification of a real great man than that all the great men of early Corinth should have been clean swept from the popular memory to make way for an unmeaning Pantheon of degraded and forgotten gods.

PROP. XLIV.—Descending lower down into the region of what has the aspect, not of metamorphic theology, but of plain human fact, we may take the names of Achilles and Theseus as examples of how far the German school is inclined to carry its peculiar tactics of finding nothing in all early tradition but theological ideas and symbols. As to Achilles, the favourite notion with most German writers is that this hero is a water god,—a notion founded on nothing that I can see, save on the etymological analogy of Achelous, the happy coincidence of Peleus with the Greek name for mud (πηλός), and the fact that the mother of the hero was a sea-goddess; and on this notion Forchhammer, I believe, or some one of the erudite fancymongers beyond the Rhine, constructed a theory that the *Iliad* is really a great geological poem, in which water power is represented by Achilles, and land power by Hector (from ἔχω, to hold, restrain, keep back)! This is really too bad. If a man in Thurso, to take a modern example, named Waters—and it is a characteristic name in that quarter,—were to marry a woman called Loch—a

well-known name in Sutherland—and a daughter, the
offspring of this marriage, should join herself in wedlock
to an English gentleman named Rivers, no sane person
could see in this conjunction of congruous etymologies
anything but one of those curious coincidences which
amuse a newspaper reader for a minute, and then are forgotten. Why, then, we ask, should the occurrence of
water, and *mud*, and a *sea-nymph*, among the family
names of an old Thessalian throne, be supposed to possess
any more profound significance, even on the supposition
that the etymologies are certain, which they certainly are
not ? And accordingly, we find this favourite water
theory discarded by the Germans themselves the moment
it does not suit the theory of the interpreter. To Max
Müller Achilles can be nothing but a solar god ; for his
imagination, fired with sunlight from the flaming east,
can see nothing in the stout battles of Greeks and Trojans
in the *Iliad* but the grand struggle between the powers
of light and darkness. Of the probability of this theory
I have sought in vain for the shadow of a proof. If Helen
of Troy, whose name can obviously be identified with
brightness ($\sigma\epsilon\lambda\alpha\varsigma$ $\sigma\epsilon\lambda\eta\nu\eta$), must on this account take her
place with her brothers, as a sidereal phenomenon (sic
Fratres Helenæ, LUCIDA SIDERA), this does seem to me an
exceeding weak foundation for the transformation of the
whole topographical and traditional heroes of the *Iliad*
into a meteoric spectacle.

If, according to the views set forth in this paper, there
is no scientific ground for raising Achilles into the category of gods, whether aquarian or solar, much stronger
are the reasons which induce us, with unsophisticated old
Plutarch, to see in Theseus no myth, but a great historical reality. If the principle be once accepted, that a

single miraculous fact or incredible story connected in the popular imagination with a great popular name shall deprive him *simpliciter* of all claim to a historical existence, we shall make strange havoc, I fear, with some of the most brilliant and the most instructive pages of national record. There is no need of believing all the wonderful stories that Athenian reverence and wonder accumulated round the name of Theseus, as little as there is of believing all the silly miracles that the Lausiac history narrates of the Egyptian ascetics; but there is certainly as little wisdom in roundly denying the historical germ to which, in all such cases, these accretions were attached.

I have thus pointed out, in a rapid and succinct way, what seem to be the leading principles on which a sound and safe interpretation of early popular myths must proceed. I have kept myself purposely within the bounds of what appears sober statement, not being ambitious of the glory of adventure in this nebulous field; and, if I shall seem to have achieved a very small thing when I keep myself within these bounds, I have at least kept myself clear of nonsense, which in mythological science is as common as sunk rocks in the Shetland seas. To Max Müller, and other Sanscrit scholars, I hope I shall always be grateful for any happy illustrations which they may supply of the general character of Aryan myths, and of occasional coincidences of the Hellenic mode of imagining with the Indian; and I think the somewhat cold and unimaginative race of English scholars are under no small obligations to him for having taught them to recognise poetical significance and religious value in some legends, which passed in their nomenclature for silly fables or worthless facts; but I profess to have been unable to derive any sure clue from the far East to the most difficult questions of Greek mythology ; nor do I expect that, when every obsolete word in the Rigveda shall have been thoroughly sifted and shaken, a single ray of intelligible light will thence flow on the Athena of the Parthenon, or the Hermes of the Cyllenian slopes.   I believe that in the region of mythology they will ultimately be found to be the wisest, who are at present content to know the least ; that, while some mythological fables are too trifling to deserve interpretation, others are too tangled to admit of it ; and that the man who, at the present day, shall attempt to interpret the Greek gods from the transliteration of Sanscrit or Hebrew words, will be found, like Ixion, to have embraced a cloud for a goddess, and to have fathered a magnificent lie from the fruitful womb of his own conceit.   There is no more dangerous passion than that which an ingenious mind conceives for the fine fancies which it begets.

ONE of the most remarkable phenomena in our recent historical literature is a tendency to whitewash all characters which had previously presented a black aspect ; to prefer the intellectual divination of a subtle modern professor to the plain testimony of a sober old chronicler ; and generally to unsettle all things that we had in previous ages been taught to look on as settled. That this tendency, dating from the gigantic excavations of Niebuhr and Wolf, had its origin in an honest love of truth, and a searching scrutiny of evidence, cannot be doubted. That its results have in the main been beneficial is equally certain ; but, on the other hand, it is not to be denied that it has sometimes run into the most wanton excesses, and has tainted not a few of the most notable historical productions of our age with a vice which will render it necessary for a future generation to repeat the work now done from a broader point of view, and with a juster criticism. Among the great works which have not escaped this prevalent contagion must be named the *History of Greece*, by George Grote. In this work, while the democratic institutions of Athens have been vindicated in the most masterly manner, and the political tone of the work may be regarded as, on the whole, sound, the author has in some prominent sections blotted his pages with the peculiarly German rage of substituting conjecture for fact, and overriding testimony by theory. And in doing this he has not only acted more like a German than an Englishman, but he has in some instances proceeded far beyond the bounds of negative criticism and bold assertion which the best German writers have observed. In no part of his work does this tendency, not only to overdo, but altogether to invert the natural order of things, appear more prominently than in his chapter on Socrates and the Sophists. In this part of his work, while he presents himself to the general reader as the chivalrous champion of injured innocence, the accurate weigher of historical evidence sees only another instance of the wonderful effect of a favourite theory in blinding a sensible man to the truth which radiates from the strongest testimony. To the reader of Mr. Grote's chapter it must certainly seem as if Socrates had spent his life most stupidly, if not most basely, in fighting with a class of men, of which he himself was one, the best among many good, and that Protagoras was a far more sensible man, and at bottom a much more profound philosopher than Plato. The effect produced by this chapter of the history has been rather increased than diminished by the distinguished historian's comment on the Protagoras and other dialogues in his recent work on Plato. Here also we are regularly given to understand that Plato was a much overrated man, and that the true objects of human admiration are rather the men whom it was the constant object of his philosophy to refute. This is even a bolder stroke of what, borrowing a phrase from mathematicians, I may call the *invertendo* style of criticism, than any with which the world has been favoured from the disintegrating school of Lachmann, Köchly, and other trans-Rhenane commentators on the Homeric poems. They, at least, while they annihilated the poet, left us the poem to admire. Here the divine objects of old reverence are thrown away as idols, and the old recognised idols are set up as the true God.

The great authority of Mr. Grote in all matters of Greek history, and the wide circulation of his work, render it expedient that a public contradiction should be given to his errors from as many independent quarters as possible; and, though I am perfectly satisfied with what I find written on this subject by an excellent scholar, Mr. Cope of Cambridge, in the *Cambridge Philological Journal*, vol. i., as also by Professor Zeller, in his *Philosophie der Griechen*, Tübingen, 1856; yet, as my own opinions have been formed altogether independently, and are based on a careful study of Plato, extending through a series of years, I have thought that a succinct statement of the bearings of this important historical question would not prove unacceptable to persons interested in the history of Greek philosophy. I proceed, therefore, to make a short statement of Mr. Grote's theory, followed by an equally short statement of how, from my point of view, his arguments ought to be met.

Mr. Grote ushers in the statement of his views by this general declaration—"I know few characters in history who have been so hardly dealt with as the Sophists; they bear the penalty of their name in its modern sense;" and the modern sense of the word, according to the whole tenor of the learned gentleman's argument, is about as far removed from the original and genuine sense, as the English word *demon* is from the Homeric word δαίμων. To restore its proper meaning, as he conceives, to this sadly misunderstood word, the learned historian brings forward, according to my analysis, six arguments.

(1.) It is plain from Plato himself—in this case we

must suppose an unwilling witness—that many of the Sophists were excellent and sensible men, and in every way capable of being the instructors of youth.

(2.) In fact, the Sophists were the great teachers of the age to which they belonged; and Socrates owed his position and his influence altogether to being one of them. The great exhibition of young democratic energy which had culminated at Marathon was now riding onward triumphantly to another and a higher development. Of this period of transition between the youth and the manhood of the Athenian intellect the Sophists were the natural representatives, and the worthy spokesmen.

(3.) Plato was a man of peculiar idiosyncrasy, a great intellect confessedly, but a crotchety pedant in some matters, and a transcendental dreamer in others. His witness—at bottom the only serious testimony against the Sophists (for of the great jester Aristophanes in such matters we need take no account)—is consequently of no value, and cannot, without the grossest injustice, be quoted against such sober, sensible, and practical thinkers as Protagoras and Gorgias.

(4.) The immoral teaching, attributed to the Sophists, and set forth by Plato through the mouth of Callicles in the *Gorgias* and of Thrasymachus in the *Republic*, must be a figment; for the whole history of the Athenian democracy shows that such doctrines would have been utterly revolting to them, and men professing such doctrines never would have been allowed the slightest influence in the education of their sons.

(5.) The Sophists, in fact, as a body, had no peculiar system of morals, either bad or good; as little had they any system of philosophic doctrine. They were a profession, not a sect.

(6.) The standing objection made to the Sophists by Plato, in almost all his Dialogues, that they were a venal and mercantile crew, because they taught philosophy for a fee, need scarcely require refutation at our hands, living, as we do, in a country where the expediency of payment for all sorts of professional work is universally recognised. One does not, indeed, see how the Sophists could have performed their duties as general Hellenic teachers, travelling from land to land, had they not exacted a considerable fee, if it were only to pay their travelling expenses.

These propositions, it will be seen, have a polemical aspect, as indeed it is both the vice and the virtue of Mr. Grote's book generally, that he is everywhere writing down an old view of Hellenic matters, and writing up a new one. In order, therefore, fully to understand the drift of his statements, we must set distinctly before us the old doctrine about the Sophists which he affects to have overturned; and though this might be done by a large array of testimonies from many quarters, it will be sufficient for our present purpose to cite two of the best known authorities, Brucker and Gillies, who may be looked on as the generally recognised exponents of the ante-Grotian doctrine with regard to the Sophists. In his *History of Philosophy*, vol. i. p. 549, the erudite old Augsburg theologian says:—" *Erant tum temporis Athenis Sophistæ, magistri docendi, quales Leontinus Gorgias, Thrasymachus, Protagoras Abderites, Prodicus Ceius, Hippias Eleus aliique, qui in eo potissimum artem consistere arrogantibus verbis jactabant, quemadmodum caussa inferior, dicendo superior evadere posset; id quod, docente* Cicerone *sententiarum magis concinnitate argutoque et circumscripto verborum ambitu quam eorum pondere*

*efficere tentabant.   Hinc homines vani, ambitiosi, avari,
quique soli sibi sapere videbantur, et omnium disciplinarum
cognitionem sibi arrogabant, non tantum hanc in utramque
partem de quavis re proposita invictis argumentis dispu-
tandi artem publice exercebant, sed et magnificis eam
promissis nobilem juventutem brevi tempore se docturos
pollicebantur.   Quae eo ardentius ad hos nugatores depro-
perabat, quod ita se utilissimam rationem discere posse
speraret, populum in suas partes trahendi, et ex civium
ad quos loquendum erat, judicio et calculo summam rerum
ad se trahendi, vel etiam in potestate semel acquisita, flexo
populi per istam eloquentiam obsequio, se confirmandi."*
And Gillies, in his well-known *History of Greece*, vol. ii.
p. 133, says, in distinct antithesis to Mr. Grote, that the
"appellation *Sophist*, in its modern sense, pretty faithfully
expresses their character," and that "their morality supplied the springs from which Epicurus watered his gardens,
and their captious logic furnished the arguments by which
Pyrrho laboured to justify his scepticism."

Now, in reference to these opposing views, my assertion is, that the old view, though not exhaustive of the
whole truth of the matter, and not recognising certain
modifications which tend to soften the harsher lines of the
portrait, is on the whole the right view; while the new
view, if containing an element of correction in some
secondary points, is on the whole a false and misleading
view, or rather a total misrepresentation and inversion of
the facts of the case.   The proof may be given, disposing
of Mr. Grote's six arguments in their order, as follows :—

(1.) The general character of the Sophists, in their
capacity of public teachers, is in no wise affected by the
fact that there were great differences in their personal
characters, and that some of them, like Protagoras, were,

as the world goes, most respectable and reputable men. The Scribes and Pharisees in the Gospel history were respectable and reputable enough, no doubt, or had at least many most respectable and reputable men in their body; but not the less were their doctrines false and their teaching pernicious. So much only we may grant to the learned historian, that if any one ever said that there were no men of average respectability among the Sophists, such an assertion is altogether unwarranted, and is contrary to the plainest indications on the very surface of Plato.

(2.) A similar admission may be made with regard to the historical significance of the Sophists generally, without, in the slightest degree, trenching on the ground occupied by Plato. That the Sophists, like everything else in the world, had their good side, might have been assumed, if it could not have been proved; and it is equally certain, that when once a body of men like the Sophists, or the Scribes and Pharisees, or the Romish priests, gets a bad name, the defects of character out of which that bad name arose are apt to occupy the whole of the canvas in historical tradition, while their virtues are altogether forgotten, or even denied. Hence arises the necessity for some sort of justification; a justification, however, which, while it may be allowed slightly to qualify, does not in any wise nullify the unfavourable character of the original verdict. A sort of plea in extenuation of this class of men was therefore, in the very nature of the case, to have been expected; and I am indebted to Professor Zeller's admirable *Geschichte der Griechischen Philosophie* for a reference to two of the earliest authorities, in which this reaction in favour of the Sophists appears. The one is Meiners, in his *Geschichte der Wissenschaften*, published at Lemgo in the year 1782, and the other that of Hegel, in his lectures on the history of philosophy delivered on various occasions soon after the commencement of the present century. Professor Meiners (vol. ii. pp. 172-599) says, " The Sophists deserve not merely to be despised and denounced, but in many views they claim respect and eulogy—a recognition which even their most violent opponents have not refused. They were the great public teachers and enlighteners of Greece; they were a necessary link in the chain of intellectual life in Greece." But while admitting this, the same author says a little further on, that " their morality was right in the teeth of the Socratic morality," and that, " on a review of the whole matter, we must agree with Xenophon, Plato, Isocrates, and those who followed them, that the Sophists did their country more harm than good, and that they corrupted more hearts than they enlightened heads." This representation deserves special notice as contrasted with Mr. Grote's; for, while it fully admits the extenuating circumstance, it does not deny the general truth of the crime charged. Hegel places the palliative circumstance in a stronger light; indeed, he purposely brings it into the foreground, as being, in his phraseology, the one " positive and truly scientific side" of the matter. But by this he means, not that the faults with which the Sophists are generally charged did not really exist, but that whatever faults a faulty thing may possess, its virtues are the only element in it which has any value to a philosophic mind. From this point of view he says, that " the Sophists were the teachers of Greece, by whom intellectual culture (*Bildung*) was brought into existence. They came into the place of the poets and rhapsodists, who were originally the only teachers. Religion in Greece did not teach. Priests offered sacrifices, soothsayers divined the future, but instruction is something quite different." This is admirable; but with this the great Berlin notionalist is far from shutting his eyes to the weak side of these teachers. He proceeds to represent them as practising a logic both superficial and unprincipled. He shows also the peculiar danger which attached to such a logic when applied to practical purposes in an atmosphere of sensual polytheism. " In our European world," he writes, " intellectual culture appeared under the protection, so to speak, and on the foundation, of a spiritual religion. But when intellectual dexterity had to do only with a religion of the imagination, it readily shook itself loose from any central holding-point, or, at all events, particular subordinate points of view might easily be made to play the part of an ultimate principle." And again, " A man of education and experience always knows how to set things in a good light to serve the occasion. In the worst action something lies which, being singled out and skilfully presented, makes it defensible. A person must have gone a very short way in his intellectual education, if he does not know how to advance fair reasons to justify the worst actions. All the evil that has happened in the world since Adam has happened with the help of fair reasons." From these passages, which I think could not possibly be better expressed, we see how little the granting of Mr. Grote's second argument has to do with the conclusion at which he so sweepingly arrives. The most comprehensive philosophical thinker of the most philosophic country in the world can see with the utmost distinctness that the Sophists were not all black, and yet that they dealt with the most important matters of human concernment in a loose and slippery fashion, which completely justified the attitude of uncompromising hostility constantly assumed towards them by both Socrates and Plato.

(3.) Hitherto Mr. Grote's arguments, so far as they present a mere plea in palliation of the Sophists, have appeared not only plausible, but in the highest degree reasonable ; and, had he stopped at this point, there would have been no question at this moment before the learned world on the matter.   But, unfortunately, the democratic historian here, by over-pleading his case, betrays the inherent weakness of his cause.   He claims a verdict of acquittal for his clients, and can do so only, as we shall now see, by attempting to override an array of historical testimonies, such as, in the general case, would make any but a thorough-paced German ideamonger shrink back in dismay.   The witnesses in this case are not few, and they are all on one side.   Let us see how the learned historian disposes of them.   In the first place, he throws Plato and Aristophanes, the greatest thinker and the greatest humorist of the age, *simpliciter,* out of court; and then, by either overlooking other testimonies, or referring them back to the twin authors of the original calumny, he tells the jury, with a gay confidence, that there is nothing more in the case.   But there is a wholesale air about this procedure, which, with a sober-minded man, only acts as a warning to use caution.   To commence with the two original framers of the indictment.   No doubt Aristophanes was a maker of jests, but he was no mere buffoon. He was a great thinker as well as a great humorist ; and his comedies expressly deal with all the principal literary, philosophical, and political questions of the age.   Such men are not apt to fling their humorous shafts at a mere imagination.   On the contrary, their strength lies in the fact that the phenomenon which they ridicule has a wide, popular recognition, and is everywhere felt to be a fact. A man of the calibre of Aristophanes could not have written such a comedy as *The Clouds*, against such a class of persons as the Sophists, had not such a class of persons existed, any more than the well-known scientific song of *The Origin of Species*, composed by a witty Scotch judge, could have existed without a Darwin and a school of Darwins. The humorist's view of the case, indeed, is not necessarily the scientific view; but it may be, and often is, the true view, or, at all events, represents strongly one true aspect of the case. Otherwise, not only would the humour be pointless, but a great humorist certainly would not meddle with the matter at all. Incidental errors, such as the confounding of Socrates with the mass of public teachers, of which he was one, do not affect the fundamental truth of the case. *The Clouds* is a play against the Sophists, not against Socrates.

But, however slight the value which a grave man may be inclined to give to the testimony of a great public humorist on a question of philosophy, if it stood alone, the case is completely altered the moment that his laughing testimony is confirmed by the serious witness of a professional thinker. The error which the greatest thinker and the greatest humorist of the age agree in condemning is not likely to have been an imagination. No doubt, in such a case, a great deal depends on the character of the philosopher; and Plato is not a name likely to forestall favour with a class of minds largely represented in this land, which rejoices to call itself pre-eminently practical, and shares in a more than Napoleonic hatred of all ideology. But let us distinguish. Plato undoubtedly had his crotchets: he was in some

things a most unpractical man, and knew that he was
so; unquestionably, also, his theory of ideas may often
have been stated in exaggerated language, and with a
paradoxical air, eminently provocative of the opposition
which, ever since Aristotle, it has encountered. But
the testimony of the philosopher in reference to the
Sophists is a thing much broader, and rooted much more
deeply, than any of his crotchets about methodizing the
sexual instinct, or building up an ideal polity. Here we
have the fact that a great philosopher of all-command-
ing mind, the founder of a great and permanent school of
thinking, who stood to his age in the same relation that
Bacon does to ours, makes it the business of his life to
write against, and represents his great master, Socrates,
as having made it the business of his life to speak against,
a class of men who professed certain principles generally
esteemed pernicious, but which, according to Mr. Grote's
view of the matter, were, in fact, most excellent and
laudable. And this testimony, so given, was accepted by
the universal voice of antiquity. It met, in fact, no
decided contradiction till the epiphany of Mr. Grote.
Now, there is nothing altogether impossible in the supposition that Mr. Grote may be right. It may sometimes be given to a Niebuhr, after a lapse of 2000 years,
to reconstruct a history of Rome; but we are not to start
with a prepossession in favour of such brilliant novelties.
They are rather to be looked on with suspicion, and require
strong backing. Plato, moreover, it must be borne in
mind, with all his tendency to one-sided exaggerations,
was by no means a narrow-minded, an ungenerous, much
less a spiteful or an ill-natured man. No man was more in
the habit of looking at both sides of a question, and more
unlikely to put up a man of straw for an adversary. His

treatment of Protagoras, Gorgias, and other Sophists, is what we would call gentlemanly in the highest degree, and gives the reader a sort of guarantee that what he alleges against the general body to which he belonged had some good foundation. In weighing the testimony of Plato and Aristophanes also, with regard to such a class of men as the Sophists are alleged to have been, we must consider the presumptions and possibilities of the case. Is there anything strange or improbable in the statement, that in a talking town like Athens, full of all sorts of quick-witted and light-witted democratic people, there should have arisen, in an age of intellectual transition, a set of shallow thinkers, who cultivated the faculty of expression at the expense of the faculty of thought and exercised their understanding with a clever logical dexterity, rather than with the earnest search after truth? To myself it seems the most natural thing in the world to suppose the existence of such a class of men—a class of men, indeed, almost certain to exist at all times wherever there is a demand for them; and particularly dangerous, as Hegel remarks, in a country where a sensuous religion exists, altogether divorced from any serious training, either of the intellect or the character.

Starting from these presumptions, I must confess I should be inclined to accept the portrait of the Sophists in every feature, and with its full colouring, as given by the god of the philosophers, and the king of the humorists, even if their testimony in this matter stood alone. But the plain and admitted fact here is, that neither the philosopher nor the humorist does stand alone; they are supported by the consenting voice of antiquity. The heritage of Greek opinion on this subject was transmitted to Cicero; and he says (*Acad.* II. 23), " *Sophistæ appel-*

lantur qui ostentationis aut quæstûs causâ philosophantur."
Among the Greeks themselves, those whose testimony
was of the highest value, and who lived nearest to the
time, and who were most interested in the subject, set
their seal in the strongest language to the witness of the
great idealist. Who are the writers whom a wise judge
would call into court, and hear with impartial eagerness
in a trial of this kind? Socrates and Xenophon, Isocrates
and Aristotle—any one of these would be sufficient, in
my judgment, to nail down, for an absolute certainty,
whatever Plato and Aristophanes might have previously
combined to testify as a prominent fact in the history of
Greek intellectual life. Of these four, though the most
remote in point of time, Aristotle is the most weighty;
and this not only on account of the accurate, inductive,
and encyclopædic character of his mind, but specially on
account of his known propensity to contradict everything
that Plato says, when it comes in his way. None of the
products of that peculiarly Platonic idiosyncrasy, which
Mr. Grote brings forward so prominently, does the Stagyrite show the slightest desire to spare. Spartan women
and Platonic ideas are two matters, in discussing which
he almost seems to lose for a moment the imperturbable
judicial coolness of his intellect. But the Sophists he
describes in exactly the same language as Plato, and in
language which forms a sufficient justification for the
peculiar use of the name in modern times. In *Soph. El.*
I. 6, he says, Ἔστι γὰρ ἡ σοφιστικὴ φαινομένη σοφία οὖσα
δὲ μὴ, καὶ ὁ σοφιστὴς χρηματιστὴς ἀπὸ φαινομένης σοφίας ἀλλ᾽
οὐκ οὔσης.

The testimonies of Socrates and Xenophon need not
be specified here in detail. They will be found below in a
note, and have been admirably handled by Mr. Cope in

the Essay to which I previously alluded.[1] Only to the witness of Isocrates I call particular attention, as that of a man who was by the general bent of his mind not at all inclined to sympathize with any transcendental notions of high-strung intellectualists like Plato, and who, as himself one of the most reputable of the class of Sophists to whom Gorgias belonged, would naturally feel no inclination to bring a charge against any large section of the fraternity, which might serve to increase the natural odium that in not a few quarters had always attached to the name. His words are as follows :—(κατὰ τῶν σοφ· ἕ).

Τίς γὰρ οὐκ ἂν μισήσειεν ἅμα καὶ καταφρονήσειε πρῶτον μὲν τῶν περὶ τὰς ἔριδας διατριβόντων, οἳ προσποιοῦνται μὲν τὴν ἀλήθειαν ζητεῖν, εὐθὺς δ' ἐν ἀρχῇ τῶν ἐπαγγελμάτων ψευδῆ λέγειν ἐπιχείρουσιν ; οἶμαι γὰρ ἅπασιν εἶναι φανερὸν, ὅτι τὰ μέλλοντα προγιγνώσκειν οὐ τῆς ἡμετέρας φύσεώς ἐστιν, ἀλλὰ τοσοῦτον ἀπέχομεν ταύτης τῆς φρονήσεως, ὥσθ' Ὅμηρος ὁ μεγίστην ἐπὶ σοφίᾳ δόξαν εἰληφὼς καὶ τοὺς θεοὺς πεποίηκεν ἔστιν ὅτε βουλευομένους ὑπὲρ αὐτῶν, οὐ τὴν ἐκείνων γνώμην εἰδὼς ἀλλ' ἡμῖν ἐνδείξασθαι βουλόμενος, ὅτι τοῖς ἀνθρώποις ἓν τοῦτο τῶν ἀδυνάτων ἐστίν.

Οὗτοι τοίνυν εἰς τοῦτο τόλμης ἐληλύθασιν, ὥστε πειρῶνται πείθειν τοὺς νεωτέρους, ὡς, ἢν αὐτοῖς πλησιάζωσιν, ἅ τε πρακτέον ἐστὶν εἴσονταὶ καὶ διὰ ταύτης τῆς ἐπιστήμης εὐδαίμονες γενήσονται. καὶ τηλικούτων ἀγαθῶν αὐτοὺς διδασκάλους καὶ κυρίους καταστήσαντες οὐκ αἰσχύνονται τρεῖς ἢ τέτταρας μνᾶς ὑπὲρ τούτων αἰτοῦντες. ἀλλ' εἰ μέν τι τῶν ἄλλων κτημάτων πολλοστοῦ μέρους τῆς ἀξίας ἐπώλουν, οὐκ ἂν ἠμφισβήτησαν, ὡς οὐκ εὖ φρονοῦντες τυγχάνουσι, σύμπασαν δὲ τὴν ἀρετὴν καὶ τὴν εὐδαιμονίαν οὕτως ὀλίγου τιμῶντες, ὡς νοῦν ἔχοντες διδάσκαλοι τῶν ἄλλων ἀξιοῦσι γίγνεσθαι. καὶ λέγουσι μὲν, ὡς οὐδὲν δέονται χρημάτων, ἀργυρίδιον καὶ χρυσίδιον τὸν πλοῦτον ἀποκαλοῦντες, μικροῦ δὲ κέρδους ὀρεγόμενοι μόνον οὐκ ἀθανάτους ὑπισχνοῦνται τοὺς συνόντας ποιήσειν.

---

[1] The contrast between the doctrine of Socrates and that of the Sophists, in reference to the origin of moral distinctions, is shown distinctly in the discussion between the former and Hippias, in Xen. *Mem.* iv. 4. 13 ; and in the same work, i. 2. 6, the well-known objection to receiv-ing μισθός for teaching morality, is stated by Socrates exactly as in Plato. Xenophon's own opinion is expressed very strongly in the last chapter of the treatise *De Venatione :* "Οἱ δὲ σοφισταὶ δ' ἐπὶ τῷ ἐξαπατᾶν λέγουσι, καὶ γράφουσιν ἐπὶ τῷ ἑαυτῶν κέρδει, καὶ οὐδένα οὐδὲν ὀφελοῦσι, κ.τ.λ."

(4.) With regard to the moral teaching of the Sophists, Mr. Grote is quite right when he says that such an un-blushing assertion of the doctrine that might is right, as is propounded by Callicles in the *Gorgias*, however wel-come to Dionysius in his rocky hold at Syracuse, would have been anything but agreeable to the Athenian de-mocracy.   But it is not necessary for those who consider that the Sophists were bad, and sometimes very bad moral guides, to maintain that they went about every-where advocating despotic principles.   Protagoras, Pro-dicus, and Gorgias, and the other members of this not-able brotherhood, whatever weak points their philosophy might offer to a sharp logician, were men of the world, and not likely to commence their teaching by rubbing their audience violently against the hair.   Neither is there the slightest reason to suppose that all of them, or the majority of them, held immoral opinions with the same grand consistency with which their spokesman pro-claims them in the *Gorgias*.   The received doctrine with regard to the sophistical ethics which the learned his-torian undertakes to refute, is simply this, that by refer-ring our ideas of right altogether to institution and con-vention, and in nowise to nature and divine necessity, they sapped the foundations of all morality, and made a justification of every iniquity easy to those who chose to argue consistently on their principles.   And that there were plenty of men in Athens only too ready to carry such a doctrine to its legitimate practical conclusion, the un-principled character of many public men in Athens, from Alcibiades to Æschines, sufficiently testifies.   The char-acter of the Athenian δῆμος may be placed as high as Mr. Grote, according to a democratic ideal, finds himself war-ranted to plant it; but it was not the δῆμος properly so called, that is, the middle and lower strata of the Athenian people, by whom the principles of the slippery sophistical ethics were principally imbibed. It was the sons of the rich men, the oligarchy, the δύνατοι, that had most leisure and most ability to frequent the lectures of such men as Protagoras, and to pay their fees ; and how grandly they profited by their instructions, the oligarchic conspiracy of the four hundred in the year 411 B.C., and the government of the thirty tyrants, proclaimed to all the world with a signature of blood, whose significance Mr. Grote would be the very last man to misinterpret.

(5.) Mr. Grote's fifth argument, that the Sophists were not a sect or body of men like the Stoics and the Platonists, holding any particular set of opinions, but only a profession, like our modern literary men, critics, and reviewers, may be disposed of in a single sentence. Nobody ever said that they were a sect, but a class of men following a particular profession, and who were distinguished generally by a certain common character and principles. Of this the French Encyclopædists, to whom the Sophists have been aptly compared, were a notable example.

(6.) The matter of the μισθός, or fee which the Sophists charged for their instructions, must not be looked at from a merely modern point of view. The Sophists were not, like our professors, public servants engaged to give a certain special training to young men, either on receipt of a salary from the public, or of single fees from individual students. They came forward voluntarily with broad general professions, to fit men for public life, by teaching both the art of public speaking and all that effective speaking implies. They professed to teach the wisdom of life, the art of getting on, and especially the art of governing men in popular assemblies. This, it is evident, is a very serious matter, and very different from the attitude that belongs to any modern teacher. What they professed to do could not be done scientifically without discussing the principles of right and wrong, and teaching virtue, ἀρετή in fact as well as ῥητορική. This is the point so ably brought out in the *Gorgias*. Now, the receiving of a fee for a large profession of this kind is a very different thing from paying a price for a pair of boots to a shoe-maker, or for so many lessons in grammar to a language master. The question might be raised on the very threshold—*Can virtue be taught?* the famous question, εἰ διδακτὸν ἡ ἀρετή, discussed in the Menon and the Prota-goras; and the strongest arguments were at hand to prove that, if it was teachable at all, it certainly was not to be taught in the same way that dancing may be learned from a dancing master, or music from a music master. A man goes to a teacher of Sanscrit, for instance, gets so many hours' grammatical exposition, appropriates the cram, passes his examination, gets an Indian appointment, and reposes comfortably upon more than the value of his fee. Here there is a definite *quid* for a definite *quo*, in the most distinct and mercantile sense. But the moral teacher must go to work in a different fashion. He does not offer a marketable article, and therefore cannot expect or demand a market price. For a mere course of lectures on the virtues, with which the scholar is to be duly crammed, will not do the business; it may prove worse than useless. A moral teacher must commence with teaching the student to see his faults, to confess his errors, and to amend his way. No man comes forward with a guinea in his hand to get instruction of this kind. No man expects to be paid for giving good but disagreeable advice to a conceited coxcomb, or a pompous pretender. And, accordingly, in our Christian churches clergymen are paid, not the value of their sermons, but, like the Platonic φύλακες, they receive a general salary for their maintenance. A sermon has no market value. No man paid the Hebrew prophets for their patriotic denunciations. The Athenians paid Socrates for his life-long speaking of all truth, and exposing of all sham, with a dungeon and a cup of hemlock. I therefore think that Socrates was right in refusing to receive a fee for teaching virtue. Besides, there is an element of convention in this matter which must not be overlooked. No public man in this country is paid, or would receive payment, for serving his country as a member of Parliament ; and if Protagoras, or any other accomplished speaker, came forward in Athens professing to teach virtue for a fee, the public conscience was entitled to be offended by the novelty, and to make a strict cross-examination of the individual who made such pretentious professions. One thing is certain, that not only in Athens, but in modern England and everywhere, the public teacher who demands no fee for his services, and can be suspected of not the slightest admixture of mercenary motives, must always stand upon a moral vantage ground that the paid teacher cannot occupy. This is the secret, or part of the secret at least, of the great influence exercised by Whitfield and other zealous evangelists in the last century, who, flinging away the golden hopes of ecclesiastical preferment, devoted themselves to field preaching and missionary work among the most abandoned classes, by whom an entirely moral service could be repaid only by a moral reward.

This paper may be most fitly concluded by an articulate statement of the heads of the sophistical doctrine, as I abstract them from the works of Plato, supported by the general testimony of the ancients :—

I. General information and alert intelligence without a philosophical basis, or a scientific method of verification.

II. The art of public speaking, considered merely as a means of moving masses of ignorant men with a view to political advancement, but not necessarily connected either with pure motives, lofty purpose, or business habits.

III. The exercise of a dexterous logic, that aimed at the ingenious, the striking, and the plausible, rather than the judicious, the solid, and the true.

IV. A theory of metaphysics which, by confounding knowledge with sensation, and subordinating the general to the particular, made wisdom consist rather in the expert use of present opportunity, than in the moulding of materials according to an intellectual principle.

V. A theory of morals which, by basing right on convention, not on nature, deprived our sensuous feelings and animal passions of the imperial control of reason, and substituted for the eternal instinct of justice in the human heart the arbitrary enactments of positive law, whose ultimate sanction is the intelligent selfishness of the individual.

ON THE PRINCIPLE OF ONOMATOPŒIA IN
LANGUAGE.

By ὀνοματοποιΐα the Greek grammarians understood that principle, or tendency in the growth of language, according to which certain words are formed by an imitation of the sounds which they signify. Thus, ὀγκ, the root of ὀγκᾶσθαι, to *bray*, may be considered to have been formed by a human mimicry of the sound uttered by that animal to which human beings of the lowest cerebral capacity are familiarly compared; and in the same way, *laogh*, the Gaelic for a *calf*, seems to contain a sound to which only the throats of Highland calves, Highland chieftains, and Highland crofters are competent. The word *onomatopœia*, like some other technical terms of the old grammarians, is not particularly happy, for it means only and generally *word-making*, or rather *name-making*, and says nothing of the principle by which the special class of words in question is made. Instead of this term, therefore, I should prefer to speak of the imitative or pictorial principle in the formation of human speech; and I should contrast the whole class of words in which the operation of this principle can be traced, with another class, derived from ideas or notions about the thing to be named in the mind of the word-maker. Thus, the modern Greeks call a cock πετεινό, that is, the *fowl*, or *flying* animal, from πέτομαι, to fly; and the Latin word, *equus*, a horse, if it comes, as Professor Müller says, from the Sanscrit adjective *âshu*,

sharp or *swift*,[1] will be another word formed on the same
principle. The roots of these words I propose to call
notional roots, as contrasted with the onomatopoetic class
of roots; which I propose to call pictorial roots, or roots
formed by *phonic imitation.*

Professor Müller, in his valuable work on the *Science
of Language*, has, in both volumes, either denied altogether the existence of this class of words, or treated
them with such marked disfavour, that in his system
they do not appear at all as effective agents in the formation of reasonable speech, but merely play a subordinate
and scarcely human part in the precincts of the poultry-
yard and the pig-sty. If, in the central table-land of
Asia, before the divarication of the great Aryan races, a
Persian pig gave a grunt, the learned Professor might
perhaps be willing to admit, or might be forced to admit,
that there was some connexion in the way of mimetic
reproduction between the sound uttered by that animal
and the words γρύζω in Greek, *grunnio* in Latin, *grunt* in
English, and *grumphie* in Scotch. If, when the sacred
chickens in their cages were observed by the Roman
augurs to give forth an attenuated indication of the
approaching fates, according to their vocal capacity, and
if the speakers of the Latin dialect of the Aryan family
agreed to designate the sound then emitted by the root
pipi, familiarly known as a verb of the fourth conjugation,
pipire, with the variety *pipilare*, applied to sparrows—
in this case also, we presume, those who disown the pictorial principle would be inclined to concede some pretty
mimicry of the small unreasoning by the great reasoning animal. Or, to take an example from an altogether
different quarter, in the word "*chirumvurumvuru*, used

---

[1] See Müller ii. 65.

by the Africans on the Zambesi river to designate a
sudden violent tornado, with lightning, thunder, and rain,
who can refuse to recognise here a beautiful imitation of
the long-continued roll of peals of thunder in a mountain
district?"[1] But then they would say that in forming such
words a man acts as a parrot and not as a man; and in
the philosophy of human speech we can take no account
of an element which denies the distinctive character—
namely, reason—of the being who forms it. It is against
this view of the part played by the imitative principle of
our nature in the formation of language that I now submit
a few observations.

In treating this matter I shall first state the arguments in favour of the extensive operation of this principle, which appear to me conclusive, and then shortly
consider the nature of the objections that have been
brought against it. But, before making a regular muster
of the arguments for or against any position, it appears to
me to be of the utmost consequence to see how the presumptions lie. When a man is tried before a jury for a
special act of felonious appropriation, the fact that he is
habit and *repute* a *thief*, although no part of the evidence
on which he can be convicted, will certainly operate
against him to some extent in the minds of the most
impartial jury. In the same way, it must have been
observed that in the discussion of the most famous literary,
scientific, and philosophical questions, there is an under-
current of presumption of some kind or other, which
secretly determines which side the reasoner will take,
more powerfully than all the arguments that are articu-
lately brought forward,—a presumption of which these

---

[1] *On the Zambesi, Notes of a long Journey.* By James Stewart. (Good Words,
Feb. 1865.)

arguments are sometimes only the servile satellites. So, in the present case, I ask, first, is there any presumption why words should not be formed by the human voice, in imitation of certain sounds emitted by or connected with objects in the external world? Man has, no doubt, been well defined a reasonable, or at least a reasoning animal; but he is no less truly, and no less largely, an imitative animal. It may be said that there are more persons in the world who can give true pictures of things by word or line, than there are who can argue about them soundly; for one instance of false portraiture in common conversation, you shall have a hundred exhibitions of bad logic. From the earliest words and actions of the child to the ripest productions of dramatic genius, you have the principle of imitation constantly and intensely at work. Many a literary reputation, exercising a powerful sway over thousands and tens of thousands of delighted readers, rests in a great measure on mimicry, on what may be called a sort of *parrot* work, in the service of reason no doubt, but not at all dependent upon any high function of reason for its potency or its popularity. It has seldom been heard that the most effective mimics are the most profound reasoners; and, on the other hand, a profound reasoner is often found deficient in that vivid power of imitating the striking points of detail which is the strength of the popular novelist, and the best spice of convivial conversation. There is therefore no presumption against the action of this so universal principle in the formation of language, but rather the contrary. And if the element by which sounds in the external world are signified in human speech is itself sound, how should we more naturally expect the one to express the other, than by some sort of imitation, more or less complete, according to the

character of the vocal organ ? I go then to nature, prepared to expect imitative phenomena in human speech ;
and I find them, not one here and one there, but everywhere in the richest abundance. Can any one hear the
English words *smash, dash, thump, dumb, squeak, creep,
clatter, chatter, click-clack, ding-dong, sigh, sob, moan,
groan, hurry-skurry, skimble-skamble, wiggle-waggle,* and
not believe that these words were framed by the human
voice, with the express intention, more or less successfully
realized, of giving a dramatic representation of the thing
signified ? This is so obvious, that, as already stated,
Professor Müller has been forced to admit it, to a certain
extent ; but, at the same time, watches with the sternest
jealousy that the action of such a principle shall not be
allowed to travel beyond the narrow precincts of the
poultry-yard and the pig-sty. But, however he may
wish to circumscribe the action of the principle, it is quite
certain that it operates, not only most powerfully in the
low region here indicated, but that this pictorial power of
words is one of the most powerful instruments by which
human speech is made to affect the human imagination,
and an instrument in the skilful wielding of which one of
the great merits of a great poet has always been felt to
consist. When, for instance, Homer says :—

Δουπῆσεν τε πεσὼν ἀραβῆσε δὲ τεύχεα ἐπ' αὐτῷ—
" *With a hollow sound he smote the ground, and his armour rattled o'er him ;*"

or Goethe—

> " *Aus dem hohlen dunklen Thor
> Drängt sich ein buntes Gewimmel hervor,*"

every one feels that the poet, under the influence of the
rhythmical instinct which is an expression of reason, is
only using the materials of language for producing an

æsthetical effect, on the same imitative principle by which
these materials themselves were originally framed. And
we can prove the actual making of words on this principle
from observation. A happy father calls his child " *little
goo-goo !* " Why ? Because the little creasy-armed,
chubby-faced Hopeful has a throat, and *g* is a guttural
letter ; and, therefore, as naturally as a chicken cries *pip,
pip,* the baby sends forth *goo-goo,* as the first notice of its
march into the realm of articulate speech ; and the delighted parent, by the exercise of the parrot faculty, immediately forms a name for his son, which might have
remained for ever, as the only name it should get, did not
the conventional rights of baptism interfere, not to mention the long prescriptive claim in favour of *baby* and *boy,*
which the labial letters from old Greek and Roman days
have succeeded in establishing against the guttural. For
I certainly do believe, whatever may be said to the contrary, that the Hebrew word *em,* the Greek μαῖα and
μήτηρ, the German *Amme,* and the common English *ma',
pa',* and *baby,* have something to do with the use of the
labial letters, so natural to the toothless gums of children,
and so obvious in the cries of certain animals. Of the
consonants indeed, which brutes use to modify their vocal
cries, of which the vowel is always the grand element, the
labials and gutturals, along with the snarling R, the rolling L, and the sibilant S, seem to be the most common.
We shall not therefore be surprised to find an ox called
Bo in Latin, Greek, and Gaelic, or to hear the bellow of
oxen called μυκᾶσθαι in Greek, while the bleat of sheep is
called μηκᾶσθαι, and the cry of goats in German *meckern,*
for which last I do not know that we have a specific word
in English. And if the Greeks say ὑλακτῶ for the bark of a
dog, it is not because their language is not mimetic in this

case, while ours certainly is, but because ὑλακτῶ is merely
a lengthened derivative form of the root ὑλ, which is only
a feebler form of our English *howl*, German *heulen*. In
the same way, that the letter R in the Greek κορώνη, the
Latin *corvus*, the Hebrew עֹרֵב, and the English *crow*, has
something to do with the sound uttered by that class of
animals, I shall continue to believe, so long as in the
world of animated voice neither swallows shall have been
heard to grunt on the eaves, nor pigs to twitter in the
sty, nor bulls to mew in Bashan, nor cats to bellow at
the old English gentleman's fireside.

Let so much therefore be allowed,—be held as admitted,—though not without manifest unwillingness, by
those who disown the principle we now advocate. But
now comes the more important question, for the sake of
which alone the preceding examples have been given, as
a sort of postulate, rather than as demanding proof. Is
this all ? If only a few names of animals, and certain
phenomena in nature always accompanied by sound, are
to be explained by the principle of pictured articulation,
we are advanced but a very short way, and the great body
of the roots of a language, expressing not *sounds* but
notions, remains unexplained. When I express the idea
of thinking in Latin by the root *med*, in Greek by μητ,
and in Sanscrit by *man*, what possible connexion can such
words have with screaming, or grunting, or twittering, or
with the cry of any unreasoning animal ? For man, as a
reasoning animal, must have a method of proceeding in
forming his language, altogether different from the procedure which would suffice for unreasoning brutes ; his discourse is not only φωνή, mere *voice*, but it is λόγος, that
is simply the outside of reason, and expressed in Greek
(as all the world knows) by the word which likewise

signifies reason.   Depend upon it, all the important roots
of a language must be *notional;* otherwise, we suppose
man acting without reason, and our philosophy sinks into
the lowest sensationalism of the French school of the last
century.

Now, before answering this argument, I must again
protest distinctly against the presumption here implied,
that the assertion that we do anything without the intervention of conscious notions and ideas is degrading to
man, and ignores that reason which is his characteristic.
We eat, drink, sleep, love, hate, dance, fly into sublime
passions, and write lofty poetry, not without reason,
indeed, but certainly in nowise by virtue of consciously
worked out products of reason, called abstract ideas.   If
it should be found, therefore, that certain words denoting
mental action are only a secondary application of words
originally painting an outward mechanical action or position, or even a mere sound, I see nothing to be ashamed
of in the matter.   A man may make himself a pig, or
worse than a pig in many ways, but certainly not merely
by painting a pig-sty or by ventriloquizing a grunt, or
even by borrowing a grunt, for the expression of some
moral or metaphysical idea.   The degradation to a reasonable being in the matter of language consists, not in the
borrowing from physical sources, but in not submitting
the borrowed physical material to a native metaphysical
treatment.

This premised, we remark that it is a known tendency
of language to grow, not by the creation of new roots,
when they are not necessary, but by a dexterous use of
the stock already acquired.   In harmony with this fact,
we have a right to suppose that the original framers of
language having succeeded, by the principle of phonic

imitation, in making a vocabulary to express the sounds made by animals or sounding bodies, and the related names by which these should be known, would not stop here, but would proceed to apply the same principle to a much wider and more important range of ideas. Nor was the stepping-stone far to seek, by which they soon learned to pass from the domain of single imitated sounds to that of actions generally, and of all sorts of ideas. For if we attend to the process of nature, in such cases, we shall observe three facts which would necessarily help, from the original stock of strictly pictorial words imitating mere sounds to work out a large class of words, including all the most important verbs, which language in its early stages required. The first of these facts is, that most actions which attract the notice of men are, in the first place, accompanied by certain sounds or noises, which serve to indicate the approach, and to express the manner and intensity of the movement. The second fact is, that between sounds and certain feelings and ideas, not accompanied by any sound, there are certain strong analogies, such as that which the blind man indicated, when he said that he thought scarlet colour was like the sound of a trumpet ; and these analogies, taken advantage of by the dexterous and economic framers of language, would necessarily lead to the designation of a number of ideas expressive of noiseless vision or touch, by words possessing some vocal and audible analogy. The third fact is, that all external impressions made upon our senses, which, if not the cause, are certainly one of the necessary factors of all human knowledge, never take place without the production of certain pleasant or unpleasant feelings, and a certain affection of the nervous system, on which the utterance of articulate sound depends ; and as effects always correspond to causes, it cannot but be that the vocal utterance from within educed by any strong impression from without, shall in some way or other represent the character of the source from which it sprang. Let us examine these three facts separately, and see to what classes of results in the formation of language they unavoidably lead. Take the word *Kill* to begin with. You ask what connexion is there between the sound of this word and the action signified? I reply, that I do not know, because there are many words in all languages, derivative both in meaning and form, whose original type is not now recoverable; but there is another *English* word, *Slay*, signifying the same thing, the original form of which is the German word *Schlagen*, to *strike*, and here I distinctly see a phonic congruity between the rough action signified and the rough word *Schlag*, by which it is expressed. The act of striking is generally accompanied by a hard, sharp noise; and so, hard, sharp syllables, as in the English words, *knock*, *rap*, are used to express that act. Or take the Sanscrit root MAR, of which Müller has made so much, and who does not see that it expresses something rude and harsh, as much as the English word *crush*, and the French word *écraser*? In the same way the root AR, signifying to plough, and which appears in the Hebrew הָאָרֶץ the earth, as well as in the Greek adverb ἔραζε, is evidently a phonetic expression of the rough sound of earth or gravel when stirred, containing a combination of letters which appears in *gravel*, *grain*, γράφω, *scratch*, χαράσσω, and other the like words.

In the same way, actions accompanied by slender soft sounds are expressed by weak vowels, as to *creep*, to *sneak*, and to *shirk*. Is it not also plain, that whether we take the Greek κλέπτω or the English *steal*, we find that these words are so formed as to present a dramatic contrast to ἁρπάζω and *rob*, which signify the same kind of abstraction, accompanied with violence and noise ? And if you say that the Latin *fūr* does not express anything of this kind, I thank you for the observation, and reply that the Greek verb φωράω, from which *fūr* is derived, does not originally imply the silent stealthiness of felonious appropriation, but rather the sudden, rude act, by which a thief is apprehended. Contrast with these words the English word *tumble*, and you will observe that the awkward, clumsy, hollow roll with which the act of accidental falling is generally accompanied, finds expression here to such a degree that the words to *tumble* and to *stand* seem as much opposed to one another as a round rowley-powley pudding is to the sharp, thin, clear knife which cuts it. And this brings me to my second great fact—Why has the word *knife* a *k* in it? Why the Gaelic *sgian*, why the Latin *culter* ? Is this altogether accidental ? Certainly not. K is a sharp letter, perhaps the sharpest in the alphabet, and therefore in all languages appears in words which signify sharpness, as in the Latin word *acies*, Greek ἄκρος, Sanscrit *kärt*, to *cut*, with which the Latin *cædo*, and probably the Gaelic *cath*, a *battle*. The Greek κόπτω contains the same initial letter, although from the intrusion of the labial π it is a less perfect word to express a clean, sharp stroke than the simple dental which appears in the other roots. For the labials, being uttered by rounded, unpointed organs, are naturally used to express bluntness, as the very word *blunt*, Greek ἀμβλύς, plainly proves. Hollow vowels and soft consonants will in all cases be applied to express the reverse of what is sharp and thin. So *tundo* in Latin is to beat, not sharply, like our word *rap*, but broadly and bluntly, as with a mallet. Hence

obtundere aures, to bore a person with talking, to be
constantly beating, and thumping, and drumming your
crotchets upon the tympanum of his ear.   So, when a
man's intellect is not very sharp, he is said to be *muddled*
or *fuddled ;* and if muddled is only a verbal form of *mud*,
you will easily understand that something soft, broad,
round, not at all clear, and not very stable, is understood by the verb as well as by the noun.   We thus see
how not only sound, but everything perceptible to vision
or to touch—that is to say, the whole range of pheno-
menal knowledge—comes under the derided principle of
ὀνοματοποιία ; and if there can be any stronger proof given
of the unlimited range of articulate sound, in mimetically
expressing things which have nothing to do with sound,
the English word *mum*, for silence, contains that proof.
M is the labial which most completely closes the lips, and
sends the breath up through the nose ; hence it appears
in the Latin *mutus*, the Greek μύω for closing or shutting,
not the mouth, but the eyes, and in the English *dumb*,
which in German is *dumm*, stupid, because stupid people
have often the sense to sit silent in company, and thus
not betray their stupidity.   I conclude these illustrations
of the second of the three great facts by a remark on the
word *stand*, previously used.   This word, which is a bas-
tard present, formed from the old past tense, like the
Alexandrian Greek στέκω, has for its root the Sanscrit
sthâ, in Latin *stare*.   Now, any one may see that this
word stands more firmly on its legs than the word *tumble*,
with which we contrasted it.   Why is this ?   There is no
firmness or decision in any part of this word, just as in
the cognate word *mumble* there is a plain want of deter-
minative emphasis in the conglomeration of the letters.
But when I say *sta*, I bring my teeth together with a

decision which shows that I am suiting the word to the action, and that the firmness which I exhibit in the muscles of my legs is not to be accompanied with any looseness in the action of my jaws. And that this is not a mere fancy will be obvious to any one who considers the wide application which this combination of letters enjoys in words expressive of strength and decision in all languages. Thus in English, *stop, strength, strike, stride, sturdy, start;* in Greek, στράγγω, στρέφω, στρήνης, στρυφνός, στέμβω, most of which have their Latin representatives, as *stringo, strenuus, stipo.* So in German, *starr, streng, stössig;* and many others. There remains now, to complete the pictorial process by which language is formed, the third fact mentioned above—according to which all external expressions necessarily affect in a certain way the whole nervous system and mental economy, and through the motion in the vital spirits thereby produced, modify in a corresponding way the articulation of human speech. Here we have a different principle altogether, as it would appear at first sight, from mere ὀνοματοποιία; for to imitate an internal sound, and to express an internal feeling, seem not only different, but quite contrary actions. Nevertheless, they are in their effects, as in their origin, substantially one; and Professor Müller has accordingly put what he calls the Pooh! pooh! theory as much under his ban as the Bow-wow! For the fact of the matter is, that an interjection, such as *ah!* or οἴμοι, or *eheu*, and all such vocal expressions of pleasure or pain, must, by the laws of vitality, exhibit a certain correspondence with the sensations of which they are the expression. Thus any oppressive, heavy feeling in the chest will naturally cause a slow, protracted, dull flow of breath to proceed from the throat. The vowels *a* and ω, the diphthongs *ai* and *oi*, are exactly such a flow of breath. Hence the interjections ω, αι, οι, amplified into the verbs ὤζω, αἰάζω, οἰμώζω.

There is here, therefore, a sort of natural drama enacted—a correspondence of the *within* and *without*—which springs fundamentally out of the same root as the ὀνοματοποιΐα proper. When Aristotle called all poetry mimetic, he probably meant something of this kind; for while dramatic poetry only is strictly imitative of outward objects, lyric poetry is dramatically expressive of inward feelings; and to this the *Bow-wow* and the *Pooh! pooh!* departments of early word-making plainly correspond.

If we now inquire what the objections are that are brought against these facts, indicative of the operation of the pictorial principle in the world of vocal utterance, we find that they require no very laboured refutation, but resolve themselves into a few misunderstandings and prejudices, which a single touch can brush aside. In the first place, if it ever was asserted by any writer that all the presently existing roots in any language are onomatopoetic, and that all current words are to be explained on this principle alone, with such assertion I have nothing to do. I only maintain that the original stock of which language was made up consisted of such roots, and that a great proportion of them, after the changes of thousands of years, bear their origin distinctly on their face. I do not say, however, that all the words now existing in a language are to be dealt with on the supposition that they contain some pictorial element of the original phonic drama of human speech. Syllables are like sixpences, and are apt to be rubbed down in the course of time, till their original image and superscription can no more be traced.

Besides, as in the Greek language the word ἀδελφός, signifying *uterinus,* or born of the same womb, took the place of φράτωρ, which no doubt originally was used as *frater* in Latin, *bhrâtar* in Sanscrit, and *brother* in English, so many of the oldest dramatically significant roots of language may have been replaced by secondary roots, in which the real character that belonged to the first pictorial roots is lost. I do not therefore deny that *equus* may come from the root *ashu* to be *swift,* and a horse signify the swift animal; and though I have no doubt that *bo,* an ox, is merely a human imitation of the bovine sound, I by no means insist that all animals should have received their names from the cries which they make. I only say that, in the original formation of language, this was one of the simplest and most obvious methods of designation, and a method that extended a great deal further than superficial observation might lead the modern speculator to believe.

As little can I see why Professor Müller should feel it his duty to declare war wholesale against onomatopœia in language, because on this or the other occasion some men have handled it wildly, and ridden rough-shod with it over Grimm's law, and the whole body of ascertained facts with regard to phonic transmigrations and transmutations. A man may talk ingenious nonsense on any branch of philological science with the utmost ease, in the teeth of Grimm's law, or even with the help of it; but that great principle of interlingual change has nothing to do with the question how roots, variable according to certain laws of phonic change, were originally formed. The Sanscrit *pitar* may become the English *father,* and the Scotch *faether,* without touching the question whether *PA* and *MA* have anything to do with imitation by

parents of the first untutored labial utterances of a child.
Finally, I must be allowed to express my conviction that
I apprehend the opposition to onomatopœia arises in the
minds of some speculators partly from a certain horror
of a sort of merely animal element in the creation of
language, which in ancient times had found acceptance
with the low sensuous philosophy of Epicurus,[1] and
partly, so far as the Germans are concerned, from a certain instinct in them which leads them to prefer what is
remote to what is obvious, what is conceptional to what
is sensational, what is fanciful to what is real, what is
mystical to what is plain.   If they blame us, not unjustly
altogether, for having no ideas in our scholarship, we may
with equal reason retort that they have too many, and
use them often with a wild ingenuity, rather than with a
sober discretion.   If we do not make such brilliant discoveries as they do beyond the flaming walls of the universe, we do not, on the other hand, so often fail to see
what lies directly before our nose.   The same national habit
of thought which led Forchhammer to find in the *Iliad* a
geological account of the struggle betwixt land and water
in the Troad, and leads Professor Müller to discover in
the same great historic tradition a mythological fight between light and darkness, seems to determine the position of this distinguished philologer, in reference to the
original formation and growth of roots in language.   How
they were formed he nowhere tells us ; he does not pretend to know ; but of one thing he feels assured, that
there is more of mystery in the matter than the easy
mimicry of natural sounds can explain.   " Are not Abana
and Pharpar rivers of Damascus ? may I not wash in

---

[1] Müller, vol. ii. p. 87, quotes a passage of Epicurus as having sug- gested his soubriquet of the *Bow-wow* theory.

them and be clean?" He will have nothing to do with word-painting, because it is too simple a process, seems to deal with facts rather than with ideas, and is not at all mysterious. For my own part, I think all is mysterious with language in one sense, nothing in another. It is as natural for men to speak as for birds to sing and fountains to flow; and that, when they did speak, they spoke originally from the imitation of natural sounds, and a cunning adaptation of the expressive power of the audible element, not only to things audible, but also to things visible and tangible, I shall continue to believe till some principle shall be propounded that may explain all known facts in a manner equally obvious and satisfactory.

I have only to say in conclusion, that my faith in imitation as the great principle in the formation of the original stock of human speech is not in any degree affected by the vexed question whether man was originally created full-grown or a baby, whether he made language for himself, or got it, as some think there is a peculiar piety in imagining, ready-made from the Deity. I do not believe that Adam got language ready-made from his Creator, for the very plain reason that we get nothing ready-made from the Creator, but we make it ourselves after a fashion, by the indwelling power of His infinite virtue and grace, who is never far from the meanest of His creatures. But even if the Supreme Being did make a present to our primal sire of a ready-made language (though I think this contrary to the words of Moses in Genesis ii. 19), still the fact remains that the grand vocal organism so presented bears on its front the most evident marks of an onomatopoetic or imitative construction. Those, therefore, who hold that God made human language must maintain that He made it on the same principle on which I maintain that man made it; for the facts are undeniable, and surely it cannot be more pious to suppose that the Father of all men coined words for the use of His reasonable children in a manner altogether arbitrary, rather than on the principle of a reasonable congruity, and a beautiful adaptation.

ON THE SPARTAN CONSTITUTION AND THE AGRARIAN LAWS OF LYCURGUS.

THE peculiar institutions and laws which go under the name of Lycurgus—in some respects a wonder and a problem to the ancients themselves—have in recent times received a very full and detailed discussion from some of the most distinguished scholars of Germany and England. Foremost among these, of course, is to be mentioned Ottfried Müller, in his great work on the Dorians; then, particularly, the historico-archæological disquisitions of C. F. Hermann and Schoemann; with the admirable summing-up the results of these investigations in the historical works of Curtius and Duncker. In our own country, after the solid and substantial substructure of Thirlwall, ground was broken by Dr. Arnold in one of the notes to his *Thucydides,* and the views there set forth were carefully sifted, and the whole question stated with complete originality and independence by the late Sir George C. Lewis in an essay in the *Cambridge Philological Museum.* After this, Mr. Grote, in the second volume of his great historical work, propounded his views on the Spartan institutions generally, with great originality and boldness, and specially on the famous Agrarian laws. After such labours of such men, it seems not unreasonable to think that we may have now arrived at some certain and indisputable conclusions, on which those who read Aristotle, Isocrates, and Xenophon some two thousand years ago, could only have very misty apprehensions. It is the intention of this discourse, accordingly, shortly to review the results which, in this most interesting field of archæological research, we seem to have arrived at; and in doing so, the method which I shall adopt is to state shortly, in the first place, the undisputed points in reference to the Spartan Constitution—that is, such points as all well-instructed scholars, being men of sound judgment, and not hunters after novelty, are now agreed on; and in the second place, to discuss in detail one of the most characteristic of the Spartan institutions, which is still lying under the severe ordeal of Mr. Grote's sceptical reprobation, and which, therefore, cannot be considered as undisputed among European scholars.

Among the undisputed points I notice the following :—

1. The political constitution of Sparta was a broad aristocracy, limited to some extent by regal rights and usages, but in no degree modified by popular influence in the modern, or even in the Roman or Athenian, sense of that term. By a *broad* aristocracy, I mean a large corporation of privileged proprietors, varying from 10,000 to 2000, with a monopoly of political power, exercised indeed by different individuals in different degrees, but altogether exclusive of the great mass of the population, who were politically null, as much, or rather a great deal more than the unenfranchised class in this country, because they were in no sense recognised as members of the body politic, were never appealed to even in the most distant way, and had no influence of any kind in public affairs. This

broad aristocracy was, in fact, the whole Spartan people, who, as Dr. Arnold properly expressed it, were " a nation of nobles,"—a brotherhood of privileged warriors, permanently encamped in a country whose native population they treated as a nullity, as much as the laity is ignored by the clergy of the Romish church. The only limitation to which the great power of this aristocracy was subject is found in the influence of the kings ; and this, connected as it was with the great element of religion and the important functions of war, must, when assisted by the weight of personal character, have often been considerable. Nevertheless, monarchy in Lacedæmon, weakened as it was by the general strength and breadth of the aristocracy, and also by the early splitting of the undivided Homeric kingship into two—itself the strongest proof of the great strength of the old aristocracy—never could have been in a position to stamp a permanently distinctive character on the constitution. Its proper type always was aristocracy : a " close, unscrupulous, and well-obeyed oligarchy," according to Mr. Grote, if any person prefers this phraseology.

2. The Spartan privileged class—that is, the whole Spartan people, so far as the rights of citizenship were concerned—were wont to meet for the management of public affairs in two bodies : the one general, called ἐκκλησία, of which the members, though select as respects the whole population, might be called a δῆμος or πλῆθος, as respects the more select body chosen out of their members ; the other the γερουσία, or senate of elders, an elective body chosen by the general mass from the members of their own body, of the greatest social weight and influence, being not less than sixty years of age. This γερουσία may just be regarded as a standing committee of the

privileged classes, constantly renovated from the general
mass by a law of merit and seniority, and intrusted with
the exclusive right of discussing all important public
questions, and proposing all legislative measures in the
first place.   In this body, therefore,—as any person practically acquainted with the working of political machinery
will at once divine—lay the real power of the government
in Lacedæmon : at least when the constitution acted nor-
mally, and was not disturbed, as it was liable to be, either
by the arbitrary power of the ephors—of which anon—or
by the preponderant personality of an energetic monarch.
As for the larger assembly—the ἐκκλησία, though by the
theory of the constitution possessing the supreme power
in the last resort—exactly after the Homeric type, so
familiarly known from the amusing scene in *Iliad*, ii.—yet
it played a very subordinate part in Spartan politics, and
makes little figure in Greek history, manifestly because its
interests and feelings were represented by its own best
members, who regularly passed into the γερουσία at the
very age when their weight as public counsellors had
reached its acme.   An opposition between the two divisions of the Spartan privileged class, such as exists in our
country between the House of Commons and the House of
Lords, never did exist, and never could exist ; because the
Spartan lower-house was in fact a house of nobles, and the
upper-house was only a select standing-committee of the
lower-house.   Anything, therefore, like popular or democratic assemblies, in our sense of the word, anything like
hostile parties within the mass of the governing body,
anything in the shape of popular measures, popular eloquence, and champions of popular rights, was altogether
unknown in Sparta.   In this regard, Professor Curtius
does not overstate the matter when he says that, " though

the Spartan people had no laws or public measures of any kind thrust upon them without their concurrence, yet, as a rule, they did not govern ; they were governed." For this reason, in the annals of their public life we hear of no Olympian Pericles, no brilliant Alcibiades, no impetuous Demades, no terrible Demosthenes, not even a correct and polished, well-balanced, well-washed, well-anointed, well-combed, well-brushed, and altogether well-bred Isocrates. They had no political literature.

The ephors, who, like the Roman tribunes, from small beginnings rose to a power that often overshadowed the kings, and even overrode the senate, have a very mysterious aspect to the student who first begins to look into the details of the Spartan government machine. But, on a little consideration, now that all the available evidence has been carefully collected, it appears to me that there cannot be the slightest doubt as to the true origin of the extraordinary authority which, at certain periods, they exercised in public affairs. The ephoralty arose from the necessity of providing a field for the energies of ambitious and adventurous young Spartans in the time of peace. The law that no person should become a senator till the ripe and safe age of sixty was for purposes of aristocratic conservation unquestionably a very wise one. But even in the most firmly-compacted aristocracies there are combustible and explosive elements which must be provided for ; and these elements exist nowhere so strong as in the hearts of young men of talent and energy. Now, in our country, the House of Commons presents exactly the sort of arena which is best adapted at once to gratify the ambition and test the capacity of such active spirits. But in Sparta, as we have seen, the ἐκκλησία could perform no such functions ; therefore, instead of public speaking and

parliamentary tactics, a sort of overseership and censor-
ship—first in smaller, and then gradually extending to
more important matters—was laid open to the adventurous and ambitious among the young Spartans, in which
field of executive activity they might blow off their
steam in time of peace, and feel that they wielded a
power in certain important matters which not even the
king or the senate could treat with contempt.   A free
career being thus laid open to the young men and the less
influential aristocracy, the ἐκκλησία was in all respects
qualified to play that acquiescent and innocent part which
it played in Spartan history.   It became, in fact, politically null; not because it had no rights, but because
there was no need for exercising its rights.   In this way
it came about that Sparta, for the space of four hundred
years, exhibited to wondering Greece the most notable
pattern of a stable conservative government, without any
disturbing opposition, that ancient history knew.   In
fact, with such a perfectly satisfied broad aristocracy, if
there arose at any time any opposition to the government,
it was either in the shape of absolute mutiny and revolt
among the helots, and unrecognised subject-classes, or in
the shape of conspiracy amongst some of the Spartans
proper, who had lost their franchise by default, that is,
either by not having conformed to the social regulations
of Lycurgus, or by not possessing the necessary property
qualification, and who were therefore no longer ὅμοιοι,
peers among peers.   Of such a conspiracy we have a well-
known example in the case of Cinadon, which took place
at the commencement of the reign of Agesilaus, B.C. 398.
The proceedings connected with the quashing of these
mutinies and conspiracies reveal to us the weak point of
the Spartan government.   A numerous subject-population,

absolutely without political rights, can be governed only by fear, and is kept in check, partly by that unity of counsel and action which belongs to all well-organized governing bodies, partly by a system of secret police, and secret execution, in that arbitrary form which is always the plague-spot of the government which employs it, and which, in the case of Sparta, was distinguished by acts of bold unscrupulousness and cold-blooded atrocity, surpassed by nothing that modern records present in the annals of Rome, Naples, Paris, or Madrid.

On the whole, therefore, we see, that notwithstanding the confessedly beneficial effect of the severe physical and moral training to which the young Spartans were subjected, the results of their political system were not such as to present a purely aristocratic government in a particularly attractive light. The Spartan system made good soldiers, drilled and maintained in notable efficiency, a small compact people of privileged proprietors brave in the use of their swords ; but it altogether failed to produce a great people. In external form only, to the superficial eye the Spartan constitution exhibits that mixed form of government com-posed of the three natural elements of king, lords, and commons, which the wisest of the ancients looked on as the best possible government ; but there was, in reality, no people, no liberty, no movement, and no enterprise. What we find instead of a great, strong, free, and happy people, is a very manly and vigorous, severely-trained, well-disciplined, and thoroughly effective aristocracy ; but an aristocracy altogether unfit to go beyond the narrow territorial limits within which it grew up, and no more qualified to produce the highest type of cultivated humanity, than the institutions of Plato's paper republic, the red-tape and pipe-clay ordinances of last century

Q

Berlin bureaucracy, or the religious exercitations of a Jesuits' college in Madrid or Rome.

So much seems undisputed. I shall now notice two points of considerable importance in the Spartan political and social organization, which, considering the weighty names who have advocated opposite views in regard to them, must be looked on as yet *sub judice* in the world of learned research. The first of these points relates to the true nature and character of those Spartans who were called ὅμοιοι, *Equals* or *Peers*. With regard to these, the late Sir G. C. Lewis, in the *Philological Review* (vol. ii. p. 64), has advanced a theory that they were in all probability " an aristocratical class within the body of the Spartans who were much employed in public offices, and had great influence with the government, originally, perhaps, selected for their merit; and afterwards their rank became hereditary." This theory has been controverted by Professor Schoemann, in an able paper in his *Opuscula Academica;* and without going into the detail of the argument, I shall only here state generally, that the passages in which mention is made of these ὅμοιοι in the Greek classics are few and incidental, and that, after a careful examination of them all, I have come to the conclusion that there is no sufficient ground in the existing authorities for the theory advanced by the learned English statesman ; and that, if we take the evidence as we have it, without adding to it in the way of conjecture, we must just simply say that the *peers* were all the Spartans who had not lost their property or other qualification. Equality, indeed, and a sort of democracy within themselves, was an essential characteristic of society in Sparta—ἰσονομία and δημοκρατία παρὰ σφίσι in the very words of Isocrates (*Panath.* 270, c.) ; and the formation of a class of superior

hereditary privileged peers, in our sense of the word, is
not to be assumed without the strongest reasons, in the
face of the plain presumptions to the contrary, arising out
of the whole constitution of oligarchy in Sparta.

But the most important of the disputed points of the
Spartan social organization is that which relates to the
Agrarian Laws. On this subject the great English historian of Greece, Mr. Grote, has lately advanced a theory,
which, as it runs counter not only to all the ancient authorities, but to the weight of learned opinion in Germany,
well deserves the serious consideration of English scholars ;
the more so that, so far as I can see, the weight justly due
to that learned gentleman's authority has had a tendency
to procure a ready admission to certain brilliant sceptical
novelties, enunciated by him, in quarters where a decided
opposition, on strong conservative principles, was rather to
have been expected ; and thus the student of ancient history comes suddenly upon the somewhat singular phenomenon, that on one point at least of Hellenic research,
while such Teutonic excavators as Ottfried Müller, C. T.
Hermann, Schoemann, Curtius, and Düncker are mar-
shalled on the side of ancient tradition and authority, in
Oxford a learned professor of ancient history [1] can declare
that Mr. Grote has proved, with " irresistible force," that
all we have hitherto been taught of Agrarian laws in
ancient Sparta is a hallucination and a dream. The two
nations thus appear to be changing sides ; the compatriots
of Niebuhr have become historical conservatives, while the
countrymen of Clinton seem eager to blow away all early
history into symbolism and myth. The mere suddenness
and completeness of this rebound might seem to indicate
that the matter had not been duly sifted, and that Mr.

[1] Rawlinson's *Herodotus*, vol. iii. Appendix I.

Grote's theory has been received more from the weight due to his authority, than from an impartial consideration of the evidence. So at least it appears to me; and it shall be my object in what remains of this discourse to state in detail the real significance of the ancient authorities on the subject, and how far they are from giving any countenance to the ingenious, but, in my opinion, baseless theory of Mr. Grote. Let it be noted, however, that when I speak of Agrarian laws as an integral part of the Lycurgean organization, I do not mean to assert that the legislator introduced these laws for the first time any more than he introduced the kingship or the senate. It belongs to God to create; the highest of mortal legislators can only use existing materials. All I say is, that, on a due consideration of all the ancient authorities, which are our only safe guides in this matter, Agrarian laws must be acknowledged as, from the earliest times, part and parcel of that singular social organization which bore the name of Lycurgus. In Lycurgus, as a man and a lawgiver, and not as a myth, a symbol, or an indefinite somebody or anybody, for reasons that I cannot here state at length, I most potently believe; but I am not in the slightest degree concerned to maintain that all the characteristic Spartan laws and customs on which his name was stamped, really proceeded originally from him; much less that we are bound to accept, as his actual scheme, every minute detail of his legislation as presented to us in the highly-finished, or, as we might say, cunningly cooked accounts of late historians.

Let us now examine Mr. Grote's position. His denial of the Spartan Agrarian laws, as a historical fact, proceeds mainly on the assertion, that, while these laws are either ignored or contradicted by all the earlier and more trust-

worthy witnesses, they are asserted only by one or two recent
and less creditable authorities. This statement of the case
is certainly very plausible. It is pretty much as if he had
·said, all the eye-witnesses knew nothing about the matter
in question, only hearsay asserts it. But the nature of
the existing authorities does not allow us to dispose of
the question in this way. There are no eye-witnesses in
the case : the oldest cited, viz., Plato, lived at least four
hundred years after the great Spartan lawgiver ; and in
such circumstances mere priority in point of date is not
of itself sufficient to outweigh other and more material
considerations. Nay, even in a common question of legal
evidence, as every lawyer knows, the mere nearness of a
witness to the time in which a disputed fact took place
will not of itself be able to secure to his testimony any
peculiar preference. I shall, therefore, adopt what appears
to me the more true method of stating the evidence in a
historical question of this kind. I shall first cite those
authors who give a distinct and deliberate testimony to
the Spartan Agrarian laws, and then inquire how far their
evidence is contradicted by any testimony to the contrary.
In the first place, we have Polybius, a Greek, a native of
the Peloponnesus, and living in the times immediately
following the Agrarian agitations of the famous Spartan
kings, Agis and Cleomenes. Of his weight and judgment
in political matters no one ever expressed a doubt ; and
his testimony to the existence of equal allotments of land
in Sparta, as one of the most characteristic elements of the
Lycurgean legislation, is given in a passage (vi. 45) where
he expressly discusses political constitutions, and draws a
direct contrast between the Cretan and Spartan systems
on this very point. A more valuable witness, therefore,
on such a matter, could not be cited. Then we have

Plutarch, in his life of Lycurgus,—an author whom it is easy to call an " old wife," but who, in fact, was one of the best-read men of his day, and a man of remarkable good sense and sound judgment.   No doubt he tells many stories which, like all historical anecdotes, may have been improved in the telling, or even invented to give point to popular opinion : unquestionably also, his philosophy of history, exhibiting the whole Spartan constitution as jumping ready-made out of the brain of Lycurgus, is far from profound ; but it remains to be proved that he has ever given false representations of great historical charac-ters, or lightly stated any important historical fact.   On the contrary, I feel convinced, that, before he sat down to write his life of Lycurgus, he had read Aristotle's famous work Περὶ Πολιτειῶν now lost ; and that the very distinct evidence given by him as to the Spartan Agrarian laws must be regarded not as his testimony merely, but *as the result of the whole mass of historical evidence, including, of course, Aristotle, which he had consulted on the subject.* And here we must observe, that in talking of the Spartan Agrarian laws, we are dealing with a matter which, if it was not a mere figment, as Mr. Grote will have it, must have been as well known in ancient Greece as it is known in modern Europe that the government of the Romish church is monarchical, and that the principle of ecclesias-tical democracy is represented by the Presbyterians in Scotland.   Facts of this kind are far too deep-fixed in their roots, and far too wide-spread in their branches, to be either invented or ignored.   If they are invented, they will not be believed ; if they are believed, it is because they cannot be ignored.   To me, therefore, the testimonies of two such writers as Polybius and Plutarch, expressly handling the subject, and summing up as they

do the whole historical tradition of antiquity, are quite
sufficient to establish the existence of Agrarian laws in
ancient Sparta, although they were not supported by any
other evidence. But this is far from being the case.
Isocrates, in his Panathenaic oration, where a contrast is
distinctly drawn between Athenian and Lacedæmonian
institutions, talks expressly (270 c.) of the equality of lots
in land, which characterized the Dorians when they first
settled in the Peloponnesus, τῆς χώρας ἧς προσήκει ἴσον ἔχειν
ἕκαστον; and Plato, in the third book of his laws (684 d.)
manifestly alludes to the same state of things. I conceive, therefore, that we have the concurrent testimony of
historians, orators, and philosophers, asserting or implying
the state of things in reference to the distribution of land
in Sparta, which Mr. Grote, with such "irresistible force,"
is said to have disproved. What, then, are the authorities by which we are called on to consider that he has
successfully rebutted the weight of the positive evidence
just adduced? His great authority, manifestly, more narrowly looked at, in fact, his only authority, is Aristotle—
a name heavy enough, perhaps, to outweigh all others, if
only it shall turn out that, in the present case, his evidence
has been duly sifted and justly weighed. But how stands
the fact? The great philosopher's great book Περὶ Πολιτειῶν on "political constitutions," which, as a matter of
course, contained a detailed account of Spartan laws and
customs, exists, as we have already stated, no more; and
we have only his work on the theory of politics, in which
some points of the Spartan polity are incidentally discussed.
These discussions occur principally in the Second Book;
and it is here that Mr. Grote finds a notable passage
(ii. 6) asserting not the equality, but the extraordinary
and abnormal inequality, of property in the Spartan

territory.   Now, in order to understand this, we must
consider carefully the whole plan and scope of the book on
Politics, and interpret the Second Book with reference to
that plan.   The work is purely a theoretical investigation,
with the view of discovering the ἀρίστη πολιτεία, or what
we call the " ideal commonwealth ;" and in order to
give a proper starting-point· for such an investigation,
the philosopher has to prove in the first place that no
best republic already exists either in theory or fact ; that
the intellectual projections of Plato and the realized work
of Lycurgus are equally at fault ; and therefore that
the speculations of the philosopher are not foreclosed ;
he may safely go on reasoning out the scheme of a best
polity, without being liable to the charge of *actum agere*.
This character of the Second Book sufficiently explains its
somewhat ungracious attitude, that of systematic fault-
finding.   The writer has merely to show that the various
constitutions which he passes under review have, as a
matter of fact, proved to be failures in certain points, and
his case is made out.   Accordingly, to use a vulgar phrase,
he sets himself—and does it with manifest gusto as an
Athenian—to pick holes in the coat of Lycurgus ; and has
no difficulty in finding that the Spartan women, so often
celebrated for their patriotism and their domestic virtues,
are in fact the most extravagant, the most blushless, and
the most domineering ladies in Greece ; and that the
lands, instead of being fairly divided, are accumulated in
the hands of a very few proprietors (which accumulation
all the ancient philosophers looked on as a great social
evil), and these proprietors principally women.   And in
accounting for this abnormal state of things, he goes on
to accuse the legislator of inconsistency, in having allowed
the free disposal of landed property by testament, while

he forbade it by sale *inter vivos.* Now this way of stating the matter, not only does not seem to me to deny, but rather plainly to imply, the existence of an equal division of landed property in the early days of the Spartan ascendency. The Stagyrite speaks in this whole book of what Sparta had become in his day, not of what it was in the days of Lycurgus. He did not require to tell his readers what everybody knew, that since the days of Lysander, Sparta was no more like what it had been under Lycurgus, than king Solomon of Palestine was like Joshua or Gideon. Whatever Lycurgus might have wished to make of Lacedæmon, he had not achieved it : the boasted Spartan constitution, which Plato and Xenophon had lauded, was a manifest failure ; and whoever felt inclined to set up that as a model of the ἀρίστη πολιτεία was contradicted by the strong staring fact, worth a whole waggon of arguments.

The evidence of Aristotle being thus disposed of, Mr. Grote's case on the authorities, according to my judgment, completely breaks down. The other witnesses whom he cites, either say nothing at all on the point, or say something quite different from what Mr. Grote supposes. That there occurs occasional mention of rich men in Sparta, as well as elsewhere, is nothing to the purpose. The Spartan magnates, in the days of Herodotus and Thucydides, might have acquired wealth in various ways, altogether independently of the original equality of the landed lots, on which the exercise of the rights of citizenship depended. The mere silence of Herodotus in a passage (lib. i.), where he is only mentioning Lycurgus in the most incidental way, can have no weight ; and the defects in the slight treatise of Xenophon are so manifest, that any mere omissions can prove nothing. The testimony of Isocrates in another passage of the oration already quoted (287 b.) has not the slightest bearing on the question; for there the orator is talking not of the original tenure of landed property under the Lycurgean institutions, but of the freedom of Sparta, during a long course of four hundred years, from violent Agrarian revolutions and other social convulsions—a freedom to be attributed principally, after the general conservative character of the government, to that original equality in the division of property, which rendered future Agrarian agitation unnecessary.

If these observations are correct, the result of our examination manifestly is, that there is no historical evidence whatever against the Spartan Agrarian laws; and if Mr. Grote's sceptical rejection is to be accepted, it must be based on grounds of internal improbability, which render all external assertion superfluous. It remains now that we look at the matter shortly from this point of view.

Agrarian laws have not been fashionable in modern times—least of all in Great Britain. They are contrary to our British instinct of individual liberty, and our national habit of leaving no more power than is absolutely necessary in the hands of the central government. We are apt to look upon them, consequently, as either ideal or revolutionary; but, though some valuable discoveries have been made in history since the time of Niebuhr, by interpreting the past through the present, nothing could lead to greater mistakes in the philosophy of ancient social life, than the supposition that it was in all respects like our own. On the contrary, it is certain that in many respects it was as much as possible unlike. It is in the contrasts, not in the identities, which ancient history presents, that great part, both of its charm, and of its instructive virtue, consists. The ancient Dalmatians, we are told by Strabo (vii. 315), made a general redivision of their lands every eighth year. Are we to disbelieve this, merely because such an Agrarian custom appears to us altogether preposterous, unjust, and impolitic ? If so, we must take up David Hume's position, and believe nothing, however well attested, that is contrary to the results of that very undefined range of induction which we call our experience. We shall, therefore, say that there is nothing improbable in the idea that an ancient legislator may have assigned his citizens equal lots of land, however much such a measure may be contrary to English instincts and modern practices. And if we look at the real position of the Dorians as a comparatively small body of invaders encamped in a hostile country which they held in subjugation, we shall see the strongest argument in favour of the existence of an Agrarian law such as was popularly attributed to Lycurgus. An uncontradicted tradition asserts that after conquering the Peloponnesus, the position of the Dorians was for a considerable period extremely uncomfortable. They had the utmost difficulty in holding their ground. Now, in such circumstances, nothing could be more dangerous to the common cause than those feuds and jealousies among themselves which are wont to arise from an unequal distribution of property. As a nation of warriors, who had acquired this new territory by the sword, they had been exposed to common perils, and were entitled to a common reward. But against this law of equal natural right to the conquered territory, the cupidity and violence of individual chiefs would no doubt prevail; and the discontent hereby caused would breed exactly that state of public danger, in which the safety of all would be consulted by giving an unlimited power of arbitration to some influential person on whom all could rely. Such a national arbiter in matters between debtor and creditor, within the strictly historical period, was Solon, in Athens; such an arbiter, specially in reference to landed property, I conceive Lycurgus to have been, when he is spoken of as the author of the Agrarian laws. I do not by any means think myself bound to inquire into the probable correctness of the details of these laws as given by Plutarch; but the fact itself carries with it all the probability that the existing circumstances, the habits of thought of the ancient mind (Müller, *Dor.* ii. p. 212, English), and the analogy of certain well-known facts in modern history can confer. The secularization of church lands at the French revolution, and the law of succession to landed property then established, operated practically as an Agrarian law, tending both to prevent immense accumulations of property in the hands of individuals, and to create among the newly-constituted proprietors, a broad, permanent interest in the new state of things. An Agrarian law of a different kind was that carried out by Baron Stein in Prussia, under the pressure of the great national humiliation subsequent to the battle of Jena in 1808. On the whole, I am so far from seeing any improbability in the alleged equality of lots, which, according to the universal testimony of the ancients, characterized the Spartan public economy, that it appears to me to be only a necessary part of their general system of equality and brotherhood, within certain well-known and narrowly-drawn limits of aristocratic privilege. Among a race of proprietors as unequal as the present English nobility and gentry, a common mess, the συσσίτιον, so characteristic of Spartan life, would have been an impossibility.

With these convictions, I need hardly say that I see
no need for having recourse to that "new canon of historical criticism" which Mr. Grote (vol. ii. p. 165, edit.
1862) brings upon the stage for the sake of solving the
difficulties connected with the alleged Agrarian law of
Lycurgus. This canon, which traces the belief in this
law to the heated enthusiasm of certain interested
dreamers in the days of Agis IV. and Cleomenes (250 and
222 B.C.), appears to me merely a special application of
the thaumaturgic German fashion of creating history out
of conjectures, against which I think our British instinct
ought to lead us emphatically to protest. The habit of
dealing negatively with old national tradition and sup-
planting it by plausible theories is always flattering to the
ingenuity of scholars, but affords a very questionable basis
for anything that can be called history. For myself I do
not believe that a royal reformer such as Agis, wishing to
move the people to an acceptance of a great measure of
Agrarian reform, could do so by appealing to a mere figment, the child of yesterday's dream; but his only hope
of success must lie in his being able to clothe the startling
aspect of his revolutionary measure with all the attractions
that belong to the rebrightening of a faded memory deeply
graven in the traditional consciousness of the people.
Generally speaking, while I would willingly admit that
the outer links and flourishes of national tradition are
often invented, I do most firmly believe the trunk and
body of any deep-rooted, widely-spread popular belief to
be a fact, a material fact in the outward fates of the
nation; as the soul of it is a moral fact, often the most
important moral fact in the history of a great people.
Such facts were the battles of Bannockburn and Drum-
clog in Scotland; the Norman conquest in England; the

legislation of Moses among the Hebrews, and of Lycurgus among the Spartans; the maritime sway of Minos in the isles of the Ægean, and the brilliant despotism of the Tarquins in early Rome. Facts of this nature, and the personalities to which they are bound, possess a tenacious vitality in the continued consciousness of a nation, altogether independent of any scrolls of written record by means of which their reality may have been externally attested.

ON THE PRE-SOCRATIC PHILOSOPHY.

THE history of origins is always interesting and generally obscure; but in the case of the early Greek philosophy a sufficient number of fragments has been saved from the wreck of tradition to enable us to have a clear view of the salient doctrines of the pre-Socratic thinkers, though not certainly an accurate knowledge of the complete organism of their speculation. The pre-Homeric poetry of Greece, of the existence of which in rich abundance there can be little doubt, can be separated from the new organism into which it was worked by the genius of Homer, only by a process more or less conjectural and slippery; but on some of the most interesting and significant utterances of the school of Greek thinkers who flourished in Asia Minor, Magna Grecia, and Sicily, for the century and a half that preceded Socrates, we are able to lay our fingers with as much certainty as on the discourses of Socrates himself reported by the pious discipleship of Xenophon; and the fragments which two hundred years ago lay scattered and untested, have in recent times been so laboriously collected, critically sifted, and organically arranged by the diligent, intelligent, and sober-minded workers of erudite Germany, that it is in the power of every fairly equipped scholar to re-create, in a more or less complete form, the main features of pre-

Socratic speculation. With the aid of the learned works
of Preller, Karsten, Zeller,[1] to give a rounded completeness to the information on this subject which we gather
from Aristotle, Plato, Eusebius, Hippolytus, Clemens,
Plutarch, and Stobæus, I have set myself to present in
one broad view whatever of most general human significance and scientific interest seemed to shine clearly
out from these early speculations; and the result of my
labours is the bird's-eye view of pre-Socratic thinking
which the present discourse contains.

With regard to the whole of this early period of Greek
thought two general remarks may be made : *first*, in reference to its locality, that it is more Asiatic than European,
the Greek colonies of Asia Minor being its cradle ; and
second, with respect to its character, that in those early
times all knowledge, thinking, and feeling was less
specialized than at the present day ; in such fashion
that, if the things known and speculated on were much
fewer, the men who knew and speculated on them were
more complete. In our time the gulf that separates the
scientific from the metaphysical, the imaginative, and the
religious man, and all these from the man of business
and affairs, is often very great, and practically impassable.
The scholar will have nothing to do with physical science ;
the student of mind ignores matter ; the dissector of brain
ignores mind ; and both seem either unable or unwilling
to bridge over the space that separates the special province of cognition from the general domain of human
spiritual instincts, aspirations, and emotions. It seems
indeed the inevitable tendency of the division of labour,
while it improves and multiplies the product, to narrow

[1] Karsten : *Philosoph. Græc. Vet. Reliq. ;* Bruxelles, 1830.
Ritter et Preller : *Historia Philos. Græc. Rom. ;* Gothæ, 1869.
Zeller : *Geschichte der Griechischen Philosophie.*

and to dwarf the producer. The ancient intellect grew
up more like a rich leafy tree with many branches,
spreading themselves out towards the sun on all sides ;
the modern man is taught to live only in a straight line,
and to extend himself, as J. S. Mill says of Jeremy Ben-
tham, infinitely in one direction. He thus loses the
central point of philosophic survey altogether, or at best
works out only one idea, which he is inclined to impose
on the universal system of things, and cultivating assiduously one side of his nature, cheats himself of the beautiful symmetry and balance of a complete growth. More
particularly we must observe that the opposition betwixt
physical science and metaphysical speculation, so common
in modern times, was not known to the ancients ; their
physics was always mixed largely with metaphysics ; or
rather we are now in the habit of treating separately subjects which then had not begun to be even thought of
as separate ; the man of physical science was at the same
time a metaphysical thinker ; the materialist was also a
spiritualist; and science stood before men, not naked as
with the exposures of a cunning dissector, but festooned
with the flowers of poetry, and fragrant with the breath
of natural piety. Hence it comes that in Empedocles, for
instance, we find that complex combination of physician,
poet, priest, and politician, so difficult for us moderns to
understand. Nature was constantly speaking to those
ancient Greek sages in the language of morals ; and
morals on the other hand did not disdain to use the language of nature. That which had never been divorced
could not be looked on as antagonistic.

It is not therefore altogether true—certainly not to
be taken in a strict and literal sense—when we read that
Socrates was the father of Moral Philosophy. Pythagoras

R

was a great moralist and a pious man more than a hundred years before him ; the so-called seven wise men, as Laertius well notes, were all not merely or mainly speculative thinkers, but active citizens, and often practical statesmen, and so could not avoid making human life, and the laws of the social organism, one of their principal studies.   The social world, in fact, could no more exist without moral philosophy in some shape or other, than the physical world could grow and blossom without the sun ; and the mission of Socrates, therefore, was not so much to create a moral philosophy which had never existed before, as (1.) to protest against a habit of physico-metaphysical speculation, which wasted itself in vague conjectures, and which in the then state of scientific observation could lead to no practical result (Xen. *Mem.* i. 14, 15) ; and (2.) by putting the weapons of an exact logic into the hands of thinking men, to teach them how to vanquish scepticism on its own battle-field, and to plant morals, as practical reason, on the high vantage ground of a demonstrative science.   This characteristically Greek tendency to identify morals with reason, and right action with true thinking, appears equally in Xenophon's dialogic reminiscences, and in Plato's argumentative dialogues, as the characteristic feature of the Socratic philosophy ; and the scientific control of morals by logic is a peculiarity marked enough to draw a strong line of distinction between the gnomic morality which inspired Homer and Hesiod no less than Pythagoras, and the systematically-built-up ethics of which Socrates and Plato were the architects.

In making a rapid summation of the results of the pre-Socratic thinkers, I shall divide them, according to what appear their most distinctive characters, into three classes:

the hylozoists, the atomists, and the metaphysical or theological philosophers.

I. By the *Hylozoists* I understand those philosophers
who found the ἀρχή or first principle of things in some external, objective, visible, tangible, material element; and
yet they were not materialists in the popular sense of the
word at all; for they knew nothing of, and could scarcely
have considered that idea, so familiar to us, of a dead
matter as opposed to mind. With them all nature was
conceived as essentially alive; "all things," as Thales
said, "are full of gods" (Diog. Laert. i. 27); hence the
technical term hylozoism, or vitalized matter. With this
class of thinkers all matter was conceived of as permeated
and interfused and moulded by a divine and reasonable
power felt to be everywhere present, but spoken of only
and mainly under some favourite bodily presentation.
What the orthodox Romanist believes to have taken place
by a special miracle through sacerdotal agency in the
elements of bread and wine consecrated in the mass, this the
Hellenic hylozoist believed constantly to take place everywhere by the eternal miracle of Nature, and specially to
be manifested in the element which he looked upon as most
entitled to the dignity of ἀρχή, or original principle. The
names which fall under this first class are five, viz., Thales,
Anaximander, Anaximenes, Heraclitus, Empedocles.

Of all these the most popularly known is Thales;
though, so far as speculative significance is concerned, his
name is to us certainly not the most interesting. The
familiarity of his name to our modern ears is doubtless
owing to his historical connexion with the famous names
of Solon and Crœsus, made public property by the pleasant
pen of Herodotus. His calculation of eclipses also fixes

him as a notable mark in the history of mathematical science; while his characteristic doctrine that water, or rather fluidity, is the ἀρχή, has perhaps received an accidental advertisement of wide circulation in the well-known initial words of Pindar's *Olympian Odes*, ἄριστον μὲν ὕδωρ. The philosophical value of this maxim is not very great; yet it confessedly announced a principle which, so far as it goes, has been confirmed and strengthened by the various investigations of modern physical science. From the salt wastes of Central Asia to the compact ice wedges of the Arctic Ocean, the most superficial view of Nature proclaims that, while solidity is almost the only thing that seems absolutely dead, fluidity is always and everywhere the cradle of life. The myriad-moving life of which a drop of water is the sphere has long been one of the favourite exhibitions of our microscopic showmen; and physiologists and organic chemists have been eager to expound to admiring popular audiences how much of this "too, too solid flesh," which we call our bodies, is really composed of the liquid dew into which Hamlet wished that it might dissolve. The fecundity of the fishy tribe was another fact of superficial Nature, on which Thales is reported to have founded his doctrine; a fact which the minute observations and calculations of modern naturalists have brought into most significant prominence. Ancient mythology, also, not only in its Hellenic, but in many far-distant forms, agreed in testifying to the great part played by water in the original creation of the world. Homer (*Iliad*, XIV. 201) sang of an Olympian dynasty older than Jove,—

" OCEAN the primal father of gods, and TETHYS the mother ; "

and with this the Babylonian tradition in Berosus of

primeval "water and darkness," and the Hindu Avatar of Brahm, as Narayana (Nereus, νερὸ *Nar*), strikingly agreed.[1] The physical truth indicated in these mythologies is distinctly stated in the Mosaic record (Gen. i. 3) ; and if for the Hebrew phrase, the רוּחַ אֱלֹהִים, or *Breath of God*, we were to substitute the Divine Reason, or λόγος, any appearance of difference would be removed which to superficial observers may now seem to separate the cosmogony of Moses from that of Thales.

A disciple of Thales was Anaximander, and, like his master, a citizen of the flourishing Ionic colony of Miletus. In the doctrine of this philosopher that the ἄπειρον is the ἀρχή we find a certain departure from the general character of the class to which he belongs ; for though this ἄπειρον, the *Infinite*, or rather the *Undetermined*, was something external and objective, it differed from the ἀρχή of Thales, and the other teachers of this school, in that it was a something neither visible, nor tangible, nor cognoscible by human senses in their ordinary action. The ἄπειρον was conceived as a sort of indeterminate basis of all existence, something, perhaps, like the protoplasm of a distinguished living physiologist, containing the possibilities of all that may be, but the reality of nothing that is ; an element neither water, nor air, nor earth, nor fire, but a common matrix out of which they are developed by a process of internal differentiation. The only value of this Anaximandrian notion seems to lie not certainly in any reality which can be proved to belong to it, but rather in the truly philosophical principle which it involves, that things are not what they seem, and that what the superficial observer calls different things, are, when nicely looked into, often only different states of the same thing. What

[1] See my *Homer*, vol. iv., note to the line quoted.

profound truth lies in this view the frequent presentation under the appliances of modern chemistry of the same body under the liquid, gaseous, and solid forms, most amply demonstrates.   Beyond this, the fragments of Anaximandrian speculation possess nothing to interest the modern thinker ; except only we must by no means omit to mention his singular anticipation of the Darwinian theory of the descent of man by a process of development from the inferior animals.   This doctrine is distinctly stated as belonging to Anaximander by Hippolytus (*Ref. Hær.*, I. 6), and by Plutarch in various places, in words as we shall now translate them.

"Anaximander says that the *first animals* were gene-rated in the *liquid* element, and were enclosed in certain thin *prickly rinds* or *skins;* that as they grew they be-came more and more consolidated, till at length the shell bursting, they came out into a different form of life" (Plac., *Phil.* v. 19).

"Anaximander says that man originally was born (developed) out of different animals ; for that, while other animals, the moment they are born, know how to help themselves and procure food, man alone requires a long nursing ; and being such as he now is, could not possibly have had his life preserved in the earliest stages" (Apud Euseb., *Præpar. Evang.*, I. 8).

"Anaximander declares that man originally had his existence as a sort of FISH among FISHES, and that being nursed in a soft element, like creatures that live in the MUD, he by degrees became strong enough to help him-self, and being cast out from his original slimy home, took to the dry land, and became a terrestrial animal" (*Quæst. Sympos.*, VIII. 8).

This theory, indeed, which has so strangely startled

modern ears, was quite familiar to the Greeks, and appears in the well-known account of the Egyptian frogs crawling, half-released, from the slime of the Nile (Ælian, *V. H.* I. 3), and in not a few other quarters. In modern times, also, Lord Monboddo was not singular in directing attention to the probable indications of an original caudal appendage in man; a French writer before him had expatiated largely on the evidence for this fact, and for that other yet more remarkable one, that the sea had at one time possessed the whole dry land—at which period man, according to Anaximander's idea, was certainly a fish, and could, indeed, have existed in no other form.[1]

Anaximenes, the next link in this Milesian chain, need not detain us. By laying down the proposition that *air*, not *water*, was the ἀρχή, this thinker made a manifest step in advance; for air is certainly fluidity in its most perfect form: a form also of more subtle penetrative power than water—of more universal diffusiveness, and more essentially connected with all forms of vitality. But beyond this we find nothing in his doctrine of any peculiar significance. Far otherwise is the case with the next representative of this school, Heraclitus. He was a native of Ephesus, and from the manner in which he is constantly spoken of by the greatest of the ancients, it is easy to gather that as a thinker he peers high above his Ionic brethren, and disputes with Pythagoras and Parmenides the claim to being the most important name in the development of Greek speculation previous to Plato. The surname of σκοτεινός, or "the *obscure*," which he received from the Greeks, may have arisen partly from an original moodiness of disposition, partly from a fondness for the

[1] *Telliamed;* or, Discourses between an Indian Philosopher and a French Missionary. From the French of De Maillet. London, 1750.

old poetic and figurative style in philosophizing, but partly, no doubt, also from the real profundity of his cogitations. He evidently went with a decided preference into regions where darkness more or less visible must always be the best light which finite minds are capable of receiving. The most distinctive and suggestive of his dogmas are the following :—

(1.) His doctrine that πῦρ, or FIRE, is the ἀρχή, is a very decided step in advance both of Thales and Anaximenes; for chemistry has now taught us by many curious processes, what appears no doubt broadly on the general face of Nature, that heat is the power to the action of which both water and air owe their existence. Take away heat from water and it becomes ice; take away heat, and the expansiveness caused by heat, from a gas, and under the influence of strong pressure it becomes *liquid*. Heraclitus therefore proceeded by a true process of induction when he put his finger on heat as that common principle which, by producing fluidity, makes life possible.

(2.) But this fire or heat is nothing of a merely material kind, like the caloric, or matter of heat, of which our captains of physical science were once fond of talking. The fire of Heraclitus is a reasonable or rational heat; it is inspired by a λόγος; it is φρόνιμον and φρενῆρες (Hippol., IX. 10. Sext. Empir. *adv. Math.*, VII. 127); it works by a divine necessity, which is the cause of order and law in the universe, and on which the validity and stability of all human laws ultimately depend. Mind and Reason, indeed, are diffused everywhere in the universe, and are the common elements in virtue of which a harmonious and coherent whole is rendered possible. Ξύνον ἐστι πᾶσι τὸ φρονεῖν· τρέφονται γάρ πάντες οἱ ἀνθρώπινοι νόμοι ὑπὸ ἑνὸς τοῦ θείου· κρατέει γὰρ τοσοῦτον ὁκόσον ἐθέλει, καὶ ἐξαρκέει πᾶσι καὶ περιγίγνεται (Stob., *Florileg.* III. 84). To a modern ear this doctrine may probably sound very like Pantheism; and no doubt it is Pantheism, but a sort of Pantheism by no means like some of our modern Pantheisms, full cousin to Atheism. It is more like the Pantheism of Spinoza, which, if it is to receive a peculiar name, ought, according to Hegel, rather to be called *Acosmism* than *Atheism.* It annihilates the world by concentrating all the significance of the term existence in the idea of GOD.

(3.) The divine rational energy, called πῦρ, is essentially self-motive, and never at rest. Πάντα ῥεῖ—*all things are in a perpetual flux,* so that a flowing river is the most proper type of universal existence. (Plato, *Crat.* 402 A).

> "Nothing to hold itself is strong,
> But all things, like a river,
> Whirl along and swirl along,
> And bubble along for ever."

(4.) But, though the motion of existence in the cosmos is shapeless and ceaseless, it is in one important respect not like the course of a river; it is not a motion directly forward and onward; but it is a motion forward and backward, with recurrent strokes like the vibrations of the string of a lyre or a bow.[1] This implies a sort of self-contradiction inherent in the very nature of things. Life is manifested by the assertion of contraries: health, beauty, truth, and rightness of all kinds consist in a balance of opposites. This doctrine Heraclitus felt so strongly, that he did not hesitate to say that πόλεμον εἶναι πατέρα καὶ βασιλέα καὶ κύριον πάντων (Plut., *Is. Osir.* 48), "*War is the father, and king, and lord of all things;*" and in putting forth this, to us strange sentiment, he no doubt in some-

---

[1] Παλίντονος ἁρμονίη κόσμου ὅκωσπερ λύρης καὶ τόξου. Plut. *Is. Osir.* 45.

wise anticipated the famous maxim of Spinoza, adopted by Hegel—*Omnis affirmatio est negatio.*

(5.) Heraclitus further taught that at the bottom of this constant vicissitude, which we call life and the world, there is a something which never changes, an absolute sameness in the midst of relative otherness ; so that what we call death is really only another form of life ; and the life of any one thing always grows out of the death of some other thing.[1] This side of his speculations, if carried out, might have formed the basis for a doctrine of permanency, which would have been the natural and proper counterpoise to the sensuous scepticism that was only too easily deduced from his favourite doctrine of flux ; but it was reserved for the philosophers of the abstract and strictly metaphysical school to give due emphasis to this essential element of the Cosmos.

The fifth and last doctor of this class was Empedocles of Agrigentum, a man of noble family, lofty character, great talent, and various accomplishment, of whose poems, περὶ Φύσεως and καθαρμοί, considerable fragments are preserved, commented on in Karsten's collection and Preller's history of Græco-Roman philosophy. Important as was the figure which he played in his native country, in the curiously compound character of a physician, a priest, and a politician, he does not seem to have said much on philosophy that had not been already said by his predecessors. Like Plato, naturally a poet, and a man of a constructive imagination, he seems to have wished to combine into one rich whole the speculations of his predecessors, partly disguised under different names. The WATER, AIR, and FIRE of three of his predecessors he adopted, and with the very obvious addition of EARTH,

---

[1] Ὁδός ἄνω καὶ κάτω μίη καὶ ὠυτή. Hippol. IX. 10.

he constructed the universe out of our familiar four elements, which he called ῥιζώματα, *roots*, constantly submitted to the influence of the two adverse principles, Φιλία and Νεῖκος—LOVE and STRIFE. This was evidently nothing but an old mythological expression for the doctrine of balanced contraries laid down by Heraclitus ; and the only thing worth saying about it is that it suggests to modern associations more directly the attractions and repulsions of physical science made so familiar to us by the establishment of chemistry as one of the most fertile fields of discovery. The alternation of life and death, of construction and destruction, of organization and dissolution, caused by the eternal action of Νεῖκος and Φιλία, comes strongly out in some lines preserved by Simplicius (*Phys.*, 34 A), which I translate as follows :—

> " First from the MANY grew the one ; and then
> The ONE, resolved into its parts, again
> Became the MANY ; thus the changes run
> Of all that lives and dies beneath the sun ;
> Now LOVE unites their elements; and they
> Chained into one a balanced whole display,
> Now by strong HATE and STRIFE their parts resile,
> And into ruin drops the stately pile."

His fragments are remarkable for a very strongly pronounced materialism, as we would call it, not, however, without a distinct recognition of the Pythagorean λόγος, which happily withdraws him from the companionship of that gross school of thinkers who, as Plato says in the Theætetus, believe only in their fingers ; at the same time he asserts in language which, if used by a modern writer, would cause him to be set down as full brother to Helvetius, that all αἴσθησις is φρόνησις, and especially that the seat of φρόνησις is in the blood. He also shows a

decided tendency to break down the wall of partition
between man and the lower animals; nay, he asserts that
intelligence belongs to plants as well as to animals; and
that man in his present state is in the fourth degree of
gradual ascent from a less complete and more dependent
to a more complete and less dependent state of existence
(Plut., *Plac. Phil.* v. 19). He thus shares with Anaximander the fame or the folly, as it may turn out, of the
development theory of animal life, so attractively put
forward by Darwin.

II. Of the second great class of the pre-Socratic
philosophers the distinguished head was Democritus of
Abdera. He was the greatest naturalist and traveller,
and the most encyclopædic man of his day—a sort of
Humboldt of the fifth century B.C., and a precursor of
Aristotle; and it is as a man of science and universal
knowledge rather than as a philosopher that he must
take rank in the history of intellect. The doctrine of
atoms which he originated has no doubt a certain philosophical value, though assuredly not a very profound one;
for it is easy to see that all composite masses can be
broken down, dissipated, and resolved into certain in-
finitesimally small atoms or molecules, which must be
regarded as their ultimate elements. But when the sage
of Abdera, by adding to this primitive material fact the
idea of mere force, conceived himself to have given an
explanation of the curious structure of the reasoned
system of things which we call the cosmos, he manifestly
did not advance, but rather made a great step backward
in the physico-metaphysical speculation of his predecessors.
They had always explicitly or implicitly asserted the
presence of an indwelling λόγος, or reason, as the soul of

the world : this was a living and a dynamical conception, which contained, without attempting to explain, the great mystery of a miraculous divine centre of existence ; but they never attempted mechanically to construct the universe out of mere variously-formed atoms, brought together by blind forces and fortuitous collisions. The philosophy of Democritus is in fact pure Atheism—that is, pure nothingness and nonsense ; for a reasonable world can never be conceived as the possible result of an unreasonable cause. If the maundering of a madhouse were to go on to all eternity, it could never produce sanity ; if the babblement of a host of children were to go to infinity, it could never stumble into the demonstration of a single proposition in Euclid ; and so evident is this that one cannot but feel seriously inclined to doubt whether, after all, Democritus, had we been able to submit him to a cross-examination, would have pleaded guilty to the inanity of the Epicurean Atheism of which he stands historically as the father. Certainly with regard to Protagoras, Diagoras, and a few other Greeks of this period, who are said to have professed open Atheism, it never can be proved that in their negation of all theology they meant to do more than protest against the existence of such superhuman beings as the anthropomorphic gods, which they found as objects of popular worship in their own country ; and the writings of some modern speculators, such as David Hume, teach us to believe that a subtle thinker may puzzle himself in theory with arguments tending to sap the belief in a reasonable Cause, and yet refuse to acknowledge the consequences of his argument when it lands him in the positive profession of blank Atheism. But however this be, the thinker who constructs a theory of Nature without God can have no pretensions to the

name of philosopher; the very fact of his ignoring the
only possible explanation of the existence of a reasonable
system of things is a proof that he has given up philosophy in despair. He may be a man of subtle thought,
of curious science, of universal knowledge ; but a philosopher, or an expounder of ultimate truth, he cannot
possibly be ; for the world which it was his business to
explain he not only leaves a riddle and a mystery as he
found it, but makes it absolute nonsense. We need not
be surprised, therefore, that as a philosopher Democritus
exercised no influence on the two great schools of Greek
thought which the next century saw founded in Athens :
the keen, sharp, analytic intellect of Aristotle, and the
lofty, constructive genius of Plato stood equally apart
from a pseudo-philosophy which was content to float
about blindly in a blind vacuity, and to reason upon pos-
tulates which implied the absolute negation of all reason.
No philosophy could prosper in reasoning Greece of which
λόγος in some shape or other was not the centre.

III. We now come to the third and last and most
distinguished class of early Greek thinkers, viz., those who
taught that the ἀρχή was not a thing objective, visible, or
tangible, or appreciable by the senses in any way, but an
inner, invisible, moulding, and formative principle, which
we call mind, or at least some function of mind, and
which cannot be conceived as objective or material. This
philosophy of course gave the direct contradiction to all
atheism, and therefore it may be properly called theological; it is also rightly termed metaphysical, because it
finds the ἀρχή or fundamental cause of all things in something behind and beyond that beautiful and various outside which we call the world. Now, no doubt, Thales,

Heraclitus, and Empedocles, as we have indicated, all believed in this metaphysical cause of everything physical as much as Pythagoras, Xenophanes, and Anaxagoras; but they presented this metaphysical cause always under the mask of some physical element; and the key-note of their thinking directed attention in a marked way to something external. But when Pythagoras, the great founder of the theological philosophy, declared the first principle of all things to be NUMBER, he brought the philosophical mind into an entirely new position, turned as it were the obverse side of the coin, and showed an image and super-scription there altogether different from that which had been previously exhibited. By ἀριθμός of course was meant, not a mere multitude or succession of units, but *calculated number, relation, proportion*, and all that curious construction of nicely-measured spaces on which symmetry in architecture, harmony in music, and the whole practice of the fine arts depend. In announcing this principle Pythagoras saw deeper into the nature of the cosmos than any of the pre-Socratic philosophers; he saw that the world is a world simply because it is a κόσμος, or an *order;* and order always depends on calculation, on the arrangement of units according to certain relations of number. But the relations of number are a thing purely abstract and intellectual; they are the product of think-ing; they are not derived from the senses; animals see an infinity of things, and see them often with a more keen and sharp observation than men; but animals have no calculation; the cleverest monkey is much further removed from the comprehension of the simplest arith-metical proposition than the stupidest man, for the one is separated by a gap, the other removed only by a step or steps from all abstract notions. It is plain therefore that

by asserting number as the ἀρχή, Pythagoras was only
defining the method of operation of MIND, or λόγος; and
what he called NUMBER was only another name for what
our modern men of physical science call LAW. For that
law is altogether a matter of calculation any one may see
in the constant practice of mechanical philosophers,
astronomers, and chemists; the laws of nature are only
the regularly acting forces of nature; and all regularly
acting forces are necessarily either directly or indirectly
the product of mind; as a steam-engine, for instance,
however often multiplied, is always and everywhere the
product of the calculating intellect of James Watt, propagated and perpetuated through countless imitators. In
assigning this high position to the mathematical element
in the constitution of the universe, Pythagoras certainly
deserves to be reverenced as the great prophet and anti-
cipator of our modern scientific processes; what he demonstrated with a fine preference in the case of the
musical scale, is now demonstrated in everything; not
only the motions of the stars and the arrangement of
leaves in plants, but the very winds and storms are made
the subjects of calculation. Unless indeed it be in the
flow of emotion, the flash of wit, the play of fancy, and
the fervour of passion, it is difficult now-a-days to find a
domain that can boast its freedom from the wide control
of calculated Number.

As in reference to the mundane system, the Pythagorean assertion of ἀριθμός necessarily implied the unity of
the plan of the world, and its existence as the product of
a calculating architect, so in reference to the social system
the same idea brought into prominence the principle of
order, and authority, and subordination, that at the
present day gives its leading features to what are called

Conservative politics, as opposed to the politics of a free and equal individualism. Pythagoras accordingly preceded Plato in the constitution of a republic mainly on the principle of order; and in one respect certainly far excelled his brilliant successor; for the constitution which the Athenian projected remained a dream upon paper, while the community established by the Samian was a realized fact of considerable social importance for a season. In the establishment of this community indeed he comes nearer to the founders of the great moral society of the Christian Church than any ancient philosopher; it appeared, however, that in this he occupied ground which philosophy was not competent to maintain; for the Pythagorean societies in South-Eastern Italy, being oligarchic in their character and operation, came into collision with that democratic element which was always so potent in the Greek colonies, and being cast out lost their organic consistency. This great failure no doubt gave the hint to Plato to content himself with founding a school at Athens, not a community; for it is only upon very rare occasions that political parties have ventured to interfere with the ventilation of unapplied speculations in the schools.

Less popularly known than Pythagoras, but scarcely of less significance in the history of thought, is Xenophanes of Colophon, who stands chronologically between the Samian and Heraclitus. As the founder of the Eleatic School, he, with Parmenides, stands forward as the champion of the principle of unity in the universe, adding the necessary counterpoise to the doctrine of flux and mutability, on which, as we have seen, Heraclitus so moodily rung the changes. How to bridge over the gap between the one and the many—to apprehend how the ἕν became

πολλά if we start from the one, and how the πολλά was
worked into the unity of a consistent whole, if we are to
start from the many—that of course was, and is, the great
problem of all metaphysical and theological thought. To
solve this problem, the Eleatics took the method of
Spinoza ; they asserted the one as the only really existent,
and allowed the many to shift for themselves as they best
might under the name of appearances, modifications, illusions (the Hindu *Maya*), and whatsoever you please, of
the nature of fleeting, ephemeral, and without independent root and enduring reality. God only exists; all
created things are mere passing phantoms and pheno-
menal illusions. As assertors of the self-existent ἕν, the
Eleatics were naturally opposed to that breaking down of
the divine nature into a multitude of discordant personalities which they beheld in the popular polytheism of
their country ; and it is one of the great merits of Xenophanes that he anticipated Plato by a century and a half
in publishing a vigorous protest against the contradictions,
puerilities, and immoralities of the Homeric theology.
Whether the boldness of his utterances in respect to the
popular theology may not have been the cause of his
leaving his Asiatic home, and settling, like Pythagoras, in
Southern Italy, we have no means of knowing ; the following declarations, however, which I translate from his
fragments in Karsten's collection, if they had got beyond
the author's private circle, are certainly strongly enough
worded to have made the writer's position sufficiently
uncomfortable in that part of the world where the presence of St. Paul, five centuries afterwards, raised such a
storm of blatant spite and fury among the worshippers of
the Ephesian Artemis.

I.

" There is one God, supreme above all gods and men that be ;
Not like a mortal thing in shape, nor like in thought is He.

II.

" O vain conceit, to ween that gods like men are born, and show
Our human face, and use our speech, and in our garments go !

III.

" If sheep and swine, and lions strong, and all the bovine crew,
Could paint with cunning hands, and do what clever mortals do,
Depend upon it every pig with snout so broad and blunt,
Would make a Jove that like himself would thunder with a grunt ;
And every lion's god would roar, and every bull's would bellow,
And every sheep's would baa, and every beast his worshipp'd fellow
Would find in some immortal form, and nought exist divine
But had the gait of lion, sheep, or ox, or grunting swine.

IV.

" Homer and Hesiod, whom we own great doctors of theology,
Said many things of blissful gods that cry for large apology,
That they may cheat, and rail, and lie, and give the rein to passion,
Which were a crime in men who tread the dust in mortal fashion.

V.

" All eyes, all ears, all thought is God, the omnipresent soul,
And free from toil, by force of mind He moves the mighty whole."

The only other point worthy of remark with regard to
Xenophanes is that he seems to have been the first Greek
speculator—certainly the first of whom any record is left
—who distinctly noted those curious phenomena in the
crust of the earth's surface indicative of an early disturbed
state of the globe, which, when collected and systematized,
have grown up into the interesting modern science of
Geology. The passage in which this remarkable notice
occurs is in that part of the work of Hippolytus (*Refut.
Hær.*, i. 14) which gives a review of the opinions of the
Greek philosophers ; and here he distinctly says that
" shells, and the prints of fishes, and marine animals were
found in the rocks at Syracuse, Malta, and Paros ; and

that this was evidently the result of a watery condition of
the Earth's surface, when everything was swathed in mud,
and the living creatures of the sea left the impressions of
their bodies in the soft beds, which afterwards became
dry."

The last philosopher whom our present scheme requires
us to mention is Anaxagoras, the friend of Pericles, and
the precursor of Plato in the complete emancipation of
metaphysical speculation from physical symbols.   No
doubt Socrates in a well-known passage accuses this philosopher of not having consistently applied the intellectual
principle of the world which he laid down (Plat. *Phæd.*
98 B.) ; but in declaring that the only adequate explanation of the cosmos was to be found in self-existent, self-
energizing νοῦς or MIND, the Clazomenian certainly made
a stride in advance, marking him out as well worthy of
the commendation bestowed by Aristotle, that in this
matter he spoke like a full-grown man as contrasted with
the lisping and babblement of children.   There is in
fact only a very superficial difference of expression between
the νοῦς of Anaxagoras and the ELOHIM of Moses. " In
the beginning GOD created the Heaven and the Earth."
About the exact meaning of the word "create" (בָּרָא),
of course our finite intellects always must dispute : if we
could understand that word fully, we should be not men,
but God : apart from this, however, the βασιλικὸς νοῦς of
Anaxagoras and Plato, which is the keystone of Christian
faith as well as of the highest modern thinking, is simply
another name for Θεός—GOD.   We find, therefore, in the
ἀρχή of Anaxagoras a natural and beautiful culmination
which harmonizes in one significant watchword the philosophy of Greece, the faith of Christendom, and the instincts
of a healthy humanity.

Of the Sophists as predecessors or contemporaries of Socrates it is not necessary to say anything in this paper. They were not so much founders of systems of philosophy as disputers about philosophy—corresponding to a certain class of our literary men, who talk and write on all subjects without having any strong convictions on any subject ; some of them, indeed, as Gorgias, professing only to be teachers of rhetoric, and others adding to that some superficial instruction in the principles of a worldly morality and a time-serving statesmanship. The philosophy that they taught was generally of a negative and destructive character ; and the part which it played in the history of thought was mainly to bring out in full armed strength the rational ethics of Socrates, Plato, and Aristotle. Of course I am fully aware of the attempt recently made by Mr. Grote to plant these gentlemen on a higher and more dignified platform ; but, great as are the merits of this distinguished writer in reference to the political history of Greece, I cannot but regard his chapter on the Sophists as the product of a reactionary feeling, doomed to pass away with the generation which gave it birth.

WHEN Mr. Southey, some fifty years ago, in his famous poem, *The Vision of Judgment*, resuscitated the long-laid " ghost of English hexameters," he did not do so under such favourable circumstances (so far as himself was concerned), nor with such accompaniments of public approbation, as could invite any future candidate for rhythmical distinction to imitate his bold example. Nay, the old English mastiff sent forth one of its rough conservative growls in the shape of a separate book of no less than eighty-four pages (price four shillings !) of "historical and critical remarks " on the subject, by a Reverend Fellow of Peterhouse, Cambridge.[1] Most people imagined that the effect of this combined indifference and opposition had been, to lay the unquiet spirit of metrical innovation for ever ;[2] but in these last times, amid the prevalence of many other strange fermentations, it is nothing surprising that the ghost should have again appeared. Not to mention Longfellow's *Evangeline*,—a poem which has boasted as wide a popularity as any rhythmical production of the present century,—we have had within the last twenty

---

[1] *Historical and Critical Remarks upon the modern Hexametrists :* by the Reverend S. Tillbrook, B. D., Fellow of Peterhouse, Cambridge. 1822.—A work valuable more for its facts than for its philosophy, and containing some curious points of information on the singular fates of hexameter verse in our early English literature.

[2] " I am well aware that the public are peculiarly intolerant of such innovations."—Southey, Preface to *Vision of Judgment*.

years no less than three translations of the *Iliad* in hexameter verse ;[1] besides a hexametrical version of the books
of the *Iliad* in a quarter so conservative of old English
ideas as *Blackwood's Magazine.*[2] The phenomenon is a
most remarkable one, and forces itself with a strong
æsthetical interest, both on the student of English literature and on the classical scholar. To the one it is interesting to inquire how far our admirable language, even at
the present late period, may admit of a new rhythmical
development ; while the other is even more concerned to
inquire whether, after the precedents which Pope and
Dryden and Sotheby have already established, it be yet
possible to make acceptable to the English ear a style of
translation which shall not merely transpose the soul and
the body of Greek antiquity into our Saxon speech, but
exhibit even the very attitude and posture, the vesture
and drapery of the Hellenic Muse. On this subject we
hope the few following remarks will not prove unacceptable.

The *beau ideal* of a translation as a work of art unquestionably is, that it shall be as much as possible a *likeness*
of its original ; the same in substance and in character, in
significance and expression, in spirit and detail, in a word
a FACSIMILE, as far as may be. There are pictures, copies
from the great masters, done by their disciples, with such
perfect cunning of the pencil, that even an experienced
eye cannot distinguish them from the originals. To achieve
that with words which has been achieved by lines and

---

[1] By Dart, 1865 ; Herschel, 1866 ;
and Cochran, 1867, privately printed.

[2] See *Blackwood* for the months of
March and May 1847 ; though in fairness we must mention that Christopher
North was anticipated in his patronage
of English hexameters by a writer in
the *Westminster Review*, March 1845, in
a notice of Sotheby's Homer, and "the
Iliad faithfully rendered into Homeric
verse :" by Lancelot Shadwell, Esquire.
Nos. 1 and 3. London. Pickering.

colours, were the perfection of the translator's art ; but unhappily the thing is in the general case impossible. For the translator does not work with the same materials as his original : a good black or blue in the hands of Giulio Romano may produce the same effect as in the hands of Raphael ; but no Coleridge or Shelley can in every case make the English language do that which Homer or Æschylus may have done with the Greek. A translator is often called on to make a facsimile of a golden image with brass, sometimes with hard granite or gnarled gneiss ; sometimes to reproduce upon coarse drugget and " hodden grey" that fine figured broidery which was worked by delicate hands on the velvet mantle of a king. It is in vain, therefore, to expect a perfect *facsimile* from a translator ; we can only demand a reproduction of the original, in so far as the material employed will allow ; and this necessary condition of the undertaking in the hands of a man of taste and judgment will often lead to very considerable encroachments on the original idea of an exact copy. It is impossible, for instance, even in the plainest prose, to give an Englishman ignorant of German any idea, through translation, of the style in which many German writers express themselves. A German sentence, partly by the habit of the language, partly by the vice of the writer, is often a thing so vast, complex, and involved, that it must be cut up into half a dozen separate sentences before it can assume the shape of readable and intelligible English. In like manner with the English language, it is impracticable to give an exact *facsimile* of some of the Greek metres, because the rhythmical constitution and habit of our tongue imperatively repels the attempt. Take, for instance, the splendid chorus in the opening of *The Persians*, written in what metricians call the *Ionic a minori* measure, and attempt a metrical transference of that into English :—

$$\pi\epsilon\pi\acute{\epsilon}\rho\alpha\kappa\epsilon\nu\ \mu\grave{\epsilon}\nu\ \acute{o}\ \pi\epsilon\rho\sigma\acute{\epsilon}\pi\tau o\lambda\iota s\ \mathring{\eta}\delta\eta$$
$$\beta\alpha\sigma\acute{\iota}\lambda\epsilon\iota os\ \sigma\tau\rho\alpha\tau\grave{o}s,\ \kappa.\tau.\lambda.$$

To the Greek coast, with a vast host,

Went the great king o'er the broad stream,

To which fair Helle her name gave,

When she fell down from the ram's back to the deep sea !

This, be it observed, is as near a facsimile as can be made to the Greek measure in our language, an accented syllable with us systematically performing the rhythmical function, which in Greek could only be performed by a long one ; and the effect, as the English ear at once feels, is perfectly ludicrous and absurd. Further, if the metrical translator were, on the principle of exact facsimile, to go a step beyond this, and compose English verses according to the ancient law, with a strict regard to the musical quantity alone, irrespective of the spoken accent, he would produce not merely an absurd and ludicrous rhythm, but a jargon out of which no English ear could extract anything the least approaching to harmony. The general principle, then, on which a metrical translation must proceed is plain enough. The reader of a translated work is entitled to demand a facsimile of the original ; but this *only in so far as is consistent with the grammatical and rhythmical genius of the language in which the translation is made.* Now what is included in that wide word the GENIUS of a language ? It includes two things essentially different ; but which in the criticisms that have been made on English hexameters have too often been confounded ; it includes, in the first place, and principally, whatever belongs organically to the grammatical and metrical structure of the language; and in the second place, whatever belongs by use and habit and association to the characteristic style and peculiar living expression of the language. Of metrical movements affected by essential structure, a language is either naturally capable, or capable only with considerable exertion, or absolutely incapable. Thus, the English language, by its structure, most naturally falls into the iambic movement, in which measure accordingly almost all our great poems of any length, as also our most popular songs and ballads, are written; but it is also capable, without any painful effort, of the trochaic movement; and when stirred with high lyric emotion, it does not refuse the tribrachic measure, which, however, according to its essentially accentual and not quantitative character, it mingles at random with dactyles, anapests, and every variety of the trisyllabic foot. The Italian language, on the other hand, is, by its structure, utterly foreclosed from the free use of the iambic close, so natural to us. An Italian, therefore, cannot make an exact facsimile of an English poem of which the closes of the verse are not all trochaics. But though we can write in trochaic rhythm, our language does not with the same facility—especially when rhyme is necessary—admit the trochaic close, or "double ending" as it is sometimes called. The consequence of which essential difference of structure is, that an exact rhythmical transference from Italian into English, or from English into Italian, is, in the general case, either impossible or extremely inconvenient. In this particular the Germans are infinitely more happy; for in their rich and various language, the single and double endings exist in a fair and even proportion, and suggest themselves accordingly to the poetic ear with equal facility. Let us now apply these remarks specially to the English Hexameter.

The question, whether there is anything in the organic structure of the English language adverse to the use of the hexameter verse, as Tillbrook and the anti-Hexametrists generally maintain, must be answered in the negative or the affirmative, according to the kind of hexameter verse meant; the ancient hexameter verse, which is essentially quantitative in its structure, or the modern hexameter verse so successfully cultivated by the Germans, which is as essentially accentual. Of the genuine ancient, or pure dactylic hexameter verse, the English language is altogether incapable; not only because no language whose poetry is founded on elocutional principles can, without the most gross solecism, exactly imitate the rhythm of a language whose poetry is founded on the rules and practice of music, but because there are not a sufficient number of pure dactyles and pure spondees in the English language, to make the imitation possible for any length of time, in a style consistent with the comfort of the artist, and the demands of his art. A fashion indeed has prevailed in the common grammars, of marshalling forth certain measures familiar to our lyric poetry, under the name of dactylic and anapæstic; but it requires only a simple appeal to the ear to perceive that this phraseology is most inadequate, and like many other terms of art, borrowed from the ancient Prosodians, when applied to our modern tongues, has had no effect but to beget and to perpetuate confusion. The fact of the matter is, that our English dactylic and anapæstic verses, though they admit of any number of true dactyles and anapæsts, are, as was hinted above, rather tribrachic than dactylic in their character; the tribrach occurring oftener in them than

the dactyle, and its equivalent the trochee, much more
frequently than the spondee. We have indeed in English a woeful lack of genuine spondees ; that is to say,
spondees that are both full as to quantity and of harmonious flow. For spondees by *position*, as they are
sometimes called, are in fact trochees, and must be altogether discarded from the account ; for position, which
allowed the ancients to lengthen a syllable otherwise
short, is so far from having that effect in English and
German, that the common rule for both languages is, that
a vowel before two or more consonants is short. According to this quantitative law, while *Wohl-laut* is a pure
spondee in German, *Weltmeer* is an iambic (though with
the accent on the first syllable, like λόγων in Greek), *Ab'-
hang* is a pyrrhic (though a trochee by abuse of language
accentually), and *Rauchfang* is a trochee both quantitative
and accentual. In the English language, *female, outgo,
outpour, foresee, live-long, bleach-green, wide-spread,* are
genuine spondees as to quantity ; but the number of such
words in our language is few, and those that we have are
in reality compound words only half-joined into one, and
not half so harmonious as a spondee included in a single
word ; for in these compound words each element retains,
in a manner, its separate existence, and comes upon the
ear almost with a double accent, which is not pleasant.[1]
For spondees, therefore, we are driven to depend in a
great measure upon the juxta-collocation of two long
monosyllables, as in that of Southey,—

[1] This is the reason why such words are peculiarly offensive in the close of a verse, where we expect the metrical undulation to fall smoothly, and not to jerk off abruptly. The last line of the first book of the *Iliad* in *Blackwood's* *Magazine* (May 1846) offends in this view. "This he ascended and slept ; and beside him was Hera, the *gold-throned.*" The "*procumbit humi bos,*" of Virgil, is harsh (but purposely) on the same principle.

> " In full-orbed glory yonder moon divine,
>
> Rolls through the dark blue depths."

But even this does not occur readily enough in a long composition, to enable the English translator to communicate to the English ear any impression of the stable mass of ponderous harmony which marches majestically to its goal, in the spondaic lines of Homer and Virgil. The fact of the matter is, the genius of the English language is essentially anti-spondaic ; and in no respect are the hexameters of Mr. Southey and the Homeric translator in *Blackwood,* more inferior to their original than even here. The writer in *Blackwood,* indeed, strikes us as superabundant in tribrachs and dactyles of admirable smoothness for the most part, but not sufficiently tempered and varied by spondees ; but this is the natural vice of the English hexameter ; for even in Mr. Southey's masterly rhythm, when the majestic undulation (for we cannot call it march) of the long-continued dactyle or tribrach is suspended, we feel that the trochee and pyrrhic, even when aided by a dexterous use of comma and pause, have scarcely weight enough to fill up the space which the subtraction of so many syllables takes from the rhythm.

> " Earth was hushed and still : all motion and sound was suspended,
> Neither man was heard, bird, beast, nor humming of insect."

So much for the spondee. As for the dactyles, it will be manifest to every one who will appeal to his ear, that though our hexameter verse is by no means deficient in them, yet that tribrachs are decidedly preponderant ; and these, along with the frequent trochees and pyrrhics, instead of real spondees, are apt to give a light and tripping air to the modern verse, the very opposite of that stability and steadiness which Dionysius of Halicarnassus so extols

in the ancient rhythm.   The fact is, that while the ancient
hexameter was, strictly speaking, march-time, our hexameter's musical correlative is rather jig-time, or waltz-
time ; and it requires great care in the writer, and even
more in the reciter, to give to this measure, in its modern
shape, that weight and majesty of movement which unquestionably belonged[1] to its ancient prototype.   But
to proceed.   Leaving the quantitative and musical element altogether out of view, the main question recurs,
whether there is anything in the mere structure of the
English language adverse to a rhythm formed in imitation
of the ancient hexameter, adopting the accentual, and
rejecting the quantitative law ; and to this question we
think we may answer confidently—despite of what Tillbrook and others have urged—that there is not.   This
matter indeed has been already proved by the fact ; for
though the majority of English readers may not have reconciled—perhaps never endeavoured to reconcile—their
ears to the new movement introduced to them in the
Vision of Judgment, it is most certain that the rhythm of
that poem flows most easily, smoothly, and naturally, and
that—whatever its effect may be on English feelings and
associations—it offers no violence to the natural structure
and movement of the English language.   It is hard indeed
to see how six dactylic or tribrachic feet in succession
should present anything contrary to the rhythmical movement of the English language, when the same measure in
dimeter, trimeter, and tetrameter extent is of the most
frequent occurrence in our lyric poetry, and when we
consider, as all our orthoepists inform us, that the ante-

---

[1] *Belonged,* we say strictly, not *belongs ;* for, with our present barbarous
habits of Latin reading in schools often
innocent of all elocution, it is mere affectation to pretend that Mr. Southey's
hexameters do not sound as well—ay
and a great deal better, to a well-trained
ear, than Virgil's.

penultimate, tribrachic or dactylic, accent is the favourite accent of the English tongue. How naturally our language slides into the hexameter is indeed manifest, not only from the fact that this measure sometimes presents itself without being sought for, as in that well-known instance quoted by Southey,

" Why do the | heathen | rage, and the | people i- | magine a | vain thing,"

but from many single experiments that can be made on our own lyric poetry, tending to show how slight the change is that is necessary to transmute some of our dactylic metres into hexameters. Thus the following three dimeters,—

> " Not in the desert,
> Son of Hodeirah,
> Art thou abandoned,"

if written in one line, are in fact a hexameter; but the law of Cæsura requires a slight change, thus :—

> " Not in the desert art thou, O son of Hodeirah, abandoned."

And in the same poem (*Thalaba*, Book ii.), in the very next stanza, two lines occur which, if written in one, are also a hexameter, though a very slight change is necessary for the same reason :—

> " In the Domdaniel caverns
> Under the roots of the ocean."

Altered thus :—

> " In the Domdaniel caverns beneath the roots of the ocean."

In vain, therefore, shall the nice academic ear rebel against Mr. Southey's grand innovation, on purely philological grounds. The learned Laureate knew his subject and his position too well ; and not without good reason, assuredly, had he " long been of opinion that an English metre might be constructed in imitation of the ancient hexameter, which would be perfectly consistent with the character of our language, and capable of great richness, variety, and strength."[1] But there is something more in the matter. A whole army of English habits, feelings, and associations remains behind; and these, call them prejudices if you will, are a matter which no great poet appealing through the people's language to the people's ear, and the people's heart, much less any mere translator, can afford to disregard. The fact is, even Mr. Southey himself, with the true instinct of genius, felt much less confidence in the result of this " experiment," than in that other of the unrhymed and irregular rhythm which in his *Thalaba* he ushered into the British world with such admirable propriety, as " the Arabesque ornament of an Arabian tale." *Thalaba* is an oriental epic, as singularly original and felicitous in its manner as in its matter; no student of English literature can afford to be ignorant of it; but the *Vision of Judgment* remains a pious curiosity in the subject as much as the style, and, except as a curiosity, has occupied no place in the series of the higher British poetry of the nineteenth century. What then are these feelings and associations with which we have to deal in this matter ? And are they such as should permanently stand in the way of a new school of translated literature, or are they likely to yield ? On this point our opinion decidedly is, that the feelings of the English public on this subject are strong and invincible, and that they neither can, nor ought to yield. What they are, and on what they are founded, we need not particularly inquire. Some of them, no doubt, are foolish enough, and sound when put into an articulate shape, just as all nonsense does when pertly stilting itself into the attitude of

---

[1] Preface to *Vision of Judgment.*

reason ; but in so far as they may be founded on the principle above enunciated, that the English dactylic, or more properly tribrachic measure, as the natural elocutional correlative of triple time in music, is essentially a measure of lyrical elevation ; and by its own nature, as well as by the undeviating usage of the English language, not adapted for the calm and equable flow of old epic narrative : if this be the case, as we could prove at great detail, then this host of rebellious feelings and associations is entitled to something more than a mere prudent regard at the hands of any artificer of English verse ; and in particular, it deserves serious consideration, whether the English hexameter, though unobjectionable on purely general grounds for some purposes, is therefore the fit measure, on æsthetical principles, for rendering the Homeric hexameter. For in this argument it must always be borne in mind, that the English hexameter is one thing, and the Homeric another. But, bating these considerations altogether, and treating the English feelings with regard to hexameter verse as a mere bundle of habits and associations,—still, as use and wont in all questions of language must have a great deal to say, there are the best possible reasons why, in the present matter, they should not be interfered with. No doubt Coleridge and Southey and Shelley, greeted though they were with sneers and contemptuous laughter on their first appearance, have done a great deal to enlarge the metrical conceptions of John Bull ; but a good rhymer will wisely not put his patience to too severe a test in this direction, for many valid reasons, but principally for this, that every good rhymer is neither a Southey nor a Shelley. In vain, also, shall we plead in behalf of English hexameters the example of our neighbours, the Germans ; not, indeed, because their language possesses any peculiar structural superiority which might avail them here,[1] but because the cases are not only not parallel, but altogether opposite. As a general rule, indeed, it may be laid down, that anything peculiarly and characteristically German—so different is the national mind—will not suit the English taste; but the real want of parallelism lies in this, that the German polite literature is but of yesterday. Klopstock, Goethe, and Schiller are the fathers of their literature, and were in a position, like Ennius among the Romans, and Dante among the Italians, to stamp authority upon whatsoever strange rhythm they chose to adopt. They have done so, and with the most signal success, as everybody knows; for, whatever certain narrow English critics may say, no man that has an ear for the melody of German poetry will deny that Goethe's elegies, written in the Ovidian stanza, are perfect models of rhythmical harmony, and fill the ear with as grateful a sweetness as anything in Tibullus or the Sulmonian himself. All this, however, makes nothing for us. Had Shakespeare and Milton and Dryden used the hexameter as plentifully as the three German masters just named, no doubt they were in a condition, by the mastery of their glorious minds, to prescribe a new rhythmical law to that public ear, which now, being old, and strong in a different habit, prescribes limits to the rhythmical artists of the present age. But Shakespeare, Milton, and Dryden had too much

---

[1] They have fewer monosyllables, certainly, than we have, their verbs and the cases of their nouns being mostly dissyllables from which we have cut off the termination; and the trochaic movement, commencing with the accent, is more natural to them. But practice has shown that these are merely accessory points; and that the main objections made to English hexameters, *on the score of structure*, apply equally to the German. Surely this fact might have made our Tillbrook pause a little in the fierce onset of their Quixotic wrath against the Laureate!

common sense, and sound British conservatism, if you like, to coquette with merely formal innovations of this kind. It is extremely doubtful, indeed, whether, on purely æsthetical principles, Klopstock and Goethe were defensible in what they did ; certainly if their innovation was proper, it was proper only for such a people of erudite cosmopolites as the Germans, and forms no precedent on which other nations are entitled to act.

The matter then comes to a very short issue. The man who, after the experiments which have already been made, shall sit down to write a translation of the *Iliad* in English hexameters, must do so with the full consciousness that he is making a very delicate and doubtful experiment against the literary use and wont of a highly cultivated language, and against the banded associations and prepossessions of a whole people, "peculiarly intolerant of such innovations." Is there a motive sufficiently strong to induce a literary man to embark in a literary adventure of this description ? The enterprise, no doubt, is a brave one ; it carries with it a magnificent sound ; we cannot but be carried away with so fair an idea—a literal English FACSIMILE of the world-revered

> " Blind old man of Scio's rocky isle,"

whose works are, and have been, and in all likelihood will for ever remain, at once the spelling-book and the Bible of all sublunar poetry. But let us beware of being robbed of our æsthetical senses by this one idea of a facsimile, which it must be confessed has something of the mechanical in its nature, and may achieve wonderful likenesses—as Photography does—only without the soul. A man, after he is hanged, looks sufficiently like himself before that operation ; and a man who is drunk has the

same eyes, nose, and mouth, as when he is sober. But
these likenesses are not pleasant. "Death," as Goethe
said, "is a bad portrait-painter;" so also is Drink and
Photography. In practice, indeed, the facsimile principle must be constantly modified by another one, which
we have not yet distinctly stated, though it lies involved
in the wide domain of what we have termed the style,
character, and expression of a language, and the associations connected with them. This principle is, that *a
translator is bound to transfer every measure of his
original into that measure of his own language, which,
in its style, character, associations, and effects, corresponds to his model.* It is upon this principle that
the iambic trimeter of Greek tragedy is universally,
in England, translated, not into an English trimeter,
in number of feet and order of pauses the literal counterpart of the original, but into that ten-syllabled iambic
verse, whose character and habit and expression, as
formed by the familiar use of our native poetry, correspond to the iambic trimeter as familiarly used by the
Greeks. In other words, in translating the dialogic part
of the Greek drama, we do not give the mechanical, but
the æsthetical facsimile of the Greek measure; and this
for the best of all possible reasons, that more would be
lost in the spirit by disturbing the familiar metrical
associations of our modern readers, than is gained in the
letter, by adhering with mechanical exactness to the
ancient model. That this is the true reason why no one
thinks of translating the Greek trimeters into English
ones of the same structure, is quite plain; for nothing
can be more natural to the English tongue than any
iambic movement; and Greek trimeters may be trolled
off from the British tongue, as glibly as any hexameters, so

soon as the ear is fairly won over to the trick. Thus the two first lines of the *Prometheus* might be done into Greek-English, thus—

> At léngth arríve we, at this úttermost boúrne of eárth—
> Bleak Scythia's wide-spread, lone untrodden solitude!

and so *ad infinitum, more Germanorum;* for our trans-Rhenane brethren deal in iambics as well as in hexameters, Goethe having set them a notable example in the second part of *Faust,* though truly their translators ask for no high stamp of this kind, but systematically twist and turn and torture themselves with mimetic minuteness after every iambic, trochaic or dactylic variation of which the various sweep of the Greek lyric is capable. Whether they are right in this procedure, so far as their own language is concerned, let themselves judge; we know that high names, William Humboldt among others, have sanctioned the practice; but we are extremely doubtful whether, on the principles of æsthetical science, it be defensible; we doubt much whether anything is gained by this syllabic scrupulosity which can compensate for the grace, ease, and nature, which is undoubtedly sacrificed; and we think, generally, that in this, as in some other minute points of scholarship, our Teutonic brethren, or masters should we not rather say, in scholarship, are not without a certain superstition. Accuracy is a good thing; but there are certain living hues and tints in the floating element of poetic emotion that will not be measured by inches; and a better likeness will sometimes be made without looking anxiously at every hair in a man's beard. As for ourselves, we may rest firmly assured that the British good sense, for which we are famous, will preserve us from any metrical aberrations

of this kind. English Iambic trimeters, however well suited
to our language, so far as structure is concerned, beside
their novelty, are objectionable on another ground, which,
perhaps, does not apply to hexameters. Their scope is
too great for the original from which they are copied;
that is to say, the difference of the languages is such
that an English trimeter will contain more sense and less
sound than the Greek, within the same limits. This will
be obvious to any person who compares the second line
in the *Prometheus*—

$$\Sigma\kappa\dot{\upsilon}\theta\eta\nu \ \dot{\epsilon}\varsigma \ o\hat{\iota}\mu o\nu, \ \ddot{\alpha}\beta\alpha\tau o\nu \ \epsilon\dot{\iota}\varsigma \ \dot{\epsilon}\rho\eta\mu\dot{\iota}\alpha\nu,$$

with our version above given, where we have been obliged
to interpolate a few epithets in order to fill up the room.
Now, though the line-for-line system is altogether out of
the question in translating from the ancient languages
into the modern, still there are reasons why the translator should choose a measure, where he can, of the same
compass as his original: a measure with which he can
conveniently give line for line when convenient, and
which does not throw in his way any temptation illegiti-
mately to contract or expand.

One other remark on the hexameter, and we have
done. The remark just made as to the compass of the
translating instrument contains the true reason why our
heroic couplet, used by Pope, is so difficult to handle in
the rendering of Homer or Virgil. It is not long enough
for two hexameters, and it is too long for one; this,
along with its tendency to make the pause too frequently
coincide with the rhyme, and thus break the natural flow
of the rhythm, seems to point it out as an unsuitable—at
least so far as structure is concerned, as an extremely
inconvenient—English substitute for the hexameter. If,

on account of epic associations, our ten-syllabled verse is to be used in rendering Homer, there can be no question that, in this particular matter, Cowper was nearer the mark than Pope, and that, in this case, blank verse is preferable to rhyme. But it admits, we think, of the clearest proof on the strictest æsthetical principles—principles which it might go hard even with our hardy German friends to disprove—that the proper English correlative of the Greek hexameter of Homer (Virgil may be different) is Chapman's old iambic verse of fourteen syllables; or better still—because, like dactylic verse, it commences with the accent—the trochaic measure of fifteen syllables, so felicitously used by Mr. Tennyson in his luxuriant poem, Locksley Hall. These measures, especially the latter, possess every quality that an intelligent admirer of Homer could wish for the purpose of producing a translation that shall, not merely in the letter, but in the spirit, and in the whole style and tone, be as much as possible a *facsimile* of the original.[1] The only doubt that can be stated is, whether this measure, iambic or trochaic, should be used with or without rhyme. Against rhyme it may well be pleaded that, though John Bull's prejudices in favour of this tinkling appendage are no doubt strong, the charm of novelty in the hands of some great creative genius might readily be stronger; an instance of very graceful and enjoyable English trochaic verse without rhyme our translated literature already possesses in Milman's version of the Sanscrit tale of *Nala and Damayanti*; and there seems little doubt that in regard to literal accuracy, which in such a venerable

---

[1] For specimens of Homer in trochaic verse, see "Translations" by Lord Lyttleton and the Right Honourable W. E. Gladstone. 2d edition. London, 1863; and *Blackwood's Magazine*, 1839, by Aytoun.

old minstrel as Homer will always be valued, an unrhymed version will have a certain advantage over a
rhymed one.   On the other hand, it is quite plain that it
requires a great creative genius—a man somewhat in the
position of Goethe in Germany—to disturb the rhythmical habitude of a full-grown literature like the English ;
and, in an æsthetical point of view, the want of harmonious flow in our verses arising from our abundance in
stout monosyllables, and the loss of those euphonious
terminations so characteristic of Greek and Sanscrit, finds
its natural compensation in that recurrent consonance
of final syllables at certain definite intervals which we
call rhyme.   And as for literal accuracy, for those who
want to spell Homer curiously, as a record of old Greek
times, a literal prose translation with the Greek appended,
in the fashion of Dr. Carlyle's translation of Dante, will
be found to be the only form that will satisfy all demands.
In a poetical version literal accuracy is one of the great
mistakes of the present age, fostered by the microscopic
habits of our University scholars, certain to produce a
strong reaction—the sooner the better.   It is not verbal
accuracy, but character and spirit, melody and grace, that
are required in a poetical version of a great poet ; without
which qualities indeed it has no meaning, and can show
no reason for its existence.   Your so-called " literal and
rhythmical version "—of which kind I call to mind a
rare specimen by Sewell of Æschylus' *Agamemnon*—will
always present more or less of the attitude of a dance
in fetters, which, though the links gleam with gold, and
tinkle with silver, can never improve the dancing.   To
all true poetry there belongs a spontaneity, that, like
the carols of sweet birds in the May, can hold no terms
with a constant mechanical pressure from without.

POPULAR POETRY OF MODERN GREECE.[*]

THE literature of modern Greece is a phrase that may sound strange to some ears, just as there are honourable and right honourable gentlemen who annually bring down so many brace of grouse on the Highland moors, who never heard the names of Duncan M'Intyre, Rob Donn, Alastair M'Donald, or any other of the stout band of Celtic singers, who have from time to time stirred the silence of the glens with the vigorous pulses of their Mountain Muse. But no person who has had his eyes open to what has been going on in Greece for nearly a hundred years since the contagion of the great French Revolution began to operate in that quarter will be prepared to expect, that, where the political world was shaken from its foundation, the intellectual world remained stagnant. On the contrary, it was in Greece as in Italy ; the way for political movement was paved by intellectual ferment, and scholars, thinkers, and singers appeared as the preparatory Avatar of men who afterwards drew the eyes of Europe as soldiers, diplomatists, and statesmen. No doubt modern Greek literature is still a very humble thing ; but as the botanist does not despise a plant merely because it is small, so the intelligent student of the vast

[*] 1. Carmina Popularia Græcorum. Passow. Lipsiæ, 1860.

2. Neugriechische Anthologie, von Dr. Theodor Kind. 2te Ausgabe.

3. Researches in the Highlands of Turkey, by the Rev. Henry Fanshaw Tozer. London, 1869. Chapter XXVIII.

4. Ἄσματα δημοτικὰ τῆς Ἑλλάδος ὑπὸ Ζαμπελίου. Corcyra, 1852.

literature of Greece may have good reason to look on the
artless lay whistled by some brigand boy in a Thessalian
glen as of more interest, both philologically and æsthetically,
than the most ambitious structures of the erudite Alexandrian Muse, on which some of the greatest of modern
scholars have spent the best electricity of their brains.
It was not indeed possible, in accordance with the laws of
growth which govern the moral no less than the physical
world, that a first-class Neo-Hellenic literature should
have sprung up in the present epoch of tentative national
reconstitution.   The physical, through the whole order of
things of which we are a part, is the indispensable basis of
the intellectual ; and a country grasping painfully after
the first elements of material prosperity can never produce
a rich and vigorous national literature.   As easily could
Dante have appeared in the days when Lombards,
Romans, Gauls, Normans and Saracens were fighting
about the possession of a few duchies in Apulia; as
readily could the tragic grace of Racine, and the charming
mysticism of Madame Guyon have been contemporary
with King Clovis and his rude Franks, as that a great
poet should appear amid the physical desolation and pro-
stration under which Greece has suffered for so many centuries.   All that a reasonable man can expect from the
modern Greek mind is, that it should show itself by in-
dubitable symptoms to be alive ; that there should be a
healthy national feeling in the masses ; and that it should
be in general no less true of the modern than of the
ancient Greeks,—that they " seek after wisdom." We
should hope to see among this people, if they are truly
the sons of their fathers, in the first place a large spirit of
appropriation ; for only by adopting and assimilating the
intellectual productions of the leading nations of Europe,

can the modern Greeks hope to assert their place among the cultivated nations of the West. This is the law of nature. Nations, like individuals, must learn from their superiors before they can aspire to teach. The premature originality of ignorance, or of the solitary self-taught student, is a frothy soap-bubble, easily created and easily destroyed. Of this great truth the Greeks have shown by their conduct, from the days of Adamantine Corais downwards, that they are profoundly aware. That great scholar and true patriot felt deeply two truths on which the progress of the Greek people during the last sixty years has mainly depended—*first*, that intellectual culture was with the Greeks, in competition with the Turks, the surest lever of national independence; and again, that the intellectual culture of a people with such a rich inheritance from the past must be based on a thorough knowledge of their own classical literature. Nor were these the thoughts of Corais only; they were the thoughts of the people of whom he was the most accomplished spokesman. Hence his influence; hence their whole career from the establishment of the famous schools at Kydonia, Scios, and Yannina, to the erection of such noble educational buildings as the Ἀρσακεῖον,[1] or Young Ladies' Academy, and the Othonian University of Athens. The flourishing condition of this latter establishment alone—an establishment in its place no less efficient in every sense than Oxford and Cambridge are in theirs;—this fresh-sprung University, with its well-marshalled lines of accomplished professors, and troops of eager-eyed students, would be a sufficient proof of the

[1] The Ἀρσακεῖον is a splendid new building, erected by the munificence of a private individual, on the same elevated ground on which the king's palace and the University stand, a little more to the north, and on the opposite side of the street. No man who sees this building can despair of Greece.

wonderful intellectual activity of the people, even were
there not a single printed book in the language. But
there is no lack of books. The press of Athens within
the last fifty years has been uncommonly active. A city,
whose population does not exceed that of Perth, supplies
intellectual nourishment to its inhabitants in the shape
of at least half a dozen literary and political papers, some
of which contain essays on the great questions of the
day, written with a talent and a command of language
of which the first newspaper in England would have no
cause to be ashamed. As for more bulky performances
the Greeks have now excellent systematic treatises on
most branches of science, composed by men who, to the
native shrewdness of their race, add the most varied
acquirements from the great laboratories of French acuteness and German erudition. If the works of such men
as Rangabe, Asopius, Paparogopoulos, Valettas, Bilettas,
Mistriotes, Satha, Zampelios, Maurophrudes, Basiades, and
a host of others, are not better known in this country,
it arises partly from a certain pedantic superciliousness
with which English scholars were accustomed to look on
every product of Greek literature not within a certain artificially circumscribed domain called " classical ;" partly from
the fact that these highly-gifted and well-instructed persons, as Mr. Brandis suggests,[1] have, with a patriotic self-
denial, been less anxious about their European reputation
as authors, than about their Greek usefulness as teachers.
At the present moment, indeed, Greece requires that all
the energies of her best men shall be devoted to the great
work of public instruction ; and no man who knows the
elements of which the present academic staff in Athens is
composed will doubt that she has in this respect been

[1] *Mittheilungen über Griechenland*, von C. A. Brandis, 3ter Theil. Leipzig, 1842.

most faithful to herself. All these scientific and literary works, moreover, whether original or translated, are
written in a style of Hellenic elegance and purity, which
even the Greeks themselves twenty years ago would have
deemed impossible. So swift is progress in the rhetorical
department when the nimble Greek wit sets itself seriously to use the materials offered by the rich and flexible
Greek tongue.

Of works bearing the type of a fresh nationality—
without which the best foreign appropriation could produce only a meagre result—the modern Greeks present
us in the first place with the military memoirs of Per-
rhœbus, highly esteemed by Niebuhr, and other historical
and biographical works. True it is, that the modern
Hellenes are not likely to produce an account of their
own great exploits in the late war, which shall surpass
that of our own countryman, Gordon, in accuracy and
impartiality; but a liberal dash of patriotic colouring will
be readily forgiven as much to a modern Greek Tricoupi,
as to an ancient Roman Livy; and in this department
we advise all Hellenistic students to keep their eyes open,
as new books are now issuing from the press, and others
are shortly expected, that will give to the recent national
history that prominence in the new national literature
to which it is so justly entitled. In the meantime, those
students of Greek literature who consider a modern
Hydriote Miaulis as interesting a human character as
an ancient Phormio, will find the true spirit of the Greek
revolt, perhaps, most effectively reflected in the popular
ballads, whose authorship is unknown, and in some of
the political and patriotic poetry of Alexandros Soutzos.
The popular ballads of the modern Greeks, the τραγούδια
Ρωμαικά, are indeed, as evidences of a healthy national

vitality, superior to any literary product of the national mind that has yet appeared. Popular poetry, like wild plants to the botanist, has to the man of refined taste always a certain value beyond its inherent worth as poetry, merely because it is popular. Even the vulgar epigrams of Martial, replete as they are with low. puns and filthy buffoonery, are, as the exponents of the corrupt life of imperial Rome, of far greater value to the literary historian than some of the most finished odes of Horace. Whatever faults they have, they are plants which look like the soil whence they sprung; and that is always pleasing to a scientific eye. So these Romaic ballads are simple enough, certainly; they are, many of them, mere voices or breathings of the popular life, with very little poetic genius, and little or no artistic skill; still they have a fragrance of nature about them, and a freshness, such as vigorous pedestrians delight to snuff up from brown moors and green fields, envying not at all the strong aroma that flows from exuberant prairies flushed with the living gold and purple of a tropical vegetation. Unquestionably inferior to our Scottish poetry of the same class in variety of dramatic element, in the fine play of humour, and in rhythmical compass, they are at the same time so truly popular, and so thoroughly Greek, that whosoever loves Greece must love them. For ourselves we are free to confess, that if a public bonfire of Greek lyric poetry were to be made after the fashion of Don Quixote's library in Cervantes, we should put in a strong word of intercession in favour of the lisping Homers of Souli and Maina, while the polished prettinesses of the classical anthology, and trim voluptuousness of the real and the pseudo-Anacreon were postponed. It is incredible, indeed, what a stomach certain people have for

Greek within the arbitrary line of a certain established philology, while everything beyond that is naught. Learned men will munch stone and gravel out of long-worked and authorized beds, while the honey-laden thymy banks in regions of less orthodox research are left to waste their fragrance and their sweets on solitude. There is a natural preference no doubt in favour of antiquity, which has its value without university walls as well as within them; but a wise man will not allow himself to be so befooled by a venerable old grey stone, however large, as to prefer it seriously to the magnificent dome of a living St. Peter's. A vile daub, though guaranteed from the hand of St. Luke himself, is, after all the pious and artistic sentiment you can spend upon it, only a daub; and the worst picture that ever George Harvey painted is, to a sane eye, in reality worth more, though the picture-dealers and the virtuosos talk less about it. Viewed in this light, the Romaic ballads will always form a most important department of the lyrical riches of the Greek language, even to those who know that there was not a drop of Greek blood in the body of Marco Bozzari.[1] He and the other brave Albanese heroes of the war of independence were swallowed up by the over-powering influence of Greek civilisation, and became Greeks, just as Lucan and Seneca, though Spanish born, became Romans.

To discuss this popular poetry fully, and to bring out distinctly the traits of national history and character with which it is replete, would require a volume. We can only indulge ourselves at present in giving one or two

[1] "The soldiers of Souli, and the sailors of Hydra, the bravest warriors, and the most skilful mariners, in the late struggle, were of the purest Al-banian race, unaltered by any mixture of Hellenic blood.—Finlay, *Mediæval Greece and Trebizond*, p. 39.

specimens of translation from our own portfolio. The ballad poetry is remarkable for being in the general case not rhymed ; a classical feature which we hope may conciliate some academic reader. This feature the German translator, the well-known philhellene, Wilhelm Müller, has preserved.[1] We shall generally follow his example. The following little piece was much admired by Goethe :—

CHARON AND THE SOULS.

" Why are the hills so dusky dark, so dark and sable-shrouded ?
Is it the wind that flouts the crag, or is it the rain that's beating ? "
" 'Tis not the wind that flouts the crag, 'tis not the rain that's beating ;
'Tis only Charon with his dead, that o'er the hills is treading.
The young he drives before his path, the old he drags behind him ;
The children, and the weeping babes, he on his saddle bindeth.
The old beseech the rider grim, the young with tears implore him—
' O Charon, halt where the cottage smokes, where the fountain cool is flowing,
The old will drink the water clear, the young will fling the pebbles,
The children with their tender arms, will pluck the flowers so blooming.'
' I will not halt where the cottage smokes, nor where the fount is flowing ;
For mothers would come to the fountain clear, and know their weeping children,
And wives would know their husbands dear, nor would allow the parting.' "

This Charon, or Death, is a great figure in the popular poetry of the modern Greeks, and is one of the very few, perhaps the only mythological personage which Byzantine orthodoxy, and Slavonian barbarism, have left to haunt the hills of Greece from the fair company that once peopled Olympus. Here is another in which that grim ferryman of the ferruginous boat assumes the functions of the ancient Nemesis, and rebukes the pride of life in one who is too young to know that " He that glorieth should glory in the Lord " :—

CHARON AND THE MAIDEN.

A fair young maid was boasting high she feared no harm from Charon,
Nine brothers she had, and Constantine was soon to be her husband,

---

[1] Müller's edition of the ballads was published at Leipzig in 1825, the year immediately following their publication by Fauriel at Paris.

Who owned four lofty palaces, and was lord of many houses.
But Charon changed his shape, and came like to a black-winged swallow,
And flew athwart, and shot the maid i' the heart with his deadly arrow ;
And her mother wept when she beheld, her mother wept full sorely.
"O Charon, cruel was thy aim, thy shot that smote my daughter,
My dear-loved girl, my only child, in all her youth and beauty !"
Then from the far and mountain glen came Constantine the bridegroom,
With four-score men, and sixty-two to harp the bridal music.
" Have done with glee, my trusty men ; ye harpers, cease your harping;
A cross I see before the door of my bride's mother's dwelling.
Belike, belike, her mother is dead, her mother or else her father ;
Or of her brothers one hath been sore wounded in the battle."
He spurs his steed, his good black steed, and to the church he cometh,
And finds the master-mason there, where he a tomb is building.
" God bless thee, master-mason, say, whose tomb here art thou building ? "
" For the maid so fair, with yellow hair and dark eyes, I am building ;
Nine brothers had she, and Constantine was soon to be her husband,
Who owned four lofty palaces, and was lord of many mansions."
" O master-mason, master fine, I pray thee, speed thy building,
A little larger make the tomb, a tomb to hold two bodies."
　　He took his golden-hilted sword, and in his heart he plunged it ;
And in that tomb they buried two, the maid and the youth that loved her.

The above two ballads are from Fauriel's collection, and exhibit the general type of the short Romaic τραγούδι, both in matter and manner. The rhythm is one sufficiently familiar to our ear, and handled not without a tincture of that sleepy monotony and canorous iteration— so different from the varied swing of Homer—in which the uncultivated popular ear delights. The following is from Dr. Kind's little volume, and is rhymed :—

THE CLEPTHS.

From the hills the Clepths came down,
Seeking horses to their mind ;
Horses none when they could find,
All my pretty lambs they stole,
Lambs and kids they took the whole.
　　And away, away they go !
O woe's me ! woe's me, waly wo !
　　My lambs away
　　And my kids took they ;
O woe's me, woe !

U

II.

And the pail in which I pour
The creaming milk, away they bore ;
And the pipe to which I sing,
Rudely from my hands they wring.
    And away, away they go !
    O woe's me ! woe's me, waly wo !
      My lambs away
      And my kids took they ;
    O woe's me, woe !

III.

And they took away outright,
With its horns of silver white,
My brave belwether, that outrolled
Its shaggy fleece of flowing gold.
    And away, away they go !
    O woe's me ! woe's me, waly wo !
      My lambs and my wether
      They stole together ;
    O woe's me, woe !

IV.

Would to God some vengeful hand
Might seize the lawless robber band
In their dens ; and sheer undo
Them, and all their thievish crew !
That I might see my brave belwether,
And my lambs again together
    In the fold.—O waly woe !
      My lambs away
      And my kids took they ;
    O woe's me, woe !

V.

If the All-holy in the skies
The ruthless robbers will chastise,
I will roast a lamb till it
Fall in pieces from the spit ;
Mid flowers that tell of coming May,
On holy George's festal day,
I'll feast, and bless the queen all-holy,
That laid the ruthless robbers lowly,
    O woe's me ! woe's me, waly wo !
      My lambs away
      And my kids took they ;
    O woe's me, woe !

This song is characteristic enough, both of what certain parts of Greece are now, and of what certain parts of Scotland were not much above a hundred years ago. There is nothing in Greek brigandage but what belongs to the history of all nations at a certain stage of civilisation. The last verse with its prominent imprecation of the Virgin Mary, the all-holy ($\pi a\nu a\gamma ia$) queen of heaven, and Saint George, and the act of worship of which the roasting of a whole sheep forms a principal part, is peculiarly Neo-Hellenic, and will suggest to those who have visited Greece many a pleasant picture of rustic piety of which they may have been spectators.

The Klepths, whose harsh treatment of the poor peasantry is recorded in the above, to our taste, extremely beautiful little threnody, would, however, appear to posterity in an altogether inadequate light, if such poems were all that remained of the popular estimate of their character. But so far from being talked of habitually as thieves, and robbers, and plunderers, they appear to the popular imagination rather in the glorified aspect of the Saxon Robinhood and the Gaelic MacGregor. Lawless by the necessity of their position rather than the native vice of their character, they have been handed down to posterity as the impersonations of manly independence, and the champions of national liberty. Their persistent defiance of the hated Turk has thrown, for the most part, a fair veil of charity over their occasional rude neglect of the principles of *meum* and *tuum* in their dealings with their fellow-countrymen. Forgotten or forgiven as plunderers, in popular song they are canonized as patriots ; and their achievements accordingly, not particularly interesting to the general reader now, will, to the student of history, ever remain as interesting historical records, playing, in their wild way, the natural prelude to the great national resurrection in 1821. The following are fair specimens of the specifically Klepthic ballads :—

CHRISTOS MILIONIS.

Three little birds upon the hill beside the camp had lighted ;
The one looked towards Armyros, the other towards Valtas ;
The third, the best of all the three, thus warbled and lamented :—
" Tell me, kind Sir, what thou dost know of Christos Milionia.
Where he may be ?—nor Valtos now nor Kriabrisi knows him.
He marched across the land, they say, with his brave men to Arta,
And captive took the Cadi there, and a brace of Agas with him.
This when the Mooselim did hear, his soul was wroth within him,
To Mauromati he did call, and to Moochtar Pleisoora,
' Good Sirs, if ye will eat your bread in peace, and keep your places,
Come kill me Christos, cut me down that brigand chief Milionis ;
The Sultan thus doth give command expressly by this firman !'
The Friday's sun shone bright—would God that sun had never risen—
And Sooliman was sent to find the Captain Milionis.
At Armyros he found the chief, and a friendly greeting gave him.
All night they drained the brimming cup until the day was dawning.
And when the day shone brightly forth they to the camp did wend them.
Then Sooliman thus spake aloud to Captain Milionis :—
Christos, the Sultan sends for thee, the Agas bids me seize thee,
For well they know, while Christos lives, no Turkish law he owneth.
With pointed guns they rushed and stood the one against the other,
Gave fire on fire till prostrate both upon the ground lay bleeding."

OLYMPOS AND KISSABOS.

Olympus high and Kissabos once hotly strove together.
Olympus turns to Kissabos, and thus to him he speaketh :—
" Strive not with me thou lowly hill, thou in the dust art trodden,
The old Olympus high am I, through all the world so famous.
My lofty peaks are forty-two, and sixty-two my fountains,
At every well a banner, and at every tree a brigand ;
And on my loftiest peak of all alone there sits an eagle,
And in his claws he holds the head of a valiant chief departed."
" What hast thou done, my wretched head, what sin art thou atoning ?
Eat, bird, my young and lusty flesh, and batten on my manhood,
'Twill give thy wings an ell, thy nails a span of strong addition.
A valiant Armatole was I in Xerimeros and in Louros,
In Chassia and Olympus high twelve years I lived a robber ;
Sixty Agas with my hand I killed, and burned their hamlets,
And left so many on the field of Turks, and of Albanians,
That none, thou kingly bird, can count the slaves that there lay bleeding
At last the fate of war was mine, and bloody death befell me."

Mr. Tozer, in his valuable account of a tour made through regions seldom footed by the regular tourist, has

made the just remark that there are many things both in
the tone and the contents of these ballads which remind
us forcibly of Homer. As to the tone and style of these
productions, he who does not see in them and in Homer
the peculiarly distinctive character of a floating poetry
made to be sung by the people, and not read in books,
has yet to learn the alphabet of the language that Homer
used, and which gives his poems their peculiar and characteristic value. As to the materials it is equally certain,
judging not only by the Romaic, but by the Servian and
other popular ballads, that the historical element is always
one of the strongest roots out of which they grew ; and
nothing can be further removed from the essential genius
of all Greek poetry than to wipe out from it, with an ingenious brush, every trace of strict personal reality, and to
occupy the stage of the popular memory altogether with
oriental allegories about light and darkness, dissolution
and regeneration, and other favourite figures of a panthe-
istic theology. In the great struggle which resulted in
the restoration of a little Greek kingdom in the south of
Greece, the Klepthic ballad naturally elevated itself into
the specifically historical ballad, of which the following
may be taken as a good example :—

THE TAKING OF TRIPOLITZA.

Dark and dreary was the day, all night the snow was drifting,
When Kiamel Bey the order gave to march to Tripolitza.
He saddled his horse at the midnight hour, he shoed his horse at midnight,
And as he marched along the road, thus prayed to God in heaven :—
" Give me, thou mighty God, to find the bishops and the primates,
That they their heads may pledge to me for these rebellious Rajas,
Nor let them join the brigand chiefs who rise against their masters."
When Kiamel Bey was in the fort, the Greeks encamped around him,
They hedged the Turk there closely in, with war they vexed him sorely,
And Colocotróni forward came, and cried from his tambouri :—
" Come yield thee, yield thee, Kiamel Bey, to the band of Colocotróni,
With life and limb you shall go hence, your wife, and all your children,
Your harem fine shall go with you, and all your dainty household."

'Tis well—'tis well, ye gallant Greeks, and valiant Capitani,
Brave Colocotróni's men we know ; we yield to Colocotróni.
Up then a Booluk Basha stood, and from a bastion cried he,—
" To Rajas vile we will not yield, to filthy misbelievers,
The fort is strong, the walls are sure, in Stamboul rules the Sultan.
A goodly host we count, a band of young and lusty warriors,
Five misbelieving dogs their sword, twice five their gun destroyeth,
Fifteen from horses' back they kill, and thirty from the trenches."
" Have at them, then !—and let them see," cried valiant Colocotróni,
" How true the shot of a Klepth can fly, how cuts a good Greek sabre,
How on the Turk the Greek can rush, and how the Turk can stand him."
Then Tuesday came, and Wednesday sad, and Thursday full of sorrow,
And Friday's sun shone on the Turks (they wished they had never seen it),
For then the Greeks stern counsel took to storm the fort ; and rushing,
They swooped like eagles on the foe, like hawks they pounced upon them,
And like a battery from their guns the eager shot came hailing.
Then at the gate of good St. George came valiant Colocotróni,
" Now fling your guns away, brave boys, and draw your shining sabres,
And drive like sheep into the pen, these Turkish dogs before you !"
The Turks before them flew ; the Greeks within the fort enclosed them.
Then the Kehaiah called aloud to valiant Colocotróni,
" Come, quarter, quarter ! surely now enough of Turks lie bleeding."
" Thou foul old Turk, what pratest thou—thou cursed misbeliever ?
What quarter ?—Bitter quarter thou didst give us at Vostizza,
Where our Greek brethren bled, as now thy Turks shall bleed, Kehaiah !"

So much for the warlike element ; the germ of some future Iliad all ready, if only the singing days would come back again, and the reading days cease all over the world gratefully for a season. Here follow two innocent little lullabies, that one finds it difficult to divorce from their native Greek without pain ; and a lisping address of a little girl to the moon—the φεγγάρι, as they now call it—on her way to the evening school after the hot toils of the day are over :—

LULLABIES.

(1.)

Sweet babe, your mother dear comes home ;
From the stream where laurel grows,
From the fount that sweetly flows,
She will bring bright flow'rets home,
Fragrant flowers that scent the air,
Crimson pinks and roses fair.

(2.)

Sing a lullaby, Mary mild,
Holy Sophia, sweetly sing,
Take to thee the little child !
Bear it hence away with thee,
That the little child may see
Blossoms bright on every tree ;
That the little child may hear
All the sweet birds piping clear.
Take the child and bring 't again
That its father know no pain,
And harshly chide the nurse that kept
Careless watch when baby slept ;
That its mother know no pain
When she seeks her child in vain,
That no sharp grief pierce her marrow,
And her milk run sour with sorrow.

Pretty moon that shines so brightly,
Shine on me that I may go
To the school, and trip it lightly ;
That my letters I may know,
Learn to stitch, and learn to sew,
And with my years in grace to grow,
And God's most holy will to know,
Who walked on earth long time ago,
    Pretty, pretty moon !

Inferior in interest to the popular ballads, but still not without a strong claim on the attention of the lover of poetry, are the more cultivated efforts of the young Greek lyre—not flying voices of the undistinguished people, but distinct articulations of some known singer, and professional student of verse. In this department of literature the Greeks have no doubt yet to look for their national spokesman. Instead of a poetical Napoleon, leading whole armies to the fields of harmonious conflict, and filling Europe with the sound of a succession of great battles, we have only a few expert skirmishers, and captains of the guerilla warfare of the Muses, whose exploits none hear of but those who visit the valleys where they are native. However high Panagiotes Soutzos might conceit himself to stand—and he has made some curious revelations of self-esteem in the Ἀιων and elsewhere—he may depend upon it the eyes of Europe are not directed to him at the present moment; his *Messiah,* we are afraid, will never make one-tenth part of the noise in Europe that was made by that windy production of the same name, in which Klopstock, the German Milton ("yes a *very* German Milton !") vented his vaporous piety.   On a late occasion taking it up (for Sunday reading), before getting to the end of the first act, we were so afflicted with a languid sensation, similar to what oppresses the stomach after large potations of weak tea, that we could proceed no further.   In *The Wanderer* of his brother Alexander, there are no doubt individual passages of considerable lyric power and sublimity; but, as a whole, it is merely a feeble and broken echo of *Childe Harold.*   To condemn all the larger productions of the recent Greek Muse wholesale, we will not venture, because we have not read them; but what we have read, besides a great deal of false and exaggerated sentiment, labours under the general vice of rhetorical diffuseness, which must be violently cut down, before any high excellence can be achieved.   Among the lighter warblings of the lyre, however, we have found several pieces, and hope to find more, that well deserve a place in any collection of Greek lyric poetry; and even in much that is feeble or exaggerated we have been delighted to recognise a flush of nationality that is powerful to lend an engaging charm even to weakness.   Patriotism, like charity, covers a multitude of sins.   In the following ode, for instance, of Karatsoutscas, there is much that is juvenile in style, and overworked in the sentiment;[1] but

---

[1] Kind says that the author was only twenty years of age at the publication of the volume from which this extract is taken.

is so thoroughly Greek, and expresses so powerfully from the hot heart of Hellenic patriotism the faith in a mighty past, and an impending future of national glory, that it must be read with very great pleasure by all who sympathize with the hopes at present animating the best minds in Greece :—

PANHELLENICS.

I.

With Parnassus' laurel wreath, the wreath aye green and never fading,
Green in face of frosty winter, and rude Boreas harsh-invading ;
With the laurel I will wreathe my lyre, a song of freedom raising
To my country, Greece and all her mighty glory truly praising ;
Happy if my well-nerved hand shall strike no feebly falling measure,
If the ears that love the land shall drink my loyal strain with pleasure,
If with song while I commend thee,
One kind glance of fair approval thou, my country dear, shalt lend me !

II.

For the Mars that wasted Creta, Greece a stole of sorrow weareth ;
For the Mars that crushed fair Creta, Greece her locks of beauty teareth.
Creta, when the Mars that crushed thee, marched his club of terror shaking,
Brandishing the sword, which flashing fills the tyrant's heart with quaking,
Darkened was the ray that cometh from the disk of Phœbus streaming ;
From its base in darkness rooted, to its peak with white snow gleaming,
Men beheld high Ida brightening,
Saw the seat of Jove the Thunderer flaming with the frequent lightning.

III.

In the Sultan's hall, the Sultan's wisest counsellors assemble,
Seize their white beards with their hands, and inly puzzled think and tremble,
How thy patriot fire, O Creta, they may quench with tyrant's knavery ;
And the powers of Europe lend a helping hand to fix thy slavery,
Ply with threats each dastard heart, and bait with golden wiles the traitor ;
And amid the faithless crew,—O shame, O mockery of nature !
He, whom Greece had made defender
Of her rights—her Consul—he was the first to cry—SURRENDER !

IV.

And the Greek that loves his country, when he saw his Cretan brother,
Prostrate, in his brother's breast the rising pity could he smother ?
Was that sacred fire extinguished, that with generous inspiration,
When the stranger dared to touch her, filled the wide Hellenic nation ?
Did the graves not ope their jaws, and forth with wrathful resurrection
Rush the troops of harnessed shades, to pledge their father land's protection ?
Did the past not fire the present,
In the hall of every burgher, in the hut of every peasant ?

V.

No ! that fire is not extinguished in the heart of Hellas glowing ;
It shall burn while earth shall stand, and while old Ocean's wave is flowing.
Slavery oft hath stamped on slaves the love of their own degradation :
But the type of years could never stamp with serf the free Greek nation.
Cursed be they who bind the hands of Hellas when her bonds she breaketh ;
Cursed who bar the gates of freedom, when the glorious start she taketh ;
　　　　May the curse of Greeks united
Lie upon them, like the Furies, when their breath consumes the blighted !

VI.

When the joyful news was speeded, that the sons of Crete had risen,
All the people clapp'd their hands to hail the captive from his prison,
All the women and the children leapt for joy ; and every temple
Showed the votive gifts for thee, that none on thy young rights might trample.
But the hope of Greeks was darkened, and their vows had no completion,
And the men that hate her triumphed ; and their hatred found addition.
　　　　Treachery vile hath triumphed o'er thee,
Crete ; thou liest low ; and we in vain with bitter tears deplore thee.

VII.

How should Europe, silly Europe, when the sign of death is plainly
Hung out on a nation's forehead, try to cheat strong nature vainly ?
Can a tree be bright with blossom, can its fruit be ripe and glowing,
When a worm the pith consumeth, when no juice of life is flowing ?
Even the water round the root, that with such busy care thou pourest,
Feeds the rot that eats the heart of the frail life that thou restorest.
　　　　When life's thread is broken, never
Shall the wits of all the wisest bind it with their strong endeavour.

VIII.

I will speak it in a figure : like a house with many chambers
Turkey stands—an old house hoary with the crust of long Decembers.
Many a prideful year it witnessed, now it knows the hour of sorrow ;
Tottering reels one wall to-day, and another falls to-morrow.
Let the hand of man approach it, and, before its ruin bury
Nobler piles and worthier mansions, with a wise precaution hurry
　　　　Down to cast the crazy dwelling,
And upraise a safer o'er it, and in beauty more excelling.

IX.

Europe, if a work thou seekest where thy toil shall find a blessing,
For the waste wouldst plant a garden worthy of thy nicest dressing,
List, and I will tell thee wisely how, being great, thou may'st be greater.
Near to Turkey is a land, a little land where kindly Nature
Such a power of brilliant beauty, and each comeliest grace has showered,
That no tongue can tell the store of that rich grace with which 'twas dowered.
　　　　'Tis a lovely land, concealing
Virtue, like the magnet's power, to seize the sense and charm the feeling.

X.

In this land a people dwelleth, rich in high ancestral glory ;
Clio names no race more noble in her roll of various story.
Bound in darkness lay the Earth ; the precious light of knowledge perished ;
Rule tyrannic, deeply rooted, spread its arms abroad and flourished.
The forced sweat of all the nations, and their bright blood crimson flowing,
Sucked a monstrous biform dragon, proud the double ensign showing
   Of the crown to monarchs given,
And the mitre of the priest who serves the Lord that rules in Heaven.

XI.

In the claws of this Chimera torn humanity lay bleeding.
From the East a wasting fire-flood came, and wildly westward speeding,
Spread to Earth's remotest corner, death and devastation dealing ;
But unharmed amid the deluge stood the Hellenic tribe, revealing
A miraculous virtue stable : by despotic sway surrounded,
Greece preserved her laws and freedom undisturbed and unconfounded ;
   She serene and independent,
All the world a march of tyrants, with a train of serfs attendant.

XII.

Strong and self-sustained Greece never to a sacred priestly college
Sold her right of thought : free-branching flowed the common stream of knowledge.
Brutish gods she never worshipped, crocodiles and creeping creatures,
But Apollo and the Muses, gods with bright benignant features.
Pyramids she never piled, colossal rows of Sphynxes keeping
Watch around the solemn Dead, in their cold stone-chambers sleeping ;
   But she raised the glorious temple,
With its clear sun-fronting rock, and its pillar'd ranges ample.

XIII.

In this land the seed of Poesy, by the gods benignly planted,
Swelled and grew to leafy grandeur. Orpheus here and Linus chanted
Songs that stirred the rooted forest, stayed the flood, and tamed the lion ;
Here the stones in rhythmic order rose to please thy lute, Amphion ;
Here the far career of thought first opened on the wondering nations ;
Here of every art were laid, of every science, sure foundations ;
   And all subtle searching spirits
Loved to graft their art with thoughts which all the world from Greece inherits.

XIV.

But alas ! a savage storm swept o'er the land, before whose power
Even their trees uprooted fell, the fair trees of the Grecian bower,
And the seed of truth was wafted where a cool-brained race, laborious,
Reaped, from fields which thou hadst sown, an intellectual harvest glorious ;
And, when feasting on the fragrance of thy fruitful gardens, never
Dreamt to cast a grateful glance on thee, of these fair gifts the giver.
   Greece their stumbling march assisted,
But in their conceit no Greece in all the vasty world existed.

XV.

Where the Muse of Æschylus soared on wings of solemn chorus ample,
Tartar hordes the soil of Hellas with unlettered feet did trample,
Then when Rigas, mighty martyr, gathered in the inspiration
Of his war-song all the slender hopes that still sustained his nation.
On his head the axe descended, lay his laurel crushed and bloody ;
But from that free song came forth a wondrous blossom bright and ruddy ;
   As from a mother's throes laborious
Greece was born anew in him, and Freedom rose to life victorious.

XVI.

Look upon the sleeping infant, lift, ye wise, your high doxology !
Come, diplomatists that finger nations with your cold phrenology,
Come and touch it !—a bright future in its noble features shining
Can ye read, or does that glance outrun your powers of dull divining ?
Seest thou how upon its healthful cheek the rosy beauty gloweth,
Even as fair Aurora's beauty, when her fingers red she showeth,
   And prepares the joys which follow,
When the awakened world shall blush beneath the full blaze of Apollo.

XVII.

Yes, my country, thou shalt never cheat the hopes of them that love thee ;
Glows my heart with heat from thee, whose far-shed radiance shall approve thee
To the good ; the scoffer's doubts thou shalt dispel with thy appearing.
Thou shalt be a Titan, glorious through the fields of Heaven careering,
Thou shalt ride thy car sublime, the bright-maned steeds thy word obeying,
On the green Earth's face vivific beams of light and heat outraying.
   So ! in rifts, where thou art nighing,
Opes the blue serene, and all the clouds that darkly lowered are flying !

XVIII.

In thy cradle, O my country, when thy baby-life was sleeping,
In thy veins the unseen virtue of immortal gods was leaping ;
When the sibilant brood assailed thee, basilisk and amphisbena,
With thy young arms thou didst crush them, like the strong son of Alcmena.
When their venomous spires voluminous rolled around thee, thou didst seize them,
And with sudden grasp resistless like the soft clay thou did squeeze them ;
   And before the infant scathless
Fell the terrible snake of Asia, fell the snake of Egypt breathless.

XIX.

Thou hast fought, and art victorious ; on thy laurels thou repairest
Now thy strength ; thou needest rest to heal the bleeding wounds thou bearest.
Sleep like ocean when the windless air no swelling wave is stirring,
Soft as noon of sultry summer, when no wing of bird is whirring ;
But like ocean thou shalt waken, when its ruffled evening mirror
Bristles round the pale sea-farer, with a thousand crests of terror,
   When the scowling rack is drifting,
And to smite the sheer black cliff his scourge the god of waves is lifting.

xx.

Like an old and toothless lion, when its strength is all departed,
Turkey roars. Up, Greek, and seize Alcides' club, the mighty-hearted ;
And with steady foot firm planted, and with strong hand overpowering,
Prostrate lay with deadly blow the savage monster, blood-devouring ;
Let it fall, and in its fall disgorge the innocent blood it swallowed !
Wrap its shaggy hide around thee, and bring back the great time-hallowed
   Kingdom, which the Cæsar glorious,
When the Cross subdued the nations, planted in the East victorious.

It were a waste of time to criticise in detail the faults
of this poem ; but the conception is good ; and, were the
tone considerably subdued in some parts, the effect would
be much increased. In favourable contrast with the high
rhetorical swell of the Panhellenics, stands the plaintive
simplicity of the following little poem by Alexander
Ypsilante, the ill-starred and crude originator of the first
movement of the Greek revolution in Moldavia. The
little bird represents, of course, the condition and feelings of a Greek in Europe without a Greece :—

THE BIRD'S LAMENT.

Poor little bird,
 Fluttering low,
Weary and lone,
 Where dost thou go ?
Seekest thou rest,
Near in thy nest,
 Poor little bird ?

No nest have I ;
But I flutter and fly
 To and fro.
I seek and I find
 No rest to my wing ;
Bliss is to me
A forbidden thing,
 Wherever I go.

I had a country when I was young ;
 And my hope was strong
 As I poured my song
The white-flowered myrtle trees among,
 When I was young.
 I sat on the tree,
 I sang late and early,

I had a mate, and I loved her dearly,
    And she loved me.
Down came a hawk with swift swoop from the sky
And tore my joy from before mine eye ;
        And spoiled my rest,
        And robbed my nest,
    And left me bare to lie.
Since then all cheerless and hopeless I roam,
Without a friend, without a home.

With weary wing, and wail more weary,
I wander o'er the world so dreary ;
        With the wind I roam,
        Till I find a home
Where no wing of the weary is stirred ;
    Where the monarch so proud
    Shall sleep with the crowd,
        And the hawk from the sky
        Shall harmless lie
With the poor little innocent bird.

We conclude with a little piece of some historical interest, written no doubt shortly after the taking of Constantinople by the Turks in 1453, and which points to a political consummation in which no Greek true to his blood and to his traditions refuses to indulge. We give the translation literal in the present case, with the original prefixed, that the student may have before him a fair specimen of the average popular Greek of the fifteenth century :—

Πῆραν τὴν πόλιν πῆράν την, πῆραν τὴν Σαλονίκην !
Πῆραν καὶ τὴν ἁγιὰν Σοφιὰν, τὸ μὲγα μοναστῆρι,
Π᾽ εἶχε τριακόσια σήμαντρα, καὶ ἐξήντα δύο καμπάναις·
Καθέ καμπάνα καὶ παππᾶς καθέ παππᾶς καὶ διάκος.
Σιμὰ νὰ βγοῦν τὰ ἅγια, κ᾽ ὁ βασιλεᾶς τοῦ κόσμου,
Φωνὴ τοὺς ἦρθ᾽ ἐξ οὐρανοῦ, ἀγγέλων ἀπ᾽ τὸ στόμα·
Αφῆτ᾽ αὐτὴν τὴν ψαλμωδιὰν νὰ χαμηλώσουν τ᾽ ἅγια,
Καὶ στείλτε λόγον εἰς τὴν φραγκιὰν, νὰ ἔρθουν νὰ τα πιάσουν,
Νὰ πάρουν τὸν χρυσὸν σταυρὸν, καὶ τ᾽ ἅγιον εὐαγγέλιον,
Καὶ τὴν ἁγιαν τράπεζαν νὰ μὴ τὴν ἀμολύνουν.
Σὰν τ᾽ ἄκουσει ἡ Δέσποινα, δακρύζουν ἡ εἰκόνες·
Σώπα, κυρία, δέσποινα ! μὴ κλαίῃς, μὴ δακρύζῃς,
Πάλε μὲ χρόνους, μὲ καιροὺς, πάλε δικὰ σου εἶναι.

They have taken the city—they have taken it—they have taken Thessalonica!
They have taken also St. Sophia, the large minster
Which had three hundred altar-bells, and sixty-two bells in the steeple,
And to every bell a priest and to every priest a deacon.
And when the Most Holy went out, and the Lord of the World,
A voice was wafted from heaven, from the mouth of angels,
"Leave off your singing of psalms, set down the Most Holy,
And send word to the land of the Franks, that they may come and take it;
That they may take the golden cross, and the holy gospel,
And the holy table, that the infidels may not pollute it."
When our Lady heard this her images wept;
"Be appeased, Sovran Lady, and do not weep,
For again, with the years and the seasons, again the minster will be yours."

If this lyric is destined to be anything more than a fine dream, the modern Hellenes, with such a big neighbour as Russia, and such slippery spectators as England and France, will require to learn the elements of a certain political wisdom to which they have hitherto been strangers; and, even with that wisdom, it may be as easy for the Muscovite, some fine day, to snap up Constantinople, as for a big trout to catch a fly. Perhaps, however, the patriotic minstrel only meant, that Constantinople would one day come back to the possession, not indeed of the Greek people, but of the Greek church. If this issue be enough to realize the pious prayer, then its fulfilment is more than likely; for that the cross will at no distant period take the place of the crescent on the dome of St. Sophia is one of the safest political prophecies on which, in the present state of Europe, a prudent man may venture.

ON THE PLACE AND POWER OF ACCENT
IN LANGUAGE.

On the subject of accent and quantity as elements of human speech, there has been such an immense amount of confusion, arising from vague phraseology, that in renewing the discussion nothing seems more necessary than to start with a careful and accurate definition of terms, and that a definition not taken from books, the dumb bearers of a dead tradition, but from the living facts of nature, and the permanent qualities belonging to articulated breath. Now, if we observe accurately the natural and necessary affections of words in human discourse, considered merely as a succession of compact little wholes of articulated breath, without regard to their signification, we shall find that all the affections of which they are capable amount to four. Either (1), the mass of articulated breath which we call a word is sent forth in a comparatively small volume, as in the case of a common gun, or it is sent forth in large volume, as in the case of a Lancaster gun ; this is a mere affair of bulk, in virtue of which alone it is manifest that any word rolled forth from the lungs of a Stentor must be a different thing from the same mass of sound emitted from a less capacious bellows. In common language this difference is marked by the words *loud* and *low*. A broader wave of air impelled against the acoustic machinery of the ear will always make a more powerful impression independent of any other consideration. But (2), an equal or a stronger impression may be made on the ear by a less volume of sound, if it be sent forth with such an amount of concentrated energy and force as to compensate for its deficiency in mass. A more sharp and intense clap of thunder, for instance, may in this way affect the ear more powerfully than a greater peal less vigorously sent forth and more widely spread. The affection of sound brought into action here is what in language we generally call stress or emphasis; and it depends altogether on the intensity of the projectile force, and gives to speech the qualification of more or less forcible. But (3), this force may often be, and very naturally is, accompanied with another affection of sound altogether distinct, viz., the sound may be deep and grave, or high and sharp, corresponding to what in music we call bass and treble notes. The analogy between music and articulate speech is here so striking, that it has passed into common use; as when we talk of a person speaking in a high or a low key, in a monotone, or in a deep low sepulchral tone, and so forth. And in reference to single words, we are accustomed to say, that the acute ·accent stands on syllables pronounced in an elevated tone, and the grave on those pronounced with a low tone. The only difference between the musical scale and the scale of articulate speech in this view is, that the latter, besides being much narrower in its compass, rises or sinks, not by mathematically calculated intervals, but by a mere upward or downward slide, not divided by any definite intervals. The true connexion of these slides with the general doctrine of accent has been well set forth by Mr. Walker, the author of the *Pronouncing Dictionary*, in a separate treatise.[1] (4). The fourth affection of articulated sound is that which is familiarly known to scholars and schoolboys under the name of quantity, and signifies simply the greater or less duration of time during which the sound continues to impress the ear. For it is manifest that any sound may be produced either by a sudden stroke, or jerk, or by a traction prolonged to any extent. In grammar a short vowel corresponds to a quaver or semi-quaver in music, and a long vowel to a crotchet or minim, according to the ratio of the movement.

Now it should seem to be pretty plain at the outset, to all persons whose ears have been exercised in a very slight degree to discern the differences of articulate sounds, that what is called accent in grammar has to do only with the second and third of the above four elements, and not at all with the first or fourth ; in other words, that the accent of a word is totally distinct both from the volume of voice with which the word is enunciated, and the length of time during which the speaker dwells on the syllable. Nevertheless, such is the confusion which learned writers have introduced into this subject, that it is necessary at the very outset to enter a *caveat* against a very prevalent notion that the placing of the acute accent on a syllable naturally or necessarily implies a prolongation of the sound of the accented vowel ; or, in other words, that to accent a syllable without making it long is impossible. In music no performer ever dreams that the rhythmical beat on the first, we shall say, of three quavers—that is jig time— necessarily turns the quaver into a crotchet. A musician making such an assertion would simply be deemed drunk

---

[1] A Key to the Classical Pronuncia-tion of Greek and Latin Proper Names ; with Observations on the Greek and Latin Accent and Quantity. By John Walker. London, 1827.

or mad ; nor does it make the slightest difference in the
quantity of the note receiving the musical accent, whether
in respect of elevation of tone it stands high or low in the
scale. It is understood by every girl who fingers the
piano, that the elevation of the note, the duration of the
note, and the rhythmical emphasis upon the note, are
three essentially different things which never interfere
with one another. But the moment we transfer this case
to the analogous domain of spoken accent,—the *certus
quidam dicendi cantus*, as Cicero called it,—we find ourselves involved in a region of confusion and contradiction
with regard to the simplest matters, than which few
things can be imagined more humiliating to human reason.
For however divergent the printed opinions of the learned
may sound, that the relative facts are exactly the same in
the case of spoken speech, as of song or played notes, is
beyond question. A single example will make this evident. The first syllable of *pō'-tent*, for instance, according to a well-known rule in the English language, is long;
but the first syllable of the Latin word from which the
English comes is short, *pŏt'-ens*, while the accent is on the
same syllable in both languages. Now, it surely will not
be alleged, in obedience to the dictates of any sane ear,
that in pronouncing the Latin word I am obliged to call
it *pō'-tens*, after the English fashion, on account of the
tyrannic force of the acute accent. It seems, nevertheless, that British schoolmasters and professors have acted
under the notion that some compulsion of this kind exists ;
for as a rule they say *bō'-nus*, and not *bŏn'-us*, though they
know very well that the first syllable of this word is not
long, as in the English word *pō'-tion*, but short, as in
mŏr-al. Such confusion of ideas on a very simple matter
is a phenomenon so strange, that some reason may justly

be demanded for its existence ; and on reflection I find
two reasons principally that seem to account for it.   The
first is the confounding of a really long quantity with that
predominance of a sound to the ear which is a necessary
element of all accentuation.   Thus, when I take the word
tĕp'-id, and form the abstract substantive from it—*tepĭd'-
ity*, by changing the place of the accent from the first
syllable of the adjective to the second, I certainly have
given a prominence to the short *i* which it did not possess
before, and a prominence, no doubt, which though it consists principally in force, emphasis, or stress, may also
carry along with it a certain dilatation of the tenuous
vowel, so that it is really longer in the substantive, being
accented, than when it was slurred over without emphasis
in the adjective.   But, though this is quite true, it is altogether false to say that the vowel has been made long
according to the comparative value of prosodial quantity ;
for, if the second syllable of *tepid'-ity* be compared, not
with the last syllable of the adjective *tepid*, but with the
same syllable of the substantive, as mispronounced by
some slow, deliberate Scot—*tepĭ'-dity, tepée-dity*—we shall
see that the vowel *i*, for all rhythmical purposes, still remains short.   The other cause which presents itself to
explain the confusion of English ears on this subject is
the doctrine of what the Greek and Roman grammarians
call length by position.   According to this doctrine, a
vowel before two consonants is long.   What this means
we may clearly conceive by the example of such words as
gōld, ghōst, in English, or *Pābst* or *Ōbst* in German ; but
though the vowels in these words are unquestionably long
in both languages, they are so only exceptionally, the rule
both in English and German being that a vowel before
two consonants is short.   Of this rule the word *shŏrt* itself

may be taken as an excellent example; which, if it occurred in a Greek chorus, by the law of position, would be sung *shŏrt*, with the *o* prolonged, like *o* in *shore*. Now, with this classical analogy in their ears, or rather in their head (for it is by no means certain that all those authors who have written on this subject did use their ears), when I pronounce such a word as *prĭm'-rōse* or *ĕl'-bŏw*, it is not at all uncommon for English scholars to say, and obstinately to insist, that the accent on the first syllable of these words is necessarily accompanied by a prolongation of the vowel. But this is a judgment of the question, not by the living fact of the sound, but by the doctrine of an old book about the sound. And as to what the old book says, we in fact do not know whether length by position meant a habitual prolongation of the vowel sound in common discourse, as in our words *gold, told, sold, ghost, most,* or only a poetical licence; that is to say, whether the genitive plural of ἀνήρ, of which the penult is short, was really pronounced *awndrōne* or *ăndrōne* in prose. I for one am strongly inclined to think that the latter is the true fact of the case; for, if it had been otherwise, would it not have been a more correct phraseology in the grammarian to say that a vowel before two consonants is naturally long? But when they tell us that a vowel which is naturally short becomes long when two consonants follow, this looks rather like an artificial exception than a natural rule. And I am inclined to think that such an exceptional rule was introduced from sheer necessity, like the long *o* in certain comparatives, such as σοφώτερος, because, without such a licence, really long syllables in sufficient abundance would not have been found in the language for the necessities of the early dactylico-spondaic poetry. As to any inherent natural necessity in the rule, such an idea cannot be entertained for a moment; for the vowel is then most easily prolonged—as in the English words *pŏ'-tent, nŏ'-tion, na'-tion, pā'-tent,* where it is kept separate in spelling from the influence of the succeeding consonant or consonants, which, as in *pŏr'-tion,* rather act by cutting the breath short, and preventing the prolongation of the vowel. The influence of the consonant in shortening the vowel will be apparent in comparing the words *nŏm'-inal* and *Lĕb'-anon* with *nŏ'-tional* and *lā'-bial;* nor does the addition of a second consonant in any perceptible way alter the case. If the first syllable in *prĭm* is manifestly short, it is certainly not made long by the addition of the long syllable *rose* in the noun *prĭm'-rōse,* a word which, in the relative values of its final and penult syllables, corresponds exactly to a whole host of Greek words which usher in a long final by a short accented penult, as in Πλάτων, the name of the great philosopher of Idealism, in Anglicising which, besides attenuating the vowel, we elongate the short penult, according to the practice of our own language.

It will now be distinctly understood, as a starting-point to the present inquiry, that by accent I mean merely a certain predominance, emphasis, or stress given to one syllable of a word above another, in virtue of a certain greater intensity of force in the articulated breath; this increased intensity being naturally in many cases, but not necessarily in all cases, accompanied by an elevation in the key of the voice. My observations do not include either rhetorical accent, which affects whole sentences and clauses, or national accent, which, in addition to rhetorical accent, often includes some favourite sound, note, or vocal mannerism characteristic of different peoples.

The general question to which we shall now attempt a

scientific answer is the following—What are the great leading principles on which accent, as a phenomenon of articulate speech, depends? Are there any such principles, or is it a matter of mere arbitrary association, fashion, and habit? and, in the comparison of different languages what is the standard of value in respect of their accentual character? Does æsthetical science contain any general rules which might enable us to measure the value of accents, as we do the value of sounds in language, when, for instance, we say that Italian is a more harmonious language than Gaelic, and Greek a more euphonious language than Latin? In answering this question I would remark, in the first place, that there is no such thing as a language altogether without accent; only a machine could produce a continuous series of sounds in undistinguished monotonous repetitions like the *tŭm, tŭm, tŭm* of a drum; a rational being using words for a rational purpose to manifest his thoughts and feelings necessarily accents both words and sentences in some way or other. When, therefore, we find it stated in Adam Smith's Essay on Language, and other English writers, that the French have no accent in their words, this is either a gross mistake, or it must be understood to mean that the French do not give such a decided and marked preponderance to one syllable of the word as the English do; which is very true, as any man may see in comparing the English *velocity* with the French *vélocité*. But this is merely a difference in the quantity and quality of accent, not a contrast betwixt accent and no accent. The second postulate of all rational discussion on this subject is, that the significant utterance of articulate breath, like every other manifestation of reason-moulded sense, is a part of æsthetical science, and subject to the same necessary laws which determine the excellence of a picture, a poem, or a piece of music. No doubt, in the enunciation of words as in all the fine arts, fashion may often prevail to such an extent as in some cases to usurp the place of reason and propriety; but the prevalence of false taste in any department of art does not affect the certainty of the eternal principles by which it is regulated, any more than the prevalence of murders or lies amongst any people can take away from the essential superiority of love to hatred, and of truth to falsehood, in all societies of reasonable beings. We are therefore justly entitled to look for a standard of excellence in the matter of orthoepy, no less certain than the standard of truth in morals or mathematics; as, indeed, all things in the world being either directly or indirectly the necessary effluence of the Divine reason, must, in their first roots and foundations, be equally rational and equally necessary. Now, in looking for the necessary conditions on which the comparative excellence of accentual systems may depend, we find that they may be reduced to the four following heads :—

1. Significance.   3. Variety.
2. Euphony.   4. Convenience.

And first, that Significance must be a main point in all accentual systems is manifest from the very nature of accent. For why should a man give predominance to one syllable in a word more than to another, unless that he means to call special attention to the significance of that syllable? Nay, it may often be essential to the effect intended to be produced by the word, that its most significant syllable should be emphasized, as when Lord Derby lately said that the adoption of the Prussian system of making every citizen a soldier would not bea *prógression* but a *rétrogression.* No doubt, in order to express such an accentual contrast as this, the English language departs from its usual fashion of accenting these words; but this only proves that the English method of accentuation in this case is a mere fashion, founded on no natural law, and which accordingly must yield to the higher law of emphatic significance, when nature, like murder, will out. And here we may observe that the English, as a merely derivative and mixed language, is by no means a favourable one for exhibiting the natural and normal laws of a rational accentuation. Neither, so far as I know, is there any language whose orthoepy presents so many anomalies, and where changes entirely reasonless and arbitrary require only the stamp of aristocratic or academic whim to give them currency. With regard, however, to the natural preponderance of the contrasting element in compound words, the Saxon part of our language affords obvious examples of its recognition; as when we say, *out'-side* and *in'-side, back'-wards* and *for'-wards, up'-hill* and *down'-hill, male* and *female.* So in the names of the Highland clans, as *MacBain, MacDonald, MacGrigor,* etc., the emphasis does not lie on the common element, the *Mac,* but on the distinctive element to which the other is attached; and in this view our Saxon pronunciation of *MácIntosh* and *MácIntyre* affords two very good examples of words where custom and fashion have inverted the natural and significant place of the accent. In the Greek language this most natural of all accentual laws operates in all such compounds as ἄκαρπος, ἄπαις, σύνοδος, πάροδος, with which we may contrast the English *fruitless, childless,* where the accent is on the root, and not, where it ought naturally to be, on the contrasting element of the compound. In the

same category with this I am inclined to place the accent
on the augment in Greek, as in ἔτυψα, τέτυμμαι; for it is
the augment here manifestly that contains the element of
past time which is distinctive of the tense, being equivalent in effect—whatever its original meaning may have
been—to *I* DID *strike,* as opposed to *I* AM *striking.* The
same desire to call attention to the distinctive element
may have determined the Greeks to accent the penult of
all diminutives, contrary to their usual practice, in words
with a short final syllable, as in παιδίον, παιδίσκος, κ.τ.λ.

Under this head I am sorry to record my dissent from
a German writer of acknowledged excellence on this subject—Dr. Karl Göttling.[1] This learned writer lays down
the maxim in the first place, that in the Greek language
the accent falls on the syllable containing the principal
idea of the word; and, accordingly, he says that in λέγω
and other verbs not pure it falls on the penult, because
this syllable is the root, and the root, as containing the
principal idea of the word, is naturally emphasized. Now,
looking back to the first framers of a language, I cannot
see in this case any reason why the root syllable should
have received the accent rather than the termination,
which, for the sake of distinction and contrast, is added
to the root. If we say ἄκαρπος, because we wish to call
attention to the negative particle, why should we not say
λεγώ calling attention to the personal pronoun; as, in fact,
we do say in English, *quoth I',* *quoth* HÉ? And in the
same way with regard to nouns, as the terminations of
the cases were originally expressions of relation, attached
to the noun for the sake of emphasis and contrast, I do
not see why the schoolboy fashion of declining *dominŭs-*

---

[1] *Elements of Greek Accentuation,* from the German. London: Whitaker.
1831.

i-o'-ûm—should not have been the original one. And so in the case of the German *brauer*ÉI and the Scotch *brewer*ÉE as contrasted with the English *bréwery*; for though no doubt it may be said that as the root *brew* contains the principal idea, the accent should naturally be there, and this is what Göttling says, yet it may with more right be said, that what is intended to be emphasized here is not mere brewing, but a place for brewing, and that the syllable denoting the place receives the accent as appropriately as the terminations ἥριον, εῖον, and ὦν, when used for the same purpose in Greek. Only so much truth, therefore, can I perceive to lie in Göttling's principle, as to admit that, so soon as the original signification of terminations is lost, and people commence to supply their place by prepositions, pronouns, and other separate words, whose significance is felt—then, and not till then, can the accent on the root syllable be regarded as natural and normal in language. Thus, when the German says *Hábe*, laying the stress on the first syllable of the first person singular present indicative of the verb to *have*, this is natural and normal, because the termination *e* has no significance to him, and could receive an accent only from a senseless fashion, not from a natural propriety. On the other hand, in *Ab'gábe, Hingábe, Zúgábe*, and similar compounds, the accent is properly placed on the contrasting element of the compound, of which the significance is strongly felt.

The next element we have to take into consideration in measuring the value of different accentual systems is Euphony. The simple mention of this word will suffice to show how very one-sided a notion it was in Göttling, that the accent, as a general principle, should always be on the root syllable, as being the most significant. If man were only a logical animal, this might be all very well as an *a priori* ideal of a perfect accentual system ; but he is also, if not always at starting, certainly when fairly developed, an æsthetical animal, which may be allowed on occasions to sacrifice the significance of ideas to the luxury of sounds. And, if this is true of man generally, it is certainly so *a fortiori* of the Greeks, whose whole culture grew out of music, and remained in the closest connexion with it to the very end of their classical period. Supposing, therefore, that with this most musical and artistic of all peoples a regard to the mere luxury of sound had, in certain cases, determined the position of the accent, let us ask in what way this determination would naturally manifest itself? The answer is obvious. In richly terminational languages such as the Greek, where the terminations are not insignificant little short vowels or syllables, as in the German *Gabe*, *Buche*, *Brüder*, etc., but deep, full-rolling, prolonged vowel-syllables, such as ων, οις, αο, αων, and οιο, there might exist a very natural tendency to place the accent on these syllables,—not, of course, because there is any necessary connexion, as some persons say, between accenting a syllable and lengthening it, but because when a syllable by the presence of a long vowel actually is long, the placing of the accent on it is the most certain way both to bring out the full length of the vowel, and to insure the permanence of the full musical value of the syllable, so long as the language lasts. For whatever other syllables of a word may from carelessness, or haste, or reasonless fashion, be cheated of their natural quantity, the accented syllable will always most stoutly maintain its rights, even if it be a short syllable, much more if it be a long. To illustrate this by a familiar example ; in

the famous Homeric line (*Il.* i. 49), in which the twang
of Apollo's bow is described,

δεινὴ δέ κλαγγὴ γένετ' ἀργυρέοιο βιοῖο,

it is manifest both that the euphony of the line lies
mainly in the two terminations in οιο, though these syllables are certainly not the significant ones in the verse ;
and further, that this verse is much more beautiful when
recited with the rhythmical accent on both the full-
sounding penults, than when, according to the prose accentuation, it emphasizes only the οῖ of the last word. The
coincidence of the termination with the accent therefore
is favourable to music ; and it is favourable also as a bar
to the injury which time is always ready to inflict on
final unaccented syllables. Now, with this principle to
guide us, we shall have no difficulty in seeing the cause
of one peculiar excellence which the ancient Roman
critics recognised in the Greek, as contrasted with their
own tongue, in respect of the accentual system. For,
as the Romans in no word placed the accent on the
last syllable, it followed that they could enjoy the rich
auricular luxury of a grand terminational unison of
accent and quantity only in the case of words whose
terminations are dissyllabic. Thus, they dealt largely
in final trochees—trochees both by accent and quantity, in such words as *sermō'nis, pennā'rum, domino'-
rum, lēgis, probā'vit, voluptā'tem,* and so forth, but could
not say *dominós,* or *Mæcenás,* or any word accented
in the same way as in English our *engiñéer, voluntéer,
eváde, capsíze, demise.* On the other hand, the Greek
terminational accent is pretty equally divided between
trochaic terminations such as οἶο, φιλοῦσι, τυφθεῖσα, μῦθος,
σῶμα, μᾶλλον, and oxytone endings, such as ἀγαθῶν, λαβών,

τυφθείς, φιλεῖς. Of the prevalence of the oxytone accent
in Greek, especially in large groups of adjectives and
substantives, not to mention the whole army of prepositions, and certain familiar parts of verbs, any one
may convince himself by taking a sentence at random
from a Greek book ; and the effect of this on the music of
the sentence will be evident to the dullest ear. Sometimes a whole sentence runs on with a succession of
accented terminational syllables, a peculiarity which, without any rhetorical intention, arises naturally from the
number of oxytone substantives and adjectives, and the
additional fact that all substantives of the first declension, whatever the accent of their termination may be,
receive a long rolling accent on the last syllable of the
genitive plural, while all monosyllables of the third declension, by a law common both to Greek and Sanscrit,
transfer the accent from the radical syllable to the termination in the genitive and dative cases of both numbers.
Take a passage from Plato's *Republic* as an example :—

Οἵ τε θηρευταὶ πάντες, οἵ τε μιμηταί, πολλοὶ μὲν οἱ περὶ τὰ σχήματά τε
καὶ χρώματα, πολλοὶ δὲ οἱ περὶ μουσικήν, ποιηταί τε καὶ τούτων ὑπηρέται,
ῥαψῳδοί, ὑποκριταί, χορευταί, ἐργολάβοι, σκευῶν τε παντοδαπῶν δημιουργοί,
τῶν τε ἄλλων καὶ τῶν περὶ τὸν γυναικεῖον κόσμον, καὶ δὴ καὶ διακόνων
πλειόνων δεησόμεθα. ἢ οὐ δοκεῖ δεήσειν παιδαγωγῶν, τιτθῶν, τροφῶν,
κομμωτριῶν, κουρέων, καὶ αἲ ὀψοποιῶν τε καὶ μαγείρων ; ἔτι δὲ καὶ
συβωτῶν προσδεησόμεθα.[1]

Greek, therefore, is superior to Latin in this respect,
just as an instrument with a larger is superior to one
with a smaller compass of notes. And taking Italian,
under this point of view, into the comparison, we observe
that the few oxytone accents which that beautiful language possesses all arise out of Latin words, with an

[1] *Rep.* ii. 373, B.

accented penult, whose last syllable has fallen away; thus, *podestá* from *potestate*, *amó* from *amavit*, and so forth. The same is the case with the French, as in *vélocité, variété, valeûr;* and most of our English oxytones, whether Latin or Greek, are merely curtailed forms of a final trochaic accent, as *eváde*, from *evádo, voluntéer* from *volontié're, proceed* from *procé'do, advért* from *advérto.* And it is this systematic curtailment by the way, caused by the dropping of the final unaccented vowel both in Latin and Saxon words, which has produced that lamentable deficiency in trochaic endings which makes our rhythmical language so much narrower in compass than that of Greek, Latin, German, and Italian. Only for short lyrical efforts can we manage the rhymed trochaic ending with graceful effect; all attempts to go beyond this natural limit have ended either in a manifest artificial strain, or an admixture of the comic element which is fatal to the effect of serious composition.[1]

If this rich and various disposition of the accent on terminational syllables is thus manifestly a plain element of euphony, that accentuation, on the other hand, will be justly esteemed cacophonous which, by drawing the accent back to the beginning of the word, that is to the third, fourth, or even fifth syllable from the end, has a tendency to cheat the ultimate or penultimate syllable of its full musical value; we say a tendency, because it is only in this tendency that the evil lies; for, if by careful elocution the tendency is corrected, the blot may be turned into a beauty on a principle to be mentioned under the next head.

The remark here made is a very serious consideration

---

[1] This defect is one among half-a-dozen reasons for the general want of success in our English hexametrical experiments.

for us English, as our predominant accent is decidedly antepenultimate, and the fashion seems to be increasing of throwing back the accent from the penult to the antepenult, and from the antepenult sometimes to the fourth syllable from the end. Thus we used to say *contem'plate* and *illústrate*, whereas we say now *con'template* and *illustrate*, *dispútable* has become *disputable*, and *contem'plative*, of course, must become *con'templative*. The tendency of this practice to deprive our syllabification of its natural melody is obvious enough. In such words, for instance, as *sig'nify*, and *púrify*, the tendency to rob the final *y* of its natural long quantity is strong, while in *cólumbīne*, *brigandīne*, from the fuller quality of the final syllable, it is less. But, if the danger be great in the case of the final syllable of such words, it is greater in the case of the penult, that is, the syllable immediately following the accented antepenult ; for, in the case of the final syllable, a secondary accent may come in to save the prominence of the vowel, while the long unaccented penult lies under the double disadvantage of a sinking inflexion and a feeble stress, after the combined force, it may be, of an elevated accent and a long quantity. From this cause it is that in vulgar speaking the second syllable of the verb *ed'ūcate* is liable to be shortened and turned into *ed'ĭcate ;* and so strong is this tendency, that many English scholars will tell you that to pronounce the Greek word ἄνθρωπος, with the accent on the first syllable and the second syllable long, is impossible ; and it is no doubt true that it is not so easy as saying ἄνθροπος, which the modern Greeks generally do ; but as to the alleged impossibility, we have only to look to such words as *land'holder, coálheáver, corn'deáler*, to see that it exists only in the unpractised articulating organs of the objectors. Of all languages that I know, the Gaelic is that whose euphony has suffered most from the habit of throwing the accent back to the beginning of the word. Of this there cannot be a more striking instance than words compounded with the element *mōr*, signifying *great*, which may be divided into two classes, those in which the termination *mor*, recognised in its full significance, is accented, and those in which it falls under the category of the German *lich* and our *y*—in *glücklich* and *lucky*—being used for flexional purposes without a distinct appreciation of its meaning, and therefore naturally unaccented. Of the one class of words, *Liosmō'r* and *Ben Móre*, i.e., *large garden* and *great mount*, may serve as familiar examples; of the other, *sultmhor*, '*fat*,' pronounced *sultvur*, and *grasmhor*, '*gracious*,' pronounced *grásvur*, are excellent illustrations. For in these two last words we see that the adjective *mōr*, in losing its separate significance, loses both its quantity and its natural accent; and the compound word becomes a paltry pyrrhic ˊ˘, instead of a respectable iambus, ˘ˊ, or a majestic spondee, ˊ -.

Under this head it only remains to mention the extraordinary theory of Bopp with regard to the place of the accent both in Sanscrit and Greek. That illustrious philologer, in a work entitled *System of Comparative Accentuation, or Concise Exhibition of the Points of Agreement between Greek and Sanscrit in the Doctrine of Accent*, Berlin, 1854, lays it down as a ruling principle, that the most perfect kind of accentuation generally, and that which prevailed originally in the Sanscrit language, was that in which the acute intonation is placed as nearly as possible to the beginning of a word, however long. Into the historical proofs of any such system of accentuation ever having existed, of course only a profound student of the Vedas could enter. I am authorized, however, by Professor Max Müller and Professor Aufrecht to say, that the theory of Bopp is universally recognised as baseless; and this is just what might have been expected. The mere assertion of such a principle to a man whose ears have been trained to a rich and various orthoepy is monstrous. If the accentuation of the first syllable, as in the well-known case of the Greek vocatives of the third declension, Πάτερ, ῎Απολλον, and such like, may well be explained by the eager energy with which the call was made, it does not therefore follow either that eager energy is the only thing to be looked at in a good orthoepy, or that such oxytone words as ἀγαθή and θεός may not be so enunciated as to carry an intense expression of energy to the ear of the hearer. Let this notion of Bopp, therefore, stand as only another instance of the great blunders to which great wits are subject, and which, as large experience teaches, are the natural consolation of the dunces.

That VARIETY is a necessary element of all æsthetic presentation of the highest order needs no special proof. Variety is both an indication of wealth and a preventive of monotony; and as such is no less a natural source of delight to the recipient of æsthetic pleasure than of just boast to the producer.

> Alles in der Welt lässt sich ertragen,
> Nur nicht eine Reihe von schönen Tagen,

says Goethe; and what the Weimarian sage here says of beautiful days is equally true of beautiful verses or of beautiful words. Hence arises the sure canon—

That language is superior in point of accentual effect which gives no partial predominance to any one accentual place, but gives the rising inflexion free play over all the syllables of a word, so far as the range is consistent with a full vocalization. Now, when we compare the Greek and Latin language by this rule, we find a decided and universally admitted superiority in favour of the Greek; for this language admits of the acute on any one of the three last syllables, while Latin allows it to fall only on the penultimate and the antepenultimate. English, on the other hand, in this view, asserts one point of decided superiority over both the classical languages; for words so accented as *lámentable* and *héritable*, on the fourth syllable from the end, are not at all uncommon with us, while the Greeks and Romans, who had no such accents, fell into the very natural error of thinking that they were contrary to nature. But, though with help of this peculiarity we are able to marshal a much larger army of what the ancients called proceleusmatic feet in words than either Greeks or Romans, we have gained this small advantage at a great risk in point of general weight and majesty; and we may be thankful to the graceful pedantry of our classical scholars, who, in retaining the penultimate accent of many Latin words, have done something to balance our habit of flinging the principal accent far back and skipping over the remaining part of the word. The next canon deducible from the test of variety is, that of any two compared languages, that is the more rich and beautiful in respect of accent, in which the acute accent is placed not on the long syllable but on the short, so that, while the accent gets fair play in one syllable, the quantity stands out in another, and thus a richer and more various melody is distributed over every part of the word. For this reason such words as *cólumbīne*, *rénegāde*, are more beautiful than *glō'riŏŭs* and *victō'riŏŭs*, *enginē'er* and *voluntē'er*, because in these last words, whether oxytone or proparoxytone, all the wealth of sound is spent upon one syllable, while the others remain comparatively weak and ineffective. On the same principle the Greek ἄνθρωπος is richer than the same word accented in the Latin way, ἀνθρώπος, and 'Αριστοφάνης is more beautiful than *Aristóphanes*, if, as the English habit has generally been, the final *es* of the word is pronounced short.

On the fourth principle, by which the comparative excellence of accents may be determined, I place very little value. No doubt, as languages, like buildings, are intended for use, convenience as well as theoretic excellence must be consulted; but, as utilitarian considerations have changed many an architect's noble plan for a great building into a grand incongruity, so considerations of mere convenience have spoiled many a fine language. For convenience, really, in a great majority of cases, means haste and carelessness, or sloth and laziness, and in all such cases proves eventually a hostile and destructive force acting against all excellency of organism in articulate speech. We shall only say generally, therefore, that it is always an imperfection in language when words are so accented as to produce a lumbering unwieldy heaviness in the march of syllables; and we may say also that accents ought, if possible, to be so placed as to admit of suffixes or prefixes being added without changing the intonation of the word. In this view, *contem'plative* is a more convenient accentuation than *con'templative*, because it admits of a substantive *contem'plativeness*, and an adverb *contem'platively*, being formed from it, without the necessity of either advancing the accent or allowing it to remain on the fifth syllable from the end of the new word, where its influence on the following syllables must

naturally be feeble in proportion to their remoteness from
the point of vocal energy.

Of the effect of fashion and whim and caprice, in
determining the accent of certain words, and even of
whole classes of words, contrary to every principle
whether of significance, euphony, or convenience, I say
nothing, because such arbitrary freaks belong not to the
domain of scientific knowledge, and are merely noticeable
as casual aberrations or monstrosities.

Such are the grand principles of the general doctrine
of accents, so far as I have been able to discover them.
It will be observed that they are based on a wide induction, and apply to Latin and Greek as well as to Gaelic
or Italian. It is, however, a point which has been long
maintained in the learned world, that the Greek accents
have something altogether peculiar, and not peculiar only,
but peculiarly mysterious about them, which prevents
them from being used along with examples from any
modern language as illustrations of general propositions
about accent. It is against this notion—a notion peculiarly English, and prevalent in high quarters—that I must
proceed now to make a distinct and deliberate protest ;
for, till it be removed, it will be impossible to say a single
sensible word on the doctrine of accents, from which the
most interesting language in the world shall not be with-
drawn as an example. I proceed, therefore, to show, both
from the nature of the case, and from the most authoritative evidence, that there is not the slightest ground for
the imagination that accent in the classical languages
meant anything substantially different from what it means
in English, or Italian, or modern Greek ; and, as a natural
sequel to this, I will trace the long course of scholarly
opinion on the subject, from the doctrine of Erasmus to

that of Professor Munro, Mr. Geldart, and other English scholars ; and conclude by showing practically, what I have proved in the actual work of teaching, how all the strange contradictions of this singular controversy can be reconciled, and all the imaginary difficulties be made to disappear.

As a foundation for all argument on this subject, we may assume—what no well-instructed scholar in the present state of learning will question—that the accentual marks now seen in every Greek book were first invented by Aristophanes of Byzantium, about 250 B.C., for the very same purpose that the marks of emphasis stand in our pronouncing dictionaries, viz., to insure a correct orthoepy in the reading and recitation of the language. The assertion once boldly flung forth by the early opponents of Greek accents, that they were properly marks of musical intonation, having nothing to do with spoken eloquence, can now be hazarded by no philologer. Whatever the accents meant, they were intended to direct the reading of prose ; had they been anything else indeed, it is impossible to understand how they ever found their way into the familiar notation of prose. But for the sake of those who may not be familiar with the evidence on which this point rests, we shall here set down the testimonies of two eminent grammarians : first, Dionysius Thrax, who lived at Rome about 80 B.C., and whose τέχνη γραμματική, quoted by Sextus Empiricus (*Adv. Math.*, i. 12), has been recently printed in the second volume of Bekker's *Anecdota* (p. 629). This grave authority tells us that the art of grammar, as it was then practised, consisted of six parts—

1. ἀνάγνωσις ἐντριβὴς κατὰ προσῳδίαν—assiduous reading, according to accentuation.

2. Explanation of the meaning, according to the significance of the tropes used by the writers.

3. Explanation of the historical facts and of the glosses or peculiar words.

4. Etymology.

5. Consideration of linguistical analogies.

6. A critical appreciation of the work expounded, in its beauties and defects.

Now, there can be no doubt here as to what προσῳδία means ; for, though the plural of this word sometimes is used in a wider sense, as we talk of the Hebrew points, so as to include aspirations, pauses, quantities, and every affection of which spoken and written words are capable, when used in the singular as a special technical term, it signifies accent, and nothing else.

The second grammarian whom I quote is Theodosius, who lived in the time of the Emperor Constantine, and whose treatise on grammar was published by Goettling in the year 1822. This author, in the chapter (p. 58) entitled πῶς χρὴ ἀναγιγνώσκειν, says that good reading consists in three things—

1. ὑπόκρισις, dramatic expression, arising out of a sympathetic conception of character.

2. προσῳδία—or reading κατὰ τοὺς ἀκριβεῖς τόνους—according to the exact accents—προσῳδία γάρ ο τόνος—for accent and tone are the same.

3. διαστολή, attention to pauses and punctuation.

Now, if any person further inquires whether the ancients did not read their prose according to quantity also, I answer that of this there can be no doubt; but that the prominence in correct reading is naturally given to accent, because quantity is the specialty of poetry, and unless where we talk specially of poetry, by the

word reading we are understood to mean prose. But
that correct reading of prose included quantity also,
is evident from what the same grammarian says a
sentence or two below, viz., that under προσῳδία, in a
wider sense we understand both accent and quantity,
and in this wider sense correct prosodial reading · arises
ἐκ τοῦ παραφυλάττειν τοὺς τόνους καὶ τοὺς χρόνους, from observ-
ing the *tones and the times*, and all the other affections of
articulate speech.   Now, as there was an uninterrupted
succession of grammatical teachers, from the age of the
Alexandrian Ptolemies to the time of the Roman Em-
perors, and from the establishment of the Eastern Empire
by Constantine to the taking of Constantinople by the
Turks, no historical fact can be more certain than this,
that the living accentuation with which Greek was
spoken in the great seats of learning and culture in the
third century before Christ, and by which a just orthoepy
in reading was determined, has been handed down to us in
an unbroken chain of the most authoritative testimony. If
this is not true, there is nothing now credited in the wide
sphere of linguistic tradition that rests on a sure basis.

If, then, the ancient Greeks both spoke and read by
the rule of those accents which we now see on our printed
books, what are we to understand by that accent?
Here the field of definition is happily well narrowed.
That Greek accent did not mean quantity, every page of
tradition on the subject distinctly testifies ; that it did
not mean mere volume of mass of articulate sound is
equally certain ; and no man, ancient or modern, ever
dreamt that it did.   There remain, therefore, under
which it may fall to be subsumed, only the other two
affections of articulate speech with which we started,
viz., elevation of tone and intensity of utterance.   Greek

accent must be either the one or the other of these, or both together. That it means the first, viz., elevation of tone, is plain from the mere terms ὀξὺς and βαρὺς, *sharp* and *heavy*, or *high* and *low*, by which the two familiar accents are designated. It is also distinctly stated by both Greek and Roman grammarians that accent implies change of tone in the voice, by alternate elevation and depression. The phraseology, indeed, of this matter was borrowed by the grammarians from the musicians, and had reference to the high and low notes in the musical scale, these minute speculators having justly observed that, as the voice in music rises or falls by a series of measured intervals, so in articulate speech it rises and falls by a succession of slides, what our great orthoepist Walker calls the rising and falling inflexions. Either, therefore—the acute accent of the Greeks, which is the accent properly so called—means the rising inflexion of the voice on particular syllables of a word, or it means this, *plus* a stress or emphasis on a certain syllable of a word, produced by the greater force, or stretch, or tension of the voice on that particular syllable. Now that it does not mean elevation of the voice merely, but also, and at the same time, that greater stretch or tension of the voice which produces the emphatic syllable of a word, will, I think, be evident from the following six considerations :—

1. From the natural difficulty of elevating the voice, and not at the same time giving an increased emphasis to the elevated vowel ; or, may I not say, rather the natural impossibility—for, though it is certainly possible to give a great emphasis to a syllable, and keep the voice at a low key, that is to say, though stress does not necessarily imply elevation—it certainly does not seem

very natural or very easy to raise the pitch of the voice without accompanying that high pitch with a certain emphasis. I may, for instance, pronounce the Greek word ἀνατολή, with a stress on the last syllable, and yet with the whole pronounced in monotone ; but, if I raise my voice on that syllable, it will be difficult for me to withhold from the syllable the stress which naturally accompanies the act of elevation.

2. But that Greek accent implies stress as well as elevation is manifest from the natural and obvious meaning of the terms used by the grammarians in describing the phenomena of accent. For what does τάσις mean but *stretch* or *tension ?* and is it not quite plain that as contrary as light is to darkness, so contrary is ἐπίτασις to ἄνεσις,—*i.e.*, *intension* to *remission*, *strain* to *slackness* of sound—the constant phraseology of the grammarians with regard to this matter ? The word κροῦσμα, also signifying *beat* or *strike*, which is sometimes used of the acute accent,[1] sufficiently indicates its analogy to the emphatic note in a musical bar, which certainly does not signify elevation or depression.

3. The analogy of the *ictus metricus* in rhythmical composition, suggested by the word κροῦσμα, supplies another argument to prove that the Greek and Roman accent meant stress as well as elevation. For there are some places in the poets where we can observe that a word naturally short is made long for no other reason that can be seen than that the spoken accent on the syllable favoured the poetical license, just in the same way that the rhythmical accent sometimes does. Mere elevation has no effect on quantity ; but stress or emphasis

---

[1] Theodosius, Goettling, p. 61 ; κρουστικοτέρα γιγνομένη ἡ λέξις ὀξύνεται. Schol. Dionys. Thrax. Bekker, ii. p. 690.

can easily be so manipulated by the voice as to pass over
into a long syllable, or, to use the language of the grammarians, ἐπίτασις may become ἔκτασις, *intension* may spread
itself out into *extension*.

4. That the acute accent meant stress is plain from
the inherited intonation of the modern Greeks ; for accent
is one of the most obstinate affections that belong to
spoken speech ; and no man can hear such words as καλό
παιδί, Σκοπό, and Παρνασσό in the mouth of the living
Greeks without feeling that the dead mark on our books
has here received its living interpretation ; and, if any
person objects that the modern Greek not only acutes the
last syllables of these words, but makes their quantity
long, this is all in favour of my argument ; for the length
arose and could arise naturally only from an exaggeration
of that tension of voice which was the necessary accom-
paniment of the accent.   With regard to the modern
Greek dialect generally, I would observe that, though the
place of the accent has been changed in a few classes of
words, in the great majority of cases it has been retained ;
and that in the case of curtailed words, as μάς for ἐμᾶς,
πίσω for ὀπίσω, ψάρι for ὀψάριον, παιδί for παιδίον, δὲν for
οὐδὲν, etc., it is the stress upon the medial accented syllable
which secured its permanence after the initial or final
unaccented syllable had dropped off.

5. But the most incontestable proof that accent means
emphasis lies in the doctrine of Enclitics ; for in Greek as
in English there are certain little words, such as the *pronouns* or the negative *no*, which in common cases are
purposely kept unemphatic, and pronounced so rapidly as
to appear to lean upon (ἐγκλίνω), or be taken up by the
previous or following word ; but the moment that the
necessity of speech demands these words to become pro-

minent, they receive the accent, and become emphatic.
Thus we say, "*give me the book,*" like *datemi* in Italian, as
one word, but "*give* ΜÉ *the book,*" that is, give it to *me,*
not to *you.* Now, there could not be a stronger fact than
this to prove that Greek accent meant emphasis ; for this
use of the acute accent to emphasize in particular cases
otherwise unemphatic words is quite common, as, for
example, in the case of the negative particle μὰ Δία οὐκ
ἔγωγε, contrasted with οὕτως λέγεις ἢ οὔ, do you say so, or
do you *not ?*

6. Lastly, the analogy of the modern Italian compared
with the ancient Roman plainly shows us both the obstinacy of accent as a fact in the life of language, and what
accent really meant in ancient Rome and Greece, as in
modern Rome. For nothing is more certain than that,
though its special laws were different in the two learned
languages, accent, as an accident of articulate speech, did
not mean one thing in Greece and another thing in Rome ;
but the Greek and Latin accent were in their nature and
operation identical ; so that what is predicated of the
essence of the one must be considered as predicated of the
essence of the other. If, therefore, the modern Italian
accent, in its position and power so evidently identical
with the old Latin, possesses the element of stress as a
prominent feature, it is a legitimate conclusion that the
Greek accent did so too. Altogether, it may be remarked
as a very extraordinary fact, and indicative of the operation of some strange deluding prejudice, that, while the
most formidable artillery of erudite arguments have been
brought to bear against pronouncing Greek with Greek
accents, no learned Latinist has yet written a book to
prove that Latin ought not to be pronounced with Latin
accents. When reading Latin we put the stress on the

accented syllable exactly where Cicero, and Quinctilian, and Priscian say it was placed ; but the moment a Hellenist gives the natural · predominance to the accents which he finds marked on his books, he is immediately told that accent does not mean stress, but means something that no man can understand or make use of. Whence this inconsistency ?

Having thus proved, by what may surely seem sufficiently strong arguments, that accents mean nothing in Greek which they do not equally mean in English, or Latin, or Italian, there remains only to take a bird's-eye view of the somewhat remarkable literature of this subject, from the revival of letters down to the present hour. Such a review will at once be the best justification of the principles above set forth, and will place vividly before the reader the partial and inadequate points of view from which the opposing doctrines have taken their rise.

Now, in tracing to its fountain-head the stream of confusion which this matter exhibits, it is most natural that we should, in the first place, turn to Erasmus, both because he was the most prominent scholar of European reputation in the eventful age to which he belonged, and because it is quite certain that before his time no learned man ever dreamt or could have dreamt of disowning the pronunciation of the Greek language, which Europe had received as a common legacy from the Constantinopolitan Greeks. The early scholars, indeed, were occupied with matters of far more serious import than the exact accentuation and quantification of syllables. They read the Greek books for the information they contained : ` Herodotus for history, Strabo for geography, Thucydides for political wisdom, Plato for philosophy, Aristotle for science. So long as this appetite for the stores of Hellenic thought and knowledge was the one thing needful, no man had either leisure or desire to put curious questions to himself with regard to the auricular luxury of a just orthoepy. But the time must come when this matter also would be examined : Homer and Sophocles could not be read in their mother tongue by men who used their ears as well as their eyes, without provoking questions as to the best method of bringing out the full music of that most musical of human languages which it was the happy fortune of these great poets to employ. If Greek was the language of the gods, there seemed a manifest impiety in allowing it to be enunciated by a confused, degraded, and irrational elocution. And, if such questions were to be raised, Erasmus was precisely the man, who, from his fine genius, cultivated taste, and broad human sympathies, was best fitted to raise them. Accordingly, in the famous dialogue, *De recta Latini, Græcique sermonis pronuntiatione*, published at Basle in the year 1528, the whole subject is brought under review ; and the text of his discourse is in the broadest terms, that "*nunc tota fere pronuntiatio depravata est tam apud Græcos, quam apud Latinos;*" and this is proved in a very exhaustive style in an argument extending to above two hundred pages. The powers of the different letters are critically discussed, and the relation of accent and quantity illustrated both by learned rules and by living examples. With regard to the vowel sounds, which is the first point handled, he had an easy task to prove that the slender sound, the characteristic of the Byzantine Greeks, could not have been the original sound of so many distinct vowels and diphthongs. Signs of different vowels were certainly not made originally to confound but to distinguish. The confusion in this case is always of a later birth. What Erasmus, however, failed in here, and what, from want of materials, he could not but fail in, was to show at what period this confusion commenced; for, as the most polished nations in modern times display in their speech abnormal tendencies and depravations of all kinds, which are consecrated by usage and fashion, so there is no reason why the itacism of the theologians of Byzantium should not have been practised by the philosophers of Alexandria, and even, to a certain extent, by the orators of the Periclean and Demosthenic age. However, this was not curiously looked into; and the result was that, by this assault of Erasmus, the faith of scholars in the orthoepic traditions of the Byzantine elders was shaken in all the most learned countries of Europe, and every nation set up vocalizing Greek according to what seemed good in its own eyes. Hence the motley babblement of Greek which now prevails. The old foundations were removed before the ground was opened, or the materials ready, to make new ones. And thus it has happened that an orthoepic reform, well intended, and in so far conducted on rational principles, has issued in an extremely irrational and altogether unsatisfactory result. So much for Greek vocalization. With regard to that other matter with which we are specially concerned here, we do not find, what we might perhaps have expected to find, that the great modern innovation of disowning Greek accents in reading Greek receives the slightest countenance from Erasmus. On the contrary, part of the bad pronunciation which it was his object to reform was precisely the ignorance or loose observance of the proper accents in Greek and Latin, according to the characteristic laws of each language. He saw also everywhere amongst careless, tasteless, or ignorant speakers that confusion of things so distinct as accent and quantity, which from the same causes prevails so largely at the present day. Scholars still tell you that accent and quantity annihilate each other, and cannot both be observed, meaning only, in fact, that for their particular ill-tutored and perverted auricular organs, it has become difficult, and is perhaps impossible. It certainly is impossible for a sharp, hard Aberdonian to speak with the rich silvery mellowness of a high-bred English lady ; but the difficulty lies in bad habit, not in Scottish nature. On the superinduced habitude which erudite ears have so often displayed in not being able to distinguish accent from quantity, there is a passage in the Erasmian tractate, which we shall be excused for inserting at length :—

"*Sunt quidam adeo crassi, ut non distinguant accentum à quantitate, quum sit longe diversa ratio. Aliud est enim acutum, aliud diu tinnire : sicut aliud intendi, aliud extendi : quanquam nihil vetat eandem syllabam et acutum habere tonum, et productum tempus, velut in* vidi, *et legi prœteritis. At eruditos novi, qui, quum pronunciarent illud ἀνέχου καὶ ἀπέχου, mediam syllabam, quoniam tonum habet acutum, quantum possent producerent, quum sit natura brevis, vel brevissima potius. Et ferè qui Grœca legunt, accentus observatione confundunt spatium morœ, sic enunciantes μενέλαος, quasi penultima sit brevis, et μενέδημος quasi duœ postremœ sint breves, quemadmodum in θεόδωρος παράκλητος εἴδωλα, aliisque innumeris. Nec ita multis contingit sonare Grœca, ut accentuum simul et morarum rationem observent, vel in carmine. Loquor autem non jam de vulgo, sed de eruditissimis quoque. Minus est erroris in Latinis, sed tamen illic quoque tonus acutus ac inflexus obscurat cœterarum sonum, ut in* vide-*

bimus, *congruit accentus cum quantitate, at in* legebâmus,
*sola penultima videtur esse producta, quum secunda sit
æque longa : in* amavérimus *sola antepenultima, quum ea
sit brevis, secunda producta. LE. Omnino sic obtinuit
usus, quem dediscere difficillimum est. UR. Atqui qui
degustarunt musicam, nullo negotio distinguunt inter longam, brevem, et inter acutam et gravem. Nihil enim est
aliud pronunciatio, quàm modulatio quædam vocum nume-
rosa. Est enim et in oratione soluta pedum ratio, licet
non perinde certis astricta legibus ut in carmine : quæ si
confundatur, non magis erit oratio quàm cantio in qua
graves cum acutis, longæ cum brevibus temere confun-
duntur. Unde quidam priscorum grammaticorum non
inscite dixerunt, accentum esse animam dictionis. Et
tamen hodie talis est etiam eruditorum pronunciatio, qualis
esset illa ridicula cantio. Scis opinor canere cithara.
LE. Utcunque. UR. Nónne frequenter imam chordam
pulsans producis sonos, et summam tangens brevibus in-
sonas aut contra ? LE. Frequenter, quanquam hoc discrimen evidentius est in flatili musica. UR. Unde igitur
nos sumus usque adeo ἄμουσοι, ut omnes acutas syllabas
sonemus productiore mora, graves omnes corripiamus?
Vel ab asinis licebat hoc discrimen discere, qui rudentes
corripiunt acutam vocem, imam producunt. LE. Idem
propemodum facit cuculus.*"

The only other interesting point, with regard to the
present matter, which requires to be mentioned here, is
that Erasmus distinctly teaches that *verses, both in Greek
and Latin, are to be read with an accurate observance
both of accent and quantity.* The difficulty and alleged
impossibility of doing this, so much spoken of by modern
scholars, he supposes to arise only from the gross neglect
of the art of elegant reading in modern education. How

z

far he is right in applying the spoken accent thus sweepingly to the rhythmical recitation of poetry, we shall
have occasion to consider afterwards.

But what to the fine genius and well-trained ear of
Erasmus presented no difficulty, to the gross majority
who take everything without discrimination in broad
masses was so formidable, that they do not even seem to
have had the courage to look the difficulty in the face,
but quietly settled down into a habit of confounding
accent and quantity, and making all accented syllables
long. This is distinctly mentioned by the next champion
in the field, Adolph von Meetkerche (vulgarly Mekirch),
a Flemish nobleman, born at Bruges in the very year
when Erasmus's book was published, and well known in
high circles in England, from his having lived and died
at London as an attaché of the Belgian ambassador at the
court of Elizabeth. He was, besides an able diplomatist
an accomplished scholar, and in the year 1576 published
a Discourse " *de verâ et rectâ pronuntiatione linguœ*
Grecœ,"[1] which seems to have given the first impulse to
the paradoxical movement which caused the Greek accentuation, so laboriously preserved by the Alexandrian grammarians, to be thrown overboard in the general practice
of scholars, and the vulgar Latin accentuation substituted in its place. The principal part of this work is
occupied with the question which then loomed most large
whether the Byzantine vocalization should be retained, or
a reformed one introduced, as suggested by Erasmus
but, in a short appendix, the doctrine of accents is stated
succinctly, and, what is more important, the author's
practice with regard to their observance. In the first
place, he tells us the important fact that, in his day,

---

[1] Reprinted in Havercamp's *Sylloge*, vol. i. p. 9. Lugd. Bat., 1836.

Greek was so read by many, confounding accent and quantity, as altogether to destroy the perception of any poetical rhythm. "*Manifestus est eorum error qui tonos cum temporibus confundunt, ita ut quæcunque acuenda vel flectenda est syllaba, eam producant: quæcunque deprimenda vel æquabiliter pronuncianda, eam corripiant. Ex quo fit ut in Græcâ oratione vel nullum vel potius corruptum numerum intelligas, dum multæ breves producuntur, et contra plurimæ longæ corripiuntur; ut pæne præstiterit Græca vel Latina non legere quam ita fædé depravare*" (p. 175). And no wonder, if, as he says, the accent was allowed such a power that, in the second line of the *Iliad*, ἔθηκεν was read as a dactyle, and the two final syllables of οὐλομένην as a spondee. And then he tells us of a general practice of schoolmasters, which by the way prevails in England almost universally to the present hour: "*Solent enim pædagogi vulgo ita suos erudire ut in omnibus dissyllabis penultimam producant.*" Just as in Eton and Harrow the boys were, till very recently, if indeed they are not still, taught or carelessly allowed to say, *bōnus*, and not *bŏnus*. He then goes on to show how this practical assumption that a penultimate accent must necessarily lengthen the vowel has no foundation in the real nature of accent and quantity, of which the one expresses the quality of the sound, the other the dimensions. And then, anticipating an objection often made in modern times, he goes on to say, "*Neque tamen nego brevi syllabæ temporis aliquid accedere, quando acuto signo signatur, quantum scilicet necesse est in acuendâ syllaba consumi; sed, ut minus sit brevis quam antea, minime tamen consequitur habendam esse pro longâ, sicut ab iis habetur qui* mālus *arborem a* mălo *adjectivo non distinguunt*" (p. 178). This is exactly what

Erasmus had said; and one should think it would be sufficiently patent to all ears, except those of stupid schoolmasters, careless schoolboys, and bookish scholars, whose learning is all in their eyes, and not in their ears. But things easy in speculative thought become in the hasty practice of life sometimes tolerably difficult; and, in fact, a just and true pronunciation, even in the case of the mother tongue, is not attainable without a certain amount of trouble. Meetkerche accordingly finds that his argument for accents, however just, is liable to be met with the objection which nullified so many of Solon's well-conceived legislative reforms. The laws were no doubt very good, but they were too good for the people. The best for them was not the best absolutely, but the best which they could endure. "*At enim,*" he continues, "*dices, ista* (*i.e.* the right pronunciation both of quantity and accent) *esse perdifficilia, et fortassis etiam* ἀδύνατα, *iis quidem qui diversæ pronuntiationi assueverunt. Id ego vero fateor, et in me ipso non invitus agnosco. Sed nihil vetat rectam viam aliis ostendere, etiam ut illam ingredi non possis. Certè veritas mihi dissimulanda non fuit, ut paullatim meliora probare et sequi condiscamus. Ergo, ut libere dicam quod sentio, vel tonos prorsus sublatos esse velim, tantisper dum depravata illa pronunciatio tonorum pro temporibus emendetur (quum præsentim veteres constet istos apices in scribendo non usurpasse) vel nullam eorum rationem haberi;*"[1] which simply means that he is in favour of suspending the operation of Greek accents till such time as schoolmasters—proverbially not a very teachable race—shall have learned to distinguish ὄs, a *bone*, from ōs, a *mouth*, and that *căn'ō* is a possible combination of articulate sounds, as much as *caw'nō* or *caē'nō*.

---

[1] Havercamp's *Sylloge*, vol. i. p. 179.

The next important work which falls to be noticed indicates plainly by its title—"*De Poematum cantu et viribus Rhythmi;*" Oxon. 1673—from what quarter the attacks of a section of the learned world were now to be directed against the traditional sway of Greek accents. The author of this tract was the celebrated Isaac Vossius, "unquestionably," to use the words of Markland, "a very learned man, but whose whimsicalness and love of paradox scarce leaves room for him to be considered a reasonable one."[1] Vossius, like Meetkerche, had got his ear possessed with a genuine living appreciation of the beauty of measure and rhythm in poetry, which justly resented the barbarism of those scholars who read ancient verse by accents, just as if it was so much German or English verse. In expressing his indignation strongly against these systematic murderers of the regal majesty of Latin, and the luxuriant swell of Greek verse, Voss did well; but, when he went further, and not content with the interim act of suspension passed by Meetkerche, stood up in violent revolt against the whole accredited system of accentuation in the Greek language, and cast it, to save the ship, like a Jonah, overboard, he committed a great mistake, and kicked vehemently against the pricks, where he could only wound his own legs. He declared roundly that the whole system of Greek accents, as we now have them, was a modern invention, or at least a corruption, or a monstrous compound of both ; that accents were originally musical marks, and had nothing to do with the pronunciation of the language ; that the best proof of this was the unrhythmical jar which they produced, when actually applied to the recitation of verse, whether Greek

---

[1] Letter to Foster in the Essay on Accent and Quantity. 3d edit. London, 1820. P. 207.

or Latin; and that therefore the only course left to the scholar of taste was to disregard them altogether, and use only such accent as was manifestly dictated by the march of the metre. While, however, this ingenious scholar found it comparatively easy work to pronounce a dictatorial sentence of eternal exclusion against Greek accents, of which few had any real knowledge, he found himself obstinately met by an obvious objection from the familiar practice of the Latin tongue, which, while it distinctly disowns (except in a very few exceptive cases) all oxytone accentuation, nevertheless, in verse, constantly uses an emphasis, which falls with marked effect on the last syllable of one or more words in the verse. In answering this objection, Voss fell upon an aspect of the case, which, if he had applied it to Greek poetry, might have saved him from the trouble of beating vainly against the strong bulwarks of Alexandrian and Roman and Byzantine tradition in the matter; for he distinctly says that singing is one thing and reading another, and that the Romans may have followed a different law of accentuation with regard to each. "*Quare non quidem multum refragabor, si quis in recitatione Latinorum poematum ultimas syllabas unquam productas fuisse negaverit: sed vero in* Cantu *id ipsum fieri potuisse si quis contendat, idem etiam merito affirmet et Latinos canere nescivisse.*"[1]

Close upon the traces of Vossius comes a German, Henry Christian Hennin, whose work entitled "Ἑλληνισμὸς ὀρθῳδός, Traject. ad Rhenum, 1684," with a great flourish of trumpets on its title-page, proclaims itself to prove "*Græcam linguam secundum accentus, ut vulgo ab omnibus hucusque fieri consuerit, pronunciandam non esse.*"

---

[1] *De viribus rhythmi*, p. 44. *N.B.*—By *productas* in this passage he evidently means *accented*.

The inspiration of this book—for it is full of fervour and emphasis, and a sort of lofty protestation—manifestly is the same as that of Voss's treatise; a certain school of scholars with whom the writer had been familiar, or it may be all the scholars of his time and place had got into a habit of sacrificing the rhythmical recitation of Greek poetry to the traditional accentuation of Greek prose, a usurpation, no doubt, of a most gross kind, and which it was obvious to think could best be got rid of by not only dethroning the usurper and telling him to keep to his proper place, but by killing him outright, and casting him down among the dead men with a triple volley of curse and execration. It was a procedure akin to that in political history, when democracy dethrones despotism, and acts ten times more despotically than the tyrant whom it overthrew. In conducting his indictment against the accents, the author commits in the outset the very transparent blunder of confounding the marks of the accents in printed books with the living accents in the mouth of the people who spoke the Greek language. These marks, whether present or absent in books, do not in the slightest degree affect the question; they do not exist in English books, and yet English words have a well-known accent in the voice of the English people, and made visible artificially to their eye in the pronouncing dictionaries of Walker and other orthoepists. The next great error made by Hennin lies in the theory—for it is a mere baseless theory—that the accents were invented by Aristophanes of Byzantium for some purpose quite different from that which they now subserve. This is simply to leap over the testimonies of the most learned Greek grammarians from the time of the Alexandrian scholars to the taking of Constantinople by the Turks.

And in order to make such a hypothesis possible and
even plausible, he draws a flaming picture of the barbarism
which corrupted the Greek language at a fever pace
from the Roman to the Turkish conquest.   All this,
however, is purely imaginary, as any person who has
looked even superficially into Byzantine literature must
confess.   Whatever changes in the course of time naturally might take place in the spoken language of the
Greeks, the last element that would be touched by the
change was the accentuation ; and that not only from its
own natural obstinacy, but from the very fact that the
proper place of the accent visible in most written books
presented a stereotyped norm, that checked all arbitrary
deflexion in the start.   Any other arguments that make
a parade in Hennin's book are based on the fact of which
we hear so much in these days, that certain persons
could not pronounce ἄνθρωπος without saying ἄνθροπος,
and certain other persons imagined that it was impossible
to do so.   After overleaping heroically the bristling fence
of historic testimony on the matter, the author proceeds
to lay down four rules of accentuation, which, both in the
Greek and Latin languages, are, " *sine ullâ exceptione
æternæ veritatis.*"   These rules are as follows :—

(I.) " *Omnis vox monosyllaba modulationem habet in
suâ vocali ut* Θῶς, νοῦς, *mons, pons.*"

(II.) " *Omnis vox dissyllaba modulationem habet in
syllabâ priori, ut* λόγοι, ὅδοι, φώνη."

(III.) " *Omnis vox polysyllaba penultimam longam
modulatur, ut* ἄνθρῶπος, τυπτῶμεν, *Græcorum,* jucúnda,
Romanorum."

(IV.) " *Omnis vox polysyllaba, penultima brevi, modulatur antepenultimam, ut* dóminos, ἄλογον."

This is certainly one of the most cool pieces of insolent one-sided dogmatism that the history of learning presents, the whole affair being simply an assertion that the particular method of accentuation in the Latin language, which the author had inherited from secular and ecclesiastical Rome, should be stilted up into an eternal norm of accentuation for all languages, while the most plain and obvious facts, both in ancient Greek and modern English, which contradict the theory are held as nonexistent, and excluded from the calculation; an instructive example of the truth of Goethe's remark, that truth is often disagreeable to us, because it limits the despotic sweep of our one idea, while error is grateful for this, above all other reasons, because it prostrates fact and thought and history before the triumphant march of our infallible conceit.

It was not to be supposed that the sweeping dictatorial dogmatism of this book of Hennin, backed as it substantially was by the high authority of Voss, would pass without comment from the learned of the Continent; and accordingly we find that in the year 1686 it received a long and able reply from John Rudolph Wetstein, professor of Greek in the university of Basle. Wetstein's book, by an overwhelming array of historical testimony, enforced by sound argument, demonstrates the utter untenableness of the proposition of his adversary, unwarrantable equally in the wholesale swamping of the Greek by the Latin accent, and in the elevation of this latter into a rational norm of accentuation, by which the excellence of all articulate speech is to be measured. With regard to the main difficulty which had staggered Meetkerche, the Basle professor quietly reminds his antagonist, in the words of Quinctilian, that the recitation of verse is in many respects different from the speaking of prose, "*imprimis lectio virilis et cum suavitate quâdam gravis et non quidem prosœ similis, quia carmen est.*"

The infection of this notable dispute now comes to England, and the first oracle to whom we feel inclined to propound the question for solution is, of course, the great Bentley. This massive and masculine scholar, in the short treatise on metres prefixed to his edition of Terence, has the following passage :—"*Tum vero id Latinis comicis qui fabulas suas populo placere cuperent magnopere cavendum erat ne contra linguœ genium ictus seu accentus in quoque versu syllabas verborum ultimas occuparent Id in omni metro, quoad licuit, observabatur ; ut in his*

> ' Ar'ma virúmque cáno, Trójae qui prímus ab óris,
> Itáliam fáto prófugus, Lavínia vénit
> Lítora ; multum ílle et térris jactátus et álto
> Vi súperum, saévae mémorem Junónis ob íram.'

Qui perite et modulate hos versus leget sic eos, ut hic accentus notantur, pronuntiabit, non ut pueri in scholis, ad singulorum pedum initia ;

"Italiám fató profugús, Lavinaque venit, *sed ad rhythmum totius versus.*"

Now, it in nowise concerns us to discuss the value of the remark here made as to the practice of the Latin poets ; that is a delicate matter, we believe, not so easily settled as the stout Cantab. seems to have imagined. The only significance of the passage for our present inquiry is, that the writer believed that in some way or other the structure of Latin verse was regulated by a regard to the spoken accent, and not simply by the law of quantity and the metrical beat. What truth there may be in this notion will appear in the sequel ; meanwhile it is quite plain that it leaves the matter in a state of considerable uncertainty, an uncertainty which is not at all diminished by the unquesionably rash assertion in the letter to Mill, that Greek accents were an invention of later times, which could only mislead the accurate scholar.[1] An *obiter dictum* of this kind, even from a Bentley, on a confessedly difficult question, cannot be regarded as having any real weight. It may, however, along with other causes, have contributed to produce that strange aversion to Greek accentuation so characteristic of English scholarship.

We now advance by a long stride into the middle of the great battle of accent and quantity that was fought in this country about the middle of the last century. The protagonist of this warfare is the Rev. Henry Gally, a Kentish Doctor of Divinity, and chaplain to His Majesty King George II. His dissertation against Greek accents was first published in the year 1754, seventy years after the famous works of Henninius and Wetstein; and quite recently on the back of two treatises on the same subject, which had appeared in Rome.[2] Dr. Gally wrote, quite aware of the achievements of his predecessors, but convinced that their attempts to untie the Gordian knot were unsatisfactory, and that his own method was altogether new and original; and so it is, no doubt, in some things, but novel only in the daringness of its assertions and the glaringness of its absurdity. Its absurdity consists mainly in the writer's belief that he can overturn the whole principles and practice of the Greek accentuation, by simply saying that it is irrational and absurd, as if some famous philosopher, some thousand years after this, when the English orthoepy may have become a field

---

[1] "Notæ accentuum quorum omnis hodierna ratio præpostera est atque perversa." Works by Dyce, vol. ii. p. 362.

[2] (1.) Sarpedonii dissertatio de vera Atticorum pronunciatione. Romae, 1750. (2.) Velaste dissertatio de literarum Græcarum pronunciatione. Romae, 1751.

for learned debate, were to say that *Mac'Intosh* and
Mac'Intyre could not have been pronounced with the
accent on the first syllable, because it is irrational to place
the accent on the common element of the *Mac*, instead of
on the distinguishing element, the clan; which rational
method of pronunciation, as above remarked, exists not
only in all the other Macs, but in all the Saxon names
ending in *son*, as An'derson, Péterson, not *Andersón*,
Petersón. A writer belonging to a people whose pronunciation is in all points so various, so arbitrary, and so
dependent on fashionable caprice as the English, might
surely have spared himself the inconsistency of such an
argument. In the other parts of this learned divine's
book we find merely a repetition of what had been said
by Meetkerche, Henninius, Vossius, and others. Accents,
we are told, were altogether musical, and had nothing to do
with the intonation of colloquial speech: then it is broadly
asserted that accent necessarily constitutes quantity, and
therefore *must* be wrong; and that, whatever the advocates of accents might preach in theory, in practice they
never did, because they never could observe the accent
without destroying the quantity. This practical difficulty
is, in fact, the gist of his whole treatise, as is manifest
from the very notable words with which he concludes:—
" If, therefore, we would observe uniformity, and keep to
what we can safely rely on, we must not admit of any use
of accents in the pronunciation of the ancient Greek language but what is consistent with quantity; and if we
have lost the nicer part of the ancient pronunciation, we
have the more reason to adhere to the essential part
which still subsisteth." And this way of putting the case,
viewed as an *argumentum ad hominem* addressed to the
great mass of the English scholars and teachers, is no

doubt perfectly just ; for these gentlemen had got into a
monstrous and irrational habit of writing Latin and Greek
verses with much labour and wonderful dexterity, by help
of their understanding only, against the verdict of their
ears, and treated both accent and quantity as an affair of
dead rules, not of living vital action.[1]

But English scholarship—whatever might be the
absurdities of professional pedagogy—was not destined to
surrender one of the strongholds of venerable philological
tradition at the trumpet-blast of such a windy dogmatist
as Dr. Gally. In the year 1767 a reply to his pretentious heresy was sent forth from Eton, by Foster, in
which, so far as the learning of the subject is concerned,
he showed himself as superior to Gally as Wetstein was
to Henninius. He proved beyond all possibility of denial
that accent had always been a recognised element in
Greek orthoepy, and was in no sense the barbarous creation of a decadent age and a degraded taste. He stated
also most distinctly that, while elevation of tone was the
most characteristic element in Greek accent, it also
necessarily included the element of *stress*—which Dr.
Gally also saw clearly—but that this stress or emphasis
was in no case to be confounded with the length or duration of syllables. Hence, indeed, the great superiority of
his argument to that of the Kentish D.D. ; for he not
only maintained that accent was not to be confounded
with quantity, but that, from the very nature of the case,
the intense energy of the acute accent might, in many
cases, have a tendency to shorten rather than to prolong
the emission of breath by which it was enunciated.[2]

---

[1] On this notable inconsistency of
those champions of quantity who de-
nounce accent, Mr. Foster is justly
severe ; ch. x., on accent-quantity.

[2] On this point he produces a remarkable passage from Suidas, *in voce* ὀξύ,
vol. ii. p. 1136. Bernhardy.

With regard to the main difficulty, however—the practice
of the theory, which, as we have seen, was the stumbling-
block of Dr. Gally—he does not seem to advance the
matter far.   Hear his words :—

"Nor let it be said, if we should retain these sounds,
we can never apply them to their proper use in practice.
Who can affirm that with certainty?   An English voice
was capable of doing this in the time of Henry VIII., and
why not now?   Sir John Cheke declares it not only
practicable, but that it was actually practised, and that
he knew many persons who could express these sounds
consistently with accent and quantity perfectly well.   I
know one person who, after a few trials, is now able to do
the same."   By this one person the reader will naturally
suppose that he means himself, though it is a pity he did
not say so in a manner that could not admit of ambiguity.
But whoever the individual might be who in the year of
grace 1761 had solved this easy vocal problem, curiously
imagined to be so difficult, schoolmasters who sinned
against this high ideal of classical recitation might well
reply, that to attempt to indoctrinate the ears of schoolboys with such delicate distinctions would prove as hopeless as to bring out the beautiful harmony of one of
Händel's operas from a hurdy-gurdy.   On another point
also, Foster's Essay, though victorious against Gally, did
perhaps more harm than good to the question of orthoepic
reform in the great schools.   He does not always sufficiently distinguish between the emphasis, or stress, or
intensity of utterance, which he rightly considers to belong essentially to accent, and the prolongation of sound
with which that intensity may sometimes be accompanied.
Hence he speaks of the effect of the accent in English
being habitually to lengthen the syllable ; whereas, if we

attend to our ears, words like *văp'id* and *răp'id* are just
as common in our language as *po'tent* and *pa'tent*, and no
person feels himself under any tendency or compulsion to
assimilate the pronunciation of the first two words to that
of the other pair.

Three years after the appearance of Mr. Foster's
Essay, the *Accentus Redivivus* of Primatt appeared,
the title of which seems sufficiently to indicate that in
England at least Meetkerche, and Voss, and Gally had
practically won the day, and that accents had retired
from the schools, and even from the typographic theatre
in Oxford ; for in the year 1759 an edition of Aristotle's
Rhetoric, without accentual marks, had appeared under
the imprimatur of Thomas Randolph, Vice-Chancellor of
the University. How many more Greek books, in the
same nude fashion, may have issued from the same quarter about the same time, I do not know ; but there was
certainly just cause for the champions of accents to take
the alarm ; and so Mr. Primatt marched forth, an accentual cataphract, bristling all over with Alexandrian and
Byzantine erudition, through which it was impossible to
pierce him. In his learned work he first shakes himself
free from the notion flung out by Vossius, and the extreme men of the rhythmical party, that accents, however
they might have been observed afterwards, were originally
a musical, and not an orthoepic notation. He then shows,
by a long historical deduction, that the reading of Greek
prose always was accentual, and that nothing can be more
illegitimate than to transfer to prose the laws of quantitative rhythm, which belong to poetry. But in this
second proposition, unfortunately, he is only half right,
and entangles himself and the whole subject in a network
of the most hopeless confusion ; for, in defining accent,

besides asserting with Foster that there is an overbearing tendency in English to lengthen all accented syllables,
and an invariable rule in Latin to accentuate long penults,
he lays it down in the strongest terms that the acute
accent necessarily lengthens the syllable on which it falls,
and that, in fact, when properly read, every accented
syllable in Greek prose is long.   Nay, more, so confused
are his ideas on the whole terminology of the subject
which he treats, that he actually tells us "we can hardly
read a verse in Virgil or Homer in which the *rhythm* does
not more than once break in upon the *quantity*" (p. 157),
a sentence which, according to the usage of all who write
intelligibly on such subjects, is pure nonsense, or true
only of such accented verse as we have in English and
other modern languages.   This extraordinary confusion
of two things by the ancient grammarians, kept so distinct as accent and quantity, rendered his whole discourse
nugatory.   To accept accent according to this theory was
to make a formal transference of quantity from one syllable
to another, and to acquire a habit of reading prose, which,
in the point of quantity, would require to be reversed the
moment a scholar threw down Plato, and took up
Sophocles.   In a country where the most elegant scholars,
under the guidance of such a Titan as Bentley, had
already begun to look with a curious preference on every
thing connected with metrical composition, such a startling doctrine could not be expected to make converts.

    After these violent but practically ineffective efforts,
the great strife about accents in England ceased for
thirty years, when in the year 1796 another remarkable
combatant entered the lists in the person of Samuel
Horsley, one of the most notable of the singular army of
erudite polemical bishops of which the Anglican Church

has been so fertile.[1] Into the weakness and utter untenableness of the received method of reading Greek in this
country the Bishop casts a piercing eye, and with an out-
spoken emphasis calls black black, and white white in
the matter, after a fashion to which it might have been
expected that in a country where the Church has so much
to say in the school, some serious attention might have
been given. "*A practice,*" he says, "*is adopted in this
country of reading Greek verse with the Latin accent, and
this is most absurdly called reading by quantity; and having adopted this strange practice of reading one language
by the rules of another, it is not unnatural that we should
wish to prove the practice right*" (pp. 26, 27). This is
indeed hitting the nail on the head; but the strange
practice, like many strange things in England, still continues, and we still make ourselves ridiculous by awkward
endeavours to prove that what is altogether unnatural
and monstrous is justifiable and even beautiful. How is
this? Not only, I believe, because the patient was self-
willed and obstinate, but because the physician who pronounced a most scientific diagnosis of the disease had not
the sagacity to discover the proper cure. He suggested
a cure more flattering to his own ingenuity than true to
the state of the case, or beneficial to the patient. He
was as original as Dr. Gally, in a more subtle, indeed, but
not in a more practical way. Gally's originality, as we
have seen, consisted simply in calling everything on the
doctrine of Greek accents irrational and absurd which was
contrary to his orthoepic habits or fancies, and nonsuiting
it, without more ado, as a defaulter *in foro rationis*.
Horsley, with that respect for historical fact and erudite

[1] *On the Prosodies of the Greek and Latin Languages.* London, 1796. The author's name was not given on the title-page.

testimony which became a bishop and a theologian, admitted the doctrine of accent in its full weight, as an element of which no sane reasoner on the matter of Hellenic orthoepy could get rid; but, in order to explain its operation as part of the harmony of Greek verse, he invented a theory altogether novel and altogether arbitrary, which nobody had ever proposed before, and which nobody, we may feel pretty certain, will ever propose again. This theory consists simply in acknowledging the Greek accents, as we find them in the books, as the law for the pronunciation of the separate words, but refusing to allow them their natural force under certain rhythmical conditions. Thus, he says, that at the end of a hexameter verse such a word as ἔθηκε must be pronounced ἐθήκε, because the last syllable of a hexameter verse being long, the accent, according to a well-known canon of Greek orthoepy, must fall on the penult! Now, the objection to this theory is threefold—(1.) It is not true that the last syllable of hexameter verse, as ἔθηκε, is long; it is short, and the time is filled up by the pause which belongs to the end of the line, like a rest in music; (2.) The theory proceeds on a supposed connexion between prose accent and rhythmical emphasis, which is fundamentally false; and (3.) The whole theory is a figment spun out of the brain of the writer, without a shadow of authority from ancient grammarians and metricians. This being so, the natural consequence followed;—the book explained nothing, and changed nothing. If everybody could not answer it, nobody cared to understand it.

Immediately upon the back of the learned Bishop's treatise, in 1797, appeared a little book entitled *Metron Ariston; or, a new Pleasure Recommended*, with a ruffed and bearded effigy of Meetkerche fronting the title-page,

and a motto which sufficiently indicates the temper and
direction of the writer—

> " Tollite barbarum
> Morem perpetuum, dulcia barbare
> Laedentem metra, quæ Venus
> Quintâ parte sui nectaris imbuit."

This book was not written by a scholar, but by a man
of taste and vivacity, and a gay self-reliance which stands
him in good stead against a whole host of scholastic
cuirassiers. In point of tendency and contents, this book
is nothing more than a repetition of Meetkerche and Voss,
and those writers who have maintained the right of
rhythmical as opposed to the accentual recitation of Greek
and Latin verse ; but the striking fact which the title of
the book suggests is, that the masters and teachers of the
great English schools, who certainly could not be accused
of paying any partial attention to accent, were the very
persons who had so thoroughly ignored the practice of
rhythm in their teaching, that it was a discovery to the
author of the book to find that there was such a thing as
rhythmical reading of classic verse ; and this discovery,
with a prompt philanthropy, he hastens to communicate
to the ingenuous youth of the nation under the inviting
name of " a new pleasure." This entirely agrees with the
complaint which we have just heard the right reverend
Bishop make with regard to the absurdity of reading
Greek poetry with Latin accents, and calling it reading by
quantity. No wonder that clever schoolboys on occasion
should begin to dream that the learned and reverend
doctors, by whom their ears had been indoctrinated in
the unpleasant mysteries of long and short syllables, at
bottom knew less about the matter than they might have
known themselves with the help of a little unsophisticated

juvenile instinct. And accordingly the writer of *Metron Ariston* tells us that "he always indeed had an idea that our very anomalous and irrational way of reading Greek and Latin poetry was founded on error; yet, from indolence, he had conformed, though reluctantly, to the general practice, because it was not his business to examine the error and seek its remedy." But what he did not seek for, he goes on to tell us, like Worcester's rebellion, came in his way, and he found it ; and the good Hermes, on whom he stumbled to direct him in his rhythmical wanderings one day, was a learned Italian ecclesiastic, while they were walking together in the *Campo Vaccino* at Rome one morning, and talking of Horace, and quoting the well-known line—

"Ibam forte viâ sacra sicut meus est mos."

The full musical weight with which the learned Italian recited this verse struck the Englishman with a pleasant surprise ; whereupon the priest, divining the cause of his satisfaction, began to expound to him the correct theory of classical recitation according to Meetkerche, "the great ambassador of a little state." Against this true doctrine, without which verse had no meaning, and lost more than half its suavity, the English scholars and schoolmasters were in the systematic habit of sinning, by pronouncing *ĕq'uus*, for instance, a *horse*, as if it were *aequus, equitable* —by shortening the final syllables of all words, and pronouncing *dŏm'inōs* as if it were *dóminŏs*, and *sacrā* the ablative singular, like *sacră* the nominative plural ; and by turning anapests into dactyles, dactyles into tribrachs, spondees into trochees, iambi into pyrrhics—in fact doing everything that could be done systematically to turn order into disorder in this region, and " by this most abominably absurd custom, destroying at once both sound and sense, and seeming to sin from a love of the very ugliness of sinning." These are hard words, but not, in fact, one whit more strong than those which we have quoted from the English Bishop; nor is it possible, indeed, to conceive anything at once more unscientific, more tasteless, and more unpractical than the way in which prosody and rhythm have been handled in the great English classical schools up to the present hour. On this point, certainly, the author of *Metron Ariston*, a single light-horseman, could triumphantly ride up and attack without fear a whole army of big blundering and self-contradictory hoplites. As to accents, however, about them he wisely said nothing; but allowed them quietly to lie in the state of suspended animation to which they had been condemned by his patron-god Meetkerche. If these mute, mysterious, little oblique and curved lines were ever to revive into speaking significance at the touch of some philological wizard, the author of *Metron Ariston* certainly did not possess the secret for their disenchantment; nor, indeed, if he had possessed it, would he have cared to use it; for the accents, whatever virtue they might possess, could add but little to the luxury of the new rhythmical pleasure which he had discovered.

But what were the great German scholars doing all this while,—the Heynes, the Wolfs, and the Hermanns, the founders of that stable and splendid edifice of philological learning which has placed Germany in the van of erudite and thoughtful research during the whole of the present century? In the preface to the second edition of his *Odyssey*, Wolf remarks that in the matter of the accents, "the editors of the previous centuries had shown a great laxness of procedure, a fault which had commenced

with so illustrious a name as Henry Stephanus, who in
this respect had declined from the accuracy of his predecessors, Chalcondylus and Aldus." And after a few remarks on points of detail, follows a remarkable witness to
the practical disuse into which accents had fallen in
Germany just as in England towards the end of the last
century. " In fact, no person now-a-days—and for many
centuries back—ever *hears* a Greek accent ; and only a
few, indeed, seem to believe that the doctrine of the
grammarians on this subject is a thing that belongs to a
complete course of teaching."[1] This passage is decided as
to the general disuse of accents among the Germans in
Wolf's time ; but the phrase *seit vielen Jahrhunderten* is
certainly too strong ; for the works of Meetkerche, Vossius, and Henninius are sufficient to prove the living
predominance of the Byzantine tradition in respect to
accents in the scholastic practice of their time. An
equally emphatic declaration in favour of accents is made
by Hermann in his famous work *De emendandâ ratione*
Grammatices Græcæ ;[2] but whether these two illustrious scholars contented themselves with publishing an
authoritative manifesto on the necessity of maintaining
accents as an inherited doctrine of genuine Hellenic
orthodoxy, or took any steps to put their views into that
practical shape which alone could give them significance
to articulate-speaking mortals, I have not been able to
learn. Certain it is, however, that the stagnant waters of
the schools—in Germany much more apt than in England
to deduce practice from principle—began to be moved in
this matter ; and, according to information which I have
from continental scholars of high reputation, the accents

---

[1] These extracts are taken from an historical review of the opinions of
scholars about accents in Wagner's *Accent Lehre.* Helmstadt, 1807.

[2] Ch. xiii. *De accentu.*

are now pronounced in a great number of the best German gymnasia. I myself, some forty years ago, heard Professor Boeckh, in Berlin, reading the Iambic verse of the trage-dians with a distinct and well-marked observance both of accent and quantity. The matter appears to have been left pretty much to the taste of individual teachers, and we may feel perfectly assured that the natural con-servatism of teachers would have resisted all change in this matter, unless it had been incontestably proved that the change carried with it the double advantage of scien-tific truth and practical convenience. Whilst the matter was thus not only fairly ventilated, but to a large extent embodied in the scholastic practice of Germany, in Eng-land not a single step seems to have been taken either to the recognition of the principle or the settlement of the practice of Greek accents. The well-known declaration of Porson, no doubt, in a note to the *Medea,*[1] gave the imperial *imprimatur* to certain traditional marks as a fact on paper, and of course put a stop for ever to the inchoate practice of printing Greek books without such marks; but it was a fact which seemed to remain as mysterious as a row of hieroglyphics on an obelisk before the great decipherment of Champollion. In fact, to use Scripture language, notwithstanding the authoritative dictum of the great Cantab., the doctrine has remained in England up to the present hour a meaningless thing, " having a name to live while it is dead." In Scotland, indeed, a country too much accustomed slavishly to follow English authority in classical matters, twenty years ago I pub-lished a short protest against the gross inconsistency and

---

[1] " *Si quis igitur vestrum ad accu-ratam Græcarum litterarum scientiam aspirat, is probabilem sibi accentuum rationem quam maturrime comparet in propositoque perstet, scurrarum dicacitate et stultorum derisione immotus.*"

grave practical grievance of inculcating rules about a host
of mysterious marks which gave neither ideas to the intellect nor direction to the ear;[1] it had become clear to me
as sunlight, not only from meditation on the nature of
the case, but from an accurate study of the ancient grammarians, that Greek accents contained the two elements of
elevation and stress of voice, and are, in fact, practically
identical with the accents in English, Italian, German,
and other modern languages. And this truth I have
carried out in practice for twenty years with increasing
profit and satisfaction. In England, however, as was to
have been expected, no attention was paid to a Greek
argument coming from the north side of the Tweed;
and, accordingly, in the next work, that of Chandler,[2]
which issued from the Oxford press, we find the whole
subject flung back into a grim limbo of despair, and
involved in a mantle of impenetrable . darkness. In the
preface to his work this author goes so far as to assert
that neither Porson nor any other scholar, " while sanc-
tioning the practice of accentuating Greek by their
example, has condescended to justify it by sound and
conclusive reasons." Porson specially, it is hinted in terms
more vigorous than polite, " gave assertion for proof in
the matter, actuated partly by his contempt for Wake-
field, who happened to entertain a different opinion from
his own." Then he goes on to proclaim the utter hope-
lessness of being able to arrive at any certainty with
regard to the meaning of accents ; it is not even certain
that they did not " indicate the length or shortness
of syllables ;" he denounces " the absurdity of those

---

[1] *The Pronunciation of Greek : Accent
and Quantity ; a Philological Inquiry.*
Edinburgh, 1852.

[2] *A Practical Introduction to Greek
Accentuation.* By H. W. Chandler, M.A.
Oxford, 1862.

who perpetuate in writing a something to · which they
never attend in reading, and who persist in ornamenting
their Greek with three small scratches, the very meaning
of which is doubtful and perhaps unknown," and laments
in the most pathetic terms his own evil destiny in having
had anything to do with the tangled disorder of " these
troublesome appendages."

> " There's something wrong in accents—cursed spite
> That ever I was born to set it right!"

In fact, it appears not a little extraordinary that a
writer who uses such strong language should not have
followed out consistently the practice of his predecessor
Henninius, and flung the whole cargo of Byzantine
lumber overboard ; for what task can be imagined more
irksome and more fruitless than to spend long months of
painful inquiry, with fret of brain and vexation of vision,
upon every mappik · and dagesh of a gospel in which the
writer does not believe ? Almost contemporaneously with
this remarkable book of Mr. Chandler, appeared an interesting paper on accent and quantity by Professor Munro
of Cambridge.[1] The occasion of this discourse was a Latin
inscription in accentual hexameters from Cirta in Numidia,
and supposed by the professor to belong to the third
century of our era. In commenting on these verses, of
course, the writer was led to explain both what accent
meant, and how it came to pass that accentual verse, at
so very early a date, came to usurp the place of quantitative, which only we now acknowledge as classical. In
making this explanation Professor Munro lays down the
following propositions :—

(1.) That the acute accent of the ancients was a mere

---

[1] *On a Metrical Latin Inscription,*   *Transactions of the Cambridge Philo-*
copied by Mr. Blakesley, at Cirta.—   *sophical Society,* vol. x. part 2. 1861.

elevation of the voice, without any stress on the accented syllable.

(2.) That in the composition of Greek and Latin verse, the metre was determined by quantity alone, and that accent had no influence on it direct or indirect.

(3.) That, nevertheless, the quantity of syllables was a matter which swine-herds in the days of Homer, and ploughmen in those of Plautus, had imbibed with their mother's milk, and could discriminate with the nicest precision.

(4.) That by some strange and, to us, unaccountable process, the nature of the Greek and Roman accent was suddenly changed in such fashion that, from being a mere raising or sharpening of the tone " it became a stress," " a mere stress," " a stiff and monotonous stress," a stress which is always accompanied with " the lengthening of the quantity," having nothing in common with the genuine classical accent except the name ; and that by this strange and inexplicable plunge, the accentual poetry of the mediæval hymns, and the whole of our modern metrical system, so early as the third century had started into recognised existence.

So much for the theory of the matter. With regard to the strange and unscientific practice of the English great schools and colleges, the following passage is notable :—

" It appears from what has been said, that we English, in reading Latin, place the accent generally, but by no means always, on the proper syllable. But then, we have entirely changed its nature, making it a mere stress, instead of a simple raising of the tone, without any lengthening of the quantity. And Præcilius and his contemporaries already did the same. From them, and their still more degraded descendants, the Italians, and other western nations, we inherit this debased accent, which had usurped and overthrown the rights of quantity. In the second line of the *Æneid* we read *Italiam fáto profugus* with the accent on the right syllable ; but on the same principle we ought to say—and Præcilius, indeed, and the Romans for centuries after him, did say—*Lavináque*, with the accent on the second *a*. We flatter ourselves that we thus preserve the quantity, but that is a mere delusion. It we feel by a mere mental process. Whether we pronounce *prófugus* or *profúgus*, quantity is equally violated. In the same way we read Greek with this debased Latin accent, and fancy that we preserve the quantity while sacrificing the accent. The modern Greeks read old Greek with the ancient Greek accent, debased in the same way into a mere stress. We think them, they think us, in the wrong ; and in different ways we are both equally in the wrong. *Μῆνιν ἀείδε θέα* in an English or Italian, and *μῆνιν ἄειδε θεά* in a modern Greek mouth, are equally remote from the accent and quantity given to the words by Homer or Demosthenes."

It will be observed that this passage touches exactly on the same absurdity which, sixty years earlier, had roused the sprightly indignation of the author of *Metron Ariston*, and the grave episcopal censure of Dr. Horsley.

In the *Cambridge Journal of Philology*, vol. i., for 1868, appeared an article on the English pronunciation of Greek, by W. G. Clark, then public orator, Cambridge. Mr. Clark is a scholar particularly well entitled to speak on this subject, both from his general accomplishments, which are far from being confined to the ordinary routine of an English classical scholar, and specially from his having travelled in Greece, and taken note of the actual

accents of the language as at present spoken by the
people.   In theory Mr. Clark entirely agrees with Professor Munro, that the ancient Greek accent consisted
merely in the elevation of the tone, while the accent of
the modern Greek includes "a stress precisely like our
own, which is given by prolonging the sound, as well as
by raising the note."   When it falls upon a syllable it
lengthens the vowel except before a double consonant.
Thus λόγος is pronounced λώγος, ὄνος ὤνος, and so forth.
With regard to scholastic practice Mr. Clark is of opinion
that, while our English Greek vocalization is altogether
anomalous and indefensible, and must be abandoned, the
present system of reading Greek with Latin accents
should not be touched, because the modern system of
accentuation is widely different from the ancient, and its
adoption could only tend " to confuse such ideas as we at
present possess of the rhythm of ancient Greek verse."
And again, "It is impossible in practice to recur to the
ancient system of accentuation, supposing that we have
ascertained it in theory.   Here and there a person may
be found with such an exquisite ear, and such plastic
organs of speech, as to be able to reproduce the ancient
distinction between the length and tone of syllables
accented and unaccented, and many not so gifted may
fancy that they reproduce it when they do nothing of the
kind.   For the mass of boys and men, pupils as well as
teachers, the distinction is practically impossible."   So
Mr. Clark leaves us, so far as action is concerned, in a
plight little better than that in which we were left by
Chandler,—not enveloped, indeed, in impermeable mystery, but clogged with impracticable fetters, and groaning
under a yoke of grammatical tradition which neither we
nor our fathers were able to bear.

A strange and a grateful contrast to the general current of English scholarship on this subject is presented by Mr. Geldart, of Balliol College, Oxford, in his interesting and ingenious book, entitled *The Modern Greek Language in its relation to Ancient Greek;* Oxford, 1870. In the third chapter of this work the author states views with regard to accent and quantity which lift him completely out of what has always appeared to me the sort of enchanted circle of confusion and delusion in which English scholars are involved the moment they approach this subject. Mr. Geldart is a decided advocate for accents, both in theory and practice, and he says roundly that "our prejudice against accents is for the most part insular, and deepened, to boot, by the peculiarities of our own insular pronunciation." He blows to the wind in a single sentence the vulgar error of English scholars, so often noticed in these pages, that accent has the necessary effect of lengthening the syllable on which it falls, the accented syllable in English being in fact as often short as long, as in *gĕt'-ting, pĭck'-ing,* while a long syllable is often unaccented, as *fĭnáncial, fértĭle, a prĭŏ'ri,* in which last the first syllable is nearly always pronounced long, in spite of the fact that it is short in Latin. It is accordingly a complete delusion to imagine "that the Latin accent is either an indispensable or an infallible device for marking the right quantity of Greek syllables." With regard to accent he makes the just remark that the raising of the note and the increase of the stress generally go together. He further denies altogether—and on this point he is a witness of great authority—that the modern Greeks always, or even in a majority of cases, lengthen the syllable on which the accent falls ; and in regard to the relation of accent and quantity he shows that neither is modern poetry always governed by the mere spoken accent, nor is ancient poetry altogether regardless of it, but that the real regulator, both of ancient and of modern poetry, though in very different ways, is rhythm, which is determined by the musical beat. How far the spoken accent was heard, as it were, through the rhythmical movement, depended principally upon whether the verse was sung or recited. In pure singing there might be heard only a faint glimmer of the spoken accent; in prose it was the prominent element, and directed the flow of the period; while between these two extremes there might be several intermediate styles of utterance in which the spoken accent was more or less prominent, according to the greater or less approach of the style of recitation to colloquial prose.

It will not be difficult, after this long and strange historical survey, to sum up the conclusions to which, by the consideration of the various facts and arguments, we are inevitably led. We find ourselves, in fact, after more than three centuries of confusion, one-sidedness, and hallucination, arrived at a point of view where no fact or principle necessary to a just conclusion is concealed, and all apparent contradictions find a happy conciliation. In particular, the whole history of the controversy displays the fact that, in one form or another, quantity is the bugbear, and that from Voss and Meetkerche to Munro, Chandler and Clark, a sacred regard for the rights of metre is the apology for the monstrous invasion of the province of Greek by Roman accents. But those who have attended to the course of our argument and historic survey will easily perceive that the interference of Greek accents with the laws of Greek metre is a pure hallucination; inasmuch as—

1. It has been amply proved that in the case of individual words the predominance given to one syllable by the stretch, stress, or emphasis of the voice with which the acute accent is naturally accompanied has no necessary tendency to lengthen the syllable on which it is laid. Through the whole argument of those who oppose Greek accents a confusion runs between two things, which in this matter must be kept carefully apart—a confusion between a short syllable unaccented compared with the same syllable accented, and a short accented syllable with a long syllable accented. When the three terms ἡμέρα, ἡμέ´ρα, and ἡμη´ρα are compared, the middle syllable of the middle term, while it is more prominent, and may be in some degree longer than the same syllable of the first term, is decidedly short when compared with the same syllable of the third term. If, therefore, any short syllable, whether in Greek or English, on which the accent falls, is in danger of being pronounced long, it arises not from the nature of the case, but from the ignorance, carelessness, or stupidity of the teacher ; and, in fact, a great part of the strange confusion which has so long prevailed on this subject may not unreasonably be traced to the want of the directing presence of a living rhetorical and musical culture in our great English schools and colleges.

2. The second great element of confusion which has been introduced into this matter is the gratuitous and altogether unauthorized assumption, that because our metrical composition follows the laws of spoken accent, therefore in Greek and Latin the same law was necessarily observed. In the writings of Hyphaestion and of those who lay down the canons of classical verse, there is not a single word said about the spoken accents ; and the

sure inference is, that in metrical composition they were, as Professor Munro justly remarks, systematically ignored, or, if attended to at all, only in a subordinate, exceptional, incidental, and even accidental way. Nothing, therefore, could be more mistaken than the attempt of Horsley to give a new theory of Homeric scansion, founded on the doctrine of the spoken accents. On what principle, then, it will be asked, was the Greek poetry written? Can it be supposed that a nation of refined taste and high culture could be delighted with the barbarism of pronouncing words one way in prose, and another way in verse? We answer, there is nothing at all strange in this supposition; and that, whether it appear strange or not, it was certainly the fact. To understand this, instead of transferring the laws of our modern poetry wholesale to the poetry of the Greeks, let us rather transfer ourselves from an age of books, reviews, newspapers, and reading-rooms into an age where there was no such thing as books or reading at all, where prose composition was altogether unknown, and where every composition, not purely ephemeral, was made to be sung, and had its existence only in the element of music. Now, we need not at the present day set forth a formal proof that Homer and the pre-Homeric teachers of Greece were not ἀναγνῶσται but ἀοιδοὶ, and that all hexameter verse, the current form of the oldest Greek metrical compositions, was originally sung, and not recited. Under these conditions it naturally conformed to the laws of musical composition; and what these laws were, especially in relation to spoken accent, it is not difficult to realize. What music principally demands from poetry is a mass of rich and full vocalization, to correspond with the measured flow of the notes; for the vowels are the musical element in human speech, and especially the deep broad vowels pronounced long, and not rapidly rattled over. This element, therefore, was naturally preserved in the first place : that is to say, Hellenic poetry was founded on quantity. But what of accent ? The rhythmical march of speech adapted to music, as every one knows, is secured by the element of equality expressed in the succession of equal spaces of sound, marked by recurrent emphasized pulsations ; these pulsations constitute what is called the musical accent, or beating of time, as it is vulgarly called. Now, it certainly might have been desirable to make this rhythmical accent of the music correspond in every case with the spoken accent of the words ; but this was not done, for the very simple reason that the choice of poetical language would have been too much fettered by the constant double demand on the poet of conformity in every case, both with the spoken quantity and the spoken accent. Nor should this appear at all strange. As it is, we see how often Homer—as in ἀθἄνἄτος and other words —is obliged to put an artificial length upon tribrachic feet in order to get them admitted into the dactylic march of his verse ; and how impossible it would have been to compose a long poem under the strict law of both quantitative and accentual conformity, we may see from the fact that, in our own poetry, we have contented ourselves with fettering one of the elements and leaving the other free ; that is to say, that, while we never, or very rarely, allow our spoken accent to clash with the rhythmical beat, we constantly take the liberty in our sung psalms and songs of drawing out short syllables to any length, and skipping over long ones with any amount of metrical celerity. Here, therefore, the Gordian knot is untied : the Greek poetry made to be sung is governed

2 B

by quantity, the musical element of language; the modern poetry made to be read is governed by accent, the colloquial accent.   What Nature, or rather the necessities of Art, have kept asunder, let no man bring together.   Let no man imagine that colloquial accents, whether Greek or Roman, can possibly come into collision with the laws of a poetry so essentially musical in its character as the Greek.

3. But the ancients, it will be said, though their poetry was all musical in its birth, and a verse had no meaning except as sung, certainly did recite their poetry at an early period.   Of course; and in this case it is obvious that a poetry constructed as part of the musical art was to a certain extent put out of Nature the moment it was translated into the region of spoken verse.   In this case a collision between the musical beat and the accented syllables was unavoidable, and some sort of compromise would naturally be the result.   This compromise, however, would on the whole be decidedly to the advantage of the musical rhythm, as opposed to the colloquial accent.   For metre, as we have seen, was metre only in virtue of the regularly recurrent musical beat; and to abolish this was to destroy metre, and to turn verse into prose, as, in fact, we often hear English schoolboys do, when reading Horace, and as the modern Greeks do when they read Homer accentually.   But that the ancients could not have done this is manifest both from the prominence of music in their national culture and from the effect of the rhythmical stroke in lengthening the shortest vowels, even in the verse of Virgil, which certainly was not sung.   The poet who wrote

Liminaquĕ' laurusque Dei

must have had his ear tuned to the march of a verse which gave that marked preponderance to the first syl-

lable of a foot which is musically given to the first note
of a bar, and which allowed the licence of lengthening a
short vowel in such a position after the example of Homer,
specially before a word beginning with a liquid. Meetkerche and Voss were therefore right in reading classical
verse mainly by this rhythmical beat, and practically
disregarding the spoken accent. It does not follow,
however, that though the rhythmical accent remained
dominant even in spoken verse, it therefore exercised an
exclusive sway. In many cases, of course, there would
be no clash, and this, indeed, regularly happened in the
two last feet of a Latin hexameter. But in other cases,
where a clash did occur, the occasional bringing forward
of the spoken accent might serve to break the monotony
of a merely musical rhythm, and cause it to approach
nearer to the march of dignified prose eloquence. Thus,
the first line of Virgil may either be accented

Arma virumque canō' Trojǣ' qui primus ab oris,

or

Arma virumque căn'ō Trŏ'jāe qui primus ab oris;

and in both cases the true quantities are preserved; but
in the second method the spoken accent is allowed to
control two words to the prejudice of the musical beat,
by whose regular recurrence the hexameter verse was
originally framed. In this way it was quite easy to
recite Latin hexameters or Greek iambics in such a
manner that, while the rhythmical beat mainly ruled,
and no short syllable was ever heard where the music had
a long note, the spoken accent to which the ear had been
habituated in conversation did nevertheless generally
shine through, and in special cases assert itself with that
natural emphasis which subordinates rhythm in order to
aid expression, and to prevent monotony.

4. It will now be evident how entirely Professor Munro was mistaken when he expressed surprise at the fact, that, while the rudest boor in the days of Plautus was familiar with the exact laws of quantitative metre, even well-educated gentlemen of the middle-class before the time of Constantine were apparently unable to write anything but accentual metre, constructed on the same principle as the Byzantine στίχοι πολιτικοί. The rudest boor, no doubt, could distinguish a long syllable from a short, and could discriminate the penultimate vowel in *păt'er* and *mā'ter* in a way that seems impossible to the gross ears of some of our English teachers. Our own peasants will distinguish *gŏt* from *goat*, or *god* from *goad*, exactly in the same way; but it will require more than a rhetorical flourish from Cicero to prove that the peasants of Italy, or even Attica, at any time were perfectly master of the complete doctrine of quantity as taught in the musical schools. For it must always be borne in mind that the practice of these schools was to a certain extent artificial ; it was founded on certain concessions which the currency of common life had made to the necessities of art ; and the common people, whose ears were trained mainly by the spoken accent, could not be expected either to compose verses in neglect of that accent, or to sympathize fully with its neglect in the case of verses composed by cultivated poets, except in so far as their own education had kept them in living connexion with those schools of music from which the cultivated poetry had emanated. Now in the best ages of Greece this living connexion naturally existed ; and the effect of custom and association would be such, that no other verses but those composed on the original quantitative principle would be recognised as legitimate even by the vulgar ear. But the moment that a great national

decay commenced, and schools of popular culture were neglected, from that moment the common people, left to themselves, if ever they tried poetical composition, could do so only in obedience to the instinct which governs all poetry not intimately associated with the musical art. Poetry now became a species of measured conversation to which laws were given by the spoken accent, and where the fixed musical recurrence of long and short syllables was systematically ignored. In this change there is nothing strange or mysterious ; on the contrary, it was the natural, and, we may say, necessary consequence of passing from a musical to a colloquial epoch in literature ; and as a fleet-footed man, when he leaves the ice and takes off his skates, passes to a kind of locomotion governed by different conditions and subject to different laws, so a people, shaken loose from all musical tradition and left to form a poetry for itself, will infallibly fall upon a form of verse in which the musical value of vowels will be sacrificed to the familiar control of accentually preponderant syllables.

5. One word remains on the question of scholastic practice, which has been such a bugbear to our teachers. Now, with regard to this problem, it is one of those to which, as Geldart says, the old adage applies, *solvitur ambulando*. What appears impossible in theory is often easy in practice. If you wish to learn how to use your legs, just rise up and walk. If you imagine that there is any difficulty in saying Σωκράτ-ης without saying Σωκρά´της, or *bŏn'us* without saying *bōnus*, just put yourself under a master of elocution for five minutes, and you will shortly be drilled out of your difficulty. But why should the ears of teachers be haunted by such a hallucination as that, by placing the Roman accent on the penult of all dissyllabic words, they are furnished with some sure spell against

the violation of quantity ? Is it not quite evident, rather, that the short quantity of the first syllable of βιός, a *bow*, is much more easily preserved by the natural oxytone accent than by the Latin accent βῖος on the penult ? And if the quantity of the long penult in the verb τρῖβω is more effectively brought out by the accent on that syllable than if it had been on the last, is it not manifest that the same syllable, being short in the substantive τρῐβή, is more certainly pronounced short—according to the argument of the Latinizing Hellenists themselves— with the native oxytone accent than with the imported Latin one ? Take again the word κᾰμᾰρᾱ, *a vault*, where all the vowels are doubtful, and where, of course, the quantity of each syllable can be recognised only by utterance. According to the current method, the accent, laid on the first syllable of this word, should inform me that the syllable is long by virtue of the stress, and it does inform me also, if I am to believe my ears, that the other two syllables are short. But three parts of the information thus given are false ; for the accent is not on the first syllable, and the quantity of the first syllable is short, and that of the last long. On the other hand, if I pronounce the same word according to the principles laid down in this paper, I learn not only where the accent is, but that the two first syllables are short, and the last long. The fact of the matter is, that, while the Greek accent, rightly placed, informs the ear rightly both as to the accent and the quantity of the syllables of which a word is composed, the Latin accent inverts and perverts both, and teaches, with regard to accent and quantity, only what must be unlearned. The opponents of accents, who absurdly call their Latinizing method the quantitative pronunciation of Greek, ought to bear in mind that, in practical teaching, next to pronouncing the long syllables long and the short short, the best way to teach quantity is to pronounce the accent, which either stands upon the long syllable and favours its prolongation, or stands in such a definite relation to that syllable that the quantity of the unaccented syllable is known from the place of the accented.

But the great practical difficulty to which teachers allude is, perhaps, rather rhythmical than prosodiacal. The pronunciation by the Latin accent, says Mr. Clark, is the only way we have of teaching our pupils to appreciate the measure of classical verse. Abolish the Latin accentuation of Greek prose, and you turn the organ of Homer into a hurdy-gurdy. Now, with regard to this matter, I would observe, in the first place, that if the young gentlemen who usually come to our universities were to lose all the rhythmical appreciation of Greek verse that really lives in their ear, and not merely in their understanding, they would lose little that is worth keeping. For what are the facts of the case? The observation of the Latin accent facilitates the rhythmical reading of the two last feet of a hexameter verse; this is an accident of the Latin language; that is all. But not even in the reading of Latin does the reading, according to the Latin prose accents, prevent the constant occurrence of a clash between the spoken accent and the rhythmical beat. In the Ovidian pentameter such a clash must always occur twice, and in the two most marked places of the verse. And, if the absence of the oxytone accent causes this opposition in Latin, is it not strange that we should banish this same accent from its natural place in a Greek word, in order, as we say, to avoid, but actually in a great number of cases to produce,

a collision between the rhythmical beat and that accent?
Take, for instance, this second line from "the Wasps" of
Aristophanes—

Φυλακὴν καταλύειν νυκτερινὴν διδάσκομεν,

and it is plain that in the only two places where a clash
does occur between the spoken accent and the rhythmical
beat, according to the Latinized accent, that clash disappears the moment the words are read according to their
natural Greek accentuation. And so, not only in Iambic
verse, but in every verse whatever, the introduction of
the Latin accent must jar with the rhythmical flow of
the line wherever the rhythmical stroke falls, as it constantly does, on the last syllable of a word. This practical objection therefore vanishes in smoke. That gross-
eared and ill-trained persons may be enabled to receive
the harmonies of the two last feet in a Homeric line,
with a little less trouble, or with no trouble at all, no
wise educator can deem a sufficient reason for invading
the whole inherited intonation of the finest language in
the world, with sounds which, however proper on the
banks of their native Tiber, on the banks of the Ilissus
must be felt to be a gross barbarism. The rhythmical
objection from the practical side is, in fact, only an
ingenious apology to cover carelessness, to prop prejudice,
and to mask with an attitude of apparent utility a peda-
gogic procedure, alike unscientific in principle and self-
contradictory in practice.

Finally, if those who delight themselves in exaggerat-
ing imaginary difficulties have any honest desire to see
how they disappear in the actual business of teaching, let
them come to me; for I am a practical man, and speak
from the experience of half a lifetime. I teach Greek on
the principle that the ear is the natural and legitimate

organ which must be addressed in the first place. I pronounce every word according to its just accent and quantity, allowing its own natural emphasis to sway the proper syllable of the Greek word, just as the Latin accent emphasizes the proper syllable of the Latin word, taking special care at the same time, that in no case shall the emphasis of the accent be drawn into a prolongation of a short vowel. In the matter of quantity, I allow length by position to be pronounced short, according to the English habit, partly because I do not feel sure that this length was anything but a metrical licence unknown to prose, partly because I should not think it advisable to encumber the English light-horseman with a greater weight of heavy Spondaic armour than he can conveniently carry. On the elevation of tone which naturally accompanies the stress, and indeed always seems to have done so at the end of a clause, I do not curiously insist, the accent being sufficiently marked without it. As little do I endeavour to distinguish between a long accented syllable, as in μήνη, and a circumflex, as in μᾶλλον, though I have not the slightest difficulty myself in bringing out the combination of rising and falling inflexion on the same syllable which the circumflex properly denotes. Thus, in the reading of prose, which should be continued assiduously for six months or a year before poetry is meddled with : I then take up Homer, and forthwith intimate to my students that, as the whole doctrine of Greek metres was a part of the science of music, it necessarily followed the laws of that science, and can be understood only by an entire subordination or sinking of the spoken accent in the first place, and a recitation according to the regularly recurrent beats of the rhythm. This, which teachers imagine to be so difficult, is one of the easiest things in the world. Most human beings have ears, and can beat time. Even serpents, and elephants, and dancing bears can do this. And in order that the rhythm may be thoroughly worked into the ear, I have no objection even to what may be called a little *sing-song* at starting; but the pupil, of course, as he advances, must be trained to counteract the monotony of mere rhythm by that variety which a proper attention to expression and punctuation produces. In this way the whole perplexing and tedious doctrine of accent and quantity is learned from beginning to end by the ear; the pain of prosody becomes a pleasure; accent and quantity learn to observe their proper bounds, each, happy in his recognised domain, forgetting all thought of making a hostile invasion into the territory of the other. The only difficulty in the matter arises from the necessity of teaching a number of thoughtless and indifferent young men to unlearn all that lumber of false quantities and false accents which has either been systematically built up, or carelessly allowed to accumulate in the schools; but this is a difficulty which it is in the power of schoolmasters, and of schoolmasters alone, radically to remove. And I feel convinced that, so soon as a radical reform in this matter shall be seriously undertaken by teachers, not only will the inculcation of classical Greek be much facilitated, but the organs of utterance being rendered more flexible and more amenable to training, will accommodate themselves to the characteristic peculiarities of German, French, and other living orthoepies, with an aptitude the want of which is now so frequently lamented.

Printed at the Edinburgh University Press
By Thomas and Archibald Constable, Printers to Her Majesty.

BEDFORD STREET, COVENT GARDEN, LONDON,

October 1873.

MACMILLAN & CO.'S CATALOGUE of WORKS in MATHEMATICS and PHYSICAL SCIENCE; including PURE and APPLIED MATHEMATICS; PHYSICS, ASTRONOMY, GEOLOGY, CHEMISTRY, ZOOLOGY, BOTANY; PHYSIOLOGY, ANATOMY, and MEDICAL WORKS generally; and of WORKS in MENTAL and MORAL PHILOSOPHY and Allied Subjects.

MATHEMATICS.

Airy.— Works by Sir G. B. AIRY, K.C.B., Astronomer Royal :—

ELEMENTARY TREATISE ON PARTIAL DIFFERENTIAL EQUATIONS. Designed for the Use of Students in the Universities. With Diagrams. Crown 8vo. cloth. 5*s*. 6*d*.

It is hoped that the methods of solution here explained, and the instances exhibited, will be found sufficient for application to nearly all the important problems of Physical Science, which require for their complete investigation the aid of Partial Differential Equations.

ON THE ALGEBRAICAL AND NUMERICAL THEORY OF ERRORS OF OBSERVATIONS AND THE COMBINATION OF OBSERVATIONS. Crown 8vo. cloth. 6*s*. 6*d*.

In order to spare astronomers and observers in natural philosophy the confusion and loss of time which are produced by referring to the ordinary treatises embracing both *branches of probabilities (the first*

2000. W. }
1250. D. S. } 9·73·

A

Airy (G. B.)—*continued.*

> *relating to chances which can be altered only by the changes of entire units or integral multiples of units in the fundamental conditions of the problem; the other concerning those chances which have respect to insensible gradations in the value of the element measured), this volume has been drawn up. It relates only to errors of observation, and to the rules, derivable from the consideration of these errors, for the combination of the results of observations.*

UNDULATORY THEORY OF OPTICS. Designed for the Use of Students in the University. New Edition. Crown 8vo. cloth. 6*s*. 6*d*.

> *The undulatory theory of optics is presented to the reader as having the same claims to his attention as the theory of gravitation,—namely, that it is certainly true, and that, by mathematical operations of general elegance, it leads to results of great interest. This theory explains with accuracy a vast variety of phenomena of the most complicated kind. The plan of this tract has been to include those phenomena only which admit of calculation, and the investigations are applied only to phenomena which actually have been observed.*

ON SOUND AND ATMOSPHERIC VIBRATIONS. With the Mathematical Elements of Music. Designed for the Use of Students of the University. Second Edition, revised and enlarged. Crown 8vo. 9*s*.

> *This volume consists of sections, which again are divided into numbered articles, on the following topics:—General recognition of the air as the medium which conveys sound; Properties of the air on which the formation and transmission of sound depend; Theory of undulations as applied to sound, etc.; Investigation of the motion of a wave of air through the atmosphere; Transmission of waves of soniferous vibrations through different gases, solids, and fluids; Experiments on the velocity of sound, etc.; On musical sounds, and the manner of producing them; On the elements of musical harmony and melody, and of simple musical composition; On instrumental music; On the human organs of speech and hearing.*

A TREATISE ON MAGNETISM. Designed for the Use of Students in the University. Crown 8vo. 9*s*. 6*d*.

> *As the laws of Magnetic Force have been experimentally examined,*

with philosophical accuracy, only in its connection with iron and steel, and in the influence excited by the earth as a whole, the accurate portions of this work are confined to the investigations connected with these metals and the earth. The latter part of the work, however, treats in a more general way of the laws of the connection between Magnetism on the one hand and Galvanism and Thermo-Electricity on the other. The work is divided into Twelve Sections, and each section into numbered articles, each of which states concisely and clearly the subject of the following paragraphs.

Ball (R. S., A.M.)—EXPERIMENTAL MECHANICS. A Course of Lectures delivered at the Royal College of Science for Ireland. By ROBERT STAWELL BALL, A.M., Professor of Applied Mathematics and Mechanics in the Royal College of Science for Ireland (Science and Art Department). Royal 8vo. 16s.

*The author's aim in these twenty Lectures has been to create in the mind of the student physical ideas corresponding to theoretical laws, and thus to produce a work which may be regarded either as a supplement or an introduction to manuals of theoretic mechanics. To realize this design, the copious use of experimental illustrations was necessary. The apparatus used in the Lectures and figured in the volume has been principally built up from Professor Willis's most admirable system. In the selection of the subjects, the question of practical utility has in many cases been regarded as the one of paramount importance, and it is believed that the mode of treatment which is adopted is more or less original. This is especially the case in the Lectures relating to friction, to the mechanical powers, to the strength of timber and structures, to the laws of motion, and to the pendulum. The illustrations, drawn from the apparatus, are nearly all original and are beautifully executed. "In our reading we have not met with any book of the sort in English."--*Mechanics' Magazine.

Bayma.—THE ELEMENTS OF MOLECULAR MECHANICS. By JOSEPH BAYMA, S.J., Professor of Philosophy, Stonyhurst College. Demy 8vo. cloth. 10s. 6d.

Of the twelve Books into which this treatise is divided, the first and second give the demonstration of the principles which bear directly on the constitution and the properties of matter. The next three books contain a series of theorems and of problems on the laws of motion of elementary substances. In the sixth and seventh, the mechanical constitution of molecules is investigated and determined: and by it the general properties of bodies are explained. The eighth book treats of luminiferous ether. The ninth explains some special properties of bodies. The tenth and eleventh contain a radical and lengthy investigation of chemical principles and relations, which may lead to practical results of high importance. The twelfth and last book treats of molecular masses, distances, and powers.

Boole.—Works by G. BOOLE, D.C.L., F.R.S., Professor of Mathematics in the Queen's University, Ireland :—

A TREATISE ON DIFFERENTIAL EQUATIONS. Third Edition. Edited by I. TODHUNTER. Crown 8vo. cloth. 14s.

Professor Boole has endeavoured in this treatise to convey as complete an account of the present state of knowledge on the subject of Differential Equations, as was consistent with the idea of a work intended, primarily, for elementary instruction. The earlier sections of each chapter contain that kind of matter which has usually been thought suitable for the beginner, while the latter ones are devoted either to an account of recent discovery, or the discussion of such deeper questions of principle as are likely to present themselves to the reflective student in connection with the methods and processes of his previous course. "A treatise incomparably superior to any other elementary book on the subject with which we are acquainted."— Philosophical Magazine.

A TREATISE ON DIFFERENTIAL EQUATIONS. Supplementary Volume. Edited by I. TODHUNTER. Crown 8vo. cloth. 8s. 6d.

This volume contains all that Professor Boole wrote for the purpose of enlarging his treatise on Differential Equations.

THE CALCULUS OF FINITE DIFFERENCES. Crown 8vo. cloth. 10s. 6d. New Edition revised.

In this exposition of the Calculus of Finite Differences, particular attention has been paid to the connection of its methods with those of the Differential Calculus —a connection which in some instances involves far more than a merely formal analogy. The work is in some measure designed as a sequel to Professor Boole's Treatise on Differential Equations.

Brook-Smith (J.)—ARITHMETIC IN THEORY AND PRACTICE. By J. BROOK-SMITH, M.A., LL.B., St. John's College, Cambridge; Barrister-at-Law; one of the Masters of Cheltenham College. Crown 8vo. 4*s.* 6*d.*

> *Writers on Arithmetic at the present day feel the necessity of explaining the principles on which the rules of the subject are based, but few as yet feel the necessity of making these explanations strict and complete; or, failing that, of distinctly pointing out their defective character. If the science of Arithmetic is to be made an effective instrument in developing and strengthening the mental powers, it ought to be worked out rationally and conclusively; and in this work the author has endeavoured to reason out in a clear and accurate manner the leading propositions of the science, and to illustrate and apply those propositions in practice. In the practical part of the subject he has advanced somewhat beyond the majority of preceding writers; particularly in Division, in Greatest Common Measure, in Cube Root, in the chapters on Decimal Money and the Metric System, and more especially in the application of Decimals to Percentages and cognate subjects. Copious examples, original and selected, are given.*

Cambridge Senate-House Problems and Riders,
WITH SOLUTIONS :—

1848-1851.—PROBLEMS. By FERRERS and JACKSON. 8vo. cloth. 15*s.* 6*d.*

1848-1851.—RIDERS. By JAMESON. 8vo. cloth. 7*s.* 6*d.*

1854.—PROBLEMS AND RIDERS. By WALTON and MACKENZIE. 8vo. cloth. 10*s.* 6*d.*

1857.—PROBLEMS AND RIDERS. By CAMPION and WALTON. 8vo. cloth. 8*s.* 6*d.*

1860.—PROBLEMS AND RIDERS. By WATSON and ROUTH. Crown 8vo. cloth. 7*s.* 6*d.*

1864.—PROBLEMS AND RIDERS. By WALTON and WILKINSON. 8vo. cloth. 10*s.* 6*d.*

> *These volumes will be found of great value to Teachers and Students, as indicating the style and range of mathematical study in the University of Cambridge.*

Cambridge and Dublin Mathematical Journal.
The Complete Work, in Nine Vols. 8vo. cloth. 10*l.* 10*s.*

Only a few copies remain on hand. Among contributors to this work will be found Sir W. Thomson, Stokes, Adams, Boole, Sir W. R. Hamilton, De Morgan, Cayley, Sylvester, Jellet, and other distinguished mathematicians.

Cheyne.—Works by C. H. H. CHEYNE, M.A., F.R.A.S.:—

AN ELEMENTARY TREATISE ON THE PLANETARY THEORY. With a Collection of Problems. Second Edition. Crown 8vo. cloth. 6*s.* 6*d.*

In this volume, an attempt has been made to produce a treatise on the Planetary theory, which, being elementary in character, should be so far complete as to contain all that is usually required by students in the University of Cambridge. This Edition has been carefully revised. The stability of the Planetary System has been more fully treated, and an elegant geometrical explanation of the formulæ for the secular variation of the node and inclination has been introduced. .

THE EARTH'S MOTION OF ROTATION. Crown 8vo. 3*s.* 6*d.*

The first part of this work consists of an application of the method of the variation of elements to the general problem of rotation. In the second part the general rotation formulæ are applied to the particular case of the earth.

Childe.—THE SINGULAR PROPERTIES OF THE ELLIPSOID AND ASSOCIATED SURFACES OF THE Nᴛʜ DEGREE. By the Rev. G. F. CHILDE, M.A., Author of "Ray Surfaces," "Related Caustics," &c. 8vo. 10*s.* 6*d.*

The object of this volume is to develop peculiarities in the Ellipsoid; and, further, to establish analogous properties in the unlimited congeneric series of which this remarkable surface is a constituent.

Dodgson.—AN ELEMENTARY TREATISE ON DETERMINANTS, with their Application to Simultaneous Linear Equations and Algebraical Geometry. By CHARLES L. DODGSON, M A., Student and Mathematical Lecturer of Christ Church, Oxford. Small 4to. cloth. 10*s.* 6*d.*

The object of the author is to present the subject as a continuous chain of argument, separated from all accessories of explanation or illustration. All such explanation and illustration as seemed necessary for a beginner are introduced either in the form of foot-notes, or, where that would have occupied too much room, of Appendices.

Earnshaw (S., M.A.)—PARTIAL DIFFERENTIAL EQUATIONS. An Essay towards an entirely New Method of Integrating them. By S. EARNSHAW, M.A., of St. John's College, Cambridge. Crown 8vo. 5s.

The peculiarity of the system expounded in this work is, that in every equation, whatever be the number of original independent variables, the work of integration is at once reduced to the use of one independent variable only. The author's object is merely to render his method thoroughly intelligible. The various steps of the investigation are all obedient to one general principle: and though in some degree novel, are not really difficult, but on the contrary, easy when the eye has become accustomed to the novelties of the notation. Many of the results of the integrations are far more general than they were in the shape in which they appeared in former Treatises, and many Equations will be found in this Essay integrated with ease in finite terms, which were never so integrated before.

Ferrers.—AN ELEMENTARY TREATISE ON TRILINEAR CO-ORDINATES, the Method of Reciprocal Polars, and the Theory of Projectors. By the Rev. N. M. FERRERS, M.A., Fellow and Tutor of Gonville and Caius College, Cambridge. Second Edition. Crown 8vo. 6s. 6d.

The object of the author in writing on this subject has mainly been to place it on a basis altogether independent of the ordinary Cartesian system, instead of regarding it as only a special form of Abridged Notation. A short chapter on Determinants has been introduced.

Frost.—Works by PERCIVAL FROST, M.A., late Fellow of St. John's College, Mathematical Lecturer of King's College, Cambridge :—

THE FIRST THREE SECTIONS OF NEWTON'S PRINCIPIA. With Notes and Illustrations. Also a Collection of Problems, principally intended as Examples of Newton's Methods. Second Edition. 8vo. cloth. 10s. 6d.

Frost—*continued.*

The author's principal intention is to explain difficulties which may be encountered by the student on first reading the Principia, *and to illustrate the advantages of a careful study of the methods employed by Newton, by showing the extent to which they may be applied in the solution of problems ; he has also endeavoured to give assistance to the student who is engaged in the study of the higher branches of mathematics, by representing in a geometrical form several of the processes employed in the Differential and Integral Calculus, and in the analytical investigations of Dynamics.*

AN ELEMENTARY TREATISE ON CURVE TRACING. 8vo. 12s.

The author has written this book under the conviction that the skill and power of the young mathematical student, in order to be thoroughly available afterwards, ought to be developed in all possible directions. The subject which he has chosen presents so many faces, pointing in directions towards which the mind of the intended mathematician has to radiate, that it would be difficult to find another which, with a very limited extent of reading, combines, to the same extent, so many valuable hints of methods of calculations to be employed hereafter, with so much pleasure in its present use. In order to understand the work it is not necessary to have much knowledge of what is called Higher Algebra, nor of Algebraical Geometry of a higher kind than that which simply relates to the Conic Sections. From the study of a work like this, it is believed that the student will derive many advantages. Especially he will become skilled in making correct approximations to the values of quantities, which cannot be found exactly, to any degree of accuracy which may be required.

Frost and Wolstenholme.—A TREATISE ON SOLID GEOMETRY. By PERCIVAL FROST, M.A., and the Rev. J. WOLSTENHOLME, M.A., Fellow and Assistant Tutor of Christ's College. 8vo. cloth. 18s.

Intending to make the subject accessible, at least in the earlier portions, to all classes of students, the authors have endeavoured to explain completely all the processes which are most useful in dealing with ordinary theorems and problems, thus directing the student to the selection of methods which are best adapted to the exigencies of each problem. In the more difficult portions of the subject, they have considered themselves to be addressing a higher class of students ;

and they have there tried to lay a good foundation on which to build, if any reader should wish to pursue the science beyond the limits to which the work extends.

Godfray.—Works by HUGH GODFRAY, M.A., Mathematical Lecturer at Pembroke College, Cambridge:—

A TREATISE ON ASTRONOMY, for the Use of Colleges and Schools. 8vo. cloth. 12s. 6d.

This book embraces all those branches of Astronomy which have, from time to time, been recommended by the Cambridge Board of Mathematical Studies: but by far the larger and easier portion, adapted to the first three days of the Examination for Honours, may be read by the more advanced pupils in many of our schools. The author's aim has been to convey clear and distinct ideas of the celestial phenomena. "It is a working book," says the Guardian, "taking Astronomy in its proper place in the Mathematical Sciences. . . . It is a book which is not likely to be got up unintelligently."

AN ELEMENTARY TREATISE ON THE LUNAR THEORY, with a Brief Sketch of the Problem up to the time of Newton. Second Edition, revised. Crown 8vo. cloth. 5s. 6d.

These pages will, it is hoped, form an introduction to more recondite works. Difficulties have been discussed at considerable length. The selection of the method followed with regard to analytical solutions, which is the same as that of Airy, Herschel, etc., was made on account of its simplicity; it is, moreover, the method which has obtained in the University of Cambridge. "As an elementary treatise and introduction to the subject, we think it may justly claim to supersede all former ones."—London, Edinburgh, and Dublin Phil. Magazine.

Green (George).—MATHEMATICAL PAPERS OF THE LATE GEORGE GREEN, Fellow of Gonville and Caius College, Cambridge. Edited by N. M. FERRERS, M.A., Fellow and Tutor of Gonville and Caius College. 8vo. 15s.

The publication of this book may be opportune at present, as several of the subjects with which they are directly or indirectly concerned have recently been introduced into the course of mathematical study at Cambridge. They have also an interest as being the work of an almost entirely self-taught mathematical genius. The Papers comprise the following:—An Essay on the application of Mathematical Analysis to the Theories of Electricity and Magnetism—On the Laws of the Equilibrium of Fluids analogous to the Electric Fluid—On the Determination of the Attractions of Ellipsoids of variable Densities—On the Motion of Waves in a variable Canal of small depth and width—On the Reflection and Refraction of Sound—On the Reflection and Refraction of Light at the Common Surface of two Non-Crystallized Media—On the Propagation of Light in Crystallized Media—Researches on the Vibrations of Pendulums in Fluid Media. " *It has been for some time recognized that Green's writings are amongst the most valuable mathematical productions we possess.*"—Athenæum.

Hemming.—AN ELEMENTARY TREATISE ON THE DIFFERENTIAL AND INTEGRAL CALCULUS. For the Use of Colleges and Schools. By G. W. HEMMING, M.A., Fellow of St. John's College, Cambridge. Second Edition, with Corrections and Additions. 8vo. cloth. 9s.

" *There is no book in common use from which so clear and exact a knowledge of the principles of the Calculus can be so readily obtained.*"—Literary Gazette.

Jackson.—GEOMETRICAL CONIC SECTIONS. An Elementary Treatise in which the Conic Sections are defined as the Plane Sections of a Cone, and treated by the Method of Projections. By J. STUART JACKSON, M.A., late Fellow of Gonville and Caius College. Crown 8vo. 4s. 6d.

This work has been written with a view to give the student the benefit of the Method of Projections as applied to the Ellipse and Hyperbola. When this method is admitted into the treatment of Conic Sections there are many reasons why they should be defined, not with reference to the focus and directrix, but according to the original definition from which they have their name, as Plane Sections of a Cone. This method is calculated to produce a material simplification in the treatment of these curves and to make the proof of their properties more easily understood in the first instance and more easily remembered. It is also a powerful instrument in the solution of a large class of problems relating to these curves.

Morgan.—A COLLECTION OF PROBLEMS AND EXAM-
PLES IN MATHEMATICS. With Answers. By H. A.
MORGAN, M.A., Sadlerian and Mathematical Lecturer of Jesus
College, Cambridge. Crown 8vo. cloth. 6s. 6d.

> *This book contains a number of problems, chiefly elementary, in the
> Mathematical subjects usually read at Cambridge. They have been
> selected from the Papers set during late years at Jesus College. Very
> few of them are to be met with in other collections, and by far the
> larger number are due to some of the most distinguished Mathe-
> maticians in the University.*

Newton's Principia.—4to. cloth. 31s. 6d.

> *It is a sufficient guarantee of the reliability of this complete edition of
> Newton's* Principia *that it has been printed for and under the care
> of Professor Sir William Thomson and Professor Blackburn, of
> Glasgow University. The following notice is prefixed:—" Finding
> that all the editions of the* Principia *are now out of print, we have
> been induced to reprint Newton's last edition [of* 1726] *without note
> or comment, only introducing the 'Corrigenda' of the old copy and
> correcting typographical errors." The book is of a handsome size,
> with large type, fine thick paper, and cleanly-cut figures, and is
> the only recent edition containing the whole of Newton's great
> work.*

Parkinson.—Works by S. PARKINSON, D.D., F.R.S., Fellow
and Tutor of St. John's College, Cambridge :—

AN ELEMENTARY TREATISE ON MECHANICS. For the
Use of the Junior Classes at the University and the Higher Classes
in Schools. With a Collection of Examples. Fourth Edition,
revised. Crown 8vo. cloth. 9s. 6d.

> *In preparing a fourth edition of this work the author has kept the
> same object in view as he had in the former editions—namely, to in-
> clude in it such portions of Theoretical Mechanics as can be con-
> veniently investigated without the use of the Differential Calculus,
> and so render it suitable as a manual for the junior classes in the
> University and the higher classes in Schools. With one or two short
> exceptions, the student is not presumed to require a knowledge of any*

Parkinson—*continued.*

> *branches of Mathematics beyond the elements of Algebra, Geometry, and Trigonometry. Several additional propositions have been incorporated in the work for the purpose of rendering it more complete, and the collection of Examples and Problems has been largely increased.*

A TREATISE ON OPTICS. Third Edition, revised and enlarged. Crown 8vo. cloth. 10s. 6d.

> *A collection of Examples and Problems has been appended to this work, which are sufficiently numerous and varied in character to afford useful exercise for the student. For the greater part of them, recourse has been had to the Examination Papers set in the University and the several Colleges during the last twenty years.*

Phear.—ELEMENTARY HYDROSTATICS. With Numerous Examples. By J. B. PHEAR, M.A., Fellow and late Assistant Tutor of Clare College, Cambridge. Fourth Edition. Crown 8vo. cloth. 5s. 6d.

> *This edition has been carefully revised throughout, and many new Illustrations and Examples added, which it is hoped will increase its usefulness to students at the Universities and in Schools. In accordance with suggestions from many engaged in tuition, answers to all the Examples have been given at the end of the book.*

Pratt.—A TREATISE ON ATTRACTIONS, LAPLACE'S FUNCTIONS, AND THE FIGURE OF THE EARTH. By JOHN H. PRATT, M.A., Archdeacon of Calcutta, Author of "The Mathematical Principles of Mechanical Philosophy." Fourth Edition. Crown 8vo. cloth. 6s. 6d.

> *The author's chief design in this treatise is to give an answer to the question, "Has the Earth acquired its present form from being originally in a fluid state?" This edition is a complete revision of the former ones.*

Puckle.—AN ELEMENTARY TREATISE ON CONIC SECTIONS AND ALGEBRAIC GEOMETRY. With numerous

Examples and Hints for their Solution ; especially designed for the Use of Beginners. By G. H. PUCKLE, M.A. New Edition, revised and enlarged. Crown 8vo. cloth. 7*s*. 6*d*.

This work is recommended by the Syndicate of the Cambridge Local Examinations. The Athenæum *says the author "displays an intimate acquaintance with the difficulties likely to be felt, together with a singular aptitude in removing them."*

Routh.—AN ELEMENTARY TREATISE ON THE DYNA-MICS OF THE SYSTEM OF RIGID BODIES. With numerous Examples. By EDWARD JOHN ROUTH, M.A., late Fellow and Assistant Tutor of St. Peter's College, Cambridge ; Examiner in the University of London. Second Edition, enlarged. Crown 8vo. cloth. 14*s*.

In this edition the author has made several additions to each chapter : he has tried, even at the risk of some little repetition, to make each chapter, as far as possible, complete in itself, so that all that relates to any one part of the subject may be found in the same place. This arrangement will enable every student to select his own order in which to read the subject. The Examples which will be found at the end of each chapter have been chiefly selected from the Examination Papers which have been set in the University and the Colleges in the last few years.

Smith's (Barnard) Works.—See EDUCATIONAL CATA-LOGUE.

Snowball.—THE ELEMENTS OF PLANE AND SPHERI-CAL TRIGONOMETRY ; with the Construction and Use of Tables of Logarithms. By J. C. SNOWBALL, M.A. Tenth Edition. Crown 8vo. cloth. 7*s*. 6*d*.

In preparing the present edition for the press, the text has been sub-jected to a careful revision ; the proofs of some of the more import-ant propositions have been rendered more strict and general ; and a considerable addition of more than two hundred examples, taken principally from the questions set of late years in the public exami-nations of the University and of individual Colleges, has been made to the collection of Examples and Problems for practice.

Tait and Steele.—DYNAMICS OF A PARTICLE. With numerous Examples. By Professor TAIT and Mr. STEELE. New Edition. Crown 8vo. cloth. 10s. 6d.

In this treatise will be found all the ordinary propositions, connected with the Dynamics of Particles, which can be conveniently deduced without the use of D'Alembert's Principle. Throughout the book will be found a number of illustrative examples introduced in the text, and for the most part completely worked out ; others with occasional solutions or hints to assist the student are appended to each chapter. For by far the greater portion of these, the Cambridge Senate-House and College Examination Papers have been applied to.

Taylor.—GEOMETRICAL CONICS ; including An harmonic Ratio and Projection, with numerous Examples. By C. TAYLOR, B.A., Scholar of St. John's College, Cambridge. Crown 8vo. cloth. 7s. 6d.

This work contains elementary proofs of the principal properties of Conic Sections, together with chapters on Projection and Anharmonic Ratio.

Todhunter.—Works by I. TODHUNTER, M.A., F.R.S., of St. John's College, Cambridge :—

"Perspicuous language, vigorous investigations, scrutiny of difficulties, and methodical treatment, characterize Mr. Todhunter's works."— Civil Engineer.

THE ELEMENTS OF EUCLID; MENSURATION FOR BEGINNERS; ALGEBRA FOR BEGINNERS; TRIGO- NOMETRY FOR BEGINNERS; MECHANICS FOR BEGINNERS.—See EDUCATIONAL CATALOGUE.

ALGEBRA. For the Use of Colleges and Schools. Sixth Edition. Crown 8vo. cloth. 7s. 6d.

This work contains all the propositions which are usually included in elementary treatises on Algebra, and a large number of Examples for Exercise. The author has sought to render the work easily intelligible to students, without impairing the accuracy of the demonstrations, or contracting the limits of the subject. The Examples, about Sixteen hundred and fifty in number, have been selected with

Todhunter (I.)—*continued.*

a view to illustrate every part of the subject. The work will be found peculiarly adapted to the wants of students who are without the aid of a teacher. The Answers to the Examples, with hints for the solution of some in which assistance may be needed, are given at the end of the book. In the present edition two New Chapters and Three hundred *miscellaneous Examples have been added. "It has merits which unquestionably place it first in the class to which it belongs."*—Educator.

KEY TO ALGEBRA FOR THE USE OF COLLEGES AND SCHOOLS. Crown 8vo. 10s. 6d.

AN ELEMENTARY TREATISE ON THE THEORY OF EQUATIONS. Second Edition, revised. Crown 8vo. cloth. 7s. 6d.

This treatise contains all the propositions which are usually included in elementary treatises on the theory of Equations, together with Examples for exercise. These have been selected from the College and University Examination Papers, and the results have been given when it appeared necessary. In order to exhibit a comprehensive view of the subject, the treatise includes investigations which are not found in all the preceding elementary treatises, and also some investigations which are not to be found in any of them. For the second edition the work has been revised and some additions have been made, the most important being an account of the Researches of Professor Sylvester respecting Newton's Rule. "A thoroughly trustworthy, complete, and yet not too elaborate treatise." —Philosophical Magazine.

PLANE TRIGONOMETRY. For Schools and Colleges. Fourth Edition. Crown 8vo. cloth. 5s.

The design of this work has been to render the subject intelligible to beginners, and at the same time to afford the student the opportunity of obtaining all the information which he will require on this branch of Mathematics. Each chapter is followed by a set of Examples: those which are entitled Miscellaneous Examples, *together with a few in some of the other sets, may be advantageously reserved by the student for exercise after he has made some progress in the subject. In the Second Edition the hints for the solution of the Examples have been considerably increased.*

Todhunter (I.)—*continued.*

A TREATISE ON SPHERICAL TRIGONOMETRY. Third Edition, enlarged. Crown 8vo. cloth. 4*s.* 6*d.*

> *The present work is constructed on the same plan as the treatise on Plane Trigonometry, to which it is intended as a sequel. In the account of Napier's Rules of circular parts, an explanation has been given of a method of proof devised by Napier, which seems to have been overlooked by most modern writers on the subject. Considerable labour has been bestowed on the text in order to render it comprehensive and accurate, and the Examples (selected chiefly from College Examination Papers) have all been carefully verified. "For educational purposes this work seems to be superior to any others on the subject."*—Critic.

PLANE CO-ORDINATE GEOMETRY, as applied to the Straight Line and the Conic Sections. With numerous Examples. Fourth Edition, revised and enlarged. Crown 8vo. cloth. 7*s.* 6*d.*

> *The author has here endeavoured to exhibit the subject in a simple manner for the benefit of beginners, and at the same time to include in one volume all that students usually require. In addition, therefore, to the propositions which have always appeared in such treatises, he has introduced the methods of abridged notation, which are of more recent origin: these methods, which are of a less elementary character than the rest of the work, are placed in separate chapters, and may be omitted by the student at first.*

A TREATISE ON THE DIFFERENTIAL CALCULUS. With numerous Examples. Sixth Edition. Crown 8vo. cloth. 10*s.* 6*d.*

> *The author has endeavoured in the present work to exhibit a comprehensive view of the Differential Calculus on the method of limits. In the more elementary portions he has entered into considerable detail in the explanations, with the hope that a reader who is without the assistance of a tutor may be enabled to acquire a competent acquaintance with the subject. The method adopted is that of Differential Coefficients. To the different chapters are appended Examples sufficiently numerous to render another book unnecessary; these Examples being mostly selected from College Examination Papers. This and the following work have been translated into*

Todhunter (I.)—*continued.*

*Italian by Professor Battaglini, who in his Preface speaks thus :—
" In publishing this translation of the Differential and Integral
Calculus of Mr. Todhunter, we have had no other object than to
add to the books which are in the hands of the students of our Universities, a work remarkable for the clearness of the exposition, the
rigour of the demonstrations, the just proportion in the parts, and
the rich store of examples which offer a large field for useful
exercise."*

A TREATISE ON THE INTEGRAL CALCULUS AND ITS
APPLICATIONS. With numerous Examples. Third Edition,
revised and enlarged. Crown 8vo. cloth. 10s. 6d.

*This is designed as a work at once elementary and complete, adapted
for the use of beginners, and sufficient for the wants of advanced
students. In the selection of the propositions, and in the mode of
establishing them, it has been sought to exhibit the principles clearly,
and to illustrate all their most important results. The process of
summation has been repeatedly brought forward, with the view
of securing the attention of the student to the notions which form the
true foundation of the Calculus itself, as well as of its most
valuable applications. Every attempt has been made to explain those
difficulties which usually perplex beginners, especially with reference
to the* limits *of integrations. A new method has been adopted in
regard to the transformation of multiple integrals. The last chapter
deals with the Calculus of Variations. A large collection of Exercises, selected from College Examination Papers, has been appended
to the several chapters.*

EXAMPLES OF ANALYTICAL GEOMETRY OF THREE
DIMENSIONS. Third Edition, revised. Crown 8vo. cloth. 4s.

A TREATISE ON ANALYTICAL STATICS. With numerous
Examples. Third Edition, revised and enlarged. Crown 8vo.
cloth. 10s. 6d.

*In this work on Statics (treating of the laws of the equilibrium of
bodies) will be found all the propositions which usually appear in
treatises on Theoretical Statics. To the different chapters Examples
are appended, which have been principally selected from University
Examination Papers. In the Third Edition many additions have
been made, in order to illustrate the application of the principles of
the subject to the solution of problems.*

B

Todhunter (I.)—*continued.*

A HISTORY OF THE MATHEMATICAL THEORY OF PROBABILITY, from the Time of Pascal to that of Laplace. 8vo. 18*s.*

The subject of this work has high claims to consideration on account of the subtle problems which it involves, the valuable contributions to analysis which it has produced, its important practical applications, and the eminence of those who have cultivated it ; nearly every great mathematician within the range of a century and a half comes under consideration in the course of the history. The author has endeavoured to be quite accurate in his statements, and to reproduce the essential elements of the original works which he has analysed. Besides being a history, the work may claim the title of a comprehensive treatise on the Theory of Probability, for it assumes in the reader only so much knowledge as can be gained from an elementary book on Algebra, and introduces him to almost every process and every special problem which the literature of the subject can furnish.

RESEARCHES IN THE CALCULUS OF VARIATIONS, Principally on the Theory of Discontinuous Solutions : An Essay to which the Adams' Prize was awarded in the University of Cambridge in 1871. 8vo. 6*s.*

The subject of this Essay was prescribed in the following terms by the Examiners :—"A determination of the circumstances under which discontinuity of any kind presents itself in the solution of a problem of maximum or minimum in the Calculus of Variations, and applications to particular instances. It is expected that the discussion of the instances should be exemplified as far as possible geometrically, and that attention be especially directed to cases of real or supposed failure of the Calculus." While the Essay is thus mainly devoted to the consideration of discontinuous solutions, various other questions in the Calculus of Variations are examined and elucidated ; and the author hopes he has definitely contributed to the extension and improvement of our knowledge of this refined department of analysis.

A HISTORY OF THE MATHEMATICAL THEORIES OF ATTRACTION, and the Figure of the Earth, from the time of Newton to that of Laplace. Two vols. 8vo. 24*s.*

Wilson (W. P.)—A TREATISE ON DYNAMICS. By W. P. WILSON, M.A., Fellow of St. John's College, Cambridge, and Professor of Mathematics in Queen's College, Belfast. 8vo. 9s. 6d.

Wolstenholme.—A BOOK OF MATHEMATICAL PROBLEMS, on Subjects included in the Cambridge Course. By JOSEPH WOLSTENHOLME, Fellow of Christ's College, some time Fellow of St. John's College, and lately Lecturer in Mathematics at Christ's College. Crown 8vo. cloth. 8s. 6d.

CONTENTS :—*Geometry (Euclid)—Algebra—Plane Trigonometry—Geometrical Conic Sections—Analytical Conic Sections—Theory of Equations—Differential Calculus—Integral Calculus—Solid Geometry—Statics—Elementary Dynamics—Newton—Dynamics of a Point—Dynamics of a Rigid Body—Hydrostatics—Geometrical Optics—Spherical Trigonometry and Plane Astronomy. In some cases the author has prefixed to certain classes of problems fragmentary notes on the mathematical subjects to which they relate.* " *Judicious, symmetrical, and well arranged.*"—Guardian.

PHYSICAL SCIENCE.

Airy (G. B.)—POPULAR ASTRONOMY. With Illustrations. By Sir G. B. AIRY, K.C.B., Astronomer Royal. Seventh and cheaper Edition. 18mo. cloth. 4s. 6d.

> *This work consists of Six Lectures, which are intended "to explain to intelligent persons the principles on which the instruments of an Observatory are constructed (omitting all details, so far as they are merely subsidiary), and the principles on which the observations made with these instruments are treated for deduction of the distances and weights of the bodies of the Solar System, and of a few stars, omitting all minutiæ of formulæ, and all troublesome details of calculation." The speciality of this volume is the direct reference of every step to the Observatory, and the full description of the methods and instruments of observation.*

Bastian.—Works by H. CHARLTON BASTIAN, M.D., F.R.S., Professor of Pathological Anatomy in University College, London, etc. :—

THE MODES OF ORIGIN OF LOWEST ORGANISMS: Including a Discussion of the Experiments of M. Pasteur, and a Reply to some Statements by Professors Huxley and Tyndall. Crown 8vo. 4s. 6d.

> *The present volume contains a fragment of the evidence which will be embodied in a much larger work—now almost completed—relating to the nature and origin of living matter, and in favour of what is termed the Physical Doctrine of Life. "It is a work worthy of the highest respect, and places its author in the very first class of scientific physicians. . . . It would be difficult to name an instance in which skill, knowledge, perseverance, and great reasoning power have been more happily applied to the investigation of a complex biological problem."—British Medical Journal.*

Bastian (H. C.)—*continued.*

THE BEGINNINGS OF LIFE: Being some Account of the Nature, Modes of Origin, and Transformations of Lower Organisms. In Two Volumes. With upwards of 100 Illustrations, Crown 8vo. 28*s.*

These volumes contain the results of several years' investigation on the Origin of Life, and it was only after the author had proceeded some length with his observations and experiments that he was compelled to change the opinions he started with for those announced in the present work—the most important of which is that in favour of " spontaneous generation "—the theory that life has never ceased to be actually originated. The First Part of the work is intended to show the general reader, more especially, that the logical consequences of the now commonly accepted doctrines concerning the " Conservation of Energy " and the " Correlation of the Vital and Physical Forces " are wholly favourable to the possibility of the independent origin of " living " matter. It also contains a view of the " Cellular Theory of Organisation." In the Second Part of the work, under the head " Archebiosis," the question as to the present occurrence or non-occurrence of " spontaneous generation " is considered. " It is a book that cannot be ignored, and must inevitably lead to renewed discussions and repeated observations, and through these to the establishment of truth."—A. R. WALLACE in Nature.

Birks (T. R.)—ON MATTER AND ETHER ; or, The Secret Laws of Physical Change. By THOMAS RAWSON BIRKS, M.A., Professor of Moral Philosophy in the University of Cambridge. Crown 8vo. 5*s.* 6*d.*

The author believes that the hypothesis of the existence of, besides matter, a luminous ether, of immense elastic force, supplies the true and sufficient key to the remaining secrets of inorganic matter, of the phenomena of light, electricity, etc. In this treatise the author endeavours first to form a clear and definite conception with regard to the real nature both of matter and ether, and the laws of mutual action which must be supposed to exist between them. He then endeavours to trace out the main consequences of the fundamental hypothesis, and their correspondence with the known phenomena of physical change.

Blanford (W. T.)—GEOLOGY AND ZOOLOGY OF ABYSSINIA. By W. T. BLANFORD. 8vo. 21*s.*

> *This work contains an account of the Geological and Zoological Obser-vations made by the author in Abyssinia, when accompanying the British Army on its march to Magdala and back in 1868, and during a short journey in Northern Abyssinia, after the departure of the troops. Part I. Personal Narrative; Part II. Geology; Part III. Zoology. With Coloured Illustrations and Geological Map. "The result of his labours," the* Academy *says, "is an important contribution to the natural history of the country."*

Clodd.—THE CHILDHOOD OF THE WORLD: a Simple Account of Man in Early Times. By EDWARD CLODD, F.R.A.S. Second Edition. Globe 8vo. 3*s.*

> *"Likely, we think, to prove acceptable to a large and growing class of readers."*—Pall Mall Gazette.

> PROFESSOR MAX MULLER, *in a letter to the Author, says : "I read your book with great pleasure. I have no doubt it will do good, and I hope you will continue your work. Nothing spoils our temper so much as having to unlearn in youth, manhood, and even old age, so many things which we were taught as children. A book like yours will prepare a far better soil in the child's mind, and I was delighted to have it to read to my children."*

Cooke (Josiah P., Jun.)—FIRST PRINCIPLES OF CHEMICAL PHILOSOPHY. By JOSIAH P. COOKE, Jun., Ervine Professor of Chemistry and Mineralogy in Harvard College. Crown 8vo. 12*s.*

> *The object of the author in this book is to present the philosophy of Chemistry in such a form that it can be made with profit the subject of College recitations, and furnish the teacher with the means of testing the student's faithfulness and ability. With this view the subject has been developed in a logical order, and the principles of the science are taught independently of the experimental evidence on which they rest.*

Cooke (M. C.)—HANDBOOK OF BRITISH FUNGI, with full descriptions of all the Species, and Illustrations of the Genera. By M. C. COOKE, M.A. Two vols. crown 8vo. 24*s.*

During the thirty-five years that have elapsed since the appearance of the last complete Mycologic Flora no attempt has been made to revise it, to incorporate species since discovered, and to bring it up to the standard of modern science. No apology, therefore, is necessary for the present effort, since all will admit that the want of such a manual has long been felt, and this work makes its appearance under the advantage that it seeks to occupy a place which has long been vacant. No effort has been spared to make the work worthy of confidence, and, by the publication of an occasional supplement, it is hoped to maintain it for many years as the "Handbook" for every student of British Fungi. Appended is a complete alphabetical Index of all the divisions and subdivisions of the Fungi noticed in the text. The book contains 400 figures. "Will maintain its place as the standard English book, on the subject of which it treats, for many years to come."—Standard.

Dawkins.—CAVE-HUNTING : Researches on the Evidence of Caves respecting the Early Inhabitants of Europe. By W. BOYD DAWKINS, F.R.S. Illustrated. 8vo. [*In the Press.*

Dawson (J. W.)—ACADIAN GEOLOGY. The Geologic Structure, Organic Remains, and Mineral Resources of Nova Scotia, New Brunswick, and Prince Edward Island. By JOHN WILLIAM DAWSON, M.A., LL.D., F.R.S., F.G.S., Principal and Vice-Chancellor of M'Gill College and University, Montreal, &c. Second Edition, revised and enlarged. With a Geological Map and numerous Illustrations. 8vo. 18s.

The object of the first edition of this work was to place within the reach of the people of the districts to which it relates, a popular account of the more recent discoveries in the geology and mineral resources of their country, and at the same time to give to geologists in other countries a connected view of the structure of a very interesting portion of the American Continent, in its relation to general and theoretical Geology. In the present edition, it is hoped this design is still more completely fulfilled, with reference to the present more advanced condition of knowledge. The author has endeavoured to convey a knowledge of the structure and fossils of the region in such a manner as to be intelligible to ordinary readers, and has devoted much attention to all questions relating to the nature and present or prospective value of deposits of useful minerals.

Besides a large coloured Geological Map of the district, the work is illustrated by upwards of 260 cuts of sections, fossils, animals, etc. "The book will doubtless find a place in the library, not only of the scientific geologist, but also of all who are desirous of the industrial progress and commercial prosperity of the Acadian provinces."—Mining Journal. *"A style at once popular and scientific. . . . A valuable addition to our store of geological knowledge."*—Guardian.

Flower (W. H.)—AN INTRODUCTION TO THE OSTE-OLOGY OF THE MAMMALIA. Being the substance of the Course of Lectures delivered at the Royal College of Surgeons of England in 1870. By W. H. FLOWER, F.R.S., F.R.C.S., Hunterian Professor of Comparative Anatomy and Physiology. With numerous Illustrations. Globe 8vo. 7s. 6d.

Although the present work contains the substance of a Course of Lectures, the form has been changed, so as the better to adapt it as a handbook for students. Theoretical views have been almost entirely excluded: and while it is impossible in a scientific treatise to avoid the employment of technical terms, it has been the author's endeavour to use no more than absolutely necessary, and to exercise due care in selecting only those that seem most appropriate, or which have received the sanction of general adoption. With a very few exceptions the illustrations have been drawn expressly for this work from specimens in the Museum of the Royal College of Surgeons.

Galton.—Works by FRANCIS GALTON, F.R.S. :—

METEOROGRAPHICA, or Methods of Mapping the Weather. Illustrated by upwards of 600 Printed Lithographic Diagrams. 4to. 9s.

As Mr. Galton entertains strong views on the necessity of Meteorological Charts and Maps, he determined, as a practical proof of what could be done, to chart the entire area of Europe, so far as meteorological stations extend, during one month, viz. the month of December, 1861. Mr. Galton got his data from authorities in every part of Britain and the Continent, and on the basis of these has here drawn up nearly a hundred different Maps and Charts, showing the state of the weather all over Europe during the above period. "If the various Governments and scientific bodies would perform for the

Galton—*continued.*

whole world for two or three years what, at a great cost and labour, Mr. Galton has done for a part of Europe for one month, Meteorology would soon cease to be made a joke of."—Spectator.

HEREDITARY GENIUS : An Inquiry into its Laws and Consequences. Demy 8vo. 12*s.*

"I propose," the author says, *"to show in this book that a man's natural abilities are derived by inheritance, under exactly the same limitations as are the form and physical features of the whole organic world. I shall show that social agencies of an ordinary character, whose influences are little suspected, are at this moment working towards the degradation of human nature, and that others are working towards its improvement. The general plan of my argument is to show that high reputation is a pretty accurate test of high ability ; next, to discuss the relationships of a large body of fairly eminent men, and to obtain from these a general survey of the laws of heredity in respect of genius. Then will follow a short chapter, by way of comparison, on the hereditary transmission of physical gifts, as deduced from the relationships of certain classes of oarsmen and wrestlers. Lastly, I shall collate my results and draw conclusions."* The Times *calls it "a most able and most interesting book;" and Mr. Darwin, in his "Descent of Man" (vol. i. p. 111), says, " We know, through the admirable labours of Mr. Galton, that Genius tends to be inherited."*

Geikie (A.)—SCENERY OF SCOTLAND, Viewed in Connection with its Physical Geography. With Illustrations and a new Geological Map. By ARCHIBALD GEIKIE, Professor of Geology in the University of Edinburgh. Crown 8vo. 10*s. 6d.*

" We can confidently recommend Mr. Geikie's work to those who wish to look below the surface and read the physical history of the Scenery of Scotland by the light of modern science."—Saturday Review. *" Amusing, picturesque, and instructive."*—Times.

Guillemin.—THE FORCES OF NATURE : A Popular Introduction to the Study of Physical Phenomena. By AMÉDÉE GUILLEMIN. Translated from the French by MRS. NORMAN LOCKYER ; and Edited, with Additions and Notes, by J. NORMAN

LOCKYER, F.R.S.   Illustrated by 11 Coloured Plates and 455
Woodcuts.   Second Edition.   Imperial 8vo, cloth, extra gilt.
31s. 6d.

M. Guillemin is already well known in this country as a most success-
ful populariser of the results of accurate scientific research, his
works, while eloquent, intelligible, and interesting to the general
reader, being thoroughly trustworthy and up to date.   The present
work consists of Seven Books, each divided into a number of
Chapters, the Books treating respectively of Gravity, Sound,
Light, Heat, Magnetism, Electricity, and Atmospheric Meteors.
The programme of the work has not been confined to a simple
explanation of the facts: but an attempt has been made to grasp
their relative bearings, or, in other words, their laws, and that
too without taking for granted that the reader is acquainted
with mathematics.   " The author's aim has been to smooth the way
for those who desire to extend their studies, and likewise to present
to general readers a sufficiently exact and just idea of this branch of
science."—Daily News.   *" Translator and Editor have done*
justice to their trust.   The text has all the force and flow of original
writing, combining faithfulness to the author's meaning with
purity and independence in regard to idiom ; while the historical
precision and accuracy pervading the work throughout, speak of the
watchful editorial supervision which has been given to every scientific
detail.   Nothing can well exceed the clearness and delicacy of the
illustrative woodcuts, borrowed from the French edition, or the
purity and chromatic truth of the coloured plates.   Altogether, the
work may be said to have no parallel, either in point of fulness or
attraction, as a popular manual of physical science.   . . . .
What we feel, however, bound to say, and what we say with
pleasure, is, that among works of its class no publication can stand
comparison either in literary completeness or in artistic grace with
it."—Saturday Review.

Henslow.—THE THEORY OF EVOLUTION OF LIVING
THINGS, and the Principles of Evolution applied to Religion
considered as Illustrative of the Wisdom and Beneficence of the
Almighty.   By the REV. GEORGE HENSLOW, M.A., F.R.S.
Crown 8vo.   6s.

Hooker (Dr.)—THE STUDENT'S FLORA OF THE BRITISH ISLANDS. By J. D. HOOKER, C.B., F.R.S., M.D., D.C.L., Director of the Royal Gardens, Kew. Globe 8vo. 10s. 6d.

*The object of this work is to supply students and field-botanists with a fuller account of the Plants of the British Islands than the manuals hitherto in use aim at giving. The Ordinal, Generic, and Specific characters have been re-written, and are to a great extent original, and drawn from living or dried specimens, or both. " Cannot fail to perfectly fulfil the purpose for which it is intended."—*Land and Water. *" Containing the fullest and most accurate manual of the kind that has yet appeared."—*Pall Mall Gazette.

Huxley (Professor).—LAY SERMONS, ADDRESSES, AND REVIEWS. By T. H. HUXLEY, LL.D., F.R.S. New and Cheaper Edition. Crown 8vo. 7s. 6d.

Fourteen Discourses on the following subjects:—(1) *On the Advisableness of Improving Natural Knowledge :—*(2) *Emancipation—Black and White :—*(3) *A Liberal Education, and where to find it :—*(4) *ScientificEducation :—*(5) *On the Educational Value of the Natural History Sciences:—*(6) *On the Study of Zoology:—*(7) *On the Physical Basis of Life:—*(8) *The Scientific Aspects of Positivism:—*(9) *On a Piece of Chalk:—*(10) *Geological Contemporaneity and Persistent Types of Life:—*(11) *Geological Reform:—*(12) *The Origin of Species :—*(13) *Criticisms on the " Origin of Species:"—*(14) *On Descartes' " Discourse touching the Method of using One's Reason rightly and of seeking Scientific Truth." The momentous influence exercised by Mr. Huxley's writings on physical, mental, and social science is universally acknowledged ; his works must be studied by all who would comprehend the various drifts of modern thought.*

ESSAYS SELECTED FROM LAY SERMONS, ADDRESSES, AND REVIEWS. Crown 8vo. 1s.

This volume includes Numbers 1, 3, 4, 7, 8, *and* 14, *of the above.*

CRITIQUES AND ADDRESSES. 8vo. 10s. 6d.

These " Critiques and Addresses," like the " Lay Sermons," etc., published three years ago, deal chiefly with educational, scientific, and

Huxley (Professor)—*continued.*

philosophical subjects ; and, in fact, as the author says, "indicate the high-water mark of the various tides of occupation by which I have been carried along since the beginning of the year 1870.*" The following is the list of Contents :—*1. *Administrative Nihilism.* 2. *The School Boards: what they can do, and what they may do.* 3. *On Medical Education.* 4. *Yeast.* 5. *On the Formation of Coal.* 6. *On Coral and Coral Reefs.* 7. *On the Methods and Results of Ethnology.* 8. *On some Fixed Points in British Ethnology.* 9. *Palæontology and the. Doctrine of Evolution.* 10. *Biogenesis and Abiogenesis.* 11. *Mr. Darwin's Critics.* 12. *The Genealogy of Animals.* 13. *Bishop Berkely on the Metaphysics of Sensation.*

LESSONS IN ELEMENTARY PHYSIOLOGY. With numerous Illustrations. New Edition. 18mo. cloth. 4*s.* 6*d.*

*This book describes and explains, in a series of graduated lessons, the principles of Human Physiology, or the Structure and Functions of the Human Body. The first lesson supplies a general view of the subject. This is followed by sections on the Vascular or Venous System, and the Circulation ; the Blood and the Lymph ; Respiration : Sources of Loss and of Gain to the Blood ; the Function of Alimentation ; Motion and Locomotion ; Sensations and Sensory Organs ; the Organ of Sight ; the Coalescence of Sensations with one another and with other States of Consciousness ; the Nervous System and Innervation ; Histology, or the Minute Structure of the Tissues. A Table of Anatomical and Physiological Constants is appended. The lessons are fully illustrated by numerous engravings. The new edition has been thoroughly revised, and a considerable number of new illustrations added: several of these have been taken from the Rabbit, the Sheep, the Dog, and the Frog, in order to aid those who attempt to make their knowledge real, by acquiring some practical acquaintance with the facts of Anatomy and Physiology. " Pure gold throughout."—*Guardian. " *Unquestionably the clearest and most complete elementary treatise on this subject that we possess in any language."—*Westminster Review.

Jellet (John H., B.D.)— A TREATISE ON THE THEORY OF FRICTION. By John H. Jellet, B.D.,

Senior Fellow of Trinity College, Dublin ; President of the Royal
Irish Academy. 8vo. 8s. 6d.

*The Theory of Friction, considered as a part of Rational Mechanics,
has not, the author thinks, received the attention which it deserves.
On this account many students have been probably led to regard
the discussion of this force as scarcely belonging to Rational
Mechanics at all ; whereas the theory of friction is as truly a part
of that subject as the theory of gravitation. The force with which
this theory is concerned is subject to laws as definite, and as fully
susceptible of mathematical expression, as the force of gravity.
This book is taken up with a special investigation of the laws of
friction ; and some of the principles contained in it are believed to
be here enunciated for the first time. The work consists of eight
Chapters as follows :—I. Definitions and Principles. II. Equilibrium with Frictions. III. Extreme Positions of Equilibrium.
IV. Movement of a Particle or System of Particles. V. Motion
of a Solid Body. VI. Necessary and Possible Equilibrium. VII.
Determination of the Actual Value of the Acting Force of Friction.
VIII. Miscellaneous Problems —1. Problem of the Top. 2. Friction
Wheels and Locomotives. 3. Questions for Exercise. " The book
supplies a want which has hitherto existed in the science of pure
mechanics."—*Engineer.

Jones.—THE OWENS COLLEGE JUNIOR COURSE OF
PRACTICAL CHEMISTRY. By Francis Jones, Chemical
Master in the Grammar School, Manchester. With Preface by
Professor Roscoe. 18mo. with Illustrations. 2s. 6d.

Kingsley.—GLAUCUS : OR, THE WONDERS OF THE
SHORE. By Charles Kingsley, Canon of Westminster.
New Edition, revised and corrected, with numerous Coloured
Plates. Crown 8vo. 5s.

Kirchhoff (G.)—RESEARCHES ON THE SOLAR SPEC-
TRUM, and the Spectra of the Chemical Elements. By G.
Kirchhoff, Professor of Physics in the University of Heidelberg.
Second Part. Translated, with the Author's Sanction, from the
Transactions of the Berlin Academy for 1862, by Henry R.
Roscoe, B.A., Ph.D., F.R.S., Professor of Chemistry in Owens
College, Manchester. Part II. 4to. 5s.

"It is to Kirchhoff we are indebted for by far the best and most accurate observations of these phenomena."—Edin. Review. *"This memoir seems almost indispensable to every Spectrum observer."*—Philosophical Magazine.

Lockyer (J. N.)—Works by J. NORMAN LOCKYER, F.R.S.—
ELEMENTARY LESSONS IN ASTRONOMY. With numerous Illustrations.   New Edition.   18mo.   5s. 6d.

The author has here aimed to give a connected view of the whole subject, and to supply facts, and ideas founded on the facts, to serve as a basis for subsequent study and discussion.   The chapters treat of the Stars and Nebulæ; the Sun; the Solar System; Apparent Movements of the Heavenly Bodies; the Measurement of Time; Light; the Telescope and Spectroscope; Apparent Places of the Heavenly Bodies; the Real Distances and Dimensions; Universal Gravitation. The most recent Astronomical Discoveries are incorporated.   Mr. Lockyer's work supplements that of the Astronomer Royal.   "The book is full, clear, sound, and worthy of attention, not only as a popular exposition, but as a scientific 'Index.'"— Athenæum. *"The most fascinating of elementary books on the Sciences."—* Nonconformist.

THE SPECTROSCOPE AND ITS APPLICATIONS. By J. NORMAN LOCKYER, F.R.S.   With Coloured Plate and numerous Illustrations.   Second Edition.   Crown 8vo.   3s. 6d.

This forms Volume One of "Nature Series," a series of popular Scientific Works now in course of publication, consisting of popular and instructive works, on particular scientific subjects—Scientific Discovery, Applications, History, Biography—by some of the most eminent scientific men of the day.   They will be so written as to be interesting and intelligible even to non-scientific readers.   Mr. Lockyer's work in Spectrum Analysis is widely known.   In the present short treatise will be found an exposition of the principles on which Spectrum Analysis rests, a description of the various kinds of Spectroscopes, and an account of what has already been done with the instrument, as well as of what may yet be done both in science and in the industrial art.

CONTRIBUTIONS TO SOLAR PHYSICS. With numerous Illustrations.   Royal 8vo., uniform with Roscoe's "Spectrum Analysis," Thompson's "Depths of the Sea," and Ball's "Mechanics."   31s. 6d.

Macmillan (Rev. Hugh).—For other Works by the same Author, see THEOLOGICAL CATALOGUE.

HOLIDAYS ON HIGH LANDS ; or, Rambles and Incidents in search of Alpine Plants. Crown 8vo. cloth. 6s.

> *The aim of this book is to impart a general idea of the origin, character, and distribution of those rare and beautiful Alpine plants which occur on the British hills, and which are found almost everywhere on the lofty mountain chains of Europe, Asia, Africa, and America. In the first three chapters the peculiar vegetation of the Highland mountains is fully described; while in the remaining chapters this vegetation is traced to its northern cradle in the mountains of Norway, and to its southern European termination in the Alps of Switzerland. The information the author has to give is conveyed in a setting of personal adventure. "One of the most charming books of its kind ever written."*—Literary Churchman. *"Mr. M.'s glowing pictures of Scandinavian scenery."*—Saturday Review.

FOOT-NOTES FROM THE PAGE OF NATURE. With numerous Illustrations. Fcap. 8vo. 5s.

> *"Those who have derived pleasure and profit from the study of flowers and ferns—subjects, it is pleasing to find, now everywhere popular —by descending lower into the arcana of the vegetable kingdom, will find a still more interesting and delightful field of research in the objects brought under review in the following pages."*—Preface. *"The naturalist and the botanist will delight in this volume, and those who understand little of the scientific parts of the work will linger over the mysterious page of nature here unfolded to their view."*—John Bull.

Mansfield (C. B.)—A THEORY OF SALTS. A Treatise on the Constitution of Bipolar (two-membered) Chemical Compounds. By the late CHARLES BLACHFORD MANSFIELD. Crown 8vo. 14s.

> *"Mansfield," says the editor, "wrote this book to defend the principle that the fact of voltaic decomposition afforded the true indication, if properly interpreted, of the nature of the saline structure, and of the atomicity of the elements that built it up. No chemist*

will peruse this book without feeling that he is in the presence of an original thinker, whose pages are continually suggestive, even though their general argument may not be entirely concurrent in direction with that of modern chemical thought."

Miller.—THE ROMANCE OF ASTRONOMY. By R. KALLEY MILLER, M.A., Fellow and Assistant Tutor of St. Peter's College, Cambridge. Crown 8vo. 3*s*. 6*d*.

" On the whole, the information contained is of a trustworthy character, and we cordially recommend it to the perusal of those who, without being in possession of the knowledge requisite for discussing astronomical theories, or the means by which they are arrived at, are yet desirous of becoming acquainted with some of the most interesting of astronomical conclusions."—Athenæum.

Mivart (St. George).—Works by ST. GEORGE MIVART, F.R.S. etc., Lecturer in Comparative Anatomy at St. Mary's Hospital:—

ON THE GENESIS OF SPECIES. Crown 8vo. Second Edition, to which notes have been added in reference and reply to Darwin's "Descent of Man." With numerous Illustrations. pp. xv. 296. 9*s*.

The aim of the author is to support the doctrine that the various species have been evolved by ordinary natural laws (for the most part unknown) controlled by the subordinate action of "natural selection," and at the same time to remind some that there is and can be absolutely nothing in physical science which forbids them to regard those natural laws as acting with the Divine concurrence, and in obedience to a creative fiat originally imposed on the primeval cosmos, " in the beginning," by its Creator, its Upholder, and its Lord. Nearly fifty woodcuts illustrate the letter-press, and a complete index makes all references extremely easy. Canon Kingsley, in his address to the "Devonshire Association," says, "Let me recommend earnestly to you, as a specimen of what can be said on the other side, the ' Genesis of Species,' by Mr. St. George Mivart, F.R.S., a book which I am happy to say has been received elsewhere as it has deserved, and, I trust, will be received so among you." " In no work in the English language has this great controversy been treated at once with the same broad and vigorous grasp of facts, and the same liberal and candid temper."—Saturday Review.

Mivart (St. George)—*continued.*

LESSONS IN ELEMENTARY ANATOMY. With upwards of 400 Illustrations. 18mo. 6s. 6d.

This volume is intended to form one of the series of Elementary Class-Books of Science, and the Lessons are intended in the first place for teachers and for earnest students of both sexes, not already acquainted with human anatomy. The author has endeavoured, secondly, by certain additions and by the mode of treatment, to fit them for students in medicine, and generally for those acquainted with human anatomy, but desirous of learning its more significant relations to the structure of other animals: the author therefore hopes his volume may serve as a hand-book of Human Morphology. The book is amply illustrated with carefully drawn woodcuts.

Murphy.—Works by JOSEPH JOHN MURPHY :—

HABIT AND INTELLIGENCE, in Connection with the Laws of Matter and Force : A Series of Scientific Essays. Two Vols. 8vo. 16s.

The author's chief purpose in this work has been to state and to discuss what he regards as the special and characteristic principles of life. The most important part of the work treats of those vital principles which belong to the inner domain of life itself, as distinguished from the principles which belong to the border-land where life comes into contact with inorganic matter and force. In the inner domain of ife we find two principles, which are the author believes, coextensive with life and peculiar to it: these are Habit and Intelligence. He has made as full a statement as possible of the laws under which habits form, disappear, alter under altered circumstances, and vary spontaneously. He discusses that most important of all questions, whether intelligence is an ultimate fact, incapable of being resolved into any other, or only a resultant from the laws of habit. The latter part of the first volume is occupied with the discussion of the question of the Origin of Species. The first part of the second volume is occupied with an inquiry into the process of mental growth and development, and the nature of mental intelligence. In the chapter that follows, the author discusses the science of history, and the three concluding chapters contain some ideas on the classification, the history, and the logic, of the sciences. The author's aim has been to make the subjects treated of intelligible to any ordinary intelligent man. "We are pleased

C

Murphy—*continued.*

to listen," says *the* Saturday Review, *"to a writer who has so firm
a foothold upon the ground within the scope of his immediate
survey, and who can enunciate with so much clearness and force
propositions which come within his grasp."*

THE SCIENTIFIC BASES OF FAITH. 8vo. 14s.

Nature.—A WEEKLY ILLUSTRATED JOURNAL OF
SCIENCE. Published every Thursday. Price 4d. Monthly
Parts, 1s. 4d. and 1s. 8d. ; Half-yearly Volumes, 10s. 6d. Cases for
binding Vols. 1s. 6d.

*" Backed by many of the best names among English philosophers, and
by a few equally valuable supporters in America and on the Continent of Europe."*—Saturday Review. *" This able and well-edited
Journal, which posts up the science of the day promptly, and
promises to be of signal service to students and savants."*—British
Quarterly Review.

Oliver.—Works by DANIEL OLIVER, F.R.S., F.L.S., Professor of
Botany in University College, London, and Keeper of the Herba-
rium and Library of the Royal Gardens, Kew :—

LESSONS IN ELEMENTARY BOTANY. With nearly Two
Hundred Illustrations. New Edition. 18mo cloth. 4s. 6d.

*This book is designed to teach the elements of Botany on Professor
Henslow's plan of selected Types and by the use of Schedules. The
earlier chapters, embracing the elements of Structural and Physiological Botany, introduce us to the methodical study of the Ordinal
Types. The concluding chapters are entitled, " How to Dry
Plants" and " How to Describe Plants." A valuable Glossary is
appended to the volume. In the preparation of this work free use
has been made of the manuscript materials of the late Professor
Henslow.*

FIRST BOOK OF INDIAN BOTANY. With numerous
Illustrations. Extra fcap. 8vo. 6s. 6d.

*This manual is, in substance, the author's " Lessons in Elementary
Botany," adapted for use in India. In preparing it he has had in
view the want, often felt, of some handy résumé of Indian Botany,*

*which might be serviceable not only to residents of India, but also
to anyone about to proceed thither, desirous of getting some preliminary idea of the botany of the country. It contains a well-
digested summary of all essential knowledge pertaining to Indian
Botany, wrought out in accordance with the best principles of
scientific arrangement."*—Allen's Indian Mail.

Penrose (F. C.)—ON A METHOD OF PREDICTING BY
GRAPHICAL CONSTRUCTION, OCCULTATIONS OF
STARS BY THE MOON, AND SOLAR ECLIPSES FOR
ANY GIVEN PLACE. Together with more rigorous methods
for the Accurate Calculation of Longitude. By F. C. PENROSE,
F.R.A.S. With Charts, Tables, etc. 4to. 12s.

*The author believes that if, by a graphic method, the prediction of
occultations can be rendered more inviting, as well as more expedi-
tious, than by the method of calculation, it may prove acceptable to
the nautical profession as well as to scientific travellers or amateurs.
The author has endeavoured to make the whole process as intelligible as possible, so that the beginner, instead of merely having to
follow directions imperfectly understood, may readily comprehend
the meaning of each step, and be able to illustrate the practice by the
theory. Besides all necessary charts and tables, the work contains
a large number of skeleton forms for working out cases in
practice.*

Roscoe.—Works by HENRY E. ROSCOE, F.R.S., Professor o
Chemistry in Owens College, Manchester :—

LESSONS IN ELEMENTARY CHEMISTRY, INORGANIC
AND ORGANIC. With numerous Illustrations and Chromo-
litho of the Solar Spectrum, and of the Alkalies and Alkaline
Earths. New Edition. 18mo. cloth. 4s. 6d.

*It has been the endeavour of the author to arrange the most important
facts and principles of Modern Chemistry in a plain but concise
and scientific form, suited to the present requirements of elementary
instruction. For the purpose of facilitating the attainment of
exactitude in the knowledge of the subject, a series of exercises and
questions upon the lessons have been added. The metric system of
weights and measures, and the centigrade thermometric scale, are*

Roscoe—*continued.*

*used throughout this work. The new edition, besides new wood-cuts, contains many additions and improvements, and includes the most important of the latest discoveries. " We unhesitatingly pronounce it the best of all our elementary treatises on Chemistry."—*Medical Times.

SPECTRUM ANALYSIS. Six Lectures, with Appendices, Engravings, Maps, and Chromolithographs. Royal 8vo. 21*s.*

*A Third Edition of these popular Lectures, containing all the most recent discoveries and several additional illustrations. " In six lectures he has given the history of the discovery and set forth the facts relating to the analysis of light in such a way that any reader of ordinary intelligence and information will be able to understand what 'Spectrum Analysis' is, and what are its claims to rank among the most signal triumphs of science."—*Nonconformist. *" The lectures themselves furnish a most admirable elementary treatise on the subject, whilst by the insertion in appendices to each lecture of extracts from the most important published memoirs, the author has rendered it equally valuable as a text-book for advanced students."—*Westminster Review.

Stewart (B.)—LESSONS IN ELEMENTARY PHYSICS. By BALFOUR STEWART, F.R.S., Professor of Natural Philosophy in Owens College, Manchester. With numerous Illustrations and Chromolithos of the Spectra of the Sun, Stars, and Nebulæ. New Edition. 18mo. 4*s.* 6*d.*

A description, in an elementary manner, of the most important of those laws which regulate the phenomena of nature. The active agents, heat, light, electricity, etc., are regarded as varieties of energy, and the work is so arranged that their relation to one another, looked at in this light, and the paramount importance of the laws of energy, are clearly brought out. The volume contains all the necessary illustrations. The Educational Times *calls this "the beau-ideal of a scientific text-book, clear, accurate, and thorough."*

Taylor.—SOUND AND MUSIC : A Non-Mathematical Treatise cn the Physical Constitution of Musical Sounds and Harmony,

including the Chief Acoustical Discoveries of Professor Helmholtz. By SEDLEY TAYLOR, M.A., late Fellow of Trinity Col-
ledge, Cambridge. Large crown 8vo. 8s. 6d.

*This treatise aims at placing before persons unacquainted with
Mathematics an intelligible and succinct account of that part of
the Theory of Sound which constitutes the physical basis of the
Art of Music. No preliminary knowledge, save of Arithmetic
and of the musical notation in common use, is assumed to be possessed by the reader. The importance of combining theoretical and
experimental modes of treatment has been kept steadily in view
throughout. Though the author has incorporated the chief acoustical discoveries of Professor Helmholtz, the present volume is not a
mere epitome of his work, but the result of independent study.*

Thomson.—THE DEPTHS OF THE SEA : An Account of the
General Results of the Dredging Cruises of H.M.SS. "Porcupine"
and "Lightning" during the Summers of 1868-69 and 70, under
the scientific direction of Dr. Carpenter, F.R.S., J. Gwyn Jeffreys,
F.R.S., and Dr. Wyville Thomson, F.R.S. By Dr. WYVILLE
THOMSON, Director of the Scientific Staff of the "Challenger"
Expedition. With nearly 100 Illustrations and 8 coloured Maps
and Plans. Second Edition. Royal 8vo. cloth, gilt. 31s. 6d.

*It was the important and interesting results recorded in this volume
that induced the Government to send out the great Expedition now
launched under the scientific guidance of Dr. Wyville Thomson.
The Athenæum says, "Professor Thomson's book is full of interesting matter, and is written by a master of the art of popular
exposition. It is excellently illustrated, both coloured maps and
woodcuts possessing high merit. Those who have already become
interested in dredging operations will of course make a point of
reading this work ; those who wish to be pleasantly introduced to the
subject, and rightly to appreciate the news which arrives from time
to time from the "Challenger," should not fail to seek instruction
from Professor Thomson."*

Thornton.—OLD-FASHIONED ETHICS, AND COMMON-
SENSE METAPHYSICS, with some of their Applications. By
WILLIAM THOMAS THORNTON, Author of "A Treatise on Labour."
8vo. 10s. 6d.

The present volume deals with problems which are agitating the minds of all thoughtful men. The following are the Contents :— I. Ante-Utilitarianism. II. History's Scientific Pretensions. III. David Hume as a Metaphysician. IV. Huxleyism. V. Recent Phases of Scientific Atheism. VI. Limits of Demonstrable Theism.

Thudichum and Dupré.—A TREATISE ON THE ORIGIN, NATURE, AND VARIETIES OF WINE. Being a Complete Manual of Viticulture and Œnology. By J. L. W. THUDICHUM, M.D., and AUGUST DUPRÉ, Ph.D., Lecturer on Chemistry at Westminster Hospital. Medium 8vo. cloth gilt. 25*s.*

In this elaborate work the subject of the manufacture of wine is treated scientifically in minute detail, from every point of view. A chapter is devoted to the Origin and Physiology of Vines, two to the Principles of Viticulture; while other chapters treat of Vintage and Vinification, the Chemistry of Alcohol, the Acids, Ether, Sugars, and other matters occurring in wine. This introductory matter occupies the first nine chapters, the remaining seventeen chapters being occupied with a detailed account of the Viticulture and the Wines of the various countries of Europe, of the Atlantic Islands, of Asia, of Africa, of America, and of Australia. Besides a number of Analytical and Statistical Tables, the work is enriched with eighty-five illustrative woodcuts. "A treatise almost unique for its usefulness either to the wine-grower, the vendor, or the consumer of wine. The analyses of wine are the most complete we have yet seen, exhibiting at a glance the constituent principles of nearly all the wines known in this country."—Wine Trade Review.

Wallace (A. R.)—CONTRIBUTIONS TO THE THEORY OF NATURAL SELECTION. A Series of Essays. By ALFRED RUSSEL WALLACE, Author of "The Malay Archipelago," etc. Second Edition, with Corrections and Additions. Crown 8vo. 8*s.* 6*d.* (For other Works by the same Author, see CATALOGUE OF HISTORY AND TRAVELS.)

Mr. Wallace has good claims to be considered as an independent originator of the theory of natural selection. Dr. Hooker, in his address to the British Association, spoke thus of the author: "Of Mr. Wallace and his many contributions to philosophical biology it is not easy to speak without enthusiasm : for, putting

*aside their great merits, he, throughout his writings, with a
modesty as rare as I believe it to be unconscious, forgets his own
unquestioned claim to the honour of having originated independently of Mr. Darwin, the theories which he so ably defends."*
The Saturday Review *says : "He has combined an abundance of
fresh and original facts with a liveliness and sagacity of reasoning
which are not often displayed so effectively on so small a scale."
The Essays in this volume are :—I. "On the Law which has regulated the introduction of New Species." II. "On the Tendencies
of Varieties to depart indefinitely from the Original Type." III.
"Mimicry, and other Protective Resemblances among Animals."
IV. "The Malayan Papilionidæ, as illustrative of the Theory
of Natural Selection." V. "On Instinct in Man and Animals."
VI. "The Philosophy of Birds' Nests." VII. "A Theory of
Birds' Nests." VIII. "Creation by Law." IX. "The Develop-
ment of Human Races under the Law of Natural Selection."
X. "The Limits of Natural Selection as applied to Man."*

Warington.—THE WEEK OF CREATION; OR, THE
COSMOGONY OF GENESIS CONSIDERED IN ITS
RELATION TO MODERN SCIENCE. By GEORGE WAR-
INGTON, Author of "The Historic Character of the Pentateuch
Vindicated." Crown 8vo. 4s. 6d.

*The greater part of this work is taken up with the teaching of the
Cosmogony. Its purpose is also investigated, and a chapter is
devoted to the consideration of the passage in which the difficulties
occur. "A very able vindication of the Mosaic Cosmogony, by a
writer who unites the advantages of a critical knowledge of the
Hebrew text and of distinguished scientific attainments."—*
Spectator.

Wilson.—Works by the late GEORGE WILSON, M.D., F.R.S.E.,
Regius Professor of Technology in the University of Edinburgh :—

RELIGIO CHEMICI. With a Vignette beautifully engraved after
a design by Sir NOEL PATON. Crown 8vo. 8s. 6d.

*"George Wilson," says the Preface to this volume, "had it in his heart
for many years to write a book corresponding to the* Religio Medici
of Sir Thomas Browne, with the title Religio Chemici. *Several
of the Essays in this volume were intended to form chapters of it.*

Wilson—*continued.*

These fragments being in most cases like finished gems waiting to be set, some of them are now given in a collected form to his friends and the public. In living remembrance of his purpose, the name chosen by himself has been adopted, although the original design can be but very faintly represented." The Contents of the volume are:—"Chemistry and Natural Theology." "The Chemistry of the Stars; an Argument touching the Stars and their Inhabitants." "Chemical Final Causes; as illustrated by the presence of Phosphorus, Nitrogen, and Iron in the Higher Sentient Organisms." "Robert Boyle." "Wollaston." "Life and Discoveries of Dalton." "Thoughts on the Resurrection; an Address to Medical Students." "A more fascinating volume," the Spectator *says, "has seldom fallen into our hands." The* Freeman *says: "These papers are all valuable and deeply interesting. The production of a profound thinker, a suggestive and eloquent writer, and a man whose piety and genius went hand in hand."*

THE PROGRESS OF THE TELEGRAPH. Fcap. 8vo. 1*s.*

"While a complete view of the progress of the greatest of human inventions is obtained, all its suggestions are brought out with a rare thoughtfulness, a genial humour, and an exceeding beauty of utterance."—Nonconformist.

Wilson (Daniel.)—CALIBAN: THE MISSING LINK. By Daniel Wilson, LL.D., Professor of History and English Literature in University College, Toronto. 8vo. 10*s.* 6*d.*

In the present state of the controversy as to the Origin of Man, this work of a competent scholar and critic, in which the Monster Caliban is studied from various points of view, will be of considerable interest. Besides "Caliban," the work treats of various other matters of Shakespearian interest, as "The Supernatural," "Ghosts and Witches," "Fairy Folk-Lore," "The Commentators," "The Folios." The two last chapters contain notes on "The Tempest," and "A Midsummer Night's Dream."

Winslow.—FORCE AND NATURE: ATTRACTION AND REPULSION. The Radical Principles of Energy graphically

discussed in their Relations to Physical and Morphological Development. By C. F. WINSLOW, M.D. 8vo. 14s.

The author having for long investigated Nature in many directions, has ever felt unsatisfied with the physical foundations upon which some branches of science have been so long compelled to rest. The question, he believes, must have occurred to many astronomers and physicists whether some subtle principle antagonistic to attraction does not also exist as an all-pervading element in nature, and so operate as in some way to disturb the action of what is generally considered by the scientific world a unique force. The aim of the present work is to set forth this subject in its broadest aspects, and in such a manner as to invite thereto the attention of the learned. The subjects of the eleven chapters are:—I. "Space." II. "Matter." III. "Inertia, Force, and Mind." IV. "Molecules." V. "Molecular Force." VI. "Union and Inseparability of Matter and Force." VII. and VIII. "Nature and Action of Force—Attraction—Repulsion." IX. "Cosmical Repulsion." X. "Mechanical Force." XI. "Central Forces and Celestial Physics." "Deserves thoughtful and conscientious study."—Saturday Review.

Wurtz.—A HISTORY OF CHEMICAL THEORY, from the Age of Lavoisier down to the present time. By AD. WURTZ. Translated by HENRY WATTS, F.R.S. Crown 8vo. 6s.

" The discourse, as a résumé of chemical theory and research, unites singular luminousness and grasp. A few judicious notes are added by the translator."—Pall Mall Gazette. *" The treatment of the subject is admirable, and the translator has evidently done his duty most efficiently."*—Westminster Review.

Young.—SIMPLE PRACTICAL METHODS OF CALCULATING STRAINS ON GIRDERS, ARCHES, AND TRUSSES ; with a Supplementary Essay on Economy in Suspension Bridges. By E. W. YOUNG, Member of the Institution of Civil Engineers. 8vo. 7s. 6d.

WORKS IN PHYSIOLOGY, ANATOMY, AND MEDICAL WORKS GENERALLY.

Allbutt (T. C.)—ON THE USE OF THE OPHTHALMO-SCOPE in Diseases of the Nervous System and of the Kidneys ; also in certain other General Disorders. By THOMAS CLIFFORD ALLBUTT, M.A., M.D. Cantab., Physician to the Leeds General Infirmary, Lecturer on Practical Medicine, etc. etc. 8vo. 15*s.*

The Ophthalmoscope has been found of the highest value in the investigation of nervous diseases. But it is not easy for physicians who have left the schools, and are engaged in practice, to take up a new instrument which requires much skill in using; it is therefore hoped that by such the present volume, containing the results of the author's extensive use of the instrument in diseases of the nervous system, will be found of service; and that to all students it may prove a useful hand-book. After four introductory chapters on the history and value of the Ophthalmoscope, and the manner of investigating the states of the optic nerve and retina, the author treats of the various diseases with which optic changes are associated, and describes the way in which such associations take place. Besides the cases referred to throughout the volume, the Appendix contains details of 123 cases illustrative of the subjects discussed in the text, and a series of tabulated cases to show the Ophthalmoscopic appearances of the eye in Insanity, Mania, Dementia, Melancholia and Monomania, Idiotcy, and General Paralysis. The volume is illustrated with two coloured plates of morbid appearances of the eye under the Ophthalmoscope.

THE EFFECTS OF OVERWORK AND STRAIN ON THE HEART AND GREAT BLOOD-VESSELS. (Reprinted from St. George's Hospital Reports.) 2*s.* 6*d.*

Anderson.—ON THE TREATMENT OF DISEASES OF THE SKIN : with an Analysis of Eleven Thousand Consecutive

Cases. By Dr. McCall Anderson, Professor of Practice of
Medicine in Anderson's University, Physician to the Dispensary for
Skin Diseases, etc., Glasgow. Crown 8vo. cloth. 5s.

*The first part of this work consists of a carefully tabulated and critical
analysis of 11,000 cases of skin disease, 1,000 of these having
occurred in the author's private practice, and the rest in his hospital practice. These cases are all classified under certain distinct
heads, according to the nature and cause of the disease, while a
number of the more interesting cases are alluded to in detail. The
second part of the work treats of the Therapeutics of Diseases of
the Skin, and will be found to contain many hints, the results of a
long and extensive experience, as to the most successful method of
treating their multitudinous forms.*

Anstie (F. E.)—NEURALGIA, AND DISEASES WHICH
RESEMBLE IT. By Francis E. Anstie, M D., M.R.C.P.,
Senior Assistant Physician to Westminster Hospital. 8vo. 10s. 6d.

*The present treatise is the result of many years' independent scientific
investigation into the nature and proper treatment of this most
painful disease. The author has had abundant means of studying
the subject both in his own person and in the hundreds of patients
that have resorted to him for treatment. The Introduction treats
briefly of Pain in General, and contains some ideas as to its nature
and in reference to sensation generally.*

Barwell.—THE CAUSES AND TREATMENT OF LATERAL
CURVATURE OF THE SPINE. Enlarged from Lectures
published in the *Lancet.* By Richard Barwell, F.R.C.S.,
Surgeon to and Lecturer on Anatomy at the Charing Cross Hospital.
Second Edition. Crown 8vo. 4s. 6d.

*Having failed to find in books a satisfactory theory of those conditions
which produce lateral curvature, Mr. Barwell resolved to investigate the subject for himself ab initio. The present work is the
result of long study of Spines, normal and abnormal. He
believes the views which he has been led to form account for those
essential characteristics which have hitherto been left unexplained ;
and the treatment which he advocates is certainly less irksome, and
will be found more efficacious than that which has hitherto been
pursued. Indeed, the mode in which the first edition has been*

received by the profession is a gratifying sign that Mr. Barwell's principles have made their value and their weight felt. Many pages and a number of woodcuts have been added to the Second Edition.

Corfield (Professor W. H.)—A DIGEST OF FACTS RELATING TO THE TREATMENT AND UTILIZATION OF SEWAGE. By W. H. CORFIELD, M.A., B.A., Professor of Hygiene and Public Health at University College, London. 8vo. 10s. 6d. Second Edition, corrected and enlarged.

The author in the Second Edition has revised and corrected the entire work, and made many important additions. The headings of the eleven chapters are as follow:—I. "Early Systems: Midden-Heaps and Cesspools." II. "Filth and Disease — Cause and Effect." III. "Improved Midden-Pits and Cesspools; Midden-Closets, Pail-Closets, etc." IV. "The Dry-Closet Systems." V. "Water-Closets." VI. "Sewerage." VII. "Sanitary Aspects of the Water-Carrying System." VIII. "Value of Sewage; Injury to Rivers." IX. "Town Sewage; Attempts at Utilization." X. "Filtration and Irrigation." XI. "Influence of Sewage Farming on the Public Health." An abridged account of the more recently published researches on the subject will be found in the Appendices, while the Summary contains a concise statement of the views which the author himself has been led to adopt: references have been inserted throughout to show from what sources the numerous quotations have been derived, and an Index has been added. "Mr. Corfield's work is entitled to rank as a standard authority, no less than a convenient handbook, in all matters relating to sewage."—Athenæum.

Elam (C.)—A PHYSICIAN'S PROBLEMS. By CHARLES ELAM, M.D., M.R.C.P. Crown 8vo. 9s.

CONTENTS :—"Natural Heritage." "On Degeneration in Man." "On Moral and Criminal Epidemics." "Body v. Mind." "Illusions and Hallucinations." "On Somnambulism." "Reverie and Abstraction." These Essays are intended as a contribution to the Natural History of those outlying regions of Thought and Action whose domain is the debatable ground of Brain, Nerve, and Mind. They are designed also to indicate the origin and mode of perpetuation of those varieties of organization, intelligence, and general tendencies towards vice or virtue, which seem to be so capriciously developed among mankind. They also point to causes for the infinitely varied forms of disorder of nerve and brain— organic and functional—far deeper and more recondite than those generally believed in. " The book is one which all statesmen, magistrates, clergymen, medical men, and parents should study and inwardly digest."—Examiner.

Fox.—Works by WILSON FOX, M.D. Lond., F.R.C.P., F.R.S., Holme Professor of Clinical Medicine, University College, London, Physician Extraordinary to her Majesty the Queen, etc. :—

DISEASES OF THE STOMACH: being a new and revised Edition of "THE DIAGNOSIS AND TREATMENT OF THE VARIETIES OF DYSPEPSIA." 8vo. 8s. 6d.

ON THE ARTIFICIAL PRODUCTION OF TUBERCLE IN THE LOWER ANIMALS. With Coloured Plates. 4to. 5s. 6d.

In this Lecture Dr. Fox describes in minute detail a large number of experiments made by him on guinea-pigs and rabbits for the purpose of inquiring into the origin of Tubercle by the agency of direct irritation or by septic matters. The work is illustrated by three plates, containing a number of coloured illustrations from nature.

ON THE TREATMENT OF HYPERPYREXIA, as Illustrated in Acute Articular Rheumatism by means of the External Application of Cold. 8vo. 2s. 6d.

The object of this work is to show that the class of cases included under the title, and which have hitherto been invariably fatal, may, by the use of the cold bath, be brought to a favourable termination. Details are given of the successful treatment by this method of two patients by the author, followed by a Commentary on the cases, in which the merits of this mode of treatment are discussed and compared with those of other methods. Appended are tables of the observations made on the temperature during the treatment; a table showing the effect of the immersion of the patients in the baths employed, in order to exhibit the rate at which the temperature was lowered in each case; a table of the chief details of twenty-two cases of this class recently published, and which are referred to in various parts of the Commentary. Two Charts are also introduced, giving a connected view of the progress of the two successful cases, and a series of sphygmographic tracings of the pulses of the two patients. "A clinical study of rare value. Should be read by everyone."—Medical Press and Circular.

Galton (D.)—AN ADDRESS ON THE GENERAL PRIN-CIPLES WHICH SHOULD BE OBSERVED IN THE CONSTRUCTION OF HOSPITALS. Delivered to the British Medical Association at Leeds, July 1869. By DOUGLAS GALTON, C.B., F.R.S. Crown 8vo. 3s. 6d.

In this Address the author endeavours to enunciate what are those principles which seem to him to form the starting-point from which all architects should proceed in the construction of hospitals. Besides Mr. Galton's paper the book contains the opinions expressed in the subsequent discussion by several eminent medical men, such as Dr. Kennedy, Sir James Y. Simpson, Dr. Hughes Bennet, and others. The work is illustrated by a number of plans, sections, and other cuts. "An admirable exposition of those conditions of structure which most conduce to cleanliness, economy, and convenience." —Times.

Harley (J.)—THE OLD VEGETABLE NEUROTICS, Hemlock, Opium, Belladonna, and Henbane; their Physiological Action and Therapeutical Use, alone and in combination. Being the Gulstonian Lectures of 1868 extended, and including a Complete Examination of the Active Constituents of Opium. By JOHN HARLEY, M.D. Lond., F.R.C.P., F.L.S., etc. 8vo. 12s.

The author's object throughout the investigations and experiments on which this volume is founded has been to ascertain, clearly and definitely, the action of the drugs employed on the healthy body in medicinal doses, from the smallest to the largest; to deduce simple practical conclusions from the facts observed; and then to apply the drug to the relief of the particular conditions to which its action appeared suited. Many experiments have been made by the author both on men and the lower animals; and the author's endeavour has been to present to the mind, as far as words may do, impressions of the actual condition of the individual subjected to the drug.

Hood (Wharton).—ON BONE-SETTING (so called), and its Relation to the Treatment of Joints Crippled by Injury, Rheumatism, Inflammation, etc. etc. By WHARTON P. HOOD, M.D., M.R.C.S. Crown 8vo. 4s. 6d.

> *The author for a period attended the London practice of the late Mr. Hutton, the famous and successful bone-setter, by whom he was initiated into the mystery of the art and practice. Thus he is amply qualified to write on the subject from the practical point of view, while his professional education enables him to consider it in its scientific and surgical bearings. In the present work he gives a brief account of the salient features of a bone-setter's method of procedure in the treatment of damaged joints, of the results of that treatment, and of the class of cases in which he has seen it prove successful. The author's aim is to give the rationale of the bone-setter's practice, to reduce it to something like a scientific method, to show when force should be resorted to and when it should not, and to initiate surgeons into the secret of Mr. Hutton's successful manipulation. Throughout the work a great number of authentic instances of successful treatment are given, with the details of the method of cure; and the Chapters on Manipulations and Affections of the Spine are illustrated by a number of appropriate cuts.*

Humphry.—Works by G. M. HUMPHRY, M.D., F.R.S., Professor of Anatomy in the University of Cambridge, and Honorary Fellow of Downing College :—

THE HUMAN SKELETON (including the Joints). With 260 Illustrations, drawn from nature. Medium 8vo. 28s.

> *In lecturing on the Skeleton it has been the author's practice, instead of giving a detailed account of the several parts, to request his students to get up the descriptive anatomy of certain bones, with the aid of some work on osteology. He afterwards tested their acquirements by examination, endeavouring to supply deficiencies and correct errors, adding also such information —physical, physiological, pathological, and practical— as he had gathered from his own observation and researches, and which was likely to be useful and excite an interest in the subject. This additional information forms, in great part, the material of this volume, which is intended to be supplementary to existing works on anatomy. Considerable space has been devoted to the description of the joints, because it is less fully given in other works, and because an accurate knowledge*

Humphry—*continued.*

of the structure and peculiar form of the joints is essential to a correct knowledge of their movements. The numerous illustrations were all drawn upon stone from nature; and in most instances from specimens prepared for the purpose by the author himself.

OBSERVATIONS IN MYOLOGY. 8vo. 6s.

This work includes the Myology of Cryptobranch, Lepidosiren, Dog-Fish, Ceratodus, and Pseudopus Pallasii, with the Nerves of Crypto-branch and Lepidosiren and the Disposition of Muscles in Vertebrate Animals. The volume contains a large number of illustrations.

Huxley's Physiology.—See p. 27, preceding.

Journal of Anatomy and Physiology.

Conducted by Professors HUMPHRY and NEWTON, and Mr. CLARK of Cambridge, Professor TURNER of Edinburgh, and Dr. WRIGHT of Dublin. Published twice a year. Old Series, Parts I. and II., price 7s. 6d. each. Vol. I. containing Parts I. and II., Royal 8vo., 16s. New Series, Parts I. to IX. 6s. each, or yearly Vols. 12s. 6d. each.

Leishman.—A SYSTEM OF MIDWIFERY, including the Diseases of Pregnancy and the Puerperal State. By WILLIAM LEISHMAN, M.D., Regius Professor of Midwifery in the University of Glasgow; Physician to the University Lying-in Hospital; Fellow and late Vice-President of the Obstetrical Society of London, etc. etc. 8vo. Illustrated. 30s.

The author's object in this work has been to furnish to students and practitioners a complete system of the Midwifery of the present day. There exists no text-book in English which can be compared with those of Cazeaux and Scanzoni; this want the author has endeavoured to supply by the publication of the present work, in writing which he has availed himself of all the most recent researches. The work is profusely illustrated.

Lankester.—COMPARATIVE LONGEVITY IN MAN AND THE LOWER ANIMALS. By E. RAY LANKESTER, B.A. Crown 8vo. 4s. 6d.

This Essay gained the prize offered by the University of Oxford for the best Paper on the subject of which it treats. This interesting subject is here treated in a thorough manner, both scientifically and statistically.

Maclaren.—TRAINING, IN THEORY AND PRACTICE. By ARCHIBALD MACLAREN, the Gymnasium, Oxford. 8vo. Handsomely bound in cloth, 7s. 6d.

The ordinary agents of health are Exercise, Diet, Sleep, Air, Bathing, and Clothing. In this work the author examines each of these agents in detail, and from two different points of view. First, as to the manner in which it is, or should be, administered under ordinary circumstances: and secondly, in what manner and to what extent this mode of administration is, or should be, altered for purposes of training; the object of "training," according to the author, being "to put the body, with extreme and exceptional care, under the influence of all the agents which promote its health and strength, in order to enable it to meet extreme and exceptional demands upon its energies." Appended are various diagrams and tables relating to boat-racing, and tables connected with diet and training. "The philosophy of human health has seldom received so apt an exposition."—Globe. "After all the nonsense that has been written about training, it is a comfort to get hold of a thoroughly sensible book at last."—John Bull.

Macpherson.—Works by JOHN MACPHERSON, M.D. :—

THE BATHS AND WELLS OF EUROPE; Their Action and Uses. With Notices of Climatic Resorts and Diet Cures. With a Map. New Edition, revised and enlarged. Extra fcap. 8vo. 6s. 6d.

This work is intended to supply information which will afford aid in the selection of such Spas as are suited for particular cases. It exhibits a sketch of the present condition of our knowledge on the subject of the operation of mineral waters, gathered from the author's personal observation, and from every other available source of information. It is divided into four books, and each book into several chapters:—Book I. Elements of Treatment, in which, among other matters, the external and internal uses of water are treated of. II. Bathing, treating of the various kinds of baths. III. Wells, treating of the various kinds of mineral waters.

Macpherson (J.)—*continued.*

*IV. Diet Cures, in which various vegetable, milk, and other "cures" are discussed. Appended is an Index of Diseases noticed, and one of places named. Prefixed is a sketch map of the principal baths and places of health-resort in Europe. "Dr. Macpherson has given the kind of information which every medical practitioner ought to possess."—*The Lancet. *"Whoever wants to know the real character of any health-resort must read Dr. Macpherson's book."—*Medical Times.

OUR BATHS AND WELLS : The Mineral Waters of the British Islands, with a List of Sea-bathing Places. Extra fcap. 8vo. pp. xv. 205. 3*s.* 6*d.*

*Dr. Macpherson has divided his work into five parts. He begins by a few introductory observations on bath life, its circumstances, uses, and pleasures ; he then explains in detail the composition of the various mineral waters, and points out the special curative pro-perties of each class. A chapter on "The History of British Wells" from the earliest period to the present time forms the natural transition to the second part of this volume, which treats of the different kinds of mineral waters in England, whether pure, thermal and earthy, saline, chalybeate, or sulphur. Wales, Scot-land, and Ireland supply the materials for distinct sections. An Index of mineral waters, one of sea-bathing places, and a third of wells of pure or nearly pure water, terminate the book. "This little volume forms a very available handbook for a large class of invalids."—*Nonconformist.

Maudsley.—Works by HENRY MAUDSLEY, M.D., Professor of Medical Jurisprudence in University College, London :—

BODY AND MIND : An Inquiry into their Connection and Mutual Influence, specially in reference to Mental Disorders ; being the Gulstonian Lectures for 1870. Delivered before the Royal College of Physicians. Crown 8vo. 5*s.* New Edition, with Psychological Essays added. Crown 8vo. 6*s.* 6*d.*

The volume consists of three Lectures and two long Appendices, the general plan of the whole being to bring Man, both in his physical and mental relations, as much as possible under the scope of scientific inquiry. The first Lecture is devoted to an exposition of the physical

Maudsley (H.)—*continued.*

conditions of mental function in health. In the second Lecture are sketched the features of some forms of degeneracy of mind, as exhibited in morbid varieties of the human kind, with the purpose of bringing prominently into notice the operation of physical causes from generation to generation, and the relationship of mental to other diseases of the nervous system. In the third Lecture are displayed the relations of morbid states of the body and disordered mental function. Appendix I. is a criticism of the Archbishop of York's address on " The Limits of Philosophical Inquiry." Appendix II. deals with the " Theory of Vitality," in which the author endeavours to set forth the reflections which facts seem to warrant.

THE PHYSIOLOGY AND PATHOLOGY OF MIND. Second Edition, Revised. 8vo. 16s.

This work is the result of an endeavour on the author's part to arrive at some definite conviction with regard to the physical conditions of mental function, and the relation of the phenomena of sound and unsound mind. The author's aim throughout has been twofold : I. To treat of mental phenomena from a physiological rather than from a metaphysical point of view. II. To bring the manifold instructive instances presented by the unsound mind to bear upon the interpretation of the obscure problems of mental science.

Morgan.—UNIVERSITY OARS : Being a Critical Enquiry into the After-health of the Men who rowed in the Oxford and Cambridge Boat-Race, from the year 1829 to 1869, based upon the personal experience of the Rowers themselves. By JOHN E. MORGAN, M.D., M.A. Oxon., F.R.C.P., late Captain of the John + (Coll. Univ.), Physician to the Manchester Royal Infirmary, author of "The Deterioration of Races," etc. Crown 8vo. 10s. 6d.

" *Dr. Morgan's book presents in a most admirable manner full and accurate statistics of the duration of life, and of the causes of death, of all the men who have rowed in Oxford and Cambridge boats from 1829 to 1869, and also gives letters addressed to the author by nearly every individual of the number.*"—Daily News.

Practitioner (The).—A Monthly Journal of Therapeutics and Public Health. Edited by FRANCIS E. ANSTIE, M.D. 8vo. Price 1s. 6d. Half-yearly vols., 8vo. cloth. 10s. 6d. each.

Radcliffe.—DYNAMICS OF NERVE AND MUSCLE. By CHARLES BLAND RADCLIFFE, M.D., F.R.C.P., Physician to the Westminster Hospital, and to the National Hospital for the Paralysed and Epileptic. Crown 8vo. 8s. 6d.

This work contains the result of the author's long investigations into the Dynamics of Nerve and Muscle, as connected with Animal Electricity. He endeavours to show from these researches that the state of action in nerve and muscle, instead of being a manifestation of vitality, must be brought under the domain of physical law in order to be intelligible, and that a different meaning, also based upon pure physics, must be attached to the state of rest.

Reynolds (J. R.)—A SYSTEM OF MEDICINE. Vol. I. Edited by J. RUSSELL REYNOLDS, M.D., F.R.C.P. London. Second Edition. 8vo. 25s.

"It is the best Cyclopædia of medicine of the time."—Medical Press.

Part I. General Diseases, or Affections of the Whole System. § I.—Those determined by agents operating from without, such as the exanthemata, malarial diseases, and their allies. § II.—Those determined by conditions existing within the body, such as Gout, Rheumatism, Rickets, etc. Part II. Local Diseases, or Affections of particular Systems. § I.—Diseases of the Skin.

A SYSTEM OF MEDICINE. Vol. II. Second Edition. 8vo. 25s.

Part II. Local Diseases (continued). § I.—Diseases of the Nervous System. A. General Nervous Diseases. B. Partial Diseases of the Nervous System. 1. Diseases of the Head. 2. Diseases of the Spinal Column. 3. Diseases of the Nerves. § II.—Diseases of the Digestive System. A. Diseases of the Stomach.

A SYSTEM OF MEDICINE. Vol. III. 8vo. 25s.

Part II. Local Diseases (continued). § II. Diseases of the Digestive System (continued). B. Diseases of the Mouth. C. Diseases of

the Fauces, Pharynx, and Œsophagus. D. Diseases of the In-
testines. E. Diseases of the Peritoneum. F. Diseases of the
Liver. G. Diseases of the Pancreas. § III.—Diseases of the
Respiratory System. A. Diseases of the Larynx. B. Diseases of
the Thoracic Organs.

Reynolds (O.)—SEWER GAS, AND HOW TO KEEP IT
OUT OF HOUSES. A Handbook on House Drainage. By
OSBORNE REYNOLDS, M.A., Professor of Engineering at Owens
College, Manchester, Fellow of Queen's College, Cambridge.
Second Edition. Crown 8vo. cloth. 1s. 6d.

*The author's chief object in writing on this subject is to suggest a plan
for preventing the evil which has been causing so much alarm since
the recent illness of the Prince of Wales—viz. the back-flow of gas
into our houses. Of the plan he here suggests, he has now had
four years' experience, and has, without exception, found it to answer
perfectly. He applied it to his own house, a house of the ordinary
type drained into a foul sewer, at a cost of about fifty shillings.
Before the introduction of the new plan it was never free from smells;
while since, there has been no annoyance of the kind, nor have the
drains required any attention whatever. The plan is very simple
and can be applied to any house without requiring the inside drains
to be disturbed. Besides fully explaining the plan and showing its
application by means of illustrations, the author throws out suggestions with regard to drainage generally which many will find
to be very valuable. "Professor Reynolds' admirable pamphlet will
a thousand times over repay its cost and the reader's most attentive
perusal."—*Mechanics' Magazine.

Rolleston.—THE HARVEIAN ORATION, 1873. By GEORGE
ROLLESTON, M.D., F.R.S., Linacre Professor of Anatomy and
Physiology, and Fellow of Merton College, in the University of
Oxford. Crown 8vo. 2s. 6d.

*In this Lecture the author expounds certain advances recently made
in our knowledge of the anatomy and physiology of the circulatory
organs, and gives the as yet unrecorded history of one of the many
attempts to rob Harvey of the glory of the great discovery.*

Seaton.—A HANDBOOK OF VACCINATION. By EDWARD C. SEATON, M.D., Medical Inspector to the Privy Council. Extra fcap, 8vo. 8s. 6d.

> *The author's object in putting forth this work is twofold: First, to provide a text-book on the science and practice of Vaccination for the use of younger practitioners and of medical students; secondly, to give what assistance he could to those engaged in the administration of the system of Public Vaccination established in England. For many years past, from the nature of his office, Dr. Seaton has had constant intercourse in reference to the subject of Vaccination, with medical men who are interested in it, and especially with that large part of the profession who are engaged as Public Vaccinators. All the varieties of pocks, both in men and the lower animals, are treated of in detail, and much valuable information given on all points connected with lymph, and minute instructions as to the niceties and cautions which so greatly influence success in Vaccination. The administrative sections of the work will be of interest and value, not only to medical practitioners, but to many others to whom a right understanding of the principles on which a system of Public Vaccination should be based is indispensable.*

Symonds (J. A., M.D.)—MISCELLANIES. By JOHN ADDINGTON SYMONDS, M.D. Selected and Edited, with an Introductory Memoir, by his Son. 8vo. 7s. 6d.

> *The late Dr. Symonds of Bristol was a man of a singularly versatile and elegant as well as powerful and scientific intellect. In order to make this selection from his many works generally interesting, the editor has confined himself to works of pure literature, and to such scientific studies as had a general philosophical or social interest. Among the general subjects are articles on "the Principles of Beauty," on "Knowledge," and a "Life of Dr. Prichard;" among the Scientific Studies are papers on "Sleep and Dreams," "Apparitions," "the Relations between Mind and Muscle," "Habit," etc.; there are several papers on "the Social and Political Aspects of Medicine;" and a few Poems and Translations selected from a great number of equal merit. "A collection of graceful essays on general and scientific subjects, by a very accomplished physician."—Graphic.*

WORKS ON MENTAL AND MORAL PHILOSOPHY, AND ALLIED SUBJECTS.

Aristotle. — AN INTRODUCTION TO ARISTOTLE'S RHETORIC. With Analysis, Notes, and Appendices. By E. M. COPE, Trinity College, Cambridge. 8vo. 14s.

This work is introductory to an edition of the Greek Text of Aristotle's Rhetoric, which is in course of preparation. Its object is to render that treatise thoroughly intelligible. The author has aimed to illustrate, as preparatory to the detailed explanation of the work, the general bearings and relations of the Art of Rhetoric in itself, as well as the special mode of treating it adopted by Aristotle in his peculiar system. The evidence upon obscure or doubtful questions connected with the subject is examined; and the relations which Rhetoric bears, in Aristotle's view, to the kindred art of Logic are fully considered. A connected Analysis of the work is given, and a few important matters are separately discussed in Appendices. There is added, as a general Appendix, by way of specimen of the antagonistic system of Isocrates and others, a complete analysis of the treatise called 'Ῥητορικὴ πρὸς 'Αλέξανδρον, with a discussion of its authorship and of the probable results of its teaching.

ARISTOTLE ON FALLACIES; OR, THE SOPHISTICI ELENCHI. With a Translation and Notes by EDWARD POSTE, M.A., Fellow of Oriel College, Oxford. 8vo. 8s. 6d.

Besides the doctrine of Fallacies, Aristotle offers, either in this treatise or in other passages quoted in the Commentary, various glances over the world of science and opinion, various suggestions or problems which are still agitated, and a vivid picture of the ancient system of dialectics, which it is hoped may be found both interesting and instructive. "It will be an assistance to genuine students of Aristotle."—Guardian. *"It is indeed a work of great skill."*—Saturday Review.

Birks.—FIRST PRINCIPLES OF MORAL SCIENCE; Or, a First Course of Lectures delivered in the University of Cambridge. By the Rev. T. R. BIRKS, Professor of Moral Philosophy. Crown 8vo. 8*s.* 6*d.*

Boole.— AN INVESTIGATION OF THE LAWS OF THOUGHT, ON WHICH ARE FOUNDED THE MATHEMATICAL THEORIES OF LOGIC AND PRO-BABILITIES. By GEORGE BOOLE, LL.D., Professor of Mathematics in the Queen's University, Ireland, &c. 8vo. 14*s.*

The design of this treatise is to investigate the fundamental laws of those operations of the mind by which reasoning is performed ; to give expression to them in the symbolical language of a Calculus, and upon this foundation to establish the science of Logic and construct its method ; to make that method itself the basis of a general method for the application of the mathematical doctrine of Probabilities ; and, finally, to collect from the various elements of truth brought to view in the course of these inquiries some probable intimations concerning the nature and construction of the human mind. The problem is one of the highest interest, and no one is better able than Professor Boole to treat of this side of it at any rate.

Butler (W. A.), Late Professor of Moral Philosophy in the University of Dublin :—

LECTURES ON THE HISTORY OF ANCIENT PHILO-SOPHY. Edited from the Author's MSS., with Notes, by WILLIAM HEPWORTH THOMPSON, M.A., Master of Trinity College, and Regius Professor of Greek in the University of Cambridge. Two Volumes. 8vo. 1*l.* 5*s.*

These Lectures consist of an Introductory Series on the Science of Mind generally, and five other Series on Ancient Philosophy, the greater part of which treat of Plato and the Platonists, the Fifth Series being an unfinished course on the Psychology of Aristotle, containing an able Analysis of the well known though by no means well

Butler (W. A.)—*continued.*

un 'erstood Treatise, περὶ ψυχῆς. These Lectures are the result of patient and conscientious examination of the original documents, and may be considered as a perfectly independent contribution to our knowledge of the great master of Grecian wisdom. The author's intimate familiarity with the metaphysical writings of the last century, and especially with the English and Scotch School of Psychologists, has enabled him to illustrate the subtle speculations of which he treats in a manner calculated to render them more intelligible to the English mind than they can be by writers trained solely in the technicalities of modern German schools. The editor has verified all the references, and added valuable Notes, in which he points out sources of more complete information. The Lectures constitute a History of the Platonic Philosophy—its seed-time, maturity, and decay.

SERMONS AND LETTERS ON ROMANISM.—See THEO-LOGICAL CATALOGUE.

Calderwood.—Works by the Rev. HENRY CALDERWOOD, M.A., LL.D., Professor of Moral Philosophy in the University of Edinburgh :—

PHILOSOPHY OF THE INFINITE: A Treatise on Man's Knowledge of the Infinite Being, in answer to Sir W. Hamilton and Dr. Mansel. Cheaper Edition. 8vo. 7s. 6d.

The purpose of this volume is, by a careful analysis of consciousness, to prove, in opposition to Sir W. Hamilton and Mr. Mansel, that man possesses a notion of an Infinite Being, and to ascertain the peculiar nature of the conception and the particular relations in which it is found to arise. The province of Faith as related to that of Knowledge, and the characteristics of Knowledge and Thought as bearing on this subject, are examined; and separate chapters are devoted to the consideration of our knowledge of the Infinite as First Cause, as Moral Governor, and as the Object of Worship. "A book of great ability . . . . written in a clear style, and may be easily understood by even those who are not versed in such discussions."—British Quarterly Review.

A HANDBOOK OF MORAL PHILOSOPHY. Second Edition. Crown 8vo. 6s.

"*It is, we feel convinced, the best handbook on the subject, intellectually and morally, and does infinite credit to its author.*"—Standard.

Elam.—A PHYSICIAN'S PROBLEMS. — See MEDICAL CATALOGUE, preceding.

Galton (Francis).—HEREDITARY GENIUS : An Inquiry into its Laws and Consequences. See PHYSICAL SCIENCE CATALOGUE, preceding.

Green (J. H.)—SPIRITUAL PHILOSOPHY : Founded on the Teaching of the late SAMUEL TAYLOR COLERIDGE. By the late JOSEPH HENRY GREEN, F.R.S., D.C.L. Edited, with a Memoir of the Author's Life, by JOHN SIMON, F.R.S., Medical Officer of Her Majesty's Privy Council, and Surgeon to St. Thomas's Hospital. Two Vols. 8vo. 25s.

> *The late Mr. Green, the eminent surgeon, was for many years the intimate friend and disciple of Coleridge, and an ardent student of philosophy. The language of Coleridge's will imposed on Mr. Green the obligation of devoting, so far as necessary, the remainder of his life to the one task of systematising, developing, and establishing the doctrines of the Coleridgian philosophy. With the assistance of Coleridge's manuscripts, but especially from the knowledge he possessed of Coleridge's doctrines, and independent study of at least the basal principles and metaphysics of the sciences and of all the phenomena of human life, he proceeded logically to work out a system of universal philosophy such as he deemed would in the main accord with his master's aspirations. After many years of preparatory labour he resolved to complete in a compendious form a work which should give in system the doctrines most distinctly Coleridgian. The result is these two volumes. The first volume is devoted to the general principles of philosophy; the second aims at vindicating à priori (on principles for which the first volume has contended) the essential doctrines of Christianity. The work is divided into four parts: I. "On the Intellectual Faculties and processes which are concerned in the Investigation of Truth." II. "Of First Principles in Philosophy." III. "Truths of Religion." IV. "The Idea of Christianity in relation to Controversial Philosophy."*

Huxley (Professor.)—LAY SERMONS, ADDRESSES, AND REVIEWS. See PHYSICAL SCIENCE CATALOGUE, preceding.

Jevons.—Works by W. STANLEY JEVONS, M.A., Professor of Logic in Owens College, Manchester :—

THE SUBSTITUTION OF SIMILARS, the True Principle of Reasoning. Derived from a Modification of Aristotle's Dictum. Fcap. 8vo. 2s. 6d.

"All acts of reasoning," the author says, " seem to me to be different cases of one uniform process, which may perhaps be best described as the substitution of similars.. *This phrase clearly expresses that familiar mode in which we continually argue by analogy* from like to like, *and take one thing as a representative of another. The chief difficulty consists in showing that all the forms of the old logic, as well as the fundamental rules of mathematical reasoning, may be explained upon the same principle; and it is to this difficult task I have devoted the most attention. Should my notion be true, a vast mass of technicalities may be swept from our logical text-books and yet the small remaining part of logical doctrine will prove far more useful than all the learning of the Schoolmen." Prefixed is a plan of a new reasoning machine, the* Logical Abacus, *the construction and working of which is fully explained in the text and Appendix. " Mr. Jevons' book is very clear and intelligible, and quite worth consulting."*—Guardian.

Maccoll.—THE GREEK SCEPTICS, from Pyrrho to Sextus. An Essay which obtained the Hare Prize in the year 1868. By NORMAN MACCOLL, B.A., Scholar of Downing College, Cambridge. Crown 8vo. 3s. 6d.

This Essay consists of five parts: I. "Introduction." II. "Pyrrho and Timon." III. "The New Academy." IV. "The Later Sceptics." V. " The Pyrrhoneans and New Academy contrasted."—*"Mr. Maccoll has produced a monograph which merits the gratitude of all students of philosophy. His style is clear and vigorous; he has mastered the authorities, and criticises them in a modest but independent spirit."*—Pall Mall Gazette.

M'Cosh.—Works by JAMES M'COSH, LL.D., President of Princeton College, New Jersey, U.S.

> "*He certainly shows himself skilful in that application of logic to psychology, in that inductive science of the human mind which is the fine side of English philosophy. His philosophy as a whole is worthy of attention.*"—Revue de Deux Mondes.

THE METHOD OF THE DIVINE GOVERNMENT, Physical and Moral. Tenth Edition. 8vo. 10s. 6d.

> *This work is divided into four books. The first presents a general view of the Divine Government as fitted to throw light on the character of God; the second deals with the method of the Divine Government in the physical world; the third treats of the principles of the human mind through which God governs mankind; and the fourth is on Pastoral and Revealed Religion, and the Restoration of Man. An Appendix, consisting of seven articles, investigates the fundamental principles which underlie the speculations of the treatise.* "*This work is distinguished from other similar ones by its being based upon a thorough study of physical science, and an accurate knowledge of its present condition, and by its entering in a deeper and more unfettered manner than its predecessors upon the discussion of the appropriate psychological, ethical, and theological questions. The author keeps aloof at once from the* à priori *idealism and dreaminess of German speculation since Schelling, and from the onesidedness and narrowness of the empiricism and positivism which have so prevailed in England.*"—Dr. Ulrici, in "Zeitschrift für Philosophie."

THE INTUITIONS OF THE MIND. A New Edition. 8vo. cloth. 10s. 6d.

> *The object of this treatise is to determine the true nature of Intuition, and to investigate its laws. It starts with a general view of intuitive convictions, their character and the method in which they are employed, and passes on to a more detailed examination of them, treating them under the various heads of* "*Primitive Cognitions,*" "*Primitive Beliefs,*" "*Primitive Judgments,*" *and* "*Moral Convictions.*" *Their relations to the various sciences, mental and physical, are then examined. Collateral criticisms are thrown into preliminary and supplementary chapters and sections.* "*The undertaking to adjust the claims of the sensational and intuitional*

M'Cosh (J.)—*continued.*

philosophies, and of the à posteriori *and* à priori *methods, is accomplished in this work with a great amount of success."*— Westminster Review. *"I value it for its large acquaintance with English Philosophy, which has not led him to neglect the great German works. I admire the moderation and clearness, as well as comprehensiveness, of the author's views."*—Dr. Dörner, of Berlin.

AN EXAMINATION OF MR. J. S. MILL'S PHILOSOPHY: Being a Defence of Fundamental Truth. Crown 8vo. 7s. 6d.

This volume is not put forth by its author as a special reply to Mr. Mill's "Examination of Sir William Hamilton's Philosophy." In that work Mr. Mill has furnished the means of thoroughly estimating his theory of mind, of which he had only given hints and glimpses in his logical treatise. It is this theory which Dr. M'Cosh professes to examine in this volume; his aim is simply to defend a portion of primary truth which has been assailed by an acute thinker who has extensive influence in England. "In such points as Mr. Mill's notions of intuitions and necessity, he will have the voice of mankind with him."— Athenæum. *"Such a work greatly needed to be done, and the author was the man to do it. This volume is important, not merely in reference to the views of Mr. Mill, but of the whole school of writers, past and present, British and Continental, he so ably represents."*—Princeton Review.

THE LAWS OF DISCURSIVE THOUGHT: Being a Text-book of Formal Logic. Crown 8vo. 5s.

The main feature of this Logical Treatise is to be found in the more thorough investigation of the nature of the notion, in regard to which the views of the school of Locke and Whately are regarded by the author as very defective, and the views of the school of Kant and Hamilton altogether erroneous. The author believes that errors spring far more frequently from obscure, inadequate, indistinct, and confused Notions, and from not placing the Notions in their proper relation in judgment, than from Ratiocination. In this treatise, therefore, the Notion (with the term, and the Relation of Thought to Language) will be found to occupy a larger relative place than in any logical work written since the time of the famous

M'Cosh (J.)—*continued.*

Art of Thinking. "*The amount of summarized information which it contains is very great; and it is the only work on the very important subject with which it deals. Never was such a work so much needed as in the present day.*"—London Quarterly Review.

CHRISTIANITY AND POSITIVISM : A Series of Lectures to the Times on Natural Theology and Apologetics. Crown 8vo. 7s. 6d.

These Lectures were delivered in New York, by appointment, in the beginning of 1871, as the second course on the foundation of the Union Theological Seminary. There are ten Lectures in all, divided into three series:—I. "Christianity and Physical Science" (three lectures). II. "Christianity and Mental Science" (four lectures). III. "Christianity and Historical Investigation" (three lectures). The Appendix contains articles on "Gaps in the Theory of Development;" "Darwin's Descent of Man ;" "Principles of Herbert Spencer's Philosophy." In the course of the Lectures Dr. M'Cosh discusses all the most important scientific problems which are supposed to affect Christianity.

Masson.—RECENT BRITISH PHILOSOPHY : A Review, with Criticisms ; including some Comments on Mr. Mill's Answer to Sir William Hamilton. By DAVID MASSON, M.A., Professor of Rhetoric and English Literature in the University of Edinburgh. Crown 8vo. 6s.

The author, in his usual graphic and forcible manner, reviews in considerable detail, and points out the drifts of the philosophical speculations of the previous thirty years, bringing under notice the work of all the principal philosophers who have been at work during that period on the highest problems which concern humanity. The four chapters are thus titled:—I. "A Survey of Thirty Years." II. "The Traditional Differences : how repeated in Carlyle, Hamilton, and Mill." III. "Effects of Recent Scientific Conceptions on Philosophy." IV. "Latest Drifts and Groupings." The last seventy-six pages are devoted to a Review of Mr. Mill's criticism of Sir William Hamilton's Philosophy. "We can nowhere point to a work which gives so clear an exposition of the course of philosophical speculation in Britain during the past century, or which indicates so instructively the mutual influences of philosophic and scientific thought."—Fortnightly Review.

Maurice.—Works by the Rev. FREDERICK DENISON MAURICE, M.A., Professor of Moral Philosophy in the University of Cambridge. (For other Works by the same Author, see THEOLOGICAL CATALOGUE.)

SOCIAL MORALITY. Twenty-one Lectures delivered in the University of Cambridge. New and Cheaper Edition. Crown 8vo. 10s. 6d.

In this series of Lectures, Professor Maurice considers, historically and critically, Social Morality in its three main aspects : I. "The Relations which spring from the Family—Domestic Morality." II. "The Relations which subsist among the various constituents of a Nation—National Morality." III. "As it concerns Universal Humanity—Universal Morality." Appended to each series is a chapter on "Worship:" first, "Family Worship;" second, "National Worship;" third, "Universal Worship." " Whilst reading it we are charmed by the freedom from exclusiveness and prejudice, the large charity, the loftiness of thought, the eagerness to recognize and appreciate whatever there is of real worth extant in the world, which animates it from one end to the other. We gain new thoughts and new ways of viewing things, even more, perhaps, from being brought for a time under the influence of so noble and spiritual a mind."—Athenæum.

THE CONSCIENCE : Lectures on Casuistry, delivered in the University of Cambridge. New and Cheaper Edition. Crown 8vo. 5s.

In this series of nine Lectures, Professor Maurice, with his wonted force and breadth and freshness, endeavours to settle what is meant by the word "Conscience," and discusses the most important questions immediately connected with the subject. Taking "Casuistry" in its old sense as being the "study of cases of Conscience," he endeavours to show in what way it may be brought to bear at the present day upon the acts and thoughts of our ordinary existence. He shows that Conscience asks for laws, not rules : for freedom, not chains; for education, not suppression. He

Maurice (F. D.)—*continued.*

has abstained from the use of philosophical terms, and has touched on philosophical systems only when he fancied "they were interfering with the rights and duties of wayfarers." The Saturday Review *says: "We rise from them with detestation of all that is selfish and mean, and with a living impression that there is such a thing as goodness after all."*

MORAL AND METAPHYSICAL PHILOSOPHY. New Edition and Preface. Vol. I. Ancient Philosophy and the First to the Thirteenth Centuries ; Vol. II. the Fourteenth Century and the French Revolution, with a glimpse into the Nineteenth Century. New Edition. 2 Vols. 8vo. 25*s.*

This is an Edition in two volumes of Professor Maurice's History of Philosophy from the earliest period to the present time. It was formerly scattered throughout a number of separate volumes, and it is believed that all admirers of the author and all students of philosophy will welcome this compact Edition. The subject is one of the highest importance, and it is treated here with fulness and candour, and in a clear and interesting manner. In a long introduction to this Edition, in the form of a dialogue, Professor Maurice justifies some of his own peculiar views, and touches upon some of the most important topics of the time.

Murphy.—THE SCIENTIFIC BASES OF FAITH. By JOSEPH JOHN MURPHY, Author of "Habit and Intelligence." 8vo. 14*s.*

" The book is not without substantial value ; the writer continues the work of the best apologists of the last century, it may be with less force and clearness, but still with commendable persuasiveness and tact ; and with an intelligent feeling for the changed conditions of the problem."—Academy.

Picton.—THE MYSTERY OF MATTER AND OTHER ESSAYS. By J. ALLANSON PICTON, Author of "New Theories and the Old Faith." Crown 8vo. 10*s.* 6*d.*

CONTENTS :—*The Mystery of Matter—The Philosophy of Ignorance—The Antithesis of Faith and Sight—The Essential Nature of Religion—Christian Pantheism.*

Thring (E., M.A.)—THOUGHTS ON LIFE-SCIENCE. By EDWARD THRING, M.A. (Benjamin Place), Head Master of Uppingham School. New Edition, enlarged and revised. Crown 8vo. 7s. 6d.

> *In this volume are discussed in a familiar manner some of the most interesting problems between Science and Religion, Reason and Feeling. "Learning and Science," says the author, "are claiming the right of building up and pulling down everything, especially the latter. It has seemed to me no useless task to look steadily at what has happened, to take stock as it were of men's gains, and to endeavour amidst new circumstances to arrive at some rational estimate of the bearings of things, so that the limits of what is possible at all events may be clearly marked out for ordinary readers. . . . . This book is an endeavour to bring out some of the main facts of the world."*

Venn.—THE LOGIC OF CHANCE: An Essay on the Foundations and Province of the Theory of Probability, with especial reference to its application to Moral and Social Science. By JOHN VENN, M.A., Fellow of Gonville and Caius College, Cambridge. Fcap. 8vo. 7s. 6d.

> *This Essay is in no sense mathematical. Probability, the author thinks, may be considered to be a portion of the province of Logic regarded from the material point of view. The principal objects of this Essay are to ascertain how great a portion it comprises, where we are to draw the boundary between it and the contiguous branches of the general science of evidence, what are the ultimate foundations upon which its rules rest, what the nature of the evidence they are capable of affording, and to what class of subjects they may most fitly be applied. The general design of the Essay, as a special treatise on Probability, is quite original, the author believing that erroneous notions as to the real nature of the subject are disastrously prevalent. "Exceedingly well thought and well written," says the* Westminster Review. *The* Nonconformist *calls it a "masterly book."*

LONDON : R. CLAY, SONS, AND TAYLOR, PRINTERS, BREAD STREET HILL.